THE
TIGER
AT
MIDNIGHT

THE
TIGER
AT
MIDNIGHT

SWATI TEERDHALA

KATHERINE TEGEN BOOKS
An Imprint of HarperCollins Publishers

Katherine Tegen Books is an imprint of HarperCollins Publishers.

The Tiger at Midnight

Library of Congress Control Number: 2018958508

ISBN 978-0-06-286921-0 (trade bdg.)

Typography by Carla Weise

19 20 21 22 23   PC/LSCH   10 9 8 7 6 5 4 3 2 1

❖

First Edition

To my parents and sisters.
To my family, blood and found.
You are my home.

Never greet a tiger at midnight,
for they are the manifestations
of your past misdeeds.

—FROM THE TALES OF
NARAN AND NARIA

CHAPTER 1

K unal's eyes, sharp as an eagle's, were used to studying an enemy's armor for chinks or a battle plan for
flaws. But tonight they rested on the sea.

Across the water, the outline of the coast of Dharka
looked as if it was etched into the night—a shadow of reality
compared to the starkness of the rocky Jansan cliffs below.
Kunal longed to sketch it, capture the shades of moonlight.

Chilly air tickled the stubble on his jaw as he sat, perched
on the highest wall of the Red Fortress, with his curved
longbow at his side. It had been many moons since he'd had
a moment to close his eyes and feel the wind on his skin
with such abandon. Terms for the cease-fire with the Dharkans had been drawn up that morning, so watch duty was a
formality today, but not one he was about to shirk.

Kunal stared out into the sooty darkness, his eyes unfo-
cused. No one would be out there on the abandoned battle

1

lines either, the soldiers too busy celebrating the momentary peace with rice wine and games of dice.

Except—there was movement.

He was up in a flash, peering out over the curved bell of the rampart's window. A small figure weaved her way through the encampment on the western side of the Fort with delicate steps.

Moonlight highlighted her careful movements, the red sandstone of the Fort creating an eerie glow around her. Her ivory-colored uttariya covered her head and shoulders, but Kunal caught a glimpse of her face under the shifting streams of light.

He abandoned his warm corner of the wall.

Kunal would have left the girl to find her way back to the harbor down below the cliff, but she was going the wrong way. In a quarter of an hour the conch would be blown, and soldiers would stream out of the west entrance for midnight exercises—drunk and in fighting moods. Though the war elephants wouldn't be out this late at night, it would still be chaos after tonight's celebrations. A lost girl could easily get underfoot as they practiced their chariot formations.

He'd risk a whipping for abandoning his post, but Kunal's stomach turned at the thought of anything happening to a civilian during his watch.

The girl disappeared under the towering shadow of the Fort, and Kunal raced from his perch to catch up. He ran down the tower stairs, nearly overturning a camphor lamp hanging from the ceiling as he shot through the narrow corridors. He reached the tall, stone arches at the bottom of the Fort and turned the corner at the side entrance, steadying his hands before he opened the door.

The foaming waves of the ocean crested and broke against the red cliffs that held up the south side of the Fort. To his left, the lights of the traders' ships glimmered up the beach, near the port. The girl stood farther down the path to his right, close to the edge of the cliff.

She looked up at the sky, moonlight cascading over her profile as she smiled.

Her smile.

It dragged an unwilling memory from the echoes of his mind. Of a childhood friend with dancing eyes and a challenging smile that had often led him into trouble. A friend long dead.

The memory ached in his chest, a remnant from an earlier life. A life where he didn't know four ways to kill a man quickly.

He watched her from the shadows of the door. The ocean breeze held a chill, and the girl wrapped her light brown arms under the end of her uttariya, shivering. She was clad in a simple crimson sari with a thin gold border, the bolt of stiff silk thrown over one shoulder and held up with a gold waist sash. He glanced at her feet. No toe rings, which meant she was unmarried. No anklets or earrings or ornate gold jewelry at all to denote her status. She must be one of the newly arrived traders, as they always dressed simply to show no affiliation.

Kunal felt himself relax at the realization, though he wondered why she was here—most traders should be off to the harbor by this time in the evening. Was she lost?

He revealed himself from the shadows, walking toward her.

"You're not supposed to be here," he said, stopping a pace away from her.

He saw her tense, clutching her uttariya tighter to her chest. Her eyes darted to his bronze armor, to the gold cuffs he wore at his wrists, indicating he was a soldier.

Kunal noticed the look and pulled back, swallowing his sharp tone. Of course she'd be frightened after he had said it like that. Only a few days ago, the commander of the cavalry had thrown a trader in irons for arguing with a Fort captain.

They stood there for the briefest of moments, staring at one another, neither moving as the wind crashed into them.

The girl was even more striking up close. Her chestnut eyes were huge, framed by thick, arched eyebrows. Her face shone with fear but her chin jutted out, defiant.

Kunal coughed and ventured a tentative smile. He tried to angle himself in the straining moonlight so that she would see he was unarmed and meant no harm, raising both hands for good measure. The tension in her shoulders eased and he tapped the four fingers of his right hand against his chest in greeting, the symbol of welcome and warmth in Jansa.

"I was up there and saw you going down the wrong path," he said. Kunal cleared his throat and pointed to the embrasure that jutted out. "You're not allowed—it isn't safe to be on the western side of the Fort tonight." His words came out fast, laced with a nervous energy. "Are you lost? It can be hard to navigate the trading footpaths at night. This one leads away from the harbor."

He couldn't remember the last time he had spoken to a girl at length; women had been removed from the Jansan army after the queendom had been dismantled, and the Fort was inhabited only by soldiers and the passing traders that helped it thrive. The other soldiers made trips into town on campaigns, but Kunal never partook in those celebrations.

He was used to seeing traders from all over the Southern Lands and Far Isles at the Fort and knew most of them by name, but he didn't recognize her. His eyes darted to the small pin that held together her sari pleats, shaped like a jasmine flower, which he could tell was Dharkan-made. But she had no valaya, the metal bracelet Dharkans wore from birth. No Dharkan would set foot here, near the Fort, anyway—she must be Jansan.

It was uncommon to see a Jansan wear such a pin nowadays but not impossible. Before the War of the Brothers, Jansans and Dharkans had mingled: they had loved and lived together as denizens of the Southern Lands. It was only after Jansa's queen and royal family had been murdered, ten years ago, that the war had started and the bond between their countries had fractured.

It was only after that bloody coup that Kunal's entire life had changed.

"I've seen many traders deliver their goods and then get lost while staring at the Fortress's height or numerous parapets. It's really not that special. But I suppose I think that because I live there . . ." His words trailed off as he bit his tongue, bewildered at why his mouth had decided to come to life on its own.

She looked at him for a long beat, studying his face, and Kunal had to resist the urge to say something to fill the silence. Finally, she lowered her head, demure.

"I believe I am lost." Her voice was musical, measured, and a note of uncertainty crept into it. "Would you be so kind as to tell me how to get back to the harbor? I was late in dropping off my shipment of poppy seeds; I hope you will forgive me." She bent her head, eyes lowering. "But if I don't get back to my quarter on the ship, I'll be left behind. The captain doesn't look kindly on tardiness."

He nodded briskly. Uncle Setu—known to the rest of Jansa as the revered, and feared, General Hotha—wasn't one for lateness either.

"Of course. I'll show you to the footpath that leads down to the harbor. I can take you there right now."

Something akin to relief passed over the girl's face. This captain must really have a lot in common with the general if she was that worried.

Kunal glanced up at his station at the top of the Fort. Even with the soldiers preoccupied by celebration in the courtyard inside, they would make their way outside at midnight without fail, only a quarter of an hour from now.

He would have to make this quick before the western gates opened. He made a note to remind the sentries to keep a closer eye on traders from now on.

Kunal led the way to the footpath in silence, stealing glances at the girl when her gaze was dropped. The girl's steps were jaunty for a trader, her shoulders held a bit too high. Most traders at the Fort crept about with their shoulders around their ears, in fear of invoking the general's wrath.

But this girl. Her eyes . . . they were filled with fire and the depths of water. It bothered Kunal. Fire and water didn't live together in harmony, yet in her eyes, it seemed perfectly natural. Something about her was so familiar, but Kunal couldn't place it.

Perhaps she was one of the daughters of the new trade leader? Or had just arrived on one of the trade ships from the Western Lands, across the sea?

He scuffed his toe against the stones as they crested the hill to the back entrance of the Fort where the footpath lay. One of the Fort's five sandstone pillars towered at the top of the path, the inscriptions of King Vardaan's edicts from the past decade gleaming in the light. There was a cracked white line in the stone, where a statue of the first queen of Jansa, Naria, and an eagle, the royal family's sigil, had used to stand. He still remembered the day he had asked his uncle why there was a king on Jansa's throne, instead of a queen as the gods had decreed—it had earned him his first beating.

Kunal didn't want to think about what his uncle would

say if he found out he had abandoned his post, whatever the reason. An unfitting decision for a dutiful Jansan soldier, especially now with his promotion.

"Are you all right?" the girl asked. Her words were quick and unmeasured, a stark difference from her previous tone.

Kunal nodded. She arched one dark eyebrow at him. "Do soldiers normally go around frowning at imaginary people?"

A smile tugged at the corners of his mouth. He hadn't realized he was that easy to read. "Only every other day. You caught me on a bad one."

She chuckled, low and hearty.

Where had that come from? Kunal wasn't a flirt, wasn't even one for a bawdy song.

The girl was now glancing at him as they walked, the grimness of her earlier expression gone, something mischievous in her eye.

"Is it always this chilly on this side of the coast, or did I just come on a bad day?" she asked, referring to the peninsula that the Red Fort was situated on.

"It's been getting cooler over the past years."

She made a concerned noise. "And I haven't seen any storm clouds. Good for our trading ships, but not so good for the land, I'm guessing."

"The land has become more arid. A quick dry spell, that's all," Kunal said, remembering what the Fort leadership had told them about the change in the land.

"I've heard tales of more than just a dry spell up north,"

she said, almost cautiously. When he inclined his head at her, she continued. "The price of wheat has increased this season, which I've heard is because of a lower yield due to the weather. It's even affecting the pearl market in the far east."

She was smart, that was obvious. But most of the traders who passed under the shadow of the Fort were content to know only what was going on within Jansa's borders. Kunal tried not to show his surprise at her knowledge. What made her different?

"You're right," he said. "I've heard a number of traders who were stopping by the port complain that their goods aren't selling like they used to, even in Gwali."

"Even in the capital? Must be serious," she said, chuckling. For a second she had looked as if she was going to say something else, but instead she changed the subject, asking about other news from the capital.

Kunal told her what he knew of the new cease-fire, watching her out of the corner of his eye. There was something about her, something fascinating, that compelled him to keep talking.

They arrived at the start of the graveled footpath, following the edge of the cliff the Fortress sat on down to the sandy beach below.

A tendril of black hair escaped her uttariya and fell across her cheek. Kunal wondered what it'd be like to brush it aside, draw that gaze to him.

He considered the impulse, but his hands remained at his sides.

Helping the girl was one thing. His uncle wouldn't excuse anything more. He shook his head as if to erase the thought. He needed to get back to his post before anyone noticed he was gone.

"Follow this path down to the harbor and you should be able to slip onto your ship before the captain notices," Kunal said.

"You're not going to walk me down?" she asked, angling her face up at him.

He hesitated. It was a bold question, but not without cause. He couldn't tell if she actually wanted him to, her face unreadable.

He shook his head. "No, I have to get back to my post. But I'll watch from up there," Kunal said, pointing up to his perch. "If you need anything, anything at all, wave."

Her eyes darted between him and the Fort.

"Thank you," she said, her words carrying a strange intensity. He nodded.

"It was a pleasure to meet you." He reached for her hand. Startled, she looked up and he held her gaze, refusing to give it up. Kunal brought her hand to his lips. "What is your name?"

CHAPTER 2

Esha was so unsettled by the soldier's warm gesture that she spoke before thinking.

"Esha."

She took her hand away and had to stop herself from clamping it over her mouth.

Stupid.

What had possessed her to give him her real name?

His warm eyes? The first kind expression she'd received from a boy in a while that didn't hide a secret agenda or dismiss her because of her gender?

Three weeks without regular human contact would drive anyone out of their mind, and it had turned her weak. Falling over herself and revealing her name for a handsome face and a kind word? Who was she?

She needed to remove herself from this conversation, finish her mission, and return home to feast with her friends and comrades. She'd even let herself find a boy to kiss under the stars.

Maybe Harun. But it couldn't be this one.

Esha looked at him standing across from her, his black hair blowing in the gusty wind. She took in every detail, sizing him up and folding the rest of the information away. He was a soldier, thickly muscled and sturdy, his brown skin tanned from days spent outside, she guessed. Scars crawled up his knuckles and a few dotted his shoulder, one carving into the edge of his full lips. But his pale amber eyes revealed something gentle.

If he was gentle, he wouldn't be able to survive her. If he was a brute, he would be like every other Jansan soldier and she'd be glad to end his life.

"Esha," he repeated. The corners of his eyes crinkled with genuine pleasure and Esha couldn't help but smile back. "I'm Kunal."

A violent wind ran through, causing the quiver of arrows slung across his back to rattle against his bronze cuirass, tangling with the uttariya thrown across his shoulders. He wore no turban to signify his status as many Jansan men did, but the bronze cuirass and gold cuffs were enough. In his armor, he was an arresting picture of strength, but Esha was drawn to his smile. It transformed his face from cold to surprisingly warm.

"Perhaps I'll see you around here again." There was a hopeful lift to his words. "Maybe I can convince our cook that we need to add poppy seeds to all of our bread," he said with a small grin.

"Well, your fellow soldiers might blame you when they find themselves with horrible stomachaches."

"We wouldn't want that."

Esha shook her head solemnly. "No, we wouldn't want to start a riot over a few extra poppy seeds." She squinted at him. "Think about it. 'The Poppy Seed Rebellion.' What a horrible name."

"At the very least, it would be an interesting tale. That is, if I managed to keep my head in said rebellion."

She was doing her best to defeat her own traitorous smile. "It would be the first thing to go. Your head for the extra barrel of poppy seeds."

"Pity. I do have such a nice head." He grinned at her and she grinned back.

Despite herself, she liked him.

Too bad she would have to betray him.

CHAPTER 3

She pulled her hand away first, turning to follow the path. But something stilled her steps and she looked back, shivering in the cool sea breeze of night.

The soldier unwrapped his own uttariya in one swift movement and had it around her shoulders in the next. With that he put four fingers to his chest in salute and turned around, marching up the rocky path toward the Red Fortress.

Or the Blood Fort, as it was called by everyone on her side of the water. One of the many names Dharkans had for the regime of the Pretender King of Jansa.

Esha could feel her heart beating in her chest as she fingered the thick silk of his uttariya over her own, drawing it tighter around her body. The faint remnants of a smile flitted on her lips as she saw him draw near the door—until a jeweled armband on his upper arm caught the moonlight and she realized what he was.

She scowled at his back. Only a Senap guard wore those armbands, the worst sort of Fort soldier. They offered warmth with one hand and ripped lives apart with the other. She knew the latter firsthand.

Esha took a deep breath and continued down the path, turning near the large boulder for a better look at the side door to the Fort. She ducked behind, sliding into a low crouch and patting the knife strapped to her thigh.

Esha pushed aside the old, painful memories that threatened to resurface, making space for the clarity she would need to accomplish her mission. There was a reason she had asked for this one, even demanded it be assigned to her.

If she could pull this off, it would be a great win for the Crescent Blades and her rebel team at home.

And for the girl she used to be.

She'd spent too many nights haunted by nightmares—the image of a soldier in bronze armor holding a curved blade, and Setu Hotha, the general of the Fort, behind him. His lips were always set in a pleased slant. She would never be free of that nightmare, never be able to wipe away those memories of the night Vardaan Himyad took control of Jansa by coup.

Vardaan Himyad, a former prince of Dharka, the younger brother of Dharka's reigning monarch, King Mahir. That night marked an unbelievable betrayal of both countries.

It was also the night her parents had been murdered in front of her eyes.

Setting up this mission after the cease-fire had been a masterful idea by Harun, the current crown prince of Dharka, giving her the distraction she needed to slip in. She welcomed the cease-fire, as it allowed Dharka's smaller military to recuperate and gave both nations' people a respite from the war. The conflict had started off as a simple border issue after the coup ten years ago, when the Pretender King pushed past the Ghanta Mountains, the natural border between Jansa and Dharka, to claim Dharkan land.

But both country's futures had always been closely tied—they both relied on the Bhagya River's tributaries and were bound to the land by the *janma* bond, the pact of blood and magic that Jansa's and Dharka's founders had made with the gods to keep the Southern Lands thriving and alive for all future generations. After the Pretender King had broken the *janma* bond by killing the queen and the royals, it had become an all-out fight for the future of Jansa—and the Southern Lands.

Ten years of on-and-off war and countless failed cease-fires later, she had a chance to claim a great win for Dharka, to take a step toward toppling the Pretender King. It was even more vital now, after what the scholars had told her about the *janma* bond—time was running out for Jansa and soon Dharka would be engulfed in drought as well.

The next ritual would be the last.

Her mission? Assassinate the brutal General Hotha and intercept a stolen report, one a fellow rebel had died protecting and that contained new information about the *janma* bond.

Two birds, one stone. The Blades would deliver a great blow to the Pretender King, eliminate his trusted adviser, *and* recover valuable intel. Tonight's celebration of the cease-fire, when the Fort's guard was down, would be their best, and only, chance.

Esha tilted her head around the boulder, watching the soldier slip inside the fort door. In a few seconds he disappeared behind the heavy stone.

The maid's entrance.

Or it used to be the maid's entrance, when the Fort had been a palace.

When Esha had last been here, the Fortress was alive with people and color. The land surrounding it had been healthy, and when moonlight struck the cliffs, they glimmered like hardened rubies.

Now the land was dying and the Fort stood on the top of the hill, bleak and ominous, its heart ripped out ten years ago on the night of the coup. The inner residence had been destroyed, according to their rebel reports, to make way for training grounds.

She remembered the vivid paintings on those walls, of the origins of Dharka and Jansa. The twin demigods of boy and girl, Naran and Naria, who had built their nations side by side on the peninsular Southern Lands.

She had spent so many afternoons as a child tracing

them, listening to stories from her father, learning about the two royal lineages who had descended from the twins—the Samyads of Jansa and the Himyads of Dharka. Even now, she could picture how her father's long handlebar mustache had shaken as he took on different voices to tell the stories, making her erupt in peals of laughter.

Esha sprinted up the path, desperate to avoid any watching eyes. She grabbed the edges of her sari, bunching the fabric of the dress together and pulling it through her legs to create a dhoti. She tucked the long length of fabric over one of her shoulders into her waist sash, freeing up her arms.

Esha tugged at the door. After steadying her breath, she reached out to hold the large gold lock in her shaking hands.

How had the soldier done it?

A twist to the right, a tug forward. Had the next step been clockwise or counterclockwise? She chose the latter but the lock didn't budge.

She suppressed a curse.

The soldier had given her the information she needed—she only had until midnight. She had been briefed on the Fort rituals before she left and she knew that the commander ran training exercises and drills in the evening and the early morning hours.

It wasn't a lot of time, but she had no choice. There was too much at stake for this mission, especially with the new cease-fire. Worse than failing, if she was caught, it could jeopardize everything. She had to keep her head about her.

Esha focused her breath until it steadied. The anxiety she felt now—she had felt it a million times. In every mission she had run, there was a moment when all felt lost. When the military plans had been impossible to steal, the blockade impossible to break.

This was her biggest mission to date. She focused on transforming her fear into excitement.

This was her chance, aside from all other obligation, to take the first step toward her revenge. One she had been dreaming about as frequently as she had tossed and turned from nightmares.

She took a deep breath and looked around her. The red stone walls in front of her were slabs, thick and sturdy. The walls around it were made of the same smooth, tall stone. Impossible to climb.

She tried the lock again, to no avail. By the third time, her palms were sore and frustration tore at her throat.

A faint shuffle of feet on the other side of the door shot her back to attention, and Esha shoved herself into the wall shadows. She tried to make herself as small as possible as the footsteps became louder and more clear.

A young soldier pushed through the door she had been trying to open, walking outside with an unsteady stance and a darting gaze. He moved toward the cliff and began to relieve himself, breathing heavily and barely keeping himself upright.

Esha held her breath and waited. The door wasn't open enough for her to sneak in and he hadn't moved far enough away, only about twenty paces. She kept her eyes on him as he moved back toward the door.

She moved forward to get a better look and stepped on the sharp point of a rock. Esha bit back a yelp of pain as quick as she could, but the soldier's hand stilled, and with a firm motion he threw the door shut.

He whirled around, a curved short sword in each hand, the metal shining like malicious smiles in the moonlight. Though he swayed slightly in the breeze, his eyes were alert and he stalked closer to where Esha stood, hidden in the shadows.

She berated herself—this wasn't a normal mission. Soldiers at the Blood Fort were second best to the elite Senap Guard. They weren't sell-swords or conscripted farmers but highly trained, skilled warriors.

Esha went deathly still, the only sound in the air the faint traces of laughter and loud cheers from inside the Fort. She was almost out of time.

She crouched to the ground as the soldier drew closer to her corner, reaching toward the strap around her thigh for her knife.

The soldier stopped a breath away from her spot in the shadows.

Esha grabbed a stone and chucked it far behind him, away from the door. He started and turned, looking at the stone with bewilderment.

A small movement, but the distraction she needed. Esha lunged out of the shadows, smashing the hilt of her knife into the back of his head. He groaned and caught her arm, her bad one. She winced in pain but moved to hit again as he aimed his fist at her stomach. But he hesitated when he locked eyes with her.

Good.

She clocked him in the head and then kicked him in the kidney for good measure. He tumbled over, but as he fell he grasped her ankle, pulling her with him. She fell with a grunt and fury rose in her chest. Esha gripped the hilt of her knife as she kicked him.

One slice and he would be dead.

The thought beckoned at Esha, but she chose stealth over bloodthirst. She grabbed a stone nearby, swinging it at the soldier's head to knock him unconscious.

If he never woke up, it would be the will of the gods. She had given him a chance.

Esha scrambled to her feet and tugged the unlucky soldier toward the Fort. He was heavy, and she huffed as she pulled him upright against the stone wall. She took the flask of liquor at his hip and dumped its contents on his head. She hoped anyone who found him would simply smell the pungent scent of alcohol and think no more of it.

Esha stared at him, and to be sure, slapped his cheek once, hard. Nothing.

Her hands ached, but Esha didn't stop to wrap them and ran to the entrance. She followed through the motions and this time, the door opened.

Esha fell against it in a moment of gratitude, her palms

flat, her forehead welcoming the cool touch of the smooth red stone.

With careful precision Esha pushed into the darkness of the Fort, taking care to move quieter than the wind and not let a single sound escape. She had left enough of a mess already.

She was in.

———◄o►———

Esha slipped into the general's room as the soldiers streamed out for midnight exercises below. She had almost been caught a few times, having taken a wrong staircase or two, but her memory of the palace—now turned fort—kept her from getting too lost. At last, she reached the highest floor of the Blood Fort, a towering spire that rose into the sky.

The general would be in his room, alone. Her contact had told her that the midnight trainings were run by the commander, as the general liked to turn in and rise early.

Esha readied her whip, imagining how she would sneak into the room and wrap the thin metal end around his neck as he slept. It would be a quick death, though he didn't deserve one, and she would recover the report before escaping. She could see it so clearly.

Her breath hitched as she took her first step, anticipation buzzing in her veins. She had spent years imagining this moment, the elation and relief she'd feel when the deed was done.

She had reached the top of the staircase now. No light flickered in his room.

It was silent.

Too silent. She put a hand against the door and it shifted; it was open already.

Within seconds, Esha had her knives drawn and her back to the stone wall.

What was going on? The general wouldn't have left the door open himself—she had been prepared to pick it with a special-made pin, forged for this mission. Esha thought about sprinting back down the steps, but steeled her heart. She hadn't come all this way for nothing.

If there was someone in there, she would simply kill them *and* the general.

She pushed the door with the toe of her sandal. It swung open without a sound. Only the light from the moon illuminated what had once been the queen of Jansa's bedroom, a faint smell of ash floating through the space. Esha moved as quietly as she could as she surveyed the room. It was sparse, uncluttered. There was no adornment past the bare necessities—a jute rug, a fireplace, and a dark wood desk. Weapons lined the wall across from the fireplace.

"Have you come to kill me as well?" A low voice rumbled like gravel from the bed.

Esha's heartbeat stuttered. The general's voice was a strained whisper as his eyes opened and he lifted a hand from his stomach. Blood dripped down his fingers, into the wound that pierced his stomach.

Moon Lord's mercy. Someone had gotten here first.

She lunged into action, pushing away the shock and fear

that coursed through her at the realization. She needed to leave now. The general looked weak and pale, his wound minutes old. He had lost a lot of blood by the look of his red-stained sheets.

Someone had wanted him to suffer. Or to leave him alive long enough for her to find him. Did the murderer know she was coming? Did they know about the report?

Esha sprinted over to the open windows, looking out over the thin curtains. It was too high up for a drop and there was no indication of ropes tied to the windows.

"Wait. End it. Please."

Esha whirled around, fury now overtaking her fear. She moved to his bed, her knife out.

"Why. Why in the name of the sun and the moon should I, after all you've done? How can you claim mercy as your right?" Her voice was rough, low, infused with hatred and years of pain.

Recognition alighted in his eyes. "You're not one of them. You're one of the Dharkan rebels, those Crescent Blades. What is it you say in your land? We're all the Mother's creation. We're all—"

"How dare you—"

"We're all flawed. We all deserve mercy. Right?"

"So did hundreds of innocent Dharkans. So did the soldiers you captured and tortured for simply fulfilling their duty. And especially after what you did in Sundara to those civilians . . ."

"Vardaan and I, we had grand dreams. Better dreams."

Esha recoiled at the name of the Pretender King, Vardaan Himyad, the one who had led the coup and now ruled Jansa. "But it was war—" he continued.

"It was a coup. Why am I even letting you speak? I should cut the tongue from your throat, General," she said, her voice acid.

She moved to leave but whirled back around, incensed. That this man, even when at Death's doorstep, could act so righteous. The general tried to sit up but fell back with heavy breaths.

Esha's fingers clenched into a fist. "You controlled the fabled armies of Jansa. What more could you have wanted? Was your *greed* worth it?"

"Was it greed? Or conviction? After the War in the North . . ." He seemed to be considering it, a man who realized he had but a short time to think on his life.

Esha had run out of patience. She was pulling closer, ready to slit his throat in the former bedroom of the queen he had murdered, when she spotted it.

Under the bed, to the side, was a replica of one of her whips, identical to the one strapped to her hip. Her mind leaped to action even as her hand froze.

A trap?

She grabbed at the rug underneath the whip and tugged. It rolled over, no wire or weapon tied to it. She bent to examine it, tamping down on the fear that had bubbled back up. The heft was all wrong, and the metal was different, but it looked the same as the weapon in her hand, snakes emblazoned on the handle. It was an exact replica of her whips, the weapons that characterized her as the Viper, the ones she had custom made for her by one of the rebels' top blacksmiths. Her whips were one of a kind.

Someone was trying to frame her.

"I knew I would never have a peaceful death," he said, staring at her as if he knew she only moved closer to his bed to guarantee his death. Another shaky breath, a weak tremor in the body of the once-powerful, all-knowing general. He pushed the hand against his wound tighter, screwing his eyes shut.

"You gave that up long ago." Esha took a shaky breath. "Who was it?"

"Does it matter? Does any of it matter now?"

She wanted to slap him. "You're leaving this world having ruined the *janma* bond with the land, our one gift from the gods. Everything matters. You have the chance to save people."

"Vardaan thought he could maintain the bond by himself. We were wrong, and for that, I am sorry." He closed his eyes and coughed up blood. He grabbed on to her, his bloody fingers a cuff on her wrist. "The fireplace."

"What of it?"

"The fireplace. And my nephew . . . ," he whispered.

Before she could register his words, the general of the Red Fortress, her target and mission, died with one last gasping breath. Her knife was still warm in her hand, had been ready to end his life. But just as he had cheated her in life, he cheated her in death, stealing away the moment she had longed for.

Fury coursed through her veins and she wanted to shake him for taking this from her as well. Instead, she watched as life faded out of him, etching a new memory of the man who had plagued her nightmares, fueled her hatred for years. Her ghosts whispered, and she closed her eyes, letting their insistent voices wash over her.

She should be happy. The general was dead. The first pawn to be toppled as she made her way across the board toward the Pretender King, Vardaan.

It felt hollow.

Esha heard the conch shell blow again and jumped—the soldiers would come in now from their exercises.

She ran to the small fireplace situated in the corner of the room, remembering the general's words and the report she still had to find. Was it another trap? Even if it was, there was valuable information for the rebels in this room.

A scroll had been tossed into the flames, along with a short note that was mostly burned away. Esha smothered the fire with the bottom of her sandal and picked up the note and then the scroll, hitting it against the stone floor to stop the spread of flames.

Was this the report? She hoped to the Moon Lord it was, as she was running out of time.

Something glinted in the ashes. Pain was shooting up her palm from where she had grasped the hot scroll handle, but Esha reached in to pick up the object. It was a silver pin shaped like a crescent moon, an arrow through the center.

The symbol of the Crescent Blades, the Dharkan rebel group she called her family.

No self-respecting Blade would be careless enough to leave their pin behind, Esha thought immediately.

Which meant whoever had left it had done so on purpose. Esha couldn't fathom a reason a Blade would do such a thing, unless they had turned traitor and double agent. Or it could have been left by a new foe, someone who wanted to draw the Blades into a conflict that wasn't theirs.

She might not be the only one being framed—whoever had been here had wanted the soldiers at the Fort to find the pin. And if they found it and tied the general's assassination back to the Blades, Viper or no Viper, it could be the start of a full-fledged vendetta against the rebels.

Just as the cease-fire had been struck and peace was on the horizon.

It wouldn't matter that the Blades weren't representative of Dharka's army or monarchy—Vardaan was known to end agreements, and lives, for more trivial reasons than the murder of his right-hand general. And right now, Dharka needed peace. If the Fort and Vardaan discovered that the Blades had a connection to the Dharkan throne . . .

A chill crept down her spine.

Esha shook her head. She couldn't stay here any longer if she wanted to escape and get to the bottom of this. She rushed over to the general's desk, rattling through trinkets and correspondence for any more reports. Her hand hit scrolls that were hidden in the back, in a secret compart-ment, and she grabbed them, shoving them into her waist sash.

Time to leave.

At the last minute, Esha took the whip replica and left her real one.

It was rash, reckless, stupid, an action colored by rage and disappointment. But whoever had done this had wanted to frame her, and if she let them think their plan was still working, if she let this story play out, she might get enough clues to find them.

To unravel who was behind this, who had killed the general before her.

Who might know her real identity.

CHAPTER 4

Kunal woke to a rapping sound outside his door.

He looked at the door with a sour expression. Whoever was making that noise would shortly meet his fist if they didn't stop. The sound dissipated and Kunal sighed back into his pillow, the side of his face nestling into the rough cotton fibers. The sun had barely peeked its head over the horizon, and ribbons of orange painted the sky outside his small window.

How anyone could be up this early after last night's festivities was a mystery to him. He hadn't had more than a glass of rice wine after his shift—which his body thanked him for this morning. Most of his friends had imbibed significantly more, and there would be throbbing headaches and regret today, for sure.

Midnight exercises had been a nightmare, soldiers stumbling and slurring. He had avoided the talk that inevitably followed, of conquests—militaristic and personal. It soothed his conscience to know he had been able to help that girl, after so much bloodshed.

The knock sounded again and he groaned. For once, Kunal had planned on waking late—or as late as his body would allow him. Even the commander had foreseen that need and postponed any training to later in the afternoon.

The incessant knocking started up again, and with it came a few snickers. In a fluid movement, Kunal threw his knife, which was always within reach, toward the door. It thudded into the thick rosewood and the noise ceased, besides a small yelp of surprise.

Kunal smiled into his pillow.

A string of curses came from outside the door, and Kunal smothered laughter as he recognized the voices. He was friendly with everyone in the Fort, but Alok and Laksh, the unfortunate souls outside, were the two Kunal considered to be true friends. Kunal kept his eyes shut, face resting on his forearms as he listened to his friends' movements outside the door.

A grumble and more curses, a rustle and a firm knock.

"Yes?"

"Get up, you lazy cow," Alok shouted.

When Kunal didn't respond, they banged on the door again. Vulgar shouts of complaint arose from the other soldiers' rooms outside.

Kunal groaned. His body was so used to waking with the sun that nothing could change it. But without the intrusion from his friends, he could've happily languished in bed awake, letting thoughts of chestnut eyes and thick, dark curls fill his mind.

Now he would have to get up, if only to save Alok from starting another brawl and landing in irons for the evening. Laksh would let it happen, chuckling as he watched, unwilling to interfere. Typically, Alok brought levity to their friendship and Laksh was the scales, balancing Alok's moments of ridiculousness with Kunal's tendency toward rigidity. But Laksh enjoyed watching them butt heads, only coming in at the end, if at all.

So, Kunal pulled himself out of bed and wrapped his dhoti around his waist on his way to the door. He swung it open just as Alok moved to ram it and Alok fell to the floor in a sprawl. He sprang up and dusted himself off while rubbing his shoulder, eyeing everything with round eyes. Laksh strolled in after, rolling his eyes.

Kunal said nothing, watching them both with faint amusement as he leaned against the door.

Alok gave him a dirty look. "What were you doing? Curling your hair?"

"I was sleeping. As is everyone else in the Fort," Kunal said.

Alok's brow furrowed, his frown deepening. "You were also the only one who didn't have extraordinarily too much to drink. I would've expected you to already be down in the sparring yard."

"Getting soft?" Laksh said, leaning his lanky frame

against the wall. "No longer aiming to be the best at the Fort, making us all look bad?"

"One day. I ask for one day to lounge in my bed," Kunal said.

"Well, I wish I were lucky enough to be General Hotha's nephew, then I'd have a bed and not a hard cot. You didn't get where you are by sleeping in," Alok replied. He pointed to Kunal's jeweled armband resting on the shelf. "You didn't get promoted into the Senap Guard by doing that."

Alok poked his head into the hall to yell at a nearby door, "Unlike you, Rakesh! You got exactly where you are by sleeping in and being useless. Nowhere!" He turned back to Kunal with a satisfied grin.

Kunal shook his head at him.

"Rakesh will make you pay for that later, you know," Laksh said, his mouth a wry twist.

"Yup, I'm fully aware," Alok said. "It's worth it."

"Is it?" Kunal's question ended up being rhetorical as Alok spun past him and Laksh.

Alok looked around in assessment of the room. "Sparse. Boring. Kind of like you." He moved to the shelf on the side of the room, picking up a paintbrush and Kunal's small marble miniature of the capital city of Gwali, which he tapped on its smooth bottom.

"Haven't done much with it yet, have you?" said Laksh.

Kunal had moved into this small room, which was barely more than four corners and a bed, only a week prior. Most soldiers bunked together in the rooms below, set up by regiment and squadron. The room was his first taste of power and privacy as a newly promoted Senap guard, one of the elite warrior squadrons of Jansa. Trained as hunters and deadly fighters, Senaps ran the king's most important missions and acted as his palace guard in Gwali. His training had been intense—physically and mentally.

He had yet to be officially promoted or know where he'd be posted, but his uncle had fought for him to get this room. He'd said that after all the years of strict training and difficult missions to become a Senap, he deserved a bit of a reward.

It was a rare moment of pride and affection for his nephew, and Kunal hadn't forgotten it. It was their conversation after that that hadn't been so pleasant.

Alok tossed the marble miniature up in the air and Kunal lunged forward, just as the miniature landed back safely in Alok's hand. Laksh looked up, hiding a snort at Kunal's face.

Kunal wondered, not for the first time, if Alok had a death wish or if he simply wasn't disciplined enough as a child.

"Did you come in here simply to insult my room?"

"No, that was a happy benefit. I wanted to take advantage of the fact that no one will be in the training courts. Maybe get in a round or two. You could show us that shield trick of yours?" His words had a studied nonchalance, but Kunal could see his fingers tapping on the sheath of his sword. "Your room really is a bore. Can't you at least get some jute mats or a small silk tapestry, maybe of the mountains?"

Kunal pretended a frown, which seemed more appropriate with the continuous stream of insults being thrown his way. Alok wasn't good at asking for help, preferring to bluster rather than let anyone in. The fact that he was asking was groundbreaking in and of itself.

"You think you could handle it? I don't know. I think you'd need to be leaner here"—Kunal punched Alok lightly in the gut—"and stronger here"—a swift slap to his biceps—"to really master the move. But I guess I could show you." Alok punched him back in the shoulder.

"Try me on for size, you cow."

"What is with you and calling everyone a cow today? Have you even seen one?" Laksh said, a note of exasperation in his voice as he watched the two of them.

"Yes. I grew up in the north, you dull ox. Close to the Aifora Pass."

"I didn't know you lived all the way up there. Did you ever meet any of the Yavar clansmen in the north?" Laksh asked.

"No. Definitely not. Things have been tense since the War in the North, even though that was thirty years ago. Not sure I'd want to come face-to-face with one of their horsemen, even now. I pray they never turn their eye south again."

Kunal laughed. "Maybe you can take us one day."

"That's a great idea. You know I used to have a sweetheart up there?" Alok stared off into the distance, looking forlorn, but Kunal and Laksh laughed. Alok frowned.

"Yes, true love as a child," Laksh muttered, rolling his eyes.

"It was." Alok tried to look offended. "Now I'm stuck here. Being part of the powerful 'Blood Fort' should make us irresistible to any girl, but there are none within an acre now that we're no longer on campaign."

Kunal resisted the urge to snort. He was sure girls valued many things higher than armor on a man.

"A tragedy," Kunal said, forgoing the cuirass. It had been made for him, molded to his body like a second skin, but most of the soldiers trained bare-chested anyway. It wasn't as humid down near the sea as in the rest of Jansa, but a few hours in the sun would get the training courtyard hot enough.

Alok snorted. "A tragedy for you too. You'd have had a swarm of sweethearts." Kunal heard him mutter how that might have helped him out as well.

Kunal rolled his eyes and fished around for his waist sash, tying it tightly over his pants. Alok turned toward him.

"Took you long enough. Let's go, lazybones."

———◄o►———

It had been a punishing round of training.

Alok had picked up the shield trick within minutes and used it repeatedly on Kunal's exposed sword arm side, pounding down like a battering ram.

Kunal rotated his arm in the socket, loosening the already stiffening muscles as they left the training courtyard and made their way to the mess hall on the main level.

Laksh had stayed behind to sharpen his weapons, leaving Alok and Kunal to trudge up to the dining hall.

They had gotten sparring time without any disturbances from others, a rarity in the overcrowded and overmasculine Fort. The cease-fire was a new reality, as was obvious by the uncertain faces of the soldiers who milled about the main courtyard.

Would this cease-fire hold? Would this lead to a real truce, to true peace? Or would their king simply turn his eyes to the western borders?

Kunal had less to worry about. His recent promotion into the Senap Guard gave him the possibility of being restationed to Gwali. That would mean less time on the front lines of the king's expansion campaigns. He had never loved war anyway.

The Fort housed three of the four regiments of the Jansan army—the elephanteers, cavalry, and charioteers. Most of the Fort soldiers spent their time on the front battle lines, leading the charge with war elephants and the elegant chariot formations they practiced endlessly. It was the infantry who maintained order and justice throughout the land. Without war, many of these soldiers would have to find new roles.

From what he had overheard from his uncle, there was a good chance for peace. Dharka's troops had been decimated after the most recent battle at Sundara, which had been a great victory for the Jansans, and they were looking for an end to the conflict. And for some reason, King

Vardaan also seemed committed to peace this time around. Perhaps he had finally tired of war against his brother or was working to secure a new alliance or trade partnership with the west.

"I wonder if there will be training today," Alok said, breaking into his musings. "If there is, you'll have a rough go at it, won't you, Kunal? Eh?" He waggled his eyebrows as Kunal grimaced.

The deep purple bruise spreading over his chest made Kunal wince with every breath. If this was what friendship was, perhaps he had enough friends.

Alok's happiness at having mastered the feinting move hadn't faded, and he was yammering on about the different battle potentials for the trick. That at least brought a smile to Kunal's face. Alok would wiggle away if he ever voiced it, but Kunal thought of Alok and Laksh as brothers of a sort. Their success was his own.

They trudged up the steep incline of the outer ramp that led to the main level, their bellies rumbling, when a soldier yelled down at them. Kunal waved up in greeting as they climbed. The soldier came into view, wearing the thick, jeweled armband of a Senap guard, and Kunal greeted him with four fingers to his chest.

"Saran. Glad to see you up and awake."

"Barely," Saran said with a grin. Kunal grinned back as Alok joined them.

"You look better than I would have imagined after last night," Alok said.

Kunal shot him an admonishing look. Nine years at the Fort and Alok still had trouble knowing when to keep his mouth shut. Kunal knew the Fort hadn't been Alok's first choice of home—or Laksh's. The draft had claimed them, as his uncle had claimed Kunal.

Saran was different—the descendant of career soldiers from one of the lower noble houses who had come to power under King Vardaan. He had been born and bred for this, his entire life built around the Fort, and with that came power. A few words, and he could make Alok's life miserable.

Thankfully, he laughed. "We'll all look a bit worse for the wear today. We did reach a cease-fire last night, soldier," Saran said, holding a hand to his head. The wine had clearly had its way with him. "Means the Dharkans understand they are no match for us. Our might will win."

Kunal nodded, as was required of him. That was the basic gist of what they believed at the Fort. Kunal could recite the story of the Fort's rise by heart, as clearly as their Rules of Order.

He could hear his uncle's voice behind his words, steel and smoke.

A decade ago, Jansa had been weak under Queen Shilpa and the other Samyad queens, open to threats and obedient where they should have been dominant. Conceding instead of conquering during the War in the North thirty years ago. Vardaan taking rule was the natural order of things, as might would always win. His Himyad blood, the blood of kings, and prowess as a military adviser made him a natural choice for a leader. The rightful ruler over the weak Samyad queendom.

Since then, Jansa had been ruled by martial law, city councils and courts had been dismantled, and it had become illegal for large groups of people to gather. Before, the differences between the cultures of Jansa and Dharka—Jansa's commitment to honor, Dharka's love of mercy—were celebrated as two halves of a whole. But Vardaan's rhetoric changed Jansa after the coup, drawing the nobility and upper class into the idea of regaining their honor through might. Now Dharka's mercy was seen as a weakness.

He had never agreed with that, no matter how many times his uncle had made him recite the Rules of Order or King Vardaan's new edicts. But Kunal could never voice that here.

Kunal slipped back into the conversation as they finished discussing the feast last night and who owed who a new sword after the games of dice.

"I'm glad for the cease-fire, truly, but I'm already itching for something to do after our victory at Sundara. Our Senap squadron was just given orders and I hear we're going to the coast," said Saran, before turning to Kunal. "I'm excited to welcome you to our brotherhood, Kunal."

Kunal bowed his head in thanks, four fingers to his chest, and Saran responded in kind.

"The coast?" Laksh said, appearing from behind Saran. "That's a terrific assignment. I'd wrestle you for it if I didn't think the commander would miss me."

"It's a terrible assignment, just manhandling smugglers and the odd bandit, I bet," Saran said. "We haven't even been told what our mission is yet."

"It won't be so bad. You'll have the beauty of the ocean nearby, and you can visit the old temple ruins, full of exquisite stonework and mosaic tiles. And the food. The jalebis." Kunal looked up toward the skies, and the Sun Maiden, at the thought of the syrupy fried dough. "If you're looking for a taste of divine nectar, jalebis are as close as you'll get."

Alok and Laksh exchanged eye rolls, having heard this many times from him.

Saran laughed, slapping Kunal on the shoulder. "You always have the most interesting way of saying things, Kunal. We should name you the poet of the Fort."

Kunal flushed, unsure of what to say, but Laksh cut in. "There are also plenty of gambling houses and an underground fighting ring." At that Saran's face lit up, and he and Laksh walked ahead, deep in discussion about the gambling scene up the coast.

They crossed the sun-worn stones of the open courtyard and were about to turn in to the residence wing where the dining halls were when Alok's hand shot out to stop Kunal.

Kunal's head went up in an instant, his hand at his knife.

He scanned the area. No immediate threat. Kunal relaxed his posture and followed Alok's gaze.

They hadn't noticed the soldier in irons, slumped against the sandstone in the shadows. It was common to be slapped in irons for punishment, a way to teach soldiers a lesson and make them stronger.

Kunal shook his head at Alok and moved to keep walking. He recoiled in the next instant, understanding Alok's shock.

The soldier was dead. Kunal's heart sank when he realized that he recognized him.

It was Udit, the young recruit who was born in the southwest of the Varulok region, like him. Only a week ago they had spent a meal reminiscing about their favorite childhood games in the tea plantations that covered the hills of Varulok.

His chest constricted, and he felt that familiar tug of frustration at his heart. What infraction could have possibly deserved this? His body out in the heat, uncovered.

"It's not right," Alok whispered, echoing the thoughts Kunal refused to speak. "Why wasn't his body cleaned, readied for the pyre?"

Kunal steadied his shaking hand, breathing in and out in the way Uncle Setu had taught him to master his emotions. *Control.*

"There must be a reason," he said, his voice now even. He looked away sharply from Udit. "He must have broken the Rules of Order. Or worse."

"Would that be a reason to disgrace his soul?" Alok asked, looking sidelong at Kunal.

"Alok," Kunal said, his voice a whisper. The Fort was always listening; many of the servants, and even soldiers, reported any hint of dissent directly to his uncle. "That is what happens when you break the rules." Kunal spoke fast, rushing his words.

"He was a boy, young and inexperienced," Alok whispered back. "They've branded him a traitor by leaving his body out like that."

"He is a soldier, first and foremost. We both know there can be no exceptions to the rules. And what if he was a traitor?"

"Remember the last time someone was labeled a traitor? How an innocent boy died? The commander went off the word of the accuser instead of allowing a proper trial."

Kunal remembered. It had happened only a few moons ago. He couldn't even recall the soldier's defense now, only the accusation. It had been wrong of the commander to mete out justice without a trial.

"I'm sure the general was just following the rules."

"But if the rules don't make sense?"

"Not this again." Kunal shook his head, feeling his hands clench. "If you want to survive at the Fort, you've got to uphold your duty, and that is to follow orders."

It's not worth disobeying.

Kunal had learned that early on in his ten years at the Fort. He had the scars to show.

This conversation was one that had been happening more frequently over the past couple of moons, which worried Kunal. If Alok stuck his neck out too much, it might mean more than a beating.

Alok's nostrils flared, his eyes lighting up in a way that

told Kunal he was ready to fight. Kunal grabbed him and dragged him up the ramp, away from Udit's body and prying ears.

"Alok, don't be stupid. You think things will change just like that?"

Alok only glared at him and walked away.

Kunal pressed the heels of his palms into his temples. Despite his harsh words, he felt the same as Alok.

Control.

The general wouldn't have condoned this—would he? He resolved to find out.

———◇———

Kunal closed his eyes and released his held breath as he reached the top of the spiraling stairs, willing his heart to stop thudding.

Every time.

Even now, the thought of facing Uncle Setu sent a shiver of nerves down his spine. He was certainly stronger, taller, more experienced than when he had first come to the Fort at the age of eight—but facing this door always brought back memories of the first time he had seen the menacing height of the Fort above him. His new home.

Kunal ran through his arguments, knowing heated words wouldn't win over General Setu Hotha of the Red Fortress. Uncle Setu appreciated logic and reason, so Kunal would remind his uncle of the noble houses, like House Rusala, and the textile merchants still bitter about the conscription. Leaving their sons' bodies unconsecrated wouldn't help that.

He sighed, unsure if his words would make any difference. But something stirred him to try after talking with Alok, even if he ended up in irons himself.

When he reached the door of his uncle's room, it was slightly ajar. Kunal stopped. His uncle never left the door open; he valued his privacy and didn't take kindly to visitors.

Cautiously, Kunal raised a hand and knocked.

No response.

His uncle wanted him to act more like a leader of the Fort. Take more initiative. He had said as much the last time they had spoken.

Kunal pushed open the thick door.

The bloody bed was the first thing he saw, a pool of red in a sea of stark white. Then his uncle's still body, sprawled across his beautiful embroidered pillows.

Shock hit him like a slap and he felt his heart stop, as if time itself slowed in the face of his disbelief.

He slammed against the wall, hand at his knife, quickly circling the perimeter of the room to see if the murderer was still there.

The room was clear.

That's when he broke with his training, crossing the distance to his uncle's bed in a few strides. Blood was everywhere, pooled and streaked across the sheets. Kunal grabbed his uncle's wrist. Put two fingers against his cold throat.

Disbelief, grief, fury coursed through him as he grasped his uncle's lifeless hand. Kunal felt his control, the one thing his uncle taught him to never lose his sight of, slipping.

First, he needed to alert the commander. The clotted blood around the wound and his uncle's cooling skin indicated his death had been hours ago, not recent, but he couldn't be sure.

He was a soldier and he had seen death before, but it had never been so personal.

Uncle Setu had been killed in his bed. Without a chance of fighting back. What kind of dishonorable man would do such a thing? Kunal had blood on his hands he could never clean, but it was all done on a battlefield. Honorable face-to-face fighting in the name of Jansa. Assassination was cowardice.

Kunal's blinding rage sent a searing pain to his temple and he lurched forward, gasping. This was why his uncle had taught him control, to remain calm and assess. These headaches plagued him whenever he didn't. He caught himself and leaned on the side of his uncle's ornately carved bed, an engraved golden eagle on the bed post digging into his palm.

A succession of quick footsteps resounded on the stairs. Kunal straightened immediately, trying to compose himself and just as he felt the final tremor leave his hands, the door opened.

Commander Panak swung open the door, two soldiers behind him. Their faces blanched.

"I hoped you wouldn't see this," the commander said. "I went to find pallbearers to carry him down for his rites. We found him only a quarter hour ago. We also found a soldier unconscious outside."

Kunal nodded. "I was just about to alert the Fort."

"No need, but appreciated." He gave Kunal a strained smile. "A soldier to the core."

"The killer?" Kunal's stomach was a roiling sea, but he kept his face placid as a lake. His uncle would have been proud. The commander shook his head wearily.

"Unknown."

"And the soldier outside, sir? Does he have any information to speak of?"

"He had nothing but babbles. He was found unconscious outside, smelling of honey liquor," Panak said. "I don't think he let the killer in on purpose. Most likely incompetence—drunk and disarmed by the killer—but we threw him in the stocks. What a disgrace of a soldier."

Kunal nodded mutely. The boy must have died overnight from his injuries.

The commander sighed and ran a hand through his short hair. He looked as if he had aged years in just a few hours.

"Any suspects, sir?" Kunal asked, trying to keep his emotions at bay.

Commander Panak hesitated. "One."

Kunal waited for more, but the commander didn't clarify, instead staring at Kunal as though he were considering something.

"Meet me in the Hall of Generals in an hour, Kunal." The commander's voice softened almost imperceptibly. "You'll want to be there."

CHAPTER 5

Esha glanced backward every so often as she made her way through the mud roads of Pora, the small traders' town situated in the hilly groves on the edge of the Tej rain forest.

Pora was a pit stop for weary travelers or traders on the Great Road, the main trading path that cut east and west through the Southern Lands. It was also where one of her contacts, Jiten, used an unassuming pawn shop as a cover for more unsavory business.

Jiten's shop had been her only stop on her way to the Fort. He was also one of the few non-Blades who might have a real crescent pin, as it was only given to Blades or their close associates to mark them as safe for business.

For his sake, she hoped her suspicion was wrong.

She couldn't help but feel like she was being watched as

she passed through the city center, despite knowing that no one knew she was the Viper. After finding the crescent pin and her whip in the dead general's room the night before, she couldn't be sure of anything.

Only that she would have to be on high alert now.

The empty path behind her didn't give her much comfort either. Esha knew the soldiers would be after the Viper when they found her real whip; she had bartered on it. The only comfort she had was that none of those soldiers would be looking for a girl.

A thousand questions flooded her mind, all of them leading back to one sickening realization.

What if the general's murderer knew she wasn't just the Viper, but one of the Crescent Blades? Worse, that she was one of the masterminds, a co-leader with Harun, the crown prince of Dharka?

Though the Fort soldiers fought against the Blades in border skirmishes, they were soldiers bred for war and it was the infantry who carried out the raids on the rebel outposts. But bad blood like this might coerce even the elite Senap guards to pursue the rebels and capture them.

Esha's hand immediately went to her right arm, rubbing her elbow as she remembered the last time she had encountered the Senap Guard. After the Senaps murdered her parents in front of her, they had taken her captive and held her for weeks in the citadel prison at Gwali for "questioning." One of the bones they broke never set well. She had trained around it, ignoring the way her left arm never extended as fully as the right, using her whips to make up for it.

All in the name of the lost princess, the one who got away.

Esha shivered and turned the corner, ducking under a low stone archway. The merchants' silk-covered stalls shone like uncut rubies to her left; she turned right.

Even sending a note back to Harun at the rebel base might be dangerous, especially if it was intercepted or tipped off whoever had framed her. Only a select few had known she was heading on this mission. She was on her own for now.

This wasn't the first time she'd been cornered, and she would get her answers, even if she had to beat them out of someone. Starting with Jiten, who was her only lead.

The narrow mud paths opened into the outskirts of town, where huts and tents were spread out over the low grassy hills. On the horizon she could spot the Tej rain forest, a glimmering green and gold in the hazy sunlight. It used to extend till Pora, its vines and trees crawling over buildings, but that had all changed in recent years.

Esha tugged at the straps of her pack, securing them as they slid down her sweaty back. At least the turban provided her some relief from the dust flying about, remnants of scorched earth from the drought. Everywhere she went, there were signs that the land was dying.

It had been different ten years ago. The heat had still

been punishing, but it held a gentleness, and the land turned out beautiful purple flowers and lip-puckering fruits. Nothing grew in this patch of land anymore, after the Bhagya River, their mother river, started to vanish, after the *janma* bond had been broken.

She blamed the Pretender King.

A decade ago, Vardaan Himyad had been second in line to the Dharkan throne as the younger of the two princes, but still, he wasn't satisfied. He'd joined Queen Shilpa's service in Jansa after the end of the War in the North and had slowly consolidated power along with Setu Hotha, then only a commander. Vardaan promised land and riches to those who followed his rule, recruiting two of the five noble houses of Jansa to his cause.

On the longest night of the year, as soon as the Jansan royal family had returned from their trip to the mountains to renew the *janma* bond, Vardaan and Hotha struck. Vardaan and the general took control of the capital while the army, loyal to Hotha, captured two military garrisons and the Blood Fort, murdering the royal family, their personal court, and anyone who fought back.

All the Samyads, the ruling royal family for centuries, wiped out in one night.

The story was that the royals had been plotting treason against Jansa, allying with the Yavar clansmen up north to take over the Southern Lands. But most knew the truth—that the Pretender King had taken the throne for his own power and benefit.

The day after the solstice, what was once a day to celebrate the Sun Maiden's return to the land was now known as the Night of Tears for the families that woke up to death and grief. It was whispered that the gods themselves shed tears that night, their anger turning the sky stormy, providing the wild monsoon that hid Princess Reha's path away from the palace as she escaped her aunt's murderer.

The murderer who now sat on the throne.

And the land had suffered ever since, growing more and more unpredictable. The renewal ritual for the *janma* bond was a topic ancient and arcane enough to be studied by scholars in Gwali and Mathur, but every Southern Lander knew the basics. It required a blood sacrifice from both a Samyad woman and a Himyad man, echoing the first offering to the gods from Naran and Naria.

As the direct descendants of Naran and Naria, only the Himyads and Samyads had the shape-shifting blood necessary to renew the *janma* bond. Queen Shilpa, her daughters and her sisters—they had been the last of the Samyad queens.

Now, with one half of the necessary blood wiped out, Jansa hadn't seen a monsoon in years. Without the natural, life-giving rains of the monsoon, the dry heat and winds of the summer season had turned the Jansan land barren.

Seeing the effects of the drought in person was heartbreaking. She should have been overjoyed to be heading back, eager to see her team in Mathur, the capital of Dharka. Arpiya, Harun, Bhandu, the twins. But instead a cloud hung over her head.

Esha turned a corner and almost ran into a small child and the mother running after him. She caught the little boy by his shoulders as his mother caught up, wheezing. The woman gave Esha a grateful look before admonishing the boy. Esha chuckled as she walked away.

It reminded her of Arpiya, the way she'd toss her head back and let out a long sigh at something Esha had done or said. Arpiya was two years her elder, and never one to pass up lording it over her. She didn't mind. She had always wanted a sibling. Esha missed Arpiya the most of her team, but more than anything, she missed the companionship, feeling known by someone.

Maybe that was the reason she couldn't get the chivalrous soldier out of her thoughts. It was the longest, most comfortable conversation she'd had in weeks, and she couldn't seem to stop replaying it over and over.

She shook her head. At least she would never see him again.

Esha passed the small door Jiten used for his clientele; the one she wanted was the second door, which he had hidden behind a thick jute throw.

She made short work of the throw, tossing it to the side in a heap. She eased the door open, taking care not to make a creak. Esha took up a spot in the shadows with her knife drawn, a wraith of darkness.

She would get her answers, that was for sure.

CHAPTER 6

The Hall of Generals was one of Kunal's favorite places in the Fort.

As an eight-year-old, newly arrived and adrift, he had come here often to stare at the tall statues of fabled generals. He'd marvel at the way the statues almost came to life despite being carved into the marble walls, at the paintings that hung next to each general, depicting their greatest victory. He would spend hours under the hall's gold etched ceilings.

Somehow he thought the more he studied these generals, men who his uncle had deemed "great," the more he could be like them. Mimic their poses, echo their dutiful behavior, and he'd become the soldier his uncle wanted, the nephew he wanted. Orphaned and alone, he had longed to fit in at the Fort and gain his uncle's approval.

Kunal brushed his hand against the golden mace of

General Vasu, the first general of Jansa and Naria's trusted adviser. Now the Hall of Generals was just a reminder of another family member he had lost.

Would the depiction of his uncle be accurate, conveying the contradictions of the man? His fierce commitment to duty, his cunning, his callousness, his moments of kindness, his ambition—would any of that be shown? Or would he be depicted as another "great" man, leaving aside the complicated human be had been?

The main door to the hall opened and the commander strode in, his dark hair askew. Three soldiers—Laksh, Amir, and Rakesh—trailed into the room behind him. Together, they made up the different regiments that stayed at the Fort: charioteer, elephanteer, and cavalry.

Two servants followed, carrying a bundle wrapped in the traditional white cloth, his uncle's body cleaned. It was then that he knew he couldn't escape the reality.

Uncle Setu was dead.

The stillness, the absence of a soul. Witnessing it was never easy, but he couldn't believe his uncle's fierce presence was lost forever. Without him, Kunal was . . . alone again.

Commander Panak hadn't let him carry the body down, as was custom for family, saying it wasn't part of the rules. Things were different when a general died, no matter if Kunal was his only living relative. Still, he'd been one of the first to know, instead of being told in the mess hall as usual. It made him feel the tiniest bit better.

The commander nodded at Kunal, Amir, Laksh, and

Rakesh. "I've brought you four soldiers down here to witness something, but any mention of this to the rest of the Fort before I give the order, and you can guarantee you'll be in irons for a fortnight."

Amir and Rakesh exchanged looks as Kunal walked over to Laksh.

His friend's face was pinched in confusion, his hands freshly cut open from fighting and smelling faintly of smoke and iron. He must have been training in the lower levels, near the blacksmiths, when they grabbed him. He gave Kunal a questioning look but Kunal had no words, instead nodding his head toward the body.

The other soldiers recoiled when the white sheet was lifted back, revealing the general. Kunal was the only one who didn't move a muscle, focusing his gaze down the hall.

"Our general will no longer lead this fort with the might of his sword. He was murdered in his bed last night." The commander's voice changed from soft regret to steel. "There was no attempt at subterfuge or diversion; it was a cold-blooded act. The killer wanted us to know what they had done. In fact, they left this."

With a flick of disgust, the commander pulled a whip out of his pocket and tossed it on the ground. Its metal hilt, emblazoned with dual snakes, clanged against the marble floor, the sound echoing throughout the cavernous hall.

"The Viper," Amir whispered, his tone almost reverential.

"Impossible," Laksh said.

Kunal looked up at them both sharply.

Kunal had always believed the Viper was a myth. The Viper was said to be many things: a creature with otherworldly powers of disguise gifted by the trickster spirits, a human spy who wielded two whips like the forked tongue of a serpent, a dark incarnation of Naria intent on justice. No matter what you believed, one thing was clear: the Viper's mission was to bring down the Jansan army.

Not that the famous spy couldn't be based on reality; a Dharkan who caused mischief and meted out justice was believable enough. But the Viper's exploits were so prolific that the stories bordered on the impossible.

In the course of six moons he had supposedly been all over Jansa—stopping a Jansan blockade of the port of Punohar, stealing a shipment of iron to the capital, and most troubling of all, assassinating a lower council member of the House Ayul in the west. It was whispered that the council member had been corrupt, stealing part of the royal tax he collected—but still.

Despite that, neither the Blades nor any other rebel group had ever claimed him or his exploits as their own. For all purposes, the Viper acted alone. The romance of a lone vigilante and the incredible stories had elevated the Viper to legend in the hearts and minds of both Jansans and Dharkans.

Kunal, and most of the captains, thought it was a cover for a number of rebel spies. It was possible various resistance groups even shared the title. But so far, they had no proof of that connection.

Something was off, though, like incorrect shading of a sunset. The Viper was known to leave little trinkets, all with the trademark double snakes.

But his own whip? The whips that had come to define him? Why leave one of those behind?

"This *Viper*—the coward who has destroyed our ships, killed good soldiers, taken back land we had won—deserves a reckoning. So I have a mission for you four soldiers. It won't be easy," Commander Panak said. "You have each been handpicked to represent your regiment. Whoever finds the murderer, this Viper, will be named the next commander of the Fort and will lead the next generation of soldiers—if you choose to accept."

Kunal's heartbeat quickened. This was what his uncle had wanted for Kunal, and had been pushing him toward, since he had come to the Fort as a shy eight-year-old. It would be dangerous but also an opportunity. One he wouldn't get otherwise.

Uncle Setu had been a hard man, but he had taken Kunal in and had shown him a new life when his old one had fallen to pieces. That was worth the weight of a thousand suns. He owed his uncle his life.

As a last act of gratitude to the man who had raised him, he would do this. Kunal would find the coward who had murdered his uncle and bring him back here to pay for his actions. It was a jewel on top that he could also become commander, the very thing his uncle had wanted so desperately for him.

"You will all take the guise of being part of a larger counter-resistance task force, but you will be able to act and pursue the Viper independently. Your only requirement for this mission is to check in every week at a nearby garrison. If you miss two check-ins, you'll be deemed out of action."

Kunal tried not to show his surprise. That meant the mission would be wholly theirs—to plan and to execute.

"Retrieve the Viper within the next two moons, and come back as commander." Kunal looked at the others, waiting for the catch. "Fail to capture the Viper, allow another soldier to capture the Viper first, and you will face a punishment, determined by the new commander and me. This is no normal mission, so the reward and punishment can't be either."

Kunal blanched, realizing this could mean he'd lose his promotion to the Senap Guard. Or worse, if Rakesh became commander. He swallowed his unease. He didn't plan to lose.

The commander swept his gaze across the four soldiers in front of him. "I'm giving you ample time. You have two moons before the start of the Sun Mela."

Kunal wondered why the Mela, their biennial games celebrating Naria's defeat of the Lord of Death, had been chosen as the date. He didn't have time to think on it too much as the commander looked straight at Kunal.

"Kunal Dhagan." He looked up at the sound of his name, his surname the only nod to his mother's family that his uncle had let him keep. "You're not officially a Senap yet, but I asked that you, as the nephew of the general, would represent them in this mission." His voice softened, though his expression didn't. "This will be a thankless task. I won't think less of any who ask to leave now."

Kunal's gaze didn't stray. This was expected of him; the commander had said as much. He could entertain doubts later.

The other soldiers seemed to be thinking the same, but they had less cause to stay. If they left, it wouldn't be a blot on their family's honor. It wasn't their duty to find the killer.

Kunal looked over at Laksh, whose mouth was set in a determined line, and felt a surge of gratitude, even if this meant they would eventually become competitors. He was the only other soldier he'd be happy to lose to.

"Start out in the morning, soldiers. You may work together but don't forget, whoever comes back with the Viper is my new commander." He looked around at each of them, locking eyes with Kunal in particular.

Kunal set his jaw. This was his chance to become commander, lead the Fort, and honor his uncle. His uncle wouldn't be alive to see it, but he knew this was what he would've wanted for him.

"For the glory of the king!" Commander Panak yelled, and the soldiers slapped their chests in response, repeating his words with fervor, their shouts ringing through the room.

"Find the cursed bastard and bring him to me." The commander swept out of the room, the clanging of his armor following him.

CHAPTER 7

Alok nearly dropped his bowl, looking at the two of them as if they were stupid.

"Why would you ever agree to such a mission?"

Laksh sighed. "This is a great opportunity, Alok. It would take a normal soldier ten years, at least, to become commander."

"And it's our duty, Alok," Kunal said.

It was his duty, his obligation to his uncle.

"But, Kunal, remember your last conversation with him."

"He was just upset that I had applied to be posted at Gwali. And maybe he was right, maybe my place is here," Kunal said. "At the Fort."

"He expected you to be at the Fort; that doesn't mean he was right. Think about what *you* want, Kunal."

"I want to do this."

"You don't have to—"

Kunal glared at his friend and to his surprise, Alok shut up.

"Thanks for the rousing support."

Alok looked at him with an odd expression. "I'm your friend. I don't want to see either of you dead. The Viper was able to sneak into the Fort and stab the damn general. *The general*," he said, slamming the table in front of them.

Laksh shushed him, looking around the low light of the Mess Hall.

A small thought bloomed in Kunal's head. The Viper was able to sneak into the Fort last night . . .

The hall door was thrown open and rows of soldiers turned their heads to look for the disturbance. Two soldiers brought in a body and Kunal almost shot up, before realizing it was too small to be his uncle's.

The boy they had seen in irons. His disheveled state was a stark contrast to the way his uncle's body had been treated—he hadn't been cleaned or given the proper rites.

Murmurs rippled through the hardened soldiers, mutterings and prayers.

Commander Panak rose from his seat, his hand at the sword that hung off his hip. "Let it be a warning; this soldier failed in his duty last night. In death he will not be honored, as he wouldn't be in life."

Alok gasped, so quietly only Kunal heard, but he understood. The soldier might have been alive when found, but his failure had ensured his death. Kunal had assumed wrong. He hadn't passed in the night due to injuries.

This—this was unnecessary. Nothing in Kunal's body or soul could tell him otherwise. The soldier had been so young, new to the Fort, and untrained.

Death surrounded them as soldiers, and they wielded it as they did their weapons. To be scared of death as a soldier was to invite it in to claim you. Kunal forced himself to draw his eyes up and rest on the boy's frame, which looked smaller in death. To remember and respect him, the small stories, the dreams and hopes he had nestled in his chest, as they all did.

A soldier's life was ruthless, cold, and Kunal hadn't always known how to stomach it. He inhaled, saying a small prayer over the boy's life, and then savagely brought up the walls around his heart.

Kunal let the calmness of duty and discipline settle over him, edging away any other feeling. The mess hall devolved into a mass of chatter and noise as the Fort leadership left, the servants taking the body away.

He turned off his emotions and focused back on the task at hand. He wouldn't end up like that boy, he wouldn't fail. His uncle deserved justice. And he would do whatever it took to ensure it was served.

Which meant he had a Viper to catch.

CHAPTER 8

Esha tossed the hilt of the knife in the air, catching it and flipping it up again as she waited for her contact, Jiten, to wake up.

The shop was a contradiction. Rows of teacups and other trinkets were interspersed with bronze maces and sinister-looking knives. Amid all the chaos Esha had placed Jiten, who sat in a wooden chair, out of reach of any weapon—or trinket.

Esha sighed and slapped Jiten once. He woke, sputtering and with terror in his eyes as he realized he was bound to a chair.

She crouched down until she was eye level with the sallow-faced man.

"Anything you want to tell me, Jiten?"

He shook his head, trying to fight against his bindings.

Esha raised an eyebrow. "Are you sure? You know, I thought we had built some trust between us. You even told me I was one of your best, even favorite, clients."

"You are," he stuttered.

"I am? Then why have you treated me so poorly, Jiten? Someone discovered my mission. Knew where I was going to be. The only person who knew about my mission in Jansa is, well, you," Esha said, affecting her voice to be saccharine, bordering on confused.

"I didn't tell anyone where you were going! What would poor me know? I only knew you were going south. I said nothing at all. I knew not to say anything, that's for sure. I wouldn't make that mistake. I wouldn't anger the Vi—you."

Esha tapped the side of her nose, holding eye contact until he squirmed. "A good decision. And I believe you." Jiten breathed a sigh of relief. "But now I know someone was asking about me."

She pressed the sharp tip of her knife into the delicate muscles of his hands. "Don't lie to me. I don't want to have to tell your other clientele that you've been spreading gossip like a fisherman. Do I?"

Jiten's fingers trembled as Esha tapped the tip of her knife against each one of his fingers.

"Someone stopped in asking about the Viper," he said in a rush, screwing his eyes shut.

Esha frowned. "Who?"

He hesitated. "I don't ask questions of those who are just seeking to trade in information. The man was hooded. He asked about the state of the Bhagya River, that new fellow, Dharmdev, who has been making a fuss in Gwali, and then the fading *janma* bond. Then the Viper. I thought nothing of it—even my regular clientele have asked me what I know of the famed vigilante. You—" Esha shot him a sharp look. "The Viper has made quite a name for themselves.

"You're good for business, it's true. But upon the Sun Maiden's bow, I swear I never revealed anything about your identity or mission. I don't even know what it is! I just do my business, collect the money, and stay away from all that," he said.

Esha stared at him, waiting. Her contact's eyes shifted back and forth, and Esha had seen the same tic enough to know when someone was about to reveal something unpleasant.

He gulped, withering under her gaze. "But when I checked later in the day, the Blades pin I keep hidden in the folds of my uttariya was gone," he said.

"Gone," Esha repeated, trying to find some new connection in this revelation. All it told her was that whoever had framed her was one step ahead of her, and had been. "And you didn't think to tell me?"

A bead of sweat inched across Jiten's forehead and his wan face took on a greenish tint.

"I didn't want—"

"If you ever give any details about me again, if you ever hint you know anything about me, real or legend, I'll come back and take your least favorite finger," Esha said calmly, her knife still resting delicately in the space between his knuckles.

Jiten blinked. Twice. "Least favorite? Not my most favorite?"

"You're right, I'll take both."

Esha stood up, looming over Jiten with her knife raised.

"I have more! I have more. You'll want to know this," he said. Esha tilted her head at him to continue. "A date for the peace summit has been set. Two moons from now."

She paused, realizing the importance of this information. Two moons. Which meant she had only one moon to figure out who was behind this and get back to Mathur. Any longer and she'd miss the royal party before they left.

Jiten seemed to sense the shift in her and lunged at it. "There's whispers of a Blade, not one of the usuals, roaming around in Faor up north in the hills. Big purse and looking to engage a caravan. If you're searching for someone suspicious, someone who might know too much, look there."

He paused, glancing at her face before he pushed further. "Why would a rebel be trying to leave Jansa now, when peace is on the horizon? It's suspicious, isn't it?" he asked, a sly smile splitting across his face.

Why indeed? Esha couldn't deny that it made sense.

A disgruntled Blade would be dangerous. Why an ex-Blade would murder the general and frame her, Esha couldn't say. But they had all the skills and knowledge required. They'd been clever enough to steal Jiten's pin, and she didn't want to know if killing the general had been the grand finale or if there was more to come.

She couldn't help the small shudder the realization

caused. Most of the Blades had been trained by her and Harun, which meant she would have to use caution, and not hesitate when she found this rogue rebel.

To Faor, then.

"See? I'm useful," her contact said, drawing her attention back.

"You've been useful—for now." Esha chuckled, and even Jiten cracked a smile, sensing that some of the danger had dissipated. He looked expectantly down at his bindings, giving a little kick.

Esha gathered her bag, taking care to not nick herself as she returned her knife to its hidden spot in her sari.

"I'm sure one of your servants will be in soon and untie you. Let this be a lesson. Don't lie to me again," Esha said, before stuffing a short piece of cloth into his mouth.

His muffled shouts filled the room as she slung her pack across her chest and climbed out the window.

CHAPTER 9

Kunal moved about his room, packing his things with quick precision as Alok watched. He had recruited his friend to help him gather as much information as possible that afternoon before he left—stories, rumors, tall tales, anything.

One of the first things he'd been taught during his Senap training was that all information had a pattern. Now if only he could find the Viper's pattern.

"Throw in some paper. And chalk," Alok said, his gaze tight with worry.

Kunal raised an eyebrow. "Paper and chalk? Do you think I'm going on a leisure trip to the mountains?"

"No, you daft ox. But you will make the time to keep me apprised of what's going on. I don't trust the reports from anyone else." Alok frowned. "I may not act like it all the time, but let's not forget who's older here. If something happened to you . . . well, I'm as good as next of kin. So don't be a pillock, and write me. Use the messenger hawks that always seem to love you."

Kunal paused, considering Alok's words. He was right. Without General Hotha, Alok was basically the only one left at the Fort who would care if something happened to him.

"I will. I promise," Kunal said with sincerity. The tension from Alok's shoulders lifted, as did his expression. "Though I'm not sure why you're not bothering Laksh as well."

"I tried already." A cloud passed over Alok's face, but it shifted so quickly that Kunal blinked, thinking he had imagined it.

"Anyway." He slapped Kunal on the back. "For a man facing almost certain death, you don't look too worried."

Kunal grimaced at him. "Thinking that I'm facing certain death might change that, so let's go with a man looking to avenge his uncle's honor." Alok snorted. Kunal continued, hoping to get him off his back. "And a man who plans to return as your commander. Maybe then I can get a proper lock on my door and some privacy," he muttered.

Alok looked at him with dawning comprehension. "So, that's your play. I didn't think you'd have something like that in you. Gods above, do you actually want to be commander? Or is this just your uncle talking?"

Kunal shrugged. "If this is to be my home for most of my life, I may as well have a role in leading it. Steering it in the right direction." He didn't mention that his words were ones taken almost directly from his uncle.

It was his duty to take over at the Fort, to honor their family.

Kunal had heard it so many times he could whisper it while drowning.

He knew what "steering the Fort in the right direction" meant to his uncle, but he had yet to fully determine what it meant to him. There were ideas, small hopes and inklings of changes that he believed he could make, but Kunal was hoping this journey would bring clarity.

Kunal remembered the tales his mother had told him of the Jansan army, the warriors of old, made in the image of Naria, the just and strong twin. That army had been revered, unlike now.

Maybe it *was* a dream, but as commander he could lead the army back to that era.

A whistle came from Alok, cutting through his thoughts. "I'm impressed. I thought you were doing this for some ridiculous sense of loyalty to your uncle. He was a strong general but he did you no favors."

"Of course, I am—" He stopped, realizing it would be easier to get Alok to stop worrying if he thought Kunal was doing this for himself. And Kunal couldn't deny that his uncle had been hard, didn't even want to deny that. "It's both, Alok. Honor and ambition. It's what I have now."

"Anyway, was any of the information we collected useful?" Alok asked.

"I thought it would simply be a collection of scattered and unhelpful stories. But I've noticed some patterns."

Alok raised an eyebrow and Kunal began ticking off each

with his fingers. "One, the Viper works alone—that seems to be a theme in every report. No official affiliation with the Crescent Blades or any of the other rebel groups. There are suspicions, but the Blades have never hesitated to recognize one of their agents, especially one who's created as much havoc as the Viper. Two, there are no clear depictions of the Viper's face and he often disappears quickly after a mission, which tells me he's the type of person who doesn't stand out. And finally, two whips."

Kunal paused, and Alok scooted closer. "That means stealth. The Viper relies on speed and stealth rather than brute force."

Alok let out a low whistle. "So, basically, you should have listened to me and not agreed to this crazy mission?"

Kunal looked to the skies and ignored him, tucking away rations he had left over from his last mission in the west.

"Fine, ignore me," Alok said. "You know, I was talking to Zane and he said he saw someone last night."

Kunal's head whipped around. "And you waited this long to mention it? I thought you wanted me to stay alive."

"Yes, for some reason." Alok rolled his eyes. "I had forgotten because it seemed like such a useless piece of information. He was drunker than a trader at the Moon Festival. It showed—he said he saw a girl."

Kunal froze, his hand hovering over his pack, not realizing he was holding the knife in his hand the wrong way. He looked down—a sliver of blood cut across his palm.

Alok chuckled and continued, oblivious. "Clearly he couldn't handle his wine. I *wish* there had been girls around last night." An ungainly snort escaped from Alok. "It's like he wants us to think he's lost his mind."

It was preposterous. The mythical Viper, slayer of soldiers, warrior of the rebels.

A girl?

Those chestnut eyes stabbing a knife into the general's heart?

He tried, but he couldn't paint that picture in his mind. She was a trader girl from Jansa, here to deliver poppy seeds and gone just as soon. If Kunal had thought any more, he would've been more careful, more alert. Kunal laughed along with him, brushing aside the thoughts. The guard had seen what he wanted to see.

"Alok, get off your fat ass and help me finish packing. I need to leave with the rest before sundown." Alok smirked at the insult but moved to help him, tossing Kunal's sheathed weapons onto his bed.

"Looks like I've finally rubbed off on you."

Kunal kept up the banter with Alok, glad to have his mind occupied with anything other than the girl.

CHAPTER 10

Esha looked up at the sky as the last purple of the sunset faded.

Back home in Dharka, it was monsoon season, and she checked the sky out of habit, despite knowing there would be no rain in Jansa. She settled into the small nook of the tree she had climbed, broad enough to hide her small form. The Tej rain forest was lush and thicketed with banyan trees, the perfect cover for her.

It was too risky to camp on the ground, another side effect of the broken *janma* bond. Strange things had been reported over the last two years: animals turning to blood when berries would've been their choice before, twisting tree roots that clawed at passersby in the night. Almost as if the land itself was angry.

Esha tugged out a small blanket to cover herself from bugs, pulling out the stolen report scrolls as well. She had glanced at them earlier but needed a private place to look through them. The sounds that enveloped her, the chirping and hissing animals, the breeze on the leaves of the canopy above her, all buffeted her. This was the only privacy she would find while on the run.

She squinted at the scroll in her hand, trying to take in the sloping scrawl as the last of the sunlight vanished. Already a difficult task, but someone had decided to write the cursed reports in Old Jansan, which she wasn't familiar with. There was a part of her that was hoping her years of tutelage in Old Dharkan would help, but despite sharing a script, the two languages were different enough that it made her head ache.

Esha resisted the urge to crumple up the scroll and toss it to the family of monkeys a couple of trees down. Instead, she rubbed her eyes and rolled the scroll back up, deciding to give it another shot in the morning when she reached the next town before Faor.

Night descended and all around her the trees began to emit a faint glow. Esha took a minute to marvel as the rain forest slowly came to eerily colored life. She had heard tales of the Tej since she was a child, the glowing forest, but seeing it in person always made her breath catch. It was as if the whole of the Tej had been dipped in bright green paint.

Even as the land south was stricken with drought, the luminescence of the forest continued on, though the lights were dimmer than the last time she had been here. The scholars from the college in Mathur said that the pockets of land where magic was deeper, like the Tej, wouldn't succumb as easily to the drought. Esha was just happy the *janma* bond hadn't completely died here—it comforted her. It meant hope.

The Tej always made Esha think of nights curled up in her father's lap, listening to tales of Dharka and Jansa—of how Naran and Naria had helped the gods churn the sea, how they'd pulled up the double peninsula that formed the Southern Lands from the water and had been blessed by the sun and moon with shape-shifting blood—a gift from the gods to bind together the land and their own people for eons.

A glint of silvery water caught her eye as Esha shifted in the tree, making her think of her favorite part of the story.

The sun and moon had lassoed the celestial river and gently poured it onto the land for Naran and Naria. The twins' blood, cut from the palm of each twin and intermingled, had anchored the Bhagya River to the land, guiding its tributaries to give life to the west and east of the peninsula, to Jansa and Dharka. And so the *janma* bond had been set, renewed each year on Mount Bangaar on the winter solstice with a blood offering from the direct descendants of the twins. It was a ritual shrouded in mystery, its secrets protected by the ruling families—the only non-royals privy were the scholars of arcana in each nation's college. It was hard to know what was myth and what was real anymore.

Still, the tale made her shiver even in the warmth of the night. They had taken the *janma* bond for granted, and look where they were now. Without the anchoring blood of both the royal families, Jansa was dying. And according to the scholars, Dharka was next. The next renewal ritual would be the last. It was six moons away, but they still had no solution.

Esha rubbed her eyes. It was a problem of the worst kind.

She sighed into the night, allowing its vastness to engulf her, calm her. She closed her eyes and settled back into the tree trunk, determined to get some sleep. It came for her swiftly, warm and inviting.

A whiff of smoke wafted into the air, and she woke with a start. Then a noise. It started out faint, but soon Esha couldn't deny the crackling of a fire in the distance.

Esha was up in an instant, taking care to not tumble out of the tree in her haste. The smoke wasn't far, and she couldn't bet on the intruders keeping to their camp. The banyan was a low-hanging tree, perfect for obscuring her from travelers on the well-worn paths, but not much help against anyone who stood directly underneath.

Esha shed the blanket and quickly scrambled farther up the tree, looking out from the heavy branches.

Soldiers or raiders? She had cut down a few raiders in her time, and they were quick but untrained. A soldier would be much worse.

Esha peered out over the branches, struggling to make out shapes in the camp. There looked to be about four figures moving, about three hundred paces away. Far but not far enough.

Esha cursed. Soldiers. Their armor was quiet, oiled to be silent, but the cuirasses caught the light of the fire, glinting off the trees and the moonlight. She considered her options. Stay put and hope to the gods they didn't pass her way, or try to put more distance between her and them.

Neither path was ideal. Her thoughts swirled like the edges of a dust storm, thrashing against her skull. Best case, she was able to hide until they passed. Worst, they found her and took her back to the Fort—the last place she wanted to go.

If they stayed on the path, she'd probably be fine here. But she couldn't bet on it.

Within minutes she rolled up her pack, shoved her blanket back, and crawled down the tree, staying as silent as possible and brushing off the glowing dust that clung to her body.

In half an hour she should be out of their path and far enough away to finally sleep.

CHAPTER 11

It wasn't that Kunal hated Rakesh; he just didn't particularly like him.

And of course, as luck would have it, he was one of the four soldiers who had been chosen for this mission. Kunal eyed the man, Rakesh's face turning red and his dark corkscrew curls jumping out of place as he told a story around the campfire with violent hand motions.

He had argued against building a campfire. Though they were pretending otherwise, the other soldiers feared the Tej and had built the fire to ward off trickster spirits. It was rumored that Vardaan himself had encountered a spirit during a campaign and that's why he had ordered soldiers to stay away from the Tej for the past decade, sparking whispers about its supernatural danger.

It made no sense—no spirits would dwell here anyway; legends said they preferred the windy cold of the Aifora

Range's peaks or the arid heat of the Hara Desert. Even the rice paddies of southern Dharka—anywhere there was an extreme in climate.

Not that anyone seemed to want to listen to him, even Laksh, who had shrugged and allowed the others to decide.

Kunal turned a stick in his hand, allowing the piece of hardened ghee to melt slowly over the crusty lentil cake. It was a trick he had learned over many campaigns to make rations more palatable. Something about the melted, clarified butter warmed his soul on the road.

He tried to bring his mind back into his body and listen to Rakesh's story but couldn't help wanting to roll his eyes every time the man spoke. Laksh and the other soldier, Amir, seemed to be getting a good laugh out of the tale. Or at least were better at pretending.

Kunal took another swig of the rice wine, cheaper than water at the Fort, and looked down to see that he had emptied his flask quicker than he'd thought.

Was he really that bored? Or was it the knot in the pit of his stomach that refused to go away and became tighter whenever he thought of that girl, Esha?

He shook the empty flask with an unhappy flick, trying to see if he could dredge up anything from the bottom. No such luck today.

Kunal couldn't stop thinking about it.

The Viper might be a girl. A pretty girl. A pretty, smart, funny girl.

It made perfect sense, in an indirect way. None of the

soldiers would assume that the Viper was a woman; many were happy to forget that just a decade ago Jansa had been a queendom, that women soldiers had been celebrated. It was easier on the ego for some men to assume being a cunning warrior was a right afforded only to men, Kunal supposed.

It also fit with the profile he had laid out. Trading was the only profession still open to women where they could pass through, unnoticed. She could blend in well, and her skill at stealth would only aid her.

Rakesh's words pricked at his ears as the conversation changed. The soldier had stopped boasting about his battle prowess to intimidate the others and now he was using a different tack, trying to scare them with stories of the Viper. This, Kunal was interested in.

"The Viper is pure animal," Rakesh said, leaning forward, a curl bobbing along his sweaty forehead. He sat away from the tree trunk behind him, jumping any time some of the glowing dust landed on his skin. "He can slither like a snake and sting like a scorpion."

"Are you sure that isn't just the Viper's whip? That is how he got the name." Laksh's voice was dry, and Kunal could hear the barely concealed humor underneath his words. "And I've heard the captains talking. It's possible that the Viper isn't just one person, but many."

Out of the corner of his eye, Kunal saw Rakesh edge forward and grab his knife, eyeing the tree behind him. He hid it quickly, looking around to make sure no one had seen his moment of weakness.

"That's possible, but my grandmother says that the Viper is the snake god reincarnated, his main goal to thwart the king's army and to fight for justice," Amir said, his voice dreamy yet insistent. "Just like the lost princess watches and weeps at the moon, waiting to avenge her family."

"The lost princess is a story told by the rebels to garner sympathy. The real Princess Reha passed in her sleep a week after the coup, a victim of the pox. It's ridiculous that these rumors remain that she escaped that night. The people of Jansa have nothing better to do than revel in made-up stories." Rakesh snorted, shaking his head at Amir, curls of bark piled up at his feet as he continued to strip the branches in front of him, as if for fun. "But the Viper is truly other-worldly in his abilities."

"If the Viper was indeed an animal of mythic origins, why did you all volunteer? None of you strike me as the type to have a death wish," Kunal asked in genuine puzzlement.

Laksh was the only one of the group in front of him who made sense as the commander. He was a strong fighter and had a keen mind—and a healthy ambition. Kunal hadn't had a chance to get Laksh alone and discuss all of this. He wasn't sure if he would share the information he had, but he wanted to be able to talk to his friend freely.

Amir was a dreamer through and through. Kunal could see him joining simply to say he had gotten a glimpse of the Viper and tell the story to his many children once he was released from active duty. Rakesh was a strong soldier, fierce in battle, but had never shown any aptitude for responsibility or leadership, despite his desire for it. Kunal would have to keep an eye on him.

Rakesh responded before the others could. "For the glory of the king." He hesitated and then added, "And to avenge our general."

"Not to become the next commander?" Laksh said, hurtling a stick at Rakesh's shoulder. Rakesh dodged it and turned back to him, annoyed.

"Yes, fine. That too," Rakesh said, and it looked to Kunal as if he were almost blushing. It was odd enough to Kunal that he took a closer look at him.

Sweat beaded across his forehead even in the lighter heat of the forest, and his movements were twitchy. He was a large young man—tall and barrel-chested—and had probably been accepted as a soldier due to his size alone. Rakesh had no qualms about throwing it around either.

Kunal's nostrils flared in frustration, and he scuffed the toe of his sandal deeper into the dirt of the forest. At least they had listened to him enough to go off the path and farther into the blanketed forest. Otherwise, they would have been easy pickings for raiders—or even the Viper. He—or she?—could be anywhere.

Maybe the guard *had* imagined the girl.

His heart leaped at the thought and his mind clenched an iron fist around it.

No, he was a lot of things, but he was no fool. He wouldn't shut out any possibility until he had all the facts.

His heart calmed a fraction as thoughts clicked into place.

So, he wouldn't shut out the possibility that she was innocent either. He felt the slight buzz of the rice wine in his veins and a deep, sudden need to get away from the other soldiers. And he wanted to see more of the Tej, especially at night, and they had all refused to explore. The thought of leaving this forest without seeing its beauty made no sense to Kunal.

He stood up. The boys were in the midst of another conversation about what weapons might take down the Viper, but looked up at Kunal's sudden movement. Kunal motioned at the empty flask on the ground and jerked a thumb in the direction of the forest. Attending to the call of nature was as good an excuse as any to get some time to himself.

"Don't get eaten by a tiger," Laksh said, saluting him.

"Or a Viper!" Amir added, his face breaking into a large, foolish smile. Rakesh chuckled.

Kunal said nothing, picking up his weapons and blending into the night.

———◄○►———

Kunal had marked the trees with his machete on his way into the forest, but he was still having trouble finding his way back in the dark, despite the illumination. Exploring in the middle of the night seemed less and less like a good idea as the buzz of the rice wine faded.

First, he had been distracted by the high squawk of a blue-winged parakeet and then the low growl of a feline, one he couldn't place, and so he had found himself lost in the deep rain forest. Kunal rubbed his eyes with the palms of his hands.

His entire life, it was as if animals were singing to him, drawing him into their world. Though there were elephants and horses at the Fort, being in a jungle was different, almost irresistible. A pull he couldn't escape, as if he could feel it in his very soul.

It was an enchanting song.

It was also a song that reminded him of his childhood—and his mother. Kunal remembered whispers of her voice singing to him, old folk songs and tales of Jansa's history, and it plagued his dreams on restless nights. She had been a woman full of life and music.

Memories of his mother's face still haunted him. She had been killed the night of the coup, despite only being a lady-in-waiting at court. She had been in the wrong place at the wrong time and his last memory of her was of her barricading him in their small bedroom with his nurse. Uncle Setu had found them later and had taken Kunal in, making him promise to never reveal to anyone what he had seen that night, where he had been.

He had never questioned any of it. He barely resisted when his uncle brought him back to the Fort, telling him he could be a great warrior like his father. He had fallen into the life of a soldier, hoping that it would make him forget the past and ease away the soft parts of him the general seemed to hate.

On the darkest, loneliest nights at the Fort, he wondered what life might have been like if he and his mother had escaped the palace the night of the coup. If they had left earlier . . . if his nurse hadn't dragged him away to hide him. . . .

Perhaps they'd still be together, painting side by side as they had in his childhood. He used to watch the sunset every night from the highest window in the palace with his mother, his eyes wide as she taught him the correct way to shade light, to cast shadows on canvas. He'd go to bed with splotches of paint up and down his arm, his hard-won battle scars from the day.

Kunal bit his lip, shaking his head as if it would loosen the memories from his mind and let them fall to the ground. He had barely known his father, only whispers of memories before he was gone, but his mother . . . the loss of her was still raw, ten years later. Her last name, Dhagan, was the only thing he had left of her.

There was a reason he avoided those memories.

He tried to focus in on the present, for with every passing minute, it was looking more and more like he was lost in the Tej. At least he had the mind to take his weapons with him. He nearly tripped over a large knotted root and caught himself on the tree trunk.

There was one of his marks, etched into the bark. He sighed in relief. Worst case, he would have to camp here, as it was almost midnight, and he could make his way back in the morning. He brushed his hands together, wiping off the crackle of bark and green dust on his palms.

The snap of a stick jolted him out of his skin and he

whipped around, his senses heightened after years of Senap training.

The noise wasn't far away and was moving away from him; whoever was in the forest with him must be close and didn't know of his presence yet.

An animal? Or raiders. Or the Viper?

He had the element of surprise—which meant he could scout ahead. Raiders or animals and he'd turn back to get the others. But if it was the third, the Viper, this could be his chance to get ahead in the competition.

The Tej was the only way out of the Fort aside from the main trade road. They'd already asked the patrols on the trade road if they had seen anyone leave the Fort and had turned up empty.

Kunal took the gamble and moved stealthily after the noise, his legs picking up the silent pace. It was faint, but Kunal was trained to hear the shuffle of feet after the calm silence. Whoever was there didn't want to be followed, and was trying to hide their steps.

He dropped, feeling around for impressions in the ground. The misshapen bend of a fallen branch, weighted down by a quick step. And farther up, under the flicker of moonlight, the leaves a darker shade of green where a foot had been.

He was right—they were nearby.

Kunal lunged into the small clearing, grabbing on to a twisted branch to steady himself.

A figure clothed in pants and a turban was two paces away, crouching in a good defensive stance, knife pointing outward.

Looking in the wrong direction.

Kunal recognized the dark curls flying in the soft wind.

He cleared his throat, allowing Esha a second to turn.

CHAPTER 12

Esha nearly jumped out of her skin as a deep voice whispered her name.

She jerked away from her lookout, and only a quick glance stopped her from slicing on instinct. Kunal's bright eyes regarded her with a heaviness. He said nothing, clearly waiting on her to explain her presence in the forest.

Esha's mind raced as fast as her heart. She couldn't deal with him right now. She had much, much larger things to worry about.

When she continued to remain silent, he spoke.

"What are you doing—"

"Shh," she hissed back, her heart clenching. He had given away their position.

A menacing growl echoed through the trees, and Kunal's eyes widened as he recognized the noise. His grip on her wrist grew tighter and he tried to pull her back behind him, unsheathing his sword.

Esha almost resisted, but took advantage of his protectiveness instead. One more barrier between her and the tiger lurking nearby. What did she care for a bronze-armored soldier?

She allowed him to shield her with his body, maneuvering her own knife into a killing grip. The tiger, its orange-and-black coat glimmering among the trees, bounded into the clearing without making a whisper. But it stopped, its bright yellow eyes darting between the two of them. The creature's gaze seemed to hold eons of knowledge in its depths.

Kunal seemed to be waiting, but for what, Esha had no idea. It was almost as if he was entranced by the animal in front of them. Or the animal was entranced by him. That made no sense, though; a connection with animals was a gift only royals had, along with their shape-shifting blood. He must never have seen a tiger up close before.

Tigers were common to the forests of Jansa, and revered. At least once a moon a human would go into the forest to try to capture a tiger for good luck—only a few left with all their limbs intact.

Esha searched for a way out, noticing a somewhat cleared path to a patch of tall trees with slim branches. Perfect for humans, not for large tigers. She turned, the slightest of movements. It was enough that the tiger's attention snapped to Esha, and it let out an ear-ripping shriek, a noise so unnatural it chilled Esha's bones.

"Run," she whispered in Kunal's ear.

She didn't bother to look back to see if he was following, but within seconds she heard his footsteps and heavy breathing behind her. The tiger let out another yowl and Esha pumped her legs faster.

The hairs on her neck prickled, and she could sense the tiger wasn't far behind. With frantic speed, she searched the path before them.

"There!" she said, and pointed.

She grabbed Kunal's hand and pulled him forward, dropping it as they reached the bottom of a tall banyan tree. She scrambled up, not waiting for him. The only thing she remembered about forest tigers was to get as high away from them as you could at night. The tiger wouldn't be able to follow—its abnormal size would make it too heavy even for the sturdy branches of a banyan.

Kunal climbed and collapsed beside her. In the distance, she could hear the soft shuffles of the tiger, pacing below them. She was safe for now.

Never greet a tiger at midnight, for they are the manifestations of your past misdeeds.

Esha drew a breath of relief and looked straight at Kunal, into the eyes of the man who might be looking for her, the Viper, but didn't know it yet. Stuck in a tree together till morning and her only protection a flimsy cover story about a poppy seed–selling trader girl.

It seemed she was due for her misdeeds.

———◄o►———

Their breaths evened out in the empty air of the night once the danger had passed. For the first few minutes, silence reigned. But Esha knew it wouldn't last, and prepared herself for the questions.

Kunal broke the silence first. "A forest tiger? At midnight? I thought the tiger at midnight was only a story told to scare children," he managed to get out, rubbing his side as he looked at her.

She cocked an eyebrow at the movement, but said nothing. No need to be kind to a soldier, even if he was hurting. He must have been through worse on campaigns in the northern mountains, where snow leopards prowled.

"I thought so too, but aren't you glad you knew the story? A merchant who had been cheating his customers meets a tiger at midnight, as does his brother, a virtuous scholar. Only one escapes." Esha caught the tone of her voice and changed it, made it lighter and softer. She drew a breath. "I'm glad I didn't have to face that tiger alone—and that we both made it out."

Something flickered in his face, but Esha couldn't catch it. "The last I saw you, I had left you on the path to the harbor. How in the Sun Maiden's—" He paused and schooled his face into a neutral mask with an ease she admired. "How did you end up here, in the forest?"

The lie rolled smoothly off her tongue. "I was too late. By the time I made it down to the harbor, the boat had already left—and I wasn't on it." She frowned, hoping he wouldn't press her story. "The harbormaster said I might catch them at Mulgahi. The horse I had borrowed became skittish at a noise and threw me off halfway through the forest. By the time I recovered, the horse was gone and I was lost. Thankfully, I had my pack on my body, otherwise I would've been left with nothing. I've been trying to make it back to the road since." She shivered as she bit her lip and looked up at him from under her lashes. "I thought I was going to die in this forest, miles away from my family."

To his credit, his face softened, and he didn't press further into her story. She tucked away that nugget about him—he was sentimental. It might come of use again before the night was over.

"*We're* not dying tonight," he said firmly. He seemed to hesitate and drew closer to her. "And we won't die tomorrow. You know how the tale goes—a tiger at midnight is no normal tiger. It will disappear at dawn, fading back into the land after meting out any justice. Otherworldly or no, the tiger will lose interest by morning." He focused his eyes dead center on hers. "How did you not only get yourself lost in the forest, but manage to find a tiger? Are your 'misdeeds' catching up with you?" Kunal grinned as he said it, but Esha felt her stomach turn. How little he knew.

"Apparently, my poppy seeds have caused several stomachaches," she whispered. His face relaxed and he laughed. Below, the tiger shrieked again, and Esha shivered.

Kunal's face paled and he mouthed "sorry" at her.

"We should climb higher," she said in response. "The branches up there will be a bit more out of reach and we can tie ourselves to the trunk so we don't fall while sleeping."

Esha stood up quickly, wanting to end the conversation about supernatural tigers and justice being meted out. She wobbled as she found her balance on the banyan branch, and offered him a hand. She was stuck with him for the night, misdeeds or no.

He nodded and rose to his feet. The incandescent bark was surprisingly soft and as they climbed, it began to paint them. When Esha collapsed into a wide branch, her arms, knees, and shoes were glowing a soft green. She stared at the green bark on her skin, marveling at the vivacity of the color and the way it dissolved into glittering dust at her touch.

A grunt from below reminded her she wasn't alone. The adrenaline from before was slowly leaving her veins and a deep weariness was taking hold. Kunal pulled up behind her and settled into the wide notch of the opposite branch.

"How do you know all of this?" he asked as he watched her tug a rope from her bag and hack it into two lengths. She stared back.

He was observant, which was dangerous.

"I grew up near the rain forest," she offered. A half-truth. Her grandfather's home had been in the overgrown jungles near the base of the Ghanta Mountains in Dharka—but Jansans wouldn't know the difference between a rain forest and a jungle anyway. "My father made sure we knew how to take care of ourselves."

"An interesting set of skills for a trading family," he observed. Esha felt herself tighten up but tried to keep her movements natural. "Did you see anyone pass by on the road earlier?" he asked.

She saw the trap instantly. Say yes and he would insist on her staying with the soldiers tomorrow to identify whoever she claimed she saw. Say no and gain suspicion—the path through the forest was the only road from the Fort that wasn't heavily guarded by soldiers. But the prospect of being left alone was too enticing.

She paused, acting as if she was trying to recollect her memories. "I didn't see anyone before my horse threw me. Was there someone you were looking for? I was aiming to travel fast, and undisturbed," she said, in a regretful tone.

It was then that he seemed to notice her pack and clothing, looking her up and down. She tensed again.

"You came prepared, that's for sure. Is that the reason for the outfit?"

Esha swallowed her sigh of relief, watching him with careful eyes as she tipped the turban off her head and unwrapped the fabric. "It's not that good of a disguise," he said, the corner of his mouth quirking as she shook her hair out.

She looked up sharply, unable to hide the offense on her face.

"No, I don't mean to insult," he said quickly. "I mean, it would be hard for anyone who's seen you to forget you." His words came out soft, as if he were unwilling to give them up.

He thought her pretty. The realization warmed Esha more than it should have, aside from the strategic opportunity it presented. She could work with this.

Esha relaxed into the small space that housed them both, letting her smile shine through. "You're a charmer."

He coughed, a laugh mixed in. "I'm not sure anyone who's met me would ever say that." Kunal rubbed the back of his head, his face guileless yet unreadable.

"Why are you here? In the Tej? Last time I saw *you*, you were at the Fort," Esha said, a playful smile on her face. She was glad the conversation had turned light. Banter, flirting—those she could do well as the Viper.

"I'm with a few other soldiers and we're hunting for the—we're hunting for a criminal," he said, turning to face her. Kunal's face instantly shuttered, and Esha saw her advantage clamp shut behind his hard gaze. He seemed to notice his mistake, having almost revealed their target to an unknown girl.

A normal girl would look frightened, so Esha feigned shock. "A criminal? What kind of criminal? Do you think that was the noise I heard?" Her eyes widened, and she tugged at her hair, glancing about the forest.

She moved closer to him, which seemed to do the trick.

"A murderer." He watched her reaction again, as if making sure it was normal. She was careful to let him see the disbelief and fright on her face.

"I hope you catch him," Esha said with conviction.

She did hope he would catch *him*, just not *her*.

"Best to be careful with a tiger and a criminal on the loose," he said, as if making up his mind. "I'll take you back to our camp in the morning. I'll see you safely to the next port town and get you on the ship before I leave."

She thought she heard him mutter *properly this time.*

Moon Lord's mercy. That was exactly what wasn't supposed to happen.

The idea of getting caught in a tangle of soldiers made her want to retch. If she were better armed, the idea might have given her a perverse sense of pleasure—more opportunity to get rid of a few soldiers—but as it was, she had only her knife. Her whip, her specialty, was in her pack and had to remain there if she wanted to keep pretending to be Poppy-Seed Girl. The other whip? Clearly it had been found.

There had been three other soldiers, and if they were anything like Kunal, she would be in trouble. He was smarter than she had given him credit for, his eyes watching her like a bird of prey.

It almost felt as if he saw the Viper in her, or knew something.

She had no choice; she would have to stay with him and figure out how to get away before dawn broke. With a quick nod, she moved toward Kunal, accepting his offer.

"Thank you. I was so worried. I'll feel much safer with your company." Esha was proud she kept her tone even as she spoke those words.

He gave her a nod, curt and quick. "It's the least I can do."

She could feel the tension dissipating between them, and wondered how much of his offer was his sense of duty and how much was about him liking her—the poppy-seed girl.

And if she could trust him either way. However much

she hated soldiers, she had to admit that he seemed to be one with some scraps of honor.

Kunal leaned away from her as he pulled off his armor. He unfurled the length of rope she handed him, tugging it over a branch to test whether it would hold, lashing it all together against the tree. Esha couldn't help but watch the way his arms moved, tight with corded muscle. He cut a fine figure, lean in the right places, broad in others. The first branch alone was too weak to hold his armor, so he began to gather a few of the hanging roots as well, tugging at them, when Esha saw it, the glint of silvery metal.

Esha lunged forward, yanking Kunal back. The bronze armor fell out of his hands and clanged down the tree, landing with a soft thud on the thickly covered forest floor below.

"What?" Kunal exclaimed when she removed her hand. Distrust flashed in his eyes. Esha said nothing, lifting her knife above his head.

With a quick swipe, Esha unleashed two metal traps on the branches Kunal had been reaching for. As they fell, they shaved off the branches, leaving clean stumps of wood behind. He stared at them and then her in disbelief, his mouth agape.

"Monkey traps. I just saved your arms, probably your life as well," she said. He shook his head. "I'm a trader. I can spot illegal traps. Monkey fur is prized up north, and earns a pretty coin. They're set up everywhere nowadays with the market the way it is."

She hadn't meant to save his life; she'd been acting on

instinct, having lost a fellow rebel to a trap during a mission. Having a dead soldier on her hands might have been easier than one who was looking at her the way he was now, with those piercing amber eyes. But they also shone with gratitude, and that could maybe buy her some time.

"I'm surprised you soldiers don't know about them," she finished.

Esha began to ease herself off Kunal, flushing as she realized she had thrown herself against him to hold him back. He caught her arm, his fingers like embers against her cool skin, and helped them both into more comfortable sitting positions. Dots of green dust painted her arms where his hands had held her.

"I hate to admit it, but we've never been trained to spot these things. We don't spend a lot of time in the Tej, or any forest, especially when the king is on a campaign. The other men say it's because the Tej terrifies him," Kunal said. His shock at the snares seemed to have loosened his tongue. Esha didn't mind. It was giving her information she could store away for a future mission. "Thank you, I mean. You saved me," he said.

Esha nodded, unable to do anything else in the face of his sudden warmth. The earlier mistrust had disappeared from his face and while it should have made Esha feel jubilant, it instead made her stomach swirl in confusion.

She wasn't honorable. She had acted on instinct. Tricks and lies were her entire life. What kind of Viper would she be without them?

A dead one.

She drew her breath back into her body and stood a little straighter. "You're very welcome. Least I could do after you saved me twice," she said, adding a lightness to her voice that she didn't feel. She was glad she could still play this role, this easygoing trader girl.

It was surprisingly nice to pretend.

The night around them had become unyielding despite the soft illumination of the rain forest, the buzz of cicadas, and the musty scent of the soil below. They needed to make camp for the night, and to her chagrin, she realized she didn't mind the idea of having someone watch her back for once.

She watched him as he removed the rest of his armor with more care. Streaks of green dust and moss danced along his neck, forearms, and sides. She realized she was staring and looked away sharply.

"We can't light a fire up here."

That was obvious, but she nodded and rubbed her hands together.

"I'm sorry," he said softly. The words drew Esha's gaze to his face. She tensed as the tiger shrieked again, though it was quieter this time. Kunal shifted as well, but hid it with a cough.

"About what?" She genuinely didn't know.

"Lost, chased by a tiger, stuck in a tree with me. No proper fire. A rough day for a lady."

Esha laughed at that.

"I'm not a lady, and I've had much worse," she said. If only he knew. She realized she had let her mask slip, but decided to let it go. It made sense that a trader would know the hardships of travel. "It wasn't as if I was going to be camping on a soft wool-covered bed if I hadn't run into you. I'd still be trying to escape a tiger—just alone."

"You've had worse than this? I'd like to hear that story," he said, smiling. She gave him a look that said he would have to get to know her much better to get that story out of her.

She had too many stories to count from her role as the Viper these past five years.

The glory, the tall tales, the power. Some days, the days where she felt like she had to keep everything nestled in her chest, where she was alone, again, on another long mission, she would trade it all for a genuine word that she could trust. A sliver of a real relationship with someone who saw her as a girl of seventeen, almost eighteen—a girl who, in a normal life, would already have been betrothed or apprenticed by now.

A girl who should have had her parents by her side, who should've still been daydreaming about the embroidered gold on her wedding sari and scheming about how to sneak a scroll from the library. Whose hands should've been covered in sugar from milk sweets rather than blood from a grown man.

The world was a danger to her as the Viper. And as such, she kept the world at a distance. She tried to ignore the pit in her stomach as she realized she might have to keep Harun and her team at a distance until she discovered more about the general's killer.

She wanted to believe they were loyal, but . . .

"Are you tired?" He broke the silence, mistaking her sudden quietness.

"No, not really. The excitement of everything over the past day should have me snoring like a babe, but instead my mind is racing," she said, easing back into the crook of the wide branch, trying to get comfortable.

"That's normal." She glanced up at him as he spoke, noticing the way the green light created a halo around him as he settled on the opposite branch, his body sprawled in an uncomfortable position. "I can never sleep well the night before a battle, or even before a normal scouting trip." He looked at her as if deciding whether to say more.

"I was born near the tea plantations in the western hills, where there's green as far as you can see. As soon as I could, I started climbing, to see more of the world. I usually go up to the top of the Fort the night before any excursion, to watch the stars come out and darkness fall from the open windows."

"Me too," she said softly. "I count the stars when I'm away from home, to remind me of how far I've come." She cleared her throat. "Why go so far up at the Fort?"

He smiled, as if reliving a memory. "From the highest point, you can see a glimpse of Dharka over the mountains."

"Oh?"

The mention of her home brought fresh memories to her mind, of a warm sun and the thick, moist air of summer. Dharka was flatter against the coastline, its peninsula smaller than Jansa's, leading to rolling hills and plantations, the delta soil of the Bhagya River's tributaries rich in loam. The land was still whole now, the *janma* bond still secure, and she meant to keep it that way.

What piqued her attention was that the soldier had mentioned Dharka without any of the derision she usually heard in soldiers' voices.

It made her curious. "Have you been?"

"I've been before. I think. As a child. I remember kind people and delicious food," he said.

"Maybe you'll have the chance to go back one day," she said slowly, parceling out her words.

"I'd like to. I've heard tales of its lush plateaus and striking mountains. The deep jungles." He spoke in a way that enchanted her, careful and rhythmic, as if he measured and evaluated every word.

"The tales of the jungle animals don't scare you?"

He smiled. "I've always enjoyed the company of animals," he said. "Though maybe not that tiger."

Esha couldn't say she shared the first sentiment. Animals almost seemed to hate her, which was ironic given her namesake.

She hesitated, unsure how much of herself to give away in response to his unguarded admissions. Caution won and she looked out through the trees.

"I've never been to Dharka, but I've sailed past it. It looks beautiful," Esha lied. "It doesn't sound so different from Jansa, though, despite what people say."

It was a test. Would he pass? Prove himself different from his bronze-clad brothers?

"No. No, it doesn't."

Kunal's words were soft, dissolving into the heavy night air.

He had passed easily.

CHAPTER 13

Esha watched him fall asleep as they talked, one eye cracked open, before falling into a dreamless sleep herself. She woke with the first shimmer of daylight, even though they had stayed awake talking later than she intended, and she was able to catch the fading of the forest's incandescent lights.

Something about their conversation had imbued her with a new energy. It had been a salve for her loneliness. She pushed away the other thoughts, the soft words they had exchanged about their favorite cities along the coast, the best places to eat jalebis. Now she was eager to get moving, spurred on by the plan she had formulated.

After scouting once again for any signs of the tiger, Esha quietly climbed down the tree and landed with a soft thud, her feet welcoming the feeling of solid ground. She left her pack on the ground, taking out the small metal flask inside.

First, she needed to find water. She remembered having seen a small stream to the east from the trees, close enough that she could have her flasks filled before the soldier woke. It was an innocuous reason to leave if he found her, and it would give her the ability to scout a clear path to get away. She could also scout whether the other soldiers had moved from their camp and farther into the rain forest.

For the first time since leaving the Fort, she felt in control.

The efficiency of her plan brought a smile to her face as she eased her arms toward the sky, feeling the gentle crack of her joints as her body woke up. She had left him still asleep, an arm tossed carelessly over his face, his face young and open in slumber.

Esha had looked away quickly, away from the soft slackness of his mouth that brought to mind a boy rather than a soldier.

She pushed away the memory and left for the stream.

CHAPTER 14

K unal woke with a start, the cry of a hornbill ringing in his ears.

He groaned, wondering why his bed felt so hard. A glance upward toward the blanketed canopy of trees above brought the memories of the past few days rushing back. The hoots of monkeys could be heard, and soon enough, he felt the annoying bite of gnats and mosquitoes.

He looked over and saw that the branch where Esha had been was empty, and in a second, he was up, crouching low against the tree trunk as he surveyed the area through the branches. His eyes landed on Esha's pack on the ground below, a few feet from his now dented cuirass, and his muscles relaxed.

She was still in the area. He didn't know of a girl who would leave her pack unattended while traveling. And there were no tracks surrounding it that hinted at a capture.

Kunal realized he had been worried for a moment, that he truly did want to see her safely off. Despite his suspicion that she was the Viper.

It was better to keep her close and keep an eye on her, even if most of him did believe her. He rolled his neck, letting warmth carry into his arms as he untied his rope and eased himself down the knotty branches of the tree.

He wondered what his uncle would have done. Probably clamped her in irons last night.

Act first, ask questions later.

That was the Fort's unofficial motto.

Problem was, that had never been Kunal's way. He prided himself on being calm and cool-headed, looking at all sides of a problem before arriving at an opinion. What if he was wrong and he took an innocent girl back to the Fort in chains? He would never forgive himself for acting without proof.

And therein lay a dilemma. Kunal had nothing but the words of a drunken soldier who claimed he saw a girl, and for him, it wasn't enough.

He had to be more sure before he could act. Until then, observe and report.

Kunal grabbed his cuirass and made a face at the dent in the armor, right below the breastplate. If he could find a branch or a stone, he could bring some of the shape back so it wouldn't dig into his skin. As he searched for a rock big enough, Kunal planned his next steps.

He would leave Esha outside the camp, grab his mare

before the others noticed, and then head off to the next port town. Either he would see her safely on a ship or he would put her in irons and take her back to the Fort.

The next few days would be crucial in determining which path he'd take.

A perfect rock—pointed yet curved enough to deliver an exacting blow—was nestled into the soft forest floor near Esha's canvas pack. He leaned down to pick it up—it would be perfect for hammering his cuirass back into shape—and his eye caught something silver on the ground.

A small silver pin was caught in the underbrush. He tugged at it and found it caked in dirt. As he began to rub it clean, Kunal glanced at Esha's bag next to him, which had fallen over.

The handle of a whip peeked out, a crisscross of snakes emblazoned across it. It took Kunal a moment to comprehend what he was seeing.

When he did, he almost dropped the rock.

He stood there, staring at the pack, unable to move. His heart began to hammer, his fingers fisting around the pin.

There was no denying it now. There it was—the proof he required. The matching whip, one of a pair, exactly like the one left behind in his uncle's bedroom.

His mind eased into a cool calmness, as it did before every battle started. Analyze the situation. Make a plan of attack.

Now he needed to figure out how to get her back to the soldiers' camp without raising any suspicion. She hadn't left yet, so it was possible he could continue this farce. Kunal grimaced at the thought of it. He had never been skilled at deception.

When he finally felt his limbs loosen with decision, he donned his still-dented cuirass with rapid speed and tucked the silver pin into his waist sash to examine later. He edged the whip back into her pack with the toe of his sandal, tipping the bag back over so it stood upright. The thought of touching it made him queasy.

Kunal ignored the small part of him that had seen a girl and a bit of hope. That still didn't believe she was the Viper—didn't believe she was *capable* of being the Viper. That part of him had been a fool.

A sharp crack resounded through the air. Kunal whipped around, his instincts pushing him to check out what the danger was. He shot off toward the sound.

Had the tiger returned? Had something happened to Esha?

He needed to return her to the Fort alive.

Kunal ran toward the sound but quickly realized nothing was amiss, except for a large tree branch having fallen on the paved path. He peered at the branch. It had been neatly severed—by the monkey trap.

Sun Maiden's spear.

He sprinted back toward their banyan tree camp, pumping his legs as fast as he could, defying the wind to move even faster. He had done exactly what he shouldn't have—gotten distracted. Even if it had been only for a minute.

A minute was all the Viper needed.

He cursed himself as he came upon the empty clearing, seeing what he expected.

Everything was gone—the pack, the girl.

He caught sight of her ivory-colored uttariya a few paces ahead and turned toward it, jumping through the leaves and branches to follow the trail of cotton in the air. She started moving faster.

Kunal threw himself forward, using every last bit of his speed, and caught the edge of the uttariya in his grasping fingers. The bolt of fabric streamed off her but got caught around her shoulders and torso, pulling her back. She stopped, her lips forming a perfect "O," mimicking the wideness of her shocked eyes. She hadn't expected him to catch her.

The uttariya had fallen off her head, revealing her riotous mane of dark curls. They flew in the wind, lashing her stricken face.

But in the next moment, her shock faded and she turned her head to face him. Her entire face broke into a grin, slow and coiling. Gone was every shred of meekness, every trace of the retiring, demure trader girl.

When their eyes met, he knew they both were aware the performance was over and the game had begun. No words had been exchanged, but Kunal knew in his marrow that he and Esha understood each other. She wouldn't stop running and he wouldn't stop chasing her.

She held his gaze as she tugged loose and threw off the

rest of the uttariya, her eyes flashing with a reckless danger.

Maybe it was his imagination, but he thought he also saw a hint of regret in her eyes.

Kunal leaped forward, to grab Esha, tackle her, anything. A sharp pain lanced up his shins and he tumbled to the ground, finding himself sprawled across the tangled roots that grew across the forest. By the time he got back on his feet, wincing in pain, she was gone. The source of his failure: a thin metal wire that stretched between the base of two trees.

She had been prepared. She had been planning every single moment.

Kunal was left standing, unmoving, crumpling her uttariya in his hand, the ends of it flapping in the gale storm she had left in her wake.

CHAPTER 15

He made it back to camp in the light of the late morning by way of the knife marks in the bark, her uttariya a tight ball in his fist. The other soldiers looked up from their perches around the small campfire when he stormed back into camp.

The tightness in his heart relaxed a bit as he spotted Laksh and the others. They had agreed to stay together until they left the Tej, but he hadn't been sure Rakesh would stick to it.

"Did you find the Viper hanging from a tree? Is that why you were gone an entire night for a leak?" Laksh teased. Kunal simply stared back at him, feeling a rise of fury in his blood, so hot his head ached. Laksh saw the change in Kunal and backed off, holding a hand out to Rakesh, who had lurched forward.

"He's got that look, comrades," Laksh said.

"I'm not scared of the Dhagan stare. As if he could scare me with those"—Rakesh waved his hand around—"eyes of his." He did scoot back, though, tugging at a curl.

Kunal was reaching that breaking point his uncle warned him to never cross, and it felt welcoming.

Control.

Kunal tried to tamp down on his anger, but it flashed hot. He trampled through the ashes of the unsteady fire, making a straight path for his small bedroll. He stuffed the uttariya into his pack and sat down, staring moodily across the campfire.

He hadn't felt this angry in many moons—years, even.

What an utter fool he was, thinking he could best the Viper.

"Now he just looks like someone stole his favorite sweet," Laksh said with a smirk. Rakesh opened his mouth, a grin on his face, but Amir shook his head at him.

"Shut up, you lot. What have you all been up to? Spent the night huddled in your tents, scared of the glowing forest?" Kunal said.

Rakesh turned a wonderful shade of red as Laksh whistled, yelling at the others to start cleaning up camp. Kunal sat there, feeling his fury recede and transform.

It teetered on the edge of an emotion he hadn't let himself feel in years—sadness.

He knew who the Viper was, a clear advantage in this game. He should feel determined or resolved.

As a soldier, his duty was to his general, his army, and

then himself. That was the order of things. But Kunal had always held his own code of honor, and now the edges of it were fraying, the years in service weighing on his mind.

It wasn't only that he had failed to catch her, but that he finally knew, without a doubt, that Esha was the Viper, and his sworn enemy.

And to become commander, he would have to capture her and take her back, even though she had saved his life. He might not be standing here, agonizing over what to do, if she hadn't.

Or had that been premeditated as well?

A branch lay in his path and he stepped on it ferociously, startling the other soldiers.

Kunal picked up the broken branch and spun it in his hands, feeling the heft of the wood before he brought it down with force, cracking it sharply against his knee. What was left was a sharp, jagged stick. He whipped out his machete and began to strip away at the wood, sliver by sliver, bringing it to its sharpest point.

She was the key to his future as a commander.

That was all.

Kunal studied the pointed tip of the stick and dragged it across his forearm to test the sharpness.

Blood welled up over the parted skin.

Control.

CHAPTER 16

Esha fled as if the wind itself was chasing her, racing through the tangled web of branches and leaves. Her heart hammered in her chest with an unrelenting thrum, both from the forced exertion of her body and her narrow escape.

She slowed down, her body almost collapsing in confusion at the change in pace, before her knees gave out. She tumbled to the ground and landed hard on her shins, her sandals catching on a broken tree branch. The ground had lost its soft dirt here in the outskirts of the Tej, rising into the low rolling hills and valleys that made up central Jansa.

She had never pushed herself this much, covering enough ground for two days. Even now, after almost the entire day, she could feel how close he had been. The recognition and fear in his eyes as he had caught the uttariya. A part of her had loved it, reveling in her ability to play the role of the Viper again after weeks of traveling in secret.

Esha picked off the stones imprinted into her palms, dusting her hands on her sooty, torn pants. The water from her flask was a treat, the one part of her plan she had managed to execute without a problem. It was lucky that she had gotten back in time to see the soldier descend.

And leaving her pack there, exposed.

Esha could curse herself a thousand moons over for such a careless act. If it had been anyone on her rebel team, she would have made them run loops around the city walls of Mathur till they were blue in the face.

She had stood there, frozen, watching the realization hit his face. The metal wire had been for the tiger, but had been an unexpected help. If not for it, she wouldn't have had the distraction to recover her pack.

Bracing herself with her hands, she looked out at the faint outline of the town ahead of her, nestled into the hills above the Tej. At least another day's walk, and at a steep upward slope.

Esha tried to stand up, only to realize she was stuck. She fumbled with her pack, trying to pull out the crescent pin to cut her sandal free, but she couldn't find it. With a huff, she tugged the pack into her lap, searching for the pin as a prickle of dread crept up her spine.

The pin was nowhere to be found.

Esha cursed, thoroughly. Stupid. She was so stupid.

Her mind immediately turned to the worst. What if the soldier had found the pin? If he knew anything about the

Blades, he would recognize it. And if he was clever enough, he'd put the pieces together. That the Viper worked for the Blades.

She took a calming breath, thinking of what Arpiya would say. *Don't assume,* she would say. *It only makes you look foolish.*

A coolness washed over Esha and she focused on the facts. She couldn't find the pin. That might mean the soldier had found it, but it could also mean she had dropped it somewhere in the forest. It didn't mean that her secret was out.

Esha scowled. And in any case, whoever framed her already knew her identity.

She found her knife and cut the loose thread, freeing herself. She had meant to slip in and out of the Tej without notice and be halfway on her way to Faor by now, maybe take a day to collect information if she had time. Her only suspect for the murder and her framing was in that city.

But now the soldier had seen her face, knew she was the Viper, and worst of all, might connect her to the Crescent Blades.

Esha breathed out a sigh of frustration—she couldn't do anything about it now anyway. But she would make it hard for the soldier to find her again. And without proof, it was unlikely that any of his fellow soldiers would accept that the Viper was a mere woman.

The thought brought a little smirk to her face. It never failed to delight her, knowing that all these soldiers, these men, were terrified of her.

A minute to catch her breath and she would keep going. Night had already started to fall, and she needed to make camp somewhere. Then she'd steal a horse and make her way to Faor, where she'd set the next part of her plan in motion.

To bring back her calm, Esha repeated what Arpiya would say if she was there, wishing that her friend was by her side. She was the closest thing to a real confidante in her life—her relationship with Harun, her co-leader, was more complicated.

It bolstered her spirits for a moment. Esha knew she would keep running and fighting for her freedom no matter what or who may come.

But maybe not looking like this.

She stared down at her dust-streaked pants and dirty shirt. She looked like a vagabond. First priority, new clothes and food. Maybe pick up another weapon or two.

Her hands left dirty prints on her silver flask and she made a face at her reflection.

She would kill for a bath. And she did mean it literally.

CHAPTER 17

"We separate here," Kunal said, his hand shading his eyes as he peered out from his mare, his gaze roaming over the horizon.

The soft ground turned into sandy, cracked earth to the west. To the east lay the port towns, and beyond, the glossy sheen of the sea.

He had underestimated Esha, the Viper, before. He wasn't about to do that again.

Kunal grasped the small pin he had found in his palm, fingering it as he looked to the horizon. He had remembered the pin that morning, cleaning up the mud to discover that it was the symbol of the Crescent Blades. His heartbeat had risen like a steady thrum as what it meant hit him.

It had been a stroke of luck from the gods.

It had been the clue he needed, one that would put him ahead of the others. He would have time later to unravel his excitement and terror that the Viper was one of the Blades.

Kunal couldn't know for sure that this was the right path—he had also considered that finding the pin had merely been coincidence. Maybe she had found the pin somewhere, had stolen it or kept it for a future mission.

But if it was true and she was a Blade, the pin told him something important—the Viper *didn't* work alone.

And now he had a plan for tracking her.

"Uh, why are we separating?" The question from Amir knocked Kunal out of his thoughts.

"Because this is a competition, Amir," Kunal said.

"And some of us could also do without the dead weight," Rakesh said, kicking Amir's shin.

Kunal rolled his eyes. He would miss Laksh. He was always a step ahead—analyzing and weighing everything behind those dark eyes. In fact, Laksh was probably the perfect match to go up against the Viper, and his heart clenched for a second, feeling guilt at withholding the information from his friend earlier that day. He had lied when they had discussed their plans—Laksh had decided to gather information from the iron blacksmiths and Kunal had made up a story about visiting the House Ayul.

No, this was his advantage and his Viper to find.

He had to admit, it hadn't been horrible to have the other soldiers around. If nothing else, it kept him from drowning in his thoughts. But from this point onward, he would have to be focused.

"It'll be easy enough to keep in touch if anyone's in dire

need. We all have the whistles for the messenger hawks. Don't lose them and you'll have a higher chance of coming back alive," Laksh said, sounding bored. Kunal saw the tension in his jaw, though, as if he was just as eager to separate from the others.

"Agreed. Now, where to go?" Rakesh asked as he squinted into the sunlight.

Kunal looked out with him.

The red and gold of the landscape of the northeast twinkled in the midday sun.

Kunal looked back at the other three boys, the sunlight glinting off their armor. He took in the picture: Rakesh straining at keeping his seat, Amir glancing back regretfully in the direction of the Fort, Laksh saying something to Rakesh that made him go red.

Something in the wind whispered that this moment would never return and that after this, nothing would be the same.

Rakesh's voice broke him out of his thoughts. "Don't even consider following me," he stated with simple menace before rearing his stallion back and galloping off toward the coast. The other horses whinnied, eager to be running and free as well. He could feel the muscles of his mare tense, as if she could sense the decision he was weighing.

"I guess this is goodbye, boys," Laksh said. "Can't say I wish you *all* luck."

He nodded at the two of them, throwing Kunal a

lopsided grin, four fingers to his chest. Kunal touched his fingers to his heart in response.

Laksh winked at Kunal and spurred off in the opposite direction from Rakesh.

"We're the last ones. Do you know where you're going?" Amir asked.

Kunal nodded and pulled at his reins. Forward.

CHAPTER 18

Kunal made his way to the center of the small town of Ujral, having left his horse at a stable near the outskirts of town. The market stalls and food stands stood tall against the sky, swatches of red and blue and green against the gray stone and wood buildings. They varied in size, some larger food stands set up like tents while the smaller market stalls were lined up in rows.

A welcome sight. The rumble of hunger in his belly had become an ache about a mile ago, and Kunal was dying for toasted mustard-seed flatbread and a jug of buttermilk to cool the fire of the sun beating down on his neck.

The light purple turban wound around his head was the only thing keeping him cool, and from being drenched to his toes in sweat. The heat was sweltering with a layer of bronze metal against his skin. He had forgotten how hot Jansa had become since the Bhagya River started to dry up, how oddly cool the weather down near the Fort was. It was a sweaty reminder.

Where would a Viper hide?

Ujral was the first town on the map of known rebel hideouts he'd made at the garrison he had stopped at a day ago. Faor was next, then Adartha. He'd sketched it out, adding as much as he could from memory.

He would bet on his armor that she would stop by one of the cities at some point, even if she was hidden. He'd hoped that's where his tracking skills would aid him, but the more he thought about it, the more he realized how little he knew of her.

Senaps were taught to identify targets based off their clothing, accent, or demeanor. But Esha's accent had betrayed no region—she spoke with the broadened vowels common to the Varulok region and used the contractions favored by the Parvalokh region. Her sari border didn't have the stitched insignia of any one region or house—in Jansa or Dharka. The only identifying thing he remembered was that sari pin she had worn the first night he had met her. It was in the shape of a jasmine flower, a flower that bloomed widely in Dharka.

What that spoke of her, he didn't know. All it said was that her background didn't match her mask.

So, instead, he had decided to track her based off the one thing she couldn't change.

Kunal reached into his pack, making sure the rolled piece of paper with his drawing of Esha was still there. He was so occupied by making sure his drawing was still in his pack that he didn't look where he was going or hear the shout of warning.

Kunal barreled into a wide expanse of cloth that was hanging off a stall, and it enveloped him. He stumbled, knocking over a bunch of custard apples as he righted himself.

The shopkeeper ran out, nostrils flared and eyes ablaze, shouting. Kunal ducked his head, resettling fruit as quickly as he could, an apology on his tongue.

"You will not steal from me, you . . ."

Kunal braced himself for more, but the shopkeeper stopped short about a foot from him. Before he could register the look that crossed the small man's face, the shopkeeper was prostrating himself on the gritty, sandy ground, the top of his thickly wound beige turban almost touching Kunal's feet.

Kunal looked at the man in bewilderment, reaching down in an instant to pull the man to his feet. It was his own fault he had gotten lost in his worries.

Instead of pulling the man up, he knelt in front of him and clasped him by the shoulder. The shopkeeper was babbling, something about the flimsy material and how he had told his assistant to bolt down the fabric.

It seemed to be an apology. For what, Kunal didn't know.

"Master, I humbly apologize. I had no intention of stealing and if I've done any damage to your stall, I'd like to pay for it."

Kunal removed his hand from the man, who had gone still at the contact, and reached toward his purse. The shopkeeper slapped his hand away, and then looked aghast again at his action, his eyes round as the stainless steel plates he was selling.

"I'm so sorry," the shopkeeper offered, words spilling forth. "I did not see—did not recognize—with the turban—" The shopkeeper paused. "*Emenda*, sir. No. I cannot accept it," he said, wringing his hands.

Kunal rose to his feet. He had only ever heard General Hotha be addressed as *emenda*. The honorific had only come into fashion after the king's usurping of the throne—Jansa used to be an egalitarian society.

Kunal reached out to the man, shaking his head, but the shopkeeper almost recoiled.

"Then let me purchase something," Kunal said.

The man looked as if he would protest again, and Kunal noticed the sideways glances thrown toward his cuirass and bronze cuffs.

The pieces clicked in his mind. He was a Blood Fort soldier, evidenced by his bronze armor. Normal infantry only wore leather armor.

It was easy for Kunal to forget the reputation of the soldiers of the Fort, spending most of his time ensconced within its walls or out to battle. It reminded him of Esha, how she had recoiled from him at first. Had that been an act?

He frowned at the realization but tried to relax his posture into something more welcoming. It made Kunal feel a pang of regret, that this was how they were received.

"I insist. I've been traveling and am sick to death of my rations."

He smiled at the man and the shopkeeper finally eased the tension in his shoulders. Kunal followed him into the back of the stall with an eager belly. There he picked out a few items suited for traveling—dried mangoes, soft flatbread, and fried green pea cakes—but noticed the dearth of fresh produce. What was offered on the linen-covered tables was meager, wilted, and broken. Thin stalks of sugarcane, emaciated eggplant and okra.

The surrounding shopkeepers couldn't keep their glances to themselves, circling their tent. Kunal supposed a soldier with an open purse was a prime target, but there was something about the fervency of their gazes that was hotter than normal.

Everyone looked thin, so thin, and at closer glance Kunal noticed the cracked skin of their hands, the desperation with which they offered their goods to passing travelers.

He hesitated, but found himself speaking before he knew it. "Master, do you get many soldiers traveling through this town?"

"No, no," the shopkeeper said, shaking his head. Kunal held his gaze and he faltered, though he did not step back. There was something on his mind, and Kunal felt his curiosity grow.

"Master, you can speak your mind." Kunal softened his voice, rolling a fig in his hand. "I am simply curious. I have not traveled much recently." The small man, old enough to be his grandfather, ran his gaze over Kunal. Kunal straightened, wanting to prove worthy in this man's eyes.

"Yes, we have had many soldiers pass through. But they will get no welcome here, not anymore." The shopkeeper leaned closer. "The last group stole our precious water, which has become scarce since the Bhagya River began to dry up. It's a sign of the displeasure from the Earth Mother. They should never have broken the *janma* bond."

It was clear the man intended to say more, but he stopped. Despite the ends of his curling mustache trembling, he held Kunal's gaze, and Kunal felt himself having to look away.

The general had told the soldiers the drought was only passing, a blip. There had been no reason to question the statement—the Fort relied on trade for food, instead of agriculture, and they'd always been able to fulfill all their needs. It was a privilege they were offered—other towns didn't have that option.

He hadn't realized that the bond was this fractured, hadn't questioned.

"Our *janma* bond, it is a wild thing, a creation of the gods, that is true. Yet even my grandchild knows that the ritual required the blood of a Samyad woman and a Himyad man. How the king—" The shopkeeper quickly shut up, realizing his words were bordering on treason. He backed away ever so slightly.

Kunal was not angry at his words, though, only shocked, and he wondered if the king had known of this. It was a sobering thought, one that had never occurred to Kunal before.

"We will protect our remaining wells. The town of Ujral will not be cowed."

Protect their wells.

He knew the soldiers had a tendency to be brash, single-minded even—but to take from those who were so clearly in need?

Kunal wanted to shake the thought out of his head, but the look on the man's face was one he wouldn't be able to erase. The firm, grim line of his mouth, the fear that hid behind eyes that had seen too much pain. Kunal found himself speechless.

The soldiers were tasked with protecting their people. And the Fort soldiers had endangered them instead. They had failed—*he* had failed, and he hadn't even known.

Heat surged into his veins.

To become commander might give him the power to change this—hold soldiers to their oaths, imbue honor into their training, get justice for misdeeds. He could make a difference as commander.

All he could do was grasp the man's hand and bow over it, fingers to his chest.

"You have nothing to fear from me, on my honor as Naria's child," Kunal said, invoking the old oath his mother had taught him.

The shopkeeper's eyes widened for a second, as if he couldn't believe he was hearing such an old oath of fealty from a Fort soldier. But his gaze softened and he pulled Kunal up by his shoulders, returning the salute.

A sharp crack emanated from inside the stall, startling Kunal. His head shot up, his hand going to the knives in his waist sash.

"What was that?"

The shopkeeper looked nervously at the back of the stall and Kunal strode forward to check out the noise. Contain any threat.

He had made it to the back of the stall when the shop-keeper lunged in front of him.

"Oh, it's nothing, nothing at all. Our stove makes odd noises sometimes."

But there was no stove furnace that let from the back of the stall. Kunal gave the man a look before pushing to the corner of the tent, where the noise had come from. There was a small opening, as if the canvas flap of the stall had been hastily closed.

He pulled at it, his knife at the ready.

Only to find himself in a small room, surrounded by young girls. A middle-aged woman sat at the front, on a small wooden stool, her arms raised in the air. Her voice was deep and musical.

"It's whispered that the gods foresaw the fracturing of the *janma* bond and planned for Princess Reha's birth, determining she would be our savior. On a summer morning during his first visit to Gwali, Mahir Himyad, the future king of Dharka, caught sight of a beautiful maiden walking the palace gardens and vowed to win her heart. It wasn't until later that he discovered the girl was Gauri Samyad, princess of Jansa and the younger sister of the reigning queen. A love for the ages—one that bridged the two nations.

"After marriage and the birth of a son, who became the crown prince of Dharka, Reha was born. A girl child who held claim to the Samyad queendom. She was a clever child but kind, spending her time in the libraries and stables of the palace in Mathur. Years passed in peace, both Jansa and Dharka thriving and the people happy. Little did they know what was to come.

"It is said that on the Night of Tears, the gods themselves wept with anger. The skies shook with storms, raining down a monsoon so fierce the air became a hazy gray. The queen Shilpa was dead, as were all those dear to her. And by a cruel twist of fate, Princess Reha was also there, visiting her aunt in Jansa to learn about that half of her blood, her birthright.

"The Senap Guard advanced on Princess Reha's room, their jeweled armbands bright even in the darkness of that night, their tread heavy upon the marble floors of the palace. But someone had warned her. The princess Reha ran from her room, slipping through the tunnels under Gwali and escaping into the night.

"She has been roaming the land ever since, hidden to us, readying herself to return when we need her most. Our only savior. Our only chance to complete the renewal ritual as the gods intended and heal the fractured *janma* bond.

"And if we continue to pray, she will be found."

He had never heard the story of the lost princess told this way. A memory of his mother came unbidden to him, her wide eyes as she screamed at him to run . . .

Kunal started at the hand placed on his shoulder, coming out of the memory.

"Please do not report them, *emenda*," the shopkeeper whispered, appearing at his elbow. "I beg of you. They are only girls."

Kunal's pulse quickened at his words, understanding dawning.

The king's edict against gatherings of more than six.

He had thought of it only as a counter-resistance method to deal with "malcontents," as his general called them, those who wanted to incite rebellion and unrest. Or that's what he had been told.

He was slowly realizing he had been told a lot of lies, and he had believed them all.

Kunal closed the flap and put a hand on the shopkeeper's shoulder. "You have nothing to worry about," he said, looking the shopkeeper in the eye. "As I told you, on my honor. What is this?"

It had looked to be a school of some sort, pieces of paper and chalk strewn about. A small, carved marble statue of a girl, a cowherd, had sat in the corner, on a raised platform. He'd seen the same one in the last town he had ridden through.

"We teach these girls, as no one else would. We have not the resources of a bigger city like Faor, but we make do."

"I will tell no one." Kunal crossed his hand over his heart. The shopkeeper visibly relaxed. "You don't need to be afraid of me."

Kunal hated that he had to make that clear.

"Was that the story of the lost princess? I've never heard it told that way before," he asked.

The shopkeeper looked at him askance. "That is the way all Jansans tell the story, with a few variations. But the heart is the same."

"The story we were told at the Fort was so different," Kunal said.

"I am not surprised, young man. The general is a fierce friend to the king."

Kunal started, realizing that he was speaking in the present tense. Which meant news of the general's death had not reached them yet. At the mention of his uncle, Kunal tugged out the scroll in his pack, unraveling it to show the older man. He hadn't sketched in a number of moons—but he had managed to capture the deep arch of her eyebrow, the curl of her lips. It would have to do.

"Have you seen this girl here?" he asked, a bubble of hope in his chest.

The shopkeeper shook his head. "Someone special to you?"

"You could say that." He paused, trying not to be disappointed. He would just go on to Faor. "You mentioned food before?" Kunal asked, smiling.

The shopkeeper nodded, seemingly happy to move away

from dangerous topics. He led him into the stall, away from the hidden room. Slowly, he relaxed around Kunal, answering his questions as he fried up more green pea cakes.

Kunal did love green pea cakes, but he also wanted to learn more about these people. Raju, the shopkeeper, told him more about Ujral—how it was reliant on agriculture and had begun to suffer two years ago, as the Bhagya River drought had begun. They had nothing for trading either—all of their sugarcane crops were no longer sellable, despite demand.

Their neighbors to the north didn't face the same daily hardships, as the river still ran strong there from its starting perch in the Aifora Range. That worried Kunal—it indicated there was only so much time before all of the midlands were engulfed in drought. The capital and other cities in the south could rely on the ocean and trade.

These people would have nothing.

The king held no warm place in his heart, but this felt irresponsible, cruel even. Kunal was realizing how sheltered he was from the reality of Jansa's land and its people. He had spent the past decade fighting on the borders or engaging in training missions, oblivious to all of it. Not questioning or looking beyond his own life.

For those who lived off the river, their land was all they had. They had no stake in the wars of this king who stole their land and lives.

Kunal left Raju's stall an hour later, some special homemade rotis that Raju insisted he take tucked into his pack alongside the freshly made green pea cakes he'd bought.

He had a lot to ponder, especially the realization that no one had heard the general had been killed. Perhaps the Fort was keeping it under wraps until the Viper could be found.

Instead of taking the straight path back to his mare at the outskirts of the city, Kunal veered off to explore the rest of the small town by way of narrow, cobbled alleys. He needed to see for himself all Raju had described.

Shops started to nestle together and clothing transformed, as the bright embroidered colors and big turbans of the market area's wide, open streets dissolved into the faded, muted tones of the poorer shanty streets.

After crisscrossing the rest of the town, he had unearthed no Viper but had seen more than enough—families of eight or ten crammed into huts no bigger than Raju's stall, dried wells that were abandoned.

The stares became hungrier, and something inside Kunal cracked open.

So much he had ignored, overlooked, stayed quiet about in his life. No more.

A pair of boys tumbled into the street in front of him, tugging at each other. They came to a stop in front of him, faces open in wonder—and fear.

Kunal glanced down at his armor, clinking his nails against the gold cuffs on his wrist. Two rough tugs and the cuffs were off. He knelt to the ground, dirt coating his light-colored cotton dhoti, and handed them to the boys.

He would find new clothes as well, something that

allowed him to blend in more in the towns he searched. The advantage that came with this armor wasn't one he wanted anymore. He saddled his mare, tossing the thin strap of leather and stirrups over her back. She tried to nip at his hand playfully, but he didn't have the heart to engage in their little game. Not today.

Once she was saddled, Kunal took off, telling himself it was to be efficient rather than to leave behind the images of these people's pain.

As it was, he would never be able to forget them.

CHAPTER 19

Esha stepped over the man drugged and asleep on the wooden floor, limbs sprawled like unraveled threads, to cross the room.

Half-opened scrolls littered a small table, a candle and looking glass next to them. She had hoped the sleeping man's expertise as a scholar would provide some useful insight into the scrolls she had stolen, but no luck yet.

Esha twirled in the new outfit she had acquired, the cool silk of the new sari like water against her skin. It was long enough that she was also able to strap her knife and whip to her thighs—a necessity when on the run. The sleeveless blouse was a deep blue, embroidered with gold and threads of purple, and fit her torso like a glove.

Her head jangled as she moved, a teardrop of gold adorning her forehead, her braided hair woven with thin strands of gold. A row of gold bangles sat on both of her wrists, shimmering with small crystals. Jansan fashion was bright and flashy, which was the opposite of inconspicuous. Esha rather liked the idea of hiding in plain sight among all the other baubles at the bazaar today.

She melted the tip of the kohl pencil over the small candle, dragging it over the outlines of her eyelid. Her breath came easy and she found herself with a smile on her face. A semblance of safety could do that to a girl. No one would find her here—she hadn't entered this inn room through conventional means. The actual occupant lay prone on the floor two paces to her right, knocked out with an herbal draft.

An image of Kunal, his hand tossed over his eyes as he slept, passed through her mind. Why hadn't she killed him right there in the light of the forest? One swipe and he would have been out of her hair.

But something had stayed her hand.

Despite the stories of the Viper, Esha wasn't one for unnecessary bloodshed in her missions. She did what she needed to. Nothing more, nothing less. Her ability to blend in and take on any story was ideal for a rebel spy. While she did get her hands dirty, many of the Viper's most famous exploits were embellished or pure fabrications.

Someone's sister told someone's cousin and soon enough, there were stories of her stopping an entire Senap squadron en route to the port. Not that she couldn't have accomplished some of the feats attributed to her, she just hadn't. Yet.

Killing for the sport of it would make her no better than the wretched Pretender King on Jansa's throne. Esha was a soldier and spy for her people, and she had her own duty to honor.

Esha stepped back from the mirror, admiring her handiwork. A smoky black line clung to her lashes and eyes like the last mists of a summer rain. Her lips looked bitten by berry kisses. All in all, she looked like a pampered rich girl. Esha adjusted the anklets at her feet, fiddling with the hook as she frowned.

And now she was finally ready for her mission.

She'd been planning this since leaving the Tej, riding straight for Faor as soon as she got a horse. If Jiten had given her false information, she'd go back and take his fingers for good.

She had little to go off except for the reports and whip, the latter of which she couldn't analyze till she got back to Mathur. This was her chance to discover more about why she'd been framed, and who might know her connection to the Blades.

Despite her new goal, she hadn't forgotten the previous mission Harun, her oh-so-wonderful prince, had sent her on. Aside from killing the general and retrieving the report their fellow rebel had died protecting, she was also supposed to assess the weakness of the *janma* bond and the severity of the drought in Jansa.

The river still ran cold and strong here in Faor, but Esha had noted the drought-stricken towns that might be in need on her ride in. Dharka's river was still unaffected by the fracturing of the *janma* bond, but Harun wanted updates to monitor the situation, to know where they could smuggle across supplies for the people. He said it was to garner popular support for the Crescent Blades, but Esha knew it was because of his soft heart.

She still hadn't told Harun that soldiers were after her, that one knew her identity, and that someone else had gotten to the general first and framed her. And might know more.

Esha cringed at the thought of how her prince would reply to that note. Even if the message was encoded, if it was intercepted, it could put the Blades in great danger. Better—and safer—to deliver that kind of news in person.

She had kept an ear to the ground when she had entered Faor earlier, listening to the traders' whispers around the town well. The news of the general's death, or that the Viper was the main suspect, hadn't reached them yet.

Instead the townspeople had sounded hopeful that this cease-fire would be the one to lead to lasting peace. The towns around the river hadn't taken the same brunt of warfare—razed farmlands, destroyed buildings—that the border towns had, yet there was an excitement. Relief.

Esha's heartstrings tightened, knowing that if she didn't figure out why she and the Blades had been framed, it could threaten the fragile buds of peace that were now growing.

If their connection was revealed, it would look like the Dharkan throne had been behind the general's assassination.

Vardaan could use it as a reason to attack Dharka again and more lives would be lost.

The Viper was supposed to be the protector of her people —willing to take on the injustices of Vardaan's regime. It had only been two years ago that her missions had become deadlier.

She had been young, too young, but no one else had the training or language skills she did. And she had been more than willing to take the risks. She had made Harun promise to separate himself and the Blades from the Viper, to stay unblemished.

She was already too far gone.

After being released from the dungeons of Gwali, she had been thrown on the streets with no food or money, only the clothes on her back. It was in a bazaar just like the one outside that a young noble boy had caught her picking his pocket and had grabbed her arm, noticing the valaya on her wrist, the starved look on her face. Instead of taking her to the guards, he had smuggled her into his family's caravan. King Mahir had been the one to notice that the wild-looking child that her son dragged in was the late Dharkan ambassador's daughter.

Harun and his family had taken her in when she had nothing. She would do whatever it took to ensure that the peace King Mahir desired would hold.

Esha tried to relax the crease in her brow as she tugged Arpiya's letter from her pack, smoothing it out over her lap to reread.

Hello, my darling,

The days here are hot and wet, and the jasmine bushes are blooming. The boys are as irritating as ever . . .

Missing Arpiya was constant, in a way that differed from the way she missed the others back at the base. She loved Bhandu's humor and loyalty, Aahal's wit, Farhan's quiet strength. And she and Harun had grown up together, finding purpose in their mutual loss.

But Arpiya had been there during Esha's worst moments and knew her every thought—and cared for her still. It was her friendship that had kept the broken fragments of her soul together during her nightmares, her longing for a normal life.

With a sigh she tucked the note away and moved to open the window, whistling sharply. A large owl flew down to the windowpane with unsteady lurches and perched on the edge, blinking at her.

She picked up her note to Harun, wrapped it quickly with twine, and secured it in the owl's claws. It stared at her for a minute and she blinked back in response. Realizing the problem, she clicked her tongue, pulling out a small treat, and the owl nipped at it, hooting in quick succession before setting off.

The sun was high in the sky, and Esha knew the bazaar would be opening in a matter of minutes. She tried to return her focus to the current mission and away from the dozens of questions that clashed in her mind. They wouldn't be solved by the force of her worries.

Esha moved back to the small table in the middle of the room and reached under her dress, drawing out one of the knives to sharpen. The sound of metal against stone filled the small space, but still the occupant didn't wake.

She grinned. A sleeping draft worth its hefty price—just as the merchant had promised. A person could get lost in the bazaar here in Faor.

She was counting on it for the task ahead.

Esha usually hated this part. Why did people have to betray the Blades? It was always such a mess.

But this time, if it meant answers, she was happy to clean it up.

CHAPTER 20

Kunal tugged off a hunk of the dried fig, chewing on it thoroughly as his mare came to a stop outside Faor. His mare tossed her head, seemingly annoyed that he was eating and she wasn't.

It had been almost a week since leaving the Fort. He wondered how the other soldiers were faring. Laksh would be fine, probably had already made a slew of friends up and down the river. Amir was probably enjoying the sights, and he didn't care one whit about Rakesh.

His horse whinnied, and he tore off a small bit of the fig and offered it to the animal with an absentminded gesture, rubbing her neck to calm her down. They were moving into the city, approaching a wide expanse of rubble, remnants of a stone tower. He ran a comforting hand over her back, until he felt the tension leave her shoulders.

The city in front of him was larger than the ones he had traveled through so far. And not as poor since they still had the river to rely on.

From the outskirts, he could see the outline of an old temple to the Sun Maiden and a domed market in the center of the town with a city hall at the top of the hill. City halls had fallen out of use in the past ten years—an edict from the king—but he didn't know any Jansan who didn't revere the old traditions and maintain the buildings.

King Vardaan would have razed the temples too, but even he had enough fear to not raise the ire of the gods— and the people who worshipped them.

He kept an eye on the people as he traveled into the city, noticing their health, the produce being sold. He even kept an eye out for any soldiers who might be making trouble. Kunal had spent the ride from Ujral thinking of all he had learned, wondering how he could do something.

Kunal hadn't been able to shake thoughts of the lost princess, either. He had never known the Senaps were said to have been the ones to draw their swords against the royals.

Was she alive? Could these people have it right, that she had survived? If she was alive, as they so fervently believed, she could be the key to saving the land, helping these people.

He cursed himself, wondering how he had been so blind, so content to listen and not question. Stolen bits of conversation between his uncle and other military leaders flitted back to him, words of drought and the failing *janma* bond—lies and half-truths, and he had believed it all.

It had been easier to live his life by only focusing on the next step as a soldier, on how to ease his own path.

Kunal couldn't help but wonder what else he had missed.

CHAPTER 21

The bazaar in Faor covered over half a mile, circling the small hill in the center of the town like a crown. Esha had familiarized herself with the layout yesterday, as it would be crucial to her plans today.

She had been mulling over Jiten's assertion—that there was a rebel in Faor looking to leave Jansa hastily—since Pora, trying to make sense of it. Why leave the Southern Lands when peace was so close?

Unless you knew peace wouldn't last and were looking to escape.

Unless you had framed the Viper and knew your days were numbered.

What would make someone betray the Crescent Blades? Being a Blade was actually a decent life. You were well fed and had a purpose. Esha shook her head. It didn't matter, did it? Even if they hadn't framed Esha and the Blades, they would be a deserter, and that would have the same result—death by Viper.

She had spent the past day gathering information from her contacts in Faor. One had divulged that the rebel had been coming to the bazaar every day for the past week, spending time in the jewelry stalls before going to the caravansary to bargain for passage. So far no one had agreed, as most of the caravans were booked for the traders festival in the east.

Clearly, the rebel had enough coin to book passage—which narrowed down the inns they could be staying at to four. It hadn't taken her long to bribe the underpaid maids at each inn and narrow it down to one.

If Esha's luck blew straight, she'd get ahold of her suspect today.

She'd been following her from the inn since early morning, hoping she'd go to the bazaar again. It was crowded enough that Esha would be able to confront her target without drawing undue attention, or blowing her cover.

The man in front of her, his thick beige turban teetering on the edge of his head, handed Esha what she had been looking for all morning. Esha cradled the metal cup in her hands, letting the steam of the chai waft into her nose. She nodded at the shopkeeper in thanks.

Taking a blissful sip, she remembered the way her mother used to call tea the nectar of the gods. Once, her father had brought back rolled tea leaves from the far east, a perk of being the Dharkan ambassador. The three of them had forgone their chai that day. Instead, they ate delicate pastries and drank the green tea as her father told stories of each kingdom's grand feasts and libraries filled with more scrolls than the mind could fathom.

Esha sighed, pushing away the memories. She had come to the stall for chai, but also because it gave her the perfect vantage point to observe the denizens of the bazaar and to strategize. She couldn't afford to be distracted.

Esha patted her thigh to make sure her weapons were still secure. Good. She ducked under a rolled-up carpet being carried by two men and dodged another shopkeeper with a sweet smile.

Esha had trailed her target from her inn room to the center of the bazaar, where stone arches towered above them. Why did her suspect keep coming here? This was where the most expensive imported jewelry was sold, as Esha had discovered yesterday.

She ambled across from stall to stall, her eyes trailing her target. The girl was all wide eyes and open face, almost guileless. Odd for someone who might have used their cunning to plot a brutal murder and frame the Viper for it. A small smile played across the girl's face as she lifted and inspected earrings and an intricate ruby necklace.

Esha moved closer, watching, waiting.

Her target turned to say something to the shopkeeper as a large man moved in front of Esha, almost knocking her over. She glared at the man's hairy back and resisted the urge to poke him with her knife.

Without notice, four women of all ages appeared beside the man, pulling at the ruby-encrusted bangles and sapphire earrings that were strewn across the stall, chattering away like parrots about an upcoming wedding. Esha twisted and turned to catch sight of what was happening with her target. She saw the girl hand the shopkeeper something before skittering away with glances tossed back at the loud family.

Moving quickly, Esha dodged around the family in question. She followed as best she could, only catching glimpses of the girl in the crowded bazaar.

Her target was now threading through the crowds at a quicker clip. As the minutes ticked by, the crowd grew thicker, the smell of fried dough and possibility of discounts at the bazaar becoming too tempting to resist.

They left the central covered area of the bazaar, the sky opening up above them. Esha sped up, elbowing her way through the crowd with smiles. She had learned early on that a well-placed smile got her further than anything else.

Shopkeepers shouted their wares from every direction, becoming more aggressive as Esha left the women's quarters and followed her target into the everyday goods and food stalls. She ignored the onslaught of delicious smells in spite of her growling stomach.

Mission first, eat later. A reward of sorts.

Distracted by a dancing monkey in a brimless jute hat with brass finger cymbals, the teeming crowd parted enough that Esha could slip in behind the traitor, following her until she passed a small alleyway.

Esha stumbled into her target on purpose, placing a hand lightly on her back as she got ready to pull out her whip.

The girl started at the touch, turning to look at Esha.

"I'm very sorry, *emendi*." Esha pointed down to the edge of her bead-embroidered sandals. "It looks like my sandal beads got snagged on the stone. Could you help me pull myself free? You know how flimsy these new fashions are."

The girl looked younger than Esha and it startled her. Esha covered up her reaction quickly, giving the young girl a smile that invited her in on the joke. She was doe-eyed and small-boned.

A slip of a girl.

She looked a bit confused, but the tension eased from her round face. "Of course."

The girl knelt down and reached to tug at Esha's sandal. As she bowed her head, Esha pushed her into the half-darkness of the alleyway. She wrapped the thin end of her whip around the girl's neck, leaning forward to conceal her from passersby with the billowing length of the uttariya that draped off her head.

"You have about a minute to explain why you framed me before you'll lose breath," Esha whispered.

"Wha-at?" The girl's brown eyes shot up to look at her, wide with surprise and terror, taking in Esha's cold smile and the whip cutting off her air. "Viper," she stuttered out.

Esha grinned, but it was hardly more than a baring of her teeth.

"Then you know I'm not playing any games. Tell me what I want to know and I may let you leave alive."

"I don't know what you're—"

"I'd take care not to lie," Esha said, a simmer of fury under her skin. "You've left Gwali without telling your fellow Blades, you've been asking around about caravans for hire, flashing a tidy sum of gold. Is it simply that you went beyond your orders? I understand wanting to kill the general, but framing me went a bit far."

The girl's face began to lose its color and she grabbed at Esha's hands, frantic.

"Well, it seems you don't feel like cooperating." She loosened the whip ever so slightly, easing the pressure off her vocal cords. "But I'll give you one more chance."

"It's not—what you—think," the girl managed to get out.

A gurgle rose from the girl's throat, but any sound she was trying to make was cut off by the tight hold of the whip. Esha paused, looking closer at the girl.

"Dalia," the girl said, her voice strained as she stuttered out the syllables. Esha looked at the traitor sharply, her mind racing to find any connection between this name and the general's murder. "My Dalia."

"What did you say?"

"Dalia," she whispered again, and wiggled her fingers toward her satchel. Esha reached in and pulled out a ruby necklace and a note.

Written in an exuberant scrawl was a love letter, with

a declaration of commitment to run away together and a signature: Dalia.

Moon Lord's mercy.

A young girl in love. Her name was Tana, and she wasn't running away after betraying the Blades, she was running toward a life for her and the girl she loved. If there existed such a love, she wouldn't come between it, despite this girl's past choices.

Esha looked up to tell the girl as much, to apologize.

Suddenly, Tana went limp. Esha quickly unwrapped and hid her whip, attempting to the shake the girl awake.

But she stayed unmoving, slumped against the wall.

Esha cursed.

CHAPTER 22

Kunal drifted through the bustling streets of the bazaar, keeping an eye out for anything peculiar but mostly enjoying the throngs of people around him.

He had spent time stopping and talking to townspeople the last few hours, showing them the drawing of Esha and telling a story about her being his betrothed who had run away, due to cold feet, which had worked surprisingly well. Many townspeople had been willing to talk, but he had gotten no new leads.

His only break from tracking Esha had been a note he had received by hawk that morning from Alok. Alok's reply had lifted his spirits, not just because of his friend's humor but because he felt like he had an ally again. He wasn't alone.

Kunal,
I should curse you for taking this long to write to me.

Even Laksh sent a note earlier. As for news . . .

Alok told him about trouble between Vardaan and the nobility. Vardaan had begun giving out wealth and land as gifts, often land that was already owned by a noble house that was in disfavor. One of the victims of this redistribution was Baloda, the lower noble house Rakesh was from.

Kunal had tucked away the knowledge to ponder later. For now, he looked around.

He could lose himself in a bazaar like this one—watching and reading people, drawing laughing eyes, wrinkled skin, and colorful clothes in his mind. His hand itched for a brush, but he hadn't touched a canvas in years, sticking to charcoal and chalk, which were easier to hide. It was a part of him better left in the past, according to his uncle. The sketch he had drawn of Esha was the first time he had shown anyone his work in many moons.

He had obeyed his uncle, respected him as his general, even loved him. But without Uncle Setu looking over his shoulder, maybe Kunal could finally become the man he had wanted to be—not just who his uncle had wanted him to be.

This mission he owed to his uncle, but after that?

He lifted his head high, letting the warmth of the sun settle on his cheekbones, breathing life into his thoughts.

Maybe he'd paint again, without having to hide it.

It'd once been his dream, to be a painter, when he was younger. But he had left it behind, as he had many other parts of his childhood. He could feel the idea, that hope, fly back to him on quiet, uncertain wings.

The bazaar was color come to life, texture and dimension and delicious smells of spice and fried foods. Rows of colored glass bangles were lined up to his left, richly decorated earthenware jugs to his right. A seller farther up was calling out his wares, waving around his merchandise: long sandals with beaded straps that were traditional to this area.

The scene called to Kunal, begging him to stay and live in its world for a moment.

The open-air section of the bazaar caught Kunal's eye and he wandered over. It was curiously colorful, with tented stall covers of mismatched hues stretching as far as his eye could see. The cracked, aging stone of weathered columns outlined the bazaar, casting shadows and lights in various places. The street here was wide, but he saw it narrowed as he got farther away from the center, the buildings rising higher with multistoried bell windows adorning their fronts and old stone arches connecting them to each other.

An array of paints were laid out on the sun-worn damask throw. Kunal reached out, barely brushing his fingertips against each of the bottles. Ideas bloomed in his head, shifting and turning into the images that lived in his heart.

And at the forefront were chestnut eyes—hard and calculating, soft and lost—a mystery that he longed to get on canvas. Something in his heart had opened in Ujral, a fire kindled to open his eyes to the world and not accept things as they seemed.

So he didn't fight the confusing weave of feelings that rose in his heart at the thought of the Viper, or the girl he thought he had been getting to know. Instead, Kunal let it color the painting he had in his mind's eye, feeling it swirl around the curls of her hair and the bronze sheen of her skin.

Kunal was about to engage the shopkeeper when he saw a commotion in the distance where a small crowd had gathered.

He moved forward, his curiosity piqued, listening to the murmurs of the market-goers. There was a sale on woven jasmine hair ornaments and a dancing monkey somewhere up front that one man swore was secretly a child in disguise. Some expressed anger over the king's latest edict on thievery and some were excited that mangoes were almost in season—that is, if the drought hadn't ruined the crop.

Kunal was taking in the sights around him, ambling toward the crowd in the front, when he felt it.

A tingling at the back of his neck, like he had missed something right in front of his eyes.

An instinct Kunal had learned not to ignore.

He looked through the crowd with a closer eye, and spotted movement a few paces away, an unusual tread in the crowd.

He would recognize that walk anywhere. Without a second thought, he took off in pursuit, unsheathing his knife.

CHAPTER 23

Esha winced as she held the girl, propping her up against the alley wall.

Tana awoke a few seconds later, and terror gripped her features as she noticed who was holding her up. Esha gave her the briefest of nods.

She had chased down more than a few deserters, never hesitating before—but this time felt different. It wasn't just that Esha had been wrong about her having framed her, it was that she couldn't get the note out of her head.

This runaway, this ex-Blade, was doing whatever was in her ability to fight for the life she wanted with her love—even if it meant possible death.

The icy cool that had been in her veins began to thaw, and her throat went dry with a desire that had been bottled up over years and years. To have someone to love that deeply, to be loved that deeply. It brought an image of her

159

father's kind eyes to her mind, the way he'd let her have her favorite mango-shaped sweets even after she had been naughty or had skipped a lesson with the tutor. The way he would pluck a jasmine for her every day to add to her flower braid.

"For Dalia," Esha whispered, her voice firm and resolute.

Confusion flashed in the girl's eyes, and then, gratitude. Viper or no, she wasn't in any place to question Esha's benevolence and she seemed to know it.

"Lean on me, and let's get you somewhere where you can rest. We'll talk more." Tana tilted her head in acknowledgment.

Esha patted the satchel, her fingers tracing the outline of the ruby necklace, before lifting the girl forward from the wooden beam.

She took a deep breath and they began to move, little by little. Esha pulled the girl's uttariya over her head, darkening her face as the crowds of market-goers pushed against them like a wave.

The girl tried to help, but she was clearly too light-headed. The struggle of getting them out of the bazaar was firmly on Esha's shoulders, and with a panicked glance around, Esha realized they might not make it.

Esha's grasp became sweaty and weak in the heat of the sun and she tugged at the fabric on the girl's sleeve. Never had she so wished for an extra pair of hands on a mission.

Esha tripped on an errant rock and the runaway lurched

forward. As if the gods themselves had heard, a strong pair of arms caught the fainting girl as she swooned forward.

Tana's eyes fluttered open as her cheek hit her savior's chest, flashing with terror before turning blank. An expert move executed even while fainting. It was a true pity the girl had gone and fallen in love—she would've been a perfect spy for the Blades.

Esha shielded her eyes as she looked up at the soldier holding her target, his bronze armor shining in the midday heat like an ominous sun.

CHAPTER 24

Kunal remembered the first time he visited a bazaar, when his mother had taken him for solstice shopping. The crowd was just as crushing, except now, people moved around him, eyeing the way he held his knife.

He caught up with his target and waited for the right moment.

Rakesh shouldn't have showed up here.

When Rakesh neared a side road, Kunal rammed into the man, pushing him against the wall, his knife at his neck. The man squirmed in his grasp, making sounds that only served to annoy Kunal further.

"What are you doing here, Rakesh?" Kunal whispered into his ear. His newly purchased leather forearm guards, less conspicuous than the gold cuffs he had given away, thudded against the bronze of Rakesh's cuirass. "If you were following me, you should've taken off the armor."

"I'm not following you," the man hissed back, his voice angry but tinged with fear. He inhaled a deep breath. "You're not going to kill me. You're Kunal the Perfect," he intoned.

"I've killed plenty." Kunal tightened his grip.

Rakesh attempted a brave face, but his skin paled. He kicked back his elbow, but Kunal caught his arm and kneed him below his ribs. Rakesh fell to his knees like a sack of grain.

"Sure, but only under orders. You don't do anything unless it's under orders, soldier," Rakesh managed to say, despite his rattling breaths.

That rankled Kunal, and he couldn't quite place why. He did things for himself, under the orders of no one. Kunal stepped on Rakesh's ankle.

"Enough. This isn't about me."

His nostrils flared. There was truth in Rakesh's words. Kunal wouldn't kill him, because he believed in winning in a fair fight. Eliminating a competitor in a dark alley wasn't part of his code. Somehow that thought comforted and yet bothered him at the same time.

"You're right," Rakesh groaned. "I was following Laksh, not you. He's the easier mark."

Kunal's brow furrowed, unsure what Rakesh meant.

The easier mark.

It dawned on Kunal. Rakesh had no intention to fight fair. Why should he? He didn't need a strategy of his own to track the Viper, he need only borrow another's and then eliminate them if they succeeded.

Kunal felt a rising concern for Laksh—and rage at Rakesh. He stepped on Rakesh's ankle again and the soldier yelped.

"The 'easier mark'? I might follow orders, but I'm no idiot." Laksh had better be alive, or Rakesh wouldn't leave this town with his body fully intact. "Where is he?"

Rakesh said nothing, panting heavily. Kunal pulled Rakesh's head back by the hair, his hands fisted in the tight curls, enjoying the moment when Rakesh realized that Kunal was no longer bound by orders here.

The soldier's eyes widened to the size of saucers.

"Where is Laksh?" Kunal demanded.

Rakesh said something quiet and Kunal leaned in. It was a mistake, and before Kunal could register it, Rakesh had rammed him backward into the alley wall.

Kunal doubled over, coughing as dust entered his nose and mouth.

Rakesh charged at him and Kunal ducked, barely avoiding a blow to the face as Rakesh's fist punched the stone wall instead. Rakesh fell back and cursed, cradling his hand, before taking off into the streets.

Kunal ran after him. Rakesh was moments away from blending into the huge crowd ahead when Kunal slid forward and wrapped his arms around him, shoving Rakesh against the wooden door of a nearby house, rattling the door.

He had his knife back against the soldier's throat in seconds.

A mix of ice and fire burned in Kunal's veins as he pressed

the pointed tip of the knife below the bob in Rakesh's throat, drawing a thin red line.

"Fine, fine! He's here." Panic gripped Rakesh's voice.

"Not good enough," Kunal growled, panting in heavy bursts.

Rakesh had put up a good fight and Kunal made note of it. He was not an opponent to take lightly.

"There." Rakesh tilted his head to the bazaar, which was teeming with people and bursting with color just beyond their scuffle, wincing as his neck stretched. "He's in the bazaar."

Kunal's breathing evened out and he shook his head, once. "Take me there. And if you run, I will find you. And I won't be happy," he said.

The cold brutality in his own voice surprised him.

Rakesh nodded once and Kunal let him go, then followed him into the bazaar.

CHAPTER 25

Esha watched the Fort soldier glance down at the girl in his arms and then at her. Then he looked between them again.

Esha's heart stopped and started about twenty times in the span of those few seconds.

"I can't say I've ever had a girl fall into my arms that easily before," he said, a smile spreading across his face. She considered him, all tall and lanky with shiny armor, as people gave them both a wide berth and more than a few began to whisper.

He wasn't *her* soldier.

She should be glad, for this one knew nothing of her identity. But a tiny, hated part of her felt a small pang. The other soldier, Kunal—he was an interesting puzzle, that was it.

As she drew breath in and out, calming her mind, she

composed her face into a coy smile. This game she could play with her eyes closed.

"I'm so sorry, my sister doesn't have a head for crowds." Esha spoke in a pleading rush. "The dancing monkey, especially those backflips, and then all these people, it was too much," she said, looking up at him through her lashes.

The soldier nodded as if it made perfect sense. "I'm the same way. An army full of Yavar horsemen, not a worry. A dancing monkey? Now that terrifies me."

Despite the humor in the soldier's voice, his smile didn't quite seem to warm his gaze, which was as sharp as his features.

Esha giggled, taking care to make it look believable. "I think it was more the heat, but I do have to admit the idea of a dancing monkey is one for nightmares."

"Exactly! If they can dance, what *else* can they do?" he asked with an impish waggle of his eyebrows. The coldness in his face seemed to disperse, but Esha could sense it underneath, waiting like the rapids of a frozen river.

His bronze armor glimmered in the buttery sunlight, flashing into her eyes in a way that triggered another memory, one that made her hand go without thought to the knife strapped to her leg. It would be so satisfying to kill a soldier, and this one had walked into her path. One more soldier dead, one closer to the one who had drawn his knife across her father's, and then her mother's, throat.

One less plague upon this land.

She stilled her hand. This soldier could help her move faster, if she used him well. Tana was now awake, but Esha could tell she was still feeling the effects of losing air.

"Thank you, *emenda*, but we must be going." She waited for him to say something, letting silence fall unsteadily between them.

Esha counted in her head, waiting. If he had even a shred of decency . . .

"Let me help you," the soldier said a few heartbeats later.

She unleashed her best smile upon the soldier in front of her, imagining the ways she could strangle him if he came even a little bit closer. "Really? How kind of you. My father always said soldiers were honorable men. I'll show you the way."

His chest puffed up slightly as he lifted Tana into his arms. Esha pointed vaguely ahead and they walked side by side, the townspeople clearing a path for the soldier.

"How do you like the bazaar?" the soldier asked, his eyes straying to her face whenever he thought she wasn't looking.

Esha scrunched her face up in delight. "I adore it and love to come at the end of every moon. My sister finds it well enough, but I had to convince her to sneak out to see the performances today."

Esha looked ahead, determining the distance between the closest alleyways and checking the rooftops to see if they were connected. The land sloped downward as they left the raised city center and bazaar, and Esha led them to the east, where the wealthy townsfolk lived.

Returning to the inn was not an option, as its occupant was probably abed with a nasty headache, wondering where his morning had gone. She had noted a blue-painted house during her walk in the merchants' quarter. A quick survey of the house and the gardens had told her the occupants were away.

And they had a tub.

She led them in that direction, making sure to keep the conversation light. They moved east toward the cliffs Faor was famous for, which curved around the eastern edge of the city, casting a shadow on all below.

Esha stopped them when she caught sight of the blue house and pointed at a house down the street, holding a finger to her mouth. The soldier paused and she tilted her head up at him.

"I can't have our father seeing us sneaking back in. He'll keep us housebound for another moon! And I must have new bangles for next week's festival," she said, smiling earnestly. "Put her down here and we'll sneak back up through the kitchens. If you don't mind, that is," she added, biting her lip.

"Of course," the soldier said. "I wish I could see you to the house myself . . ."

She shook her head firmly. "No, I wouldn't ask that of you. You must have so much more important things to be doing as a soldier."

His eyes seemed to refocus and he nodded, almost in

distraction, as if he had remembered something. "Nothing more important than helping a beautiful girl."

She blushed and pulled the corner of her uttariya over her eyes, letting only her smile peek out as she waved a hand.

Despite the act, Esha kept a keen eye on him as he bent down to place the girl on the ground and then looked up at her. He asked her a question, and she nodded without listening.

All Esha could think about was the way the soldier was exposing his neck, and how easy it would be, how simple to draw her knife and hide his body in the garden.

Her hand rested on her thigh. The killing instinct rose in her blood.

It was a familiar call, warm and inviting.

Before she could make a move, he had straightened, and her advantage had vanished in her moment of weakness.

———◄◊►———

Esha watched the soldier—Laksh—amble back toward the city center before she breathed a sigh of relief. He had spent a few minutes chatting with her about inane things, clearly looking to be invited in, but she had done her best to get him to leave.

This time, she had given a fake name. Esha couldn't know if there would be more soldiers in the area—she'd need to get out of here as soon as she could.

The problem was the girl. She couldn't leave her in some alleyway.

Esha looped her arm under the girl's body, dragging

her toward the garden of the blue house. She ducked them inside the basement kitchen.

The girl fell against the kitchen wall, almost knocking over a metal pot as she rubbed her neck. With a sigh, Esha collapsed against the wall too. She told herself it was just for a second, just because this girl was so heavy.

But she was tired, and it started in her heart.

"Have you dragged me all this way to kill me?" Tana asked, color finally coming back to her face.

Esha scoffed. "That would be highly inefficient. No, I chose to save you. If I wanted you dead, you'd be dead. It wasn't my original intention anyway."

Some of the wariness fell away from the girl, and she slid to the ground, leaning her head against the wall. The girl coughed, her breaths like rattling swords. "Thank you, then. I know the punishment for deserters and you didn't need to . . ." The girl paused and then finished with, ". . . weren't supposed to save me."

Esha shook her head. She was no hero, despite the girl looking at her as if she was one.

That note had been an arrow to her heart. The heart she claimed to not have or hid away deep within herself. Seeing someone risk certain death for love—would she ever find that again?

Once a killer, always a killer. Once your hands were stained, you could never be an innocent. And her hands had been stained many times over.

She wondered what her father would think of her now.

"I didn't want to desert the rebels," the girl said. "But I had—"

"I saw the necklace and the note, Tana," Esha said. Tana shifted to face her, eyes shining with gratitude.

Esha turned her face away. She had only done what she thought was right.

"It's best that we part. Take your time to rest here and gather supplies. I was never here and we never met. Find your way back to the bazaar and go to the life you want. Tell no one about me." Tana opened her mouth in protest and Esha shushed her. "Take on a different name—it'll be better for escaping notice anyway. Tana Pamina is dead after today, understand?"

Tana nodded briefly and sat up. Esha could tell she wanted to talk, something Esha did not want to do. She moved to leave, but the look on Tana's face stopped her.

"What is it?" Esha said.

"I heard something," the girl said, interrupting Esha's thoughts. Esha raised an eyebrow, waiting. "My last contact had a run-in with a few soldiers, before realizing they were Senaps—in their small town, of all places."

Senaps away from the palace or border? That was information, interesting information, though Esha couldn't be sure what it meant. She gave the girl an appraising look.

"I also heard Vardaan is moving troops from the borders back into Jansa. It might have something to do with that."

Esha pursed her lips and asked, "And the cease-fire? Any noise on the upcoming peace summit?" Tana hadn't framed her, so she shouldn't know about the general's death.

"People are happy to have a respite. Nothing much else."

What game was Vardaan playing? She knew the soldiers had found the whip, yet nothing. A few moons ago, Vardaan would've used such information to raze border villages.

"I heard Vardaan is happy, giving out jewels and land at court after the cease-fire. My gut says there's more to it, especially after he's relentlessly pursued our land for years. Something's changed. Could be an alliance, could be some advantage they've developed militarily. I just don't trust him, knowing how volatile he is," Tana said.

Esha thought of the report she had been unable to translate.

Could it have information on Vardaan securing an alliance? That would make the Pretender King happy, especially if he was planning on renewing war with Dharka in the near future.

Tana noticed Esha had gone quiet. "That's all I know," she said. Esha held a hand to the young girl's face, making sure her vital signs were strong again.

"You've been posted here for a while. Do you know of any scholars who would understand Old Dharkan?" Esha asked, her thoughts returning to the report. It was the only lead she had now.

Tana shook her head. "There are only a few scholars left who the Blades can trust. But I do have a contact in Amali who I'd trust with my life." The girl took out a small piece of paper and chalk, jotting a few notes. "As my thanks for letting me go."

Esha raised her eyebrows at the information.

Amali. A small town deep in the northern Parvalokh region. She was familiar with it.

"You sure you don't want to stay in service of the Blades?" Esha asked. Tana's eyes went wide and Esha laughed. "It's all right. I understand. But if you change your mind, just send a note to me."

"Sorry for this."

Tana's eyes flashed in confusion before Esha dipped her hand into the sleeping draft and covered Tana's mouth.

Tana looked to be only a few years younger than her, her face losing years in sleep. Not young for the rebels, but young. If she had another life to live—a small one, a happy one—who was she to stop her?

It could end up being a huge mistake, but something in Esha's gut told her Tana would never speak of the Viper or the rebels again.

Esha watched the girl for a while, her breath rising and falling, before winding her way upstairs.

CHAPTER 26

Kunal had been trailing behind Rakesh for the past ten minutes, gripping the handle of his knife tightly as the other soldier led the way through the long, winding bazaar. He was getting dangerously close to a breaking point, and hoped, for Rakesh's sake, that they found Laksh soon.

"He's here, somewhere. I swear," Rakesh said, turning back to toss a glance or two at Kunal, probably looking for a weakness or a failing on his part so he could break and run.

Kunal took a deep breath.

Focus hones the soldier into the keen edge of a blade.

The memory of his uncle's words hit him hard. He would never hear his uncle's wisdom again—never argue *against* his words of wisdom again.

Rakesh came to a sudden halt, ignoring the annoyed squawk of an old man who he had cut off. Kunal pulled up behind him and Rakesh winced, recognizing the tip of

Kunal's knife against the bottom of his spine.

Kunal's heart unclenched at the sight of Laksh a few paces away. Laksh looked up at them as he brushed a lock of wavy hair out of his eyes.

"Nice to see you both," he said, not a hint of surprise in his voice. Relief flooded through Kunal.

"What?" Laksh asked, looking between the two of them. He addressed Rakesh first. "Did you really think I didn't know you were following me? You're as tall as the western hills."

Rakesh scoffed, his face turning red.

"And you. You shouldn't be so glad to see me." Laksh shook his head slowly, looking at Kunal. "I'm competition."

Kunal's brow furrowed. He turned around to clasp Laksh by the shoulder, who waved them over to the side of the road, away from the crush of people in the center of the bazaar.

"Glad to see you alive," he whispered into Laksh's ear. The corners of Laksh's mouth tilted upward.

"I wouldn't let Rakesh get rid of me that easily. I've known he's been behind me since the last town, but I was able to slip him this time and pick up a nice poison for my knife. If he tries anything . . . ," Laksh said, his voice low, but not low enough for Rakesh to miss.

Kunal smirked and looked behind him—just in time to see Rakesh holding a knife.

In an instant, Kunal disarmed him.

Speed was the one thing Kunal had that Rakesh did not. He shoved Rakesh against the nearest wall, knocking the knife from his hand. Rakesh choked on the cloud of dust that flew out around them.

Kunal smiled. "Truce? I'm feeling generous right now. No one touches each other until we're all outside the city. Jansan's oath."

Rakesh's eyes flashed murder, but Kunal saw him swallow hard. Laksh stepped forward and held out a hand, palm up.

"I would take it, soldier," he said. "I guarantee you it's the best option this one will give you."

After a moment, Rakesh sighed. "Truce," he croaked.

Kunal let him go and Rakesh straightened, dusting off his armor and pants. "Oath as Naria's child. You're witness, Laksh."

"Now that we're back to being one big, happy family . . ." Laksh grinned as the two soldiers glared at each other. He motioned them toward a stall selling long, curved swords and round iron shields and they moved back into the teeming crowd.

A cough came from Laksh, and Kunal realized his hands were still fisted, ready for attack. Laksh held out a fine-looking shield to Rakesh, whose eyes finally dropped that hunted-animal look.

"Not that I'm *not* happy to see your shining faces, but I've just met a beautiful girl and I've got to say, you both are a bit of a disappointment after that," Laksh said. Rakesh folded his arms and leaned against the wooden post of the weaponry stall.

"Getting distracted?" Rakesh scoffed. "I'm not surprised at all. You were always a jokester. I don't even know why you were picked for this mission."

Laksh ignored him. "This girl." He whistled. "She had eyes that changed like the winds of the monsoon season."

"Are you becoming a poet now, Laksh?" Kunal asked, with one eye on Rakesh.

"No, I think I'll leave that to you, Kunal," Laksh said. "I've seen better in the royal court in Gwali, don't get me wrong. But her eyes—"

Unbidden images of Esha entered Kunal's mind, face illuminated by the moon and the light of the Tej. Kunal started, guilt painting over the image, mixing in with memories of sitting across from his uncle.

He looked around, at Rakesh, realizing he had drifted off into a daydream. Laksh was still talking, but Kunal heard only bits and pieces.

"I walked her over to the east, where there's a row of blue houses. Merchants, from the looks of it. Quite wealthy too."

Kunal remembered the houses in a vivid rush of memory, an image he had tucked away to paint and one that now stood out starkly in his mind. They had ranged from a vivid cerulean color to the deepest midnight blue, with trellises that climbed up the sides, dotting the walls with bright bursts of pink hydrangeas. That area had been almost abandoned when he had strolled through it earlier, the merchants away on their annual trip to the east.

Rakesh picked up the round shield and inspected it. Kunal watched his hand graze the opal-encrusted hilt of a curved knife that sat next to it.

"Wealthy and beautiful? Seems like a prize you don't deserve," Kunal teased.

"I do quite well for myself," Laksh said. "But this time it seemed a bit too much work even for me. Her sister had fainted due to excitement, apparently, but she seemed rather sicker than that. A protective father and a sick sister? Too much trouble."

"Not up for the challenge?" Rakesh said.

"The girl wouldn't even enter the house she was so terrified of her father," Laksh said. "Why work so hard when I'm about to become commander and can take my pick of beautiful women?"

Kunal rolled his eyes. Laksh always talked like this, but he had only occasionally joined the other soldiers on their city excursions during campaigns. And then, often only to gamble.

Something about Laksh's story seemed odd.

A protective father didn't make sense—most merchants in this region were on their pilgrimage to the eastern coast for the annual trade festival right now. Why would she lie about where she lived if her father was most likely gone?

It hit Kunal as he ran his fingers over a quiver, admiring

the delicate mirror work that created shifting illusions of color and light.

Beautiful eyes. An empty house and a story. A girl on the run.

Esha.

Laksh had just seen the Viper, spoken to her. His throat closed up at how close she had been. One wrong move and it would have been Laksh who captured her, not him.

The thought was a gut punch.

Kunal put down the quiver, imagining the different pathways to the blue house, how to get out of this ridiculous conversation, how to lead the others away.

No more distractions.

CHAPTER 27

Esha slid farther down the tub, letting her hair billow out in the water, floating like tiny snakes. Lifting her eyes, she took in the golden filigree that was etched across the ceiling and the sumptuous tapestries in shades of blue and pale cream that hung on the walls.

Tana slept soundly a few stories below, and with the amount of the draft in her body, she would stay there till the morning. By then, Esha would be gone.

Esha sighed. Faor had been a dead end on who had framed her, but something bigger was on her mind now.

Tana's information on Vardaan, that he hadn't publicized the news of the general's murder, that he was *happy*, worried her. She hoped the report she had stolen back from the general would add context. There was something in there that the Fort had wanted to protect—perhaps it was news of an alliance.

That could mean the end of peace.

The only way to know was to translate that report. She'd go to Amali next and connect with Tana's scholar contact. At least it was something.

She rubbed her eyes, letting the hot water drip down her face and onto her aching shoulders. She massaged them, taking care to work around the long scar that trailed her right shoulder, remnant of a reckless childhood. It had been worth it to draw the steaming bath, despite the effort and time it had taken. A week of grime eased off her body as she scrubbed herself raw and soaked. She let herself rest there, closing her eyes to enjoy the feeling of soothing water against her muscles.

For a few heartbeats, she let go of the constant tension that prickled under her skin, trying to enjoy the present. And the future? Experience told her that things always got worse before they improved—if they didn't simply stay that way.

The silence and hot water lulled her into peace and she sighed, content. It had been a risk, stealing into this abandoned home, but she couldn't resist a bath, hot food, and a real bed. No one would know she had arrived, and no one would know she had left.

A shadow passed over the window curtains and Esha sat up so quickly in the bath that half a bucket's worth of water spilled and splashed onto the smooth stone floor, soaking into the tasseled edge of the sumptuous brocade carpet. All the peace that had begun to accumulate under her breastbone vanished.

Her eyes flickered to her knives on the table next to her, within grasp. She set her jaw and took a calming breath. No one knew she was here.

But she was unable to reclaim the calm she had felt moments before, and decided to get ready.

Esha emerged from the water, patting herself dry with a long length of woven cotton. The room was clearly loved and lived in—scrolls and letters, jewelry and trinkets were strewn about. A silver mirror was propped up in the corner, with dust fingerprints over it, as if someone constantly peered at themselves with that mirror.

This was a home.

She might've grown up in a house like this if the coup had never happened. Esha wandered around, taking stock of the contents of the room as she dried her hair. An ivory comb sat on top of the wardrobe and Esha picked it up, letting memories wash over her.

She'd once had a comb like this. The thought made a part of her heart ache—the part she hid under rage and revenge.

Esha took a deep breath, willing away those old thoughts and wishes, combing her wet hair. Through the hanging folds of multicolored silk that hung from the lushly curved window, Esha could see that the sun was beginning to descend.

Day faded in broad purple streaks across the sky and Esha could see the rolling curve of the Ghanta Mountains to the east and the green jungles that thicketed the valleys below the mountains. In the far distance, the snowcapped peaks of the Aifora Range glittered.

Everywhere were signs of the end of the day—women in the distance hauling out their washed clothes from the river, men pulling down woven straw covers to protect their wares. It never failed to warm her heart to see that the real soul of Jansa, the people, hadn't changed.

The two countries were so similar, Esha thought. Either here or there, the men and women rose every day with the same burdens weighing on their shoulders, the same responsibilities and sorrows and joys. She would never understand how Vardaan had convinced people to see the differences between them, rather than the similarities.

Away from the capital and the Blood Fort, the old ways were remembered and the people still spoke of the lost princess with hope. Another memory came to her, unbidden.

Esha had been with the princess on the night of the coup. Her family had been the princess's royal companions on her trip to her aunt's house. On the Night of Tears, she had been in the Great Library with Reha. Esha had been the one to grab the princess and race to her family's room, where she sent her and her nurse through the passage that led to the city's tunnels.

When the soldiers found Esha and her parents later, they showed no mercy in trying to capture her, one of the Senaps having seen Esha earlier from the library window.

Her father had been the first to go, trying to save his beloved daughter. Her screams had been so loud, her grief so keen, that one of the soldiers had made the sign to ward off the Lord of Darkness. She remembered little after that, or tried not to.

Esha inhaled deeply, letting the humid air from the bath fill her lungs, warm away those cold, bleak memories. What good did it do her to indulge in the past? Esha put down the ivory comb and stepped away, trying to bury the memories the room seemed determined to drag out of her.

In the distance, she could hear the song of the cleaning women.

It was called the Lament of Naria—a song passed from mother to child in every home in Jansa. It was a song she had learned when she had lived at the summer palace as a child.

Esha hummed quietly as she helped herself to the clothes in the wardrobe, letting the sumptuous silks distract her mind from death and grief.

———◁o▷———

It wasn't until her stomach let out an ungainly growl that Esha remembered to eat.

She had taken note of the food that had been stored on the lower levels of the house when she had brought in Tana—some salted fish and dried fruit. It would be enough for now.

Esha opened the door of the bedroom she had claimed as her own and looked both ways out of habit. Arpiya always said she was a bit too suspicious. She was halfway down the stairs when she heard the noise, soft yet noticeable. Like a shuffling of feet.

Esha grabbed her knife and flattened herself against the wall.

Had the occupants returned early? There was no squeak of wheels outside, no chatter of children. And the servants would have arrived first to prepare the kitchens.

She inched up the stairs, taking care to step as light as a leopard.

It had to be Laksh, the soldier from before. Perhaps he had returned, hoping to catch her attention. A besotted boy would do such a thing.

Or worse, he had seen the whip mark on Tana's neck.

Another noise, a slow yawn of wood, but this time from above. Esha froze, paralyzed as she realized she was no longer sure what direction the noise was coming from.

Take the chance and go down? There were more entryways there, but that also meant more ways to escape. She could come back for her hidden pack.

Or go back up, try to leave by the rooftop?

Whoever it was, their tread was light, as if they had practiced sneaking about. Esha held her breath and made a choice, tiptoeing back up to her room. She had her weapons there.

The hall was empty as she turned the corner.

But she had misjudged.

Footsteps bounded behind her. The soldier grabbed her wrist and twisted her arm around her back in a swift motion, his other arm coming around her neck. His breath was hot against her skin and it shot shivers down her spine.

His hands tightened around her own, and she pushed down the immediate frantic energy that coursed through her body, searching for the calmness in her core that had gotten her through a number of tight spots.

There were people outside, the women, the fruit seller. Her eyes darted to the fluttering curtains of the window inside the room and he clamped his hand around her mouth, his fingers sears of fire against her parted lips.

"I wouldn't scream if I were you. I don't think they'll look too kindly on a girl who broke into a home that wasn't her own." Kunal leaned in closer, his words soft. "I won't hurt you."

He shuffled her forward into the bedroom and eased the door shut with a soft thud, pulling her into the center of the room. She struggled and fought wildly, but his grip was tight.

Calm. She needed to remain calm.

Esha kicked her right hip back and shifted her arm out of his grip enough to aim an elbow jab at his side. It barely glanced off his skin, causing her more pain than him, and she realized he was wearing his armor under his clothing.

Clever. He chuckled but his grip on her softened and she whirled out, cursing at the pain radiating from her elbow.

"Now, do you want to tell me why you're here? Why you left in the woods? I said I would help you get to a ship, see you off safely. Yet you left me in a tree, with no idea where you'd gone." His tone was unsettling, like steel that covered its true form in silk.

She wouldn't have thought the soldier had menace in him—but she had talked her way out of his grasp before. She just had to distract him enough to run.

Her eyes flashed to the window to the right, but she had

latched it shut. He regarded her, his light eyes unnerving in the dim light, and she couldn't help but glance over his body, assessing his weaknesses. Strong shoulders, lithe but muscled. It was clear he was strong, but she could tell from the way he moved that he would also be fast.

She'd just have to be faster.

"I was scared. How was I to know that you would see me safely back? You were kind, but how could I trust you?" she said, allowing her words to remain soft as she chewed on her lip.

He looked at her askance and she widened her eyes at him, letting her lips part.

The soldier laughed grimly. The quiet humor she had found behind his eyes in the forest was gone.

"You're good, Esha. Very good. A jewel for the rebels." He said the words without a trace of mockery, the meaning as sincere as the mistrust that now radiated from him.

Moon Lord's mercy. He knew.

How?

She let the mask fall, matching his focused gaze with a stare of her own. It was as if in those few seconds, he understood every facet of her, light and dark, and didn't back away.

There was no warmth, as there had been days ago. No lightness, no levity.

His eyes remained steady on her and Esha released a held breath.

But his face showed no fear. He wasn't scared of her. Something about that called to her, reminded her of her friend from a lifetime ago who hadn't backed away from her wild, younger self, all wide eyes and skinned knees.

"I'll ask again. Why did you flee from me in the forest?"

He stepped closer and she resisted the instinct to step back. Why was he asking when he knew the answer? It was as if he wanted to hear it come from her mouth, to hear her curse herself with her own words.

His shoulders blocked out the light around her, shrouding him in darkness so that the planes of his face looked as if they'd been cut from marble.

"I left. I didn't flee."

"Esha, why did you leave? Tell me I'm wrong. I'd like to hear it. That you aren't the Viper. That you didn't use me to sneak into the Fort and kill General Hotha."

His words were strangled, and he looked distressed, as if he had revealed more than he had wanted. The soldier was inches away from her now and Esha's heart began to beat faster, in accompaniment to the rush of blood to her face. She saw his eyes widen in response, as if he sensed the change in her body. The silky light of the lone candle in the room flickered over his head, casting an intimate glow.

She wished she had her knife in her hand, her whip around his throat. Even a sharp pointed rock would do.

Esha broke away from his stare to glance at the door, the window. She was cornered, and when she looked back, his gaze was still on her, the heat of it weighing her down.

So she did the only thing she could think of.

"I did it. I killed him. Your general."

CHAPTER 28

He glanced at her, startled at the confession. Esha felt her eyes go wide, betraying her own surprise.

Once the words were out of her mouth, she had no idea why she had wanted to say it, why she had lied. Maybe he would've believed her if she had told the truth, but it was better to watch him, to see what he might reveal.

"Why would you admit it?" He seemed puzzled, a frown on his face, as if expecting a trick.

She shrugged, her mind racing.

"You asked," she pointed out, her brow furrowing. "Maybe it's because my friends say I like to be contrary. Maybe it's because I'm trying to confuse you." She felt the words take on their own life as she looked at his face. "Maybe it's because you seem to like me and I wonder if you will even after knowing."

That hit too close to the truth that was beating in her heart.

He shook his head. "You admitted it. Whether I like you or not has no bearing on what I must do now. If you killed the general, you must be brought to justice." A look like regret passed across his face. "Even if I owe you a debt."

With just a few words, the rising fire in her belly flickered out and anger replaced it, warming her limbs with a different kind of heat.

"Must I? For killing one person when he's slaughtered thousands?" Her face was stony.

This was the behavior Harun always said would get her killed. She was challenging a soldier who had the advantage on her. The last thing she should be doing was provoking him, but she couldn't help it.

"You've probably killed more people in one fortnight than I have my entire life. Where's the justice in that?"

"Whoever I killed was on a battlefield." Irritation bloomed on his face, darkening his brow. "It was by the rules. You slaughtered him in his bed."

"Well, these are my rules. I'm not a soldier. I'm the Viper."

Kunal's face remained impassive but his fingers began tapping.

"Even rebels have rules they must follow."

"I'm not associated with those reb—"

Kunal flashed the Crescent Blades pin in front of her.

She tried to snatch it, but he caught her wrist, tucking the pin away.

"We've always suspected that there was a connection between the Viper and a rebel group. I always thought the stories couldn't possibly have come from one person. But now having met you—"

"Don't pretend to know me, soldier."

"If you were told to become the Viper . . . ," he said, looking thoughtful. "That would be different. You wouldn't be at fault then."

The vicious part of her wanted to squash that thought.

"Have you considered that I may have *chosen* to become the Viper? Took it on out of my own sense of duty to my people? You of all people should understand that, soldier."

Esha fell back into her hatred and it settled around her like an old blanket. It was a relief to feel it, instead of whatever he had been making her feel minutes ago.

"No? Because I have this face I can't possibly be in control of my own destiny? I used to think so too. Your *king*"—she spat the word—"seems to think so too, removing all women from military service." She stepped back, only to find herself even closer to the corner of the room. The thick brocade of a tapestry brushed her arm. "I'll not feel a shred of remorse for sending that general to the pyre. He has sent hundreds, thousands, of families to weep at the pyres of their loved ones. He's one less monster roaming the streets."

One less soldier with the power to destroy families like her own.

"And you don't owe me any debt. I would rather be sacrificed to that tiger in Tej than be helped by a bronze-armored, yellow-bellied Fort soldier," Esha finished.

Something warred on Kunal's face, as if two halves of him were struggling to make a whole, fighting for dominance. She eyed him warily as he moved toward the door. In seconds, he had broken the latch to the window, so that it was stuck in place.

They were now on different ends of the room, Kunal moving to stand in front of the door and Esha in the corner opposite.

"You're right," Kunal said. She stared at him, shocked. "No matter how much I hate to admit it, he was a harsh man. Cruel when he could have been merciful, tough when kindness would have worked just as well. He may have been my—my mentor, but even I knew he wasn't always a good man."

He agreed? What was she supposed to say to that?

She had an outline of him in her mind, bronze and blood. But now the gaps were filled in with gray—an unknown. And she hated it.

He shook his head. "But it still doesn't matter. My orders are to take you back. You'll face a trial and justice will be meted out. That's how I will repay my debt. You'll not be killed under my watch."

Esha burst into laughter and he looked up, startled.

"'A fair trial'? Ignorance truly is bliss." Her tone was biting.

"I will get no trial. You're full of lies," she hissed, feeling more like her namesake than ever. "I will be barely tossed a glance before I'm thrown into a cell or left for the buzzards. Gone are the days when Jansans respected women and viewed them as equal under the law. In ten years, centuries of equality were stolen from the women of Jansa because of your king's greed and fear."

Kunal looked surprised, as if he hadn't thought she would be so apprised of Jansa and its politics. She took pleasure in that, in surprising him—she was more than one thing.

"Not only am I a woman, but I'm a murderer. The men who become soldiers are not those who value women—and definitely not a woman who has managed to discard their notions of female fragility with a slice of her knife."

Once again, his brows rose and she knew she was giving away more than she should. Revealing her cultured and educated upbringing, her passionate interest in what had happened to Jansa.

"You don't know those men. They're not all bad."

"But they're not all good. All you need is a few bad grapes to ruin the wine."

Kunal opened his mouth to respond but shut it quickly, as if he realized the truth in her words. He sighed deeply and glanced away before running a hand through his hair, which had grown longer than the traditional short soldier cut. His sharp amber eyes snapped to hers, and Esha thought she could read the emotion in them.

His face warred between annoyance, frustration, and

something else. It seemed he didn't know what to do with her.

The feeling was mutual.

———◄○►———

If there was one compliment Esha could give him, it was that he never seemed to speak without thinking and considering all sides. She supposed that was useful for a soldier who wanted to lead, probably why he had risen into the Senap Guard as well.

But that had never been her style and she was growing impatient with him.

He pointed at her. "You make some valid points, but it doesn't change what I must do. You will go back. You will stand trial—I will make sure of it. Justice will reign. I don't know about the rest of Jansa, but in the Fortress, when I'm the next commander, that's how it will happen."

His brow was furrowed and his hands fidgeted with tension. The meaning of his words hit Esha full in the stomach, thinking back to the other soldiers in the forest.

"Ah, one of you will be named commander."

Kunal began to speak but seemed to think better of it. He curled his fingers into a fist and sat back.

She had just wasted precious moments arguing with this fellow, who could be the next commander of the Fort. It didn't matter what her heart told her, her mind was screaming at her to run or to fight. Do something. Her words wouldn't convince him and she needed to get to Amali.

She took his momentary speechlessness to lunge toward

the bed, where she had hidden her whips. She had barely taken a step when she was thrown backward, a knife catching the edge of her uttariya, lodging her, and the cloth, into the wooden wardrobe behind her.

Kunal moved forward, grimacing.

"I'm no idiot, Esha. Though you seem to think so."

That was exactly the opposite of how she felt. Esha was so stunned that she kept still, realizing the knife had missed the muscle of her shoulder by inches.

"If I didn't think all Fort soldiers were scum, I'd ask you to teach me that trick."

She glared at him.

He moved toward her, golden in the dim light of the candle. "It's not a trick. It came from many moons of hard work and focus." He considered her. "But I could teach you. Later."

Esha's heart lifted at that and she hated herself for it.

She shook her head.

He was mad.

She was mad for caring.

He owed her a life debt. Apparently, he was one of those Jansans who still went by the old codes of honor, which were precious to Naria's children. Beyond that, there was nothing real here. What in the moon's name was happening to her anyway? Esha had no illusions about what would happen if he managed to get her back to the Fort, lie or no lie.

She watched him move with silent, fluid motions as he expertly tied her hands together in a tight knot and dislodged the knife from her tangled uttariya.

In other circumstances, Esha would have been pleased at meeting her match.

Now she just wanted to kick him. He deftly avoided her blow, squeezing her hands tighter behind her back.

"Don't make me tie your feet too."

Esha stared at him, her eyes wild. He was a madman to think she would let him take her back, that she wouldn't fight tooth and nail the whole way. She wouldn't make it easy.

But the soldier was one step ahead of her. He did bind her feet together.

She had to applaud him for it—he learned quickly.

Next he searched her, patting her down efficiently for any weapons. His hands skimmed over the contours of her body, causing her cheeks to flush. His face betrayed nothing, stony and stoic as his hands searched.

She would've liked some sort of reaction—she did have a curve or two she was proud of.

Esha finally noticed a faint pain slinking through her torso—hunger—and behind it a sense of weakness. Instead of dinner, Kunal had shown up, and she hadn't eaten in almost two days, gulping down water and a few fruits and nuts whenever she had a spare moment. Her dinner was down in the kitchens.

Maybe she would rest for just a second. It didn't seem like she'd be able to get out of here when he was awake anyway. Her stomach growled, a noise loud enough that Kunal noticed.

"When's the last time you ate?" he asked.

Esha mumbled something about how running for her life wasn't really good for the appetite and how he had interrupted her dinner. He shook his head as he picked her up, gently curving his arms under her knees and back. She looked up at him, wondering if he would soften if she pretended to faint or cry. Her pride kept her from doing either.

This soldier was a true mystery. It didn't make sense—why he was kind to her, why he was honoring a way of life his countrymen had largely abandoned, why she felt there was a depth to him she wanted to know more about.

He put her down on the floor, propping her up between the bathtub and door. From his pack on the table he produced roti and green pea cakes. He portioned it out with expert care, as if he had done this a thousand times.

Esha supposed he had. Someone had to oversee rations while at war. He put her portion on a small cloth on the floor next to her. She looked up at him, her mouth pursed, a sour expression on her face.

"How am I supposed to eat this? With my feet?" His brow furrowed. Esha smiled sweetly at him. "If you untie me, I promise I won't run. I'll just stuff my face with food and settle back into a peaceful slumber."

He snorted at that, and a ghost of a smile flitted over Esha's mouth.

"I don't hear you promising not to kill me in my sleep, so I think I'll pass."

He crouched before her, close enough that she could

see the flutter of his eyelashes and smell the faint scent of clove and sandalwood on him. He tore a piece of the roti and offered it to her. She glared at him before opening her mouth and he popped it in. Her taste buds alighted and she savored the morsel.

This roti, dusted with spices and seeds, was definitely worth losing her dignity.

Or that was what she was telling herself. He fed her with careful attentiveness but the smirk never left.

It made her want to hit him again.

"It's so easy to read your thoughts right now."

She scoffed at this. No one said that about the Viper. He looked at her as he tapped his nose.

"You're imagining all the ways you want to hit me. I bet a punch square to the nose is looking pretty good to you."

For just a moment she felt like a normal girl being teased by a handsome boy. She could almost forget that he was one of the soldiers she had dedicated the past ten years to fighting, and would soon be the dreaded commander if he succeeded in taking her back.

It helped that her hands and feet were still tied, bringing her back to reality.

She looked away quickly from his eyes, which had become too warm, too familiar.

"Yes, direct to the nose. It is a bit too straight."

He laughed, and she tried to stop the small grin on her face.

"It's a prerequisite for entrance into the Fortress. 'Must

have perfect, straight nose.'" His mouth quirked into a sardonic smile. "Do you want more?"

The rest of his rations were on the floor and she realized he had barely eaten his share. She began to shake her head no but the rumble in her stomach betrayed her. He broke the rest of his roti into pieces, dipping it, folding it around the spicy mixture like a small parcel, and offering it to her.

"I meant it when I said I wouldn't hurt you. I'm not one to lie."

His voice was soft and she jerked away, not meeting his eyes.

"Perhaps not. But you are still a soldier," she said evenly.

"I owe you a debt and I will not hurt you, on my honor as Naria's child." His jaw tightened. "But you killed a man. Outside the norms and laws of battle." He sighed. "I would take anyone back. It's my duty."

She stared at him. "Tell me something I don't know, soldier."

CHAPTER 29

That word again. Soldier. He hated how her use of that word reduced him to one of those thin flaps of wood, one-dimensional and facet-less.

"Fine. Here's something," he said, his brow furrowing. "I never wanted to be a soldier." That seemed to get her attention.

"What did you want to be, then?"

Kunal hesitated. But he had already started and he wanted her to see him as he saw himself: complex. Good, in spite of having done things he'd rather forget about.

"An artist, perhaps a painter. But I never would have been allowed. I was given a bow and blade instead. Lucky me, I happened to be good at fighting and whatever I wanted for my own life disappeared. I was to become a soldier."

In the likeness of Uncle Setu.

He heard his voice turned bitter and she cocked an

eyebrow at him. Kunal knew he was telling too much to her, his enemy.

But the story brought out feelings he had made himself put aside, for they had no place in his life. After his mother's death, he had clung on to the one thing his uncle approved of, the one thing that made him look at him with something akin to pride. He had believed his uncle when he had said he was carrying on his tradition and the tradition of Kunal's father by becoming a soldier. And so he had abandoned dreams of art, hiding them away for those moments when he was alone.

But now he was realizing he was simply a tool of a king who cared little for his people or their land. From the drought-stricken town of Ujral to the broken-down city halls in Faor, Kunal was slowly seeing a new side to Jansa. One where people cowered and justice crumbled under might.

His uncle he had deferred to—he had given him respect. He was his only remaining blood relative, after all. But Vardaan . . .

Kunal stopped. His thoughts had turned treasonous, and they felt different now, as if there was a power behind them. It surprised him, the intensity with which they hit him. Her words of challenge brought up his own fraught thoughts since Ujral.

He glanced back up to see Esha watching him, a thoughtful look on her face.

"I wouldn't have thought you, all muscled and menacing, would have wanted to do anything other than slice your blades through bodies. I guess I was wrong. You do have a heart under all that bronze."

She smirked, eyeing him up and down, causing his stomach to tighten. Her next look only made the knots in his stomach worsen.

"Makes it all the more difficult to hate you," she said quietly, her eyes softening.

She said nothing more, letting the space between them turn quiet.

Why had she become the Viper? Why had she killed his uncle?

He wanted to understand this frustrating woman. More than that, he wanted to fight back, assert that all he had done was follow orders and he had believed he was protecting their country. Yet he knew it wasn't an excuse.

But she didn't seem to be interested in talking anymore, her mouth a tight line.

"Fine, continue thinking I'm a heartless pawn of the king," he said, anger winning.

"When you've seen the bodies of your friends found, unrecognizable due to torture, then you can talk to me about soldiers and their worth." Esha tilted her chin up, defiance written across her face. Her eyes flashed with barely concealed contempt.

"I gave you my word. I owe you my life. You will get a fair trial," he said back with uncontained force, more so because he had no idea if he could guarantee that.

"Oh? Did any of my fellow Blades get a fair trial after the

last raid? Or the one before?"

He only stared at her. Suddenly Esha looked very tired, and the fight in her seemed to blink out. "You know what would be fair? If you let me sleep on that bed tonight."

Kunal began to shake his head.

"I'm not asking you to untie me, just let me on the bed, Kunal. I'm exhausted, I've been sleeping in trees for weeks, and going forward I'll only have howler monkeys as companions."

He blinked at her. It was the first time she had called him anything besides soldier.

"All right."

"Really?"

She looked shocked. He nodded, unsure why he had agreed, and a real smile broke across her face. He bit the inside of his cheek to stop the small flip his stomach did at the sight of it.

It wasn't as if he would get any sleep with her staring at him from across the room. With a soft tug, he brought her to her feet, letting his hands linger on the soft curve of her waist.

She smelled like smoke and wood, and beneath it, a hint of night rose, which only bloomed in the harsh summer heat.

Kunal helped her to the edge of the bed and she hopped and tumbled in.

It took him a few seconds to still his heart as he pulled his shirt and uttariya off. He hesitated and then slid his armor off as well, cleaning it with care before lining it up neatly against the wall. Within a few minutes, she had fallen into a deep sleep. Then he eased himself onto the bed, fighting the fluttering of his lids as he stared at her sleeping form.

Her presence next to him was like a blaze under his skin, but it was no match for the overwhelming weariness of the past few days. Sleep took him quickly and he slumbered, plagued by the scent of night rose.

———◄○►———

When he woke up in the morning, she was gone. The surprise he should have felt was replaced by a dull acceptance.

All that was left of her was the warm impression where her body had lain on the bed and a small note. As he bent to pick it up, he saw on the floor the remains of the ropes that had bound her wrists, sawed off in sheaves.

> *You searched me for weapons, but you didn't look everywhere.*

Kunal glanced at the next line, and he quickly looked aside, his cheeks blazing hot at the image she painted.

His eyes skimmed over the rest of the note.

> *A truce. No killing you in your sleep, soldier. You let me live and I did the same. Now catch me if you can.*

Kunal could almost see the gleam in Esha's eyes as he read the words.

P.S. Trade for trade. You wanted to be an artist.
I wanted to be a troupe performer, though my mother
would have never allowed it. Life didn't quite work out
for either of us.

He smiled at the postscript even as he crumpled the piece of paper in his fist.

She had slipped right through his fingers. Again. But she had told him something.

A troupe performer. He never would've guessed.

Catch me if you can.

It was a challenge, and Kunal didn't like to lose.

CHAPTER 30

Kunal ran out into the street, the crumpled note still clenched in his fist. He hadn't wasted time donning his armor or uttariya, choosing to go bare-chested in the heat.

When folding the note, he had noticed the ink had still been fresh—fluid enough to smudge. These were the things he was trained to notice. She couldn't have escaped more than fifteen minutes ago.

He remembered she had mentioned howler monkeys in her exhaustion last night; only the jungles at the base of the Ghanta Mountains housed them. Kunal had spent enough time on the borders to be familiar with the wildlife, his first mission in the thick jungles and high groves of the Mauna Valley.

She must be going toward the valley—toward Chinta or Amali, the only towns around there.

Kunal took off to the right, toward the northern path out of the city, which followed the river. He cursed his own stupidity.

Kunal swerved into a dark alleyway, kicking up a cloud of dust with his sandals as he sped up, almost colliding into one of the many stray dogs that resided in Faor. The stone walls looked sturdy and were uneven enough that Kunal could hold on. Kunal grabbed on to the highest one he could reach, his muscles straining as he pulled himself up the wall.

In a few minutes, he was on the roof and running and leaping over the blazing-hot stones from one rooftop to another. The buildings tapered off toward the north.

With his armor and pack still behind in the blue house, he would be at a disadvantage. But he would be cursed if he let her escape that easily.

A troupe performer.

A troupe performer with a killer instinct.

The heat of the sun burned as he came to a stop, looking out over the wide expanse of land to the north of the town. Specks of color dotted the horizon—other towns—and green seeped into gray mountain in the far distance.

The sky was a brilliant blue that illuminated it all. Kunal looked around hurriedly, peering over the front and back of the rooftop he was on. This was the tallest one in the town, from what he could tell. It was a long shot, but from up here he could see everyone and everything.

He peered above the crowds, hoping he had picked the right roof to give him the vantage point he needed. There.

A small figure, curly hair peeking out of her uttariya, moved against the current of traders bustling their way to the market after sunup. His training as a Senap helped him sift through the unnecessary, and he felt his eyes go sharp as he focused on the contrary figure.

Kunal knew in his bones that it was Esha. He traced her through the crowds, watched her start moving faster toward the eastern gate. His headache began to recede, and with it went that steady drumbeat in his head that always seemed to call to him.

Control.

Kunal climbed down from the rooftop to land on the street with a soft thud.

She wouldn't get far.

CHAPTER 31

Esha moved as quickly as she could without drawing notice.

She worked her way through the outer edge of the bazaar, winding her way to the river. Perhaps she could find—steal—a small boat or convince someone to help her go north toward Amali. Either way, it felt good to put distance between herself and the soldier.

The colors of the bazaar faded as she began to take the small, narrow passageways toward the east. She kept her head down, letting her uttariya slip down to cover her face.

As she rounded the corner, she collided with someone coming from the other way. Esha stumbled back and looked up to apologize when her heart stopped.

Kunal stood in front of her, his armor gone and bare chest heaving with exertion. His eyes flashed as he drew closer.

"Going somewhere, Esha?"

"I merely stepped out to get some fruit."

Esha reached a hand into her pack and he grabbed her wrist, inches away.

"I read your note."

"Good, did you enjoy it? Like the image I painted?" He ignored her, though a faint blush crept up his neck. He reached into her pack with his other hand and pulled out a mango.

She noticed the slight pucker of his brow with glee.

"A mango?"

"*Mangoes*," she corrected him.

"Mangoes."

"They're delicious, aren't they? Juicy, sweet." He began to look at her as if she were losing her mind, and she angled her body, her other arm sliding down to her waist sash. "You look confused."

"I would've thought you'd have a better excuse than that."

"Better than mangoes? Impossible. They're the royalty of the fruit world." She almost chuckled, but she saw his eyes dart to her other hand and knew she had to pause her fun. "And, soldier, you really should get smarter if you want to play with me."

Esha threw herself into his side, hitting him with enough force that he let go of her wrist and tumbled to the ground. With her other hand, she brought the hilt of her knife down, aiming for his head, but he caught her hand inches away from his skull, twisting her wrist.

Her body twisted with it and she rolled into the fall, landing and jumping up.

Now she ran.

She tugged at her sack as she fled, pulling out her real whip and tucking it into the palm of her hand. It wasn't a weapon she could use just anywhere, so she'd have to draw him into a dark corner.

Esha smiled, a tight line. Dark corners were her specialty.

The smile slipped a bit as she turned a corner, keeping to the shadows. She had meant it—he would have to be smarter to play at her level. But somehow the idea of playing had started to lose its appeal.

How many moons ago had she sat with Arpiya, sitting on the steps of the training ground at the rebel base, talking about the glory of serving their country and bringing back balance, the power they felt when they brought down their enemies?

Never had they talked about the loneliness, or the fear. Last night had been a respite, one she hadn't expected. To just tell the truth, and have someone see both faces she wore.

But she had a bigger purpose now. She couldn't entertain these ideas when the cease-fire the king had worked so hard for, that the country needed, might be at stake.

Until then, she was the Viper. She would be the nightmare everyone thought she was. The darkness in her soul overcame her, one that was familiar and an old friend.

Within a minute, another set of footsteps could be heard behind her.

Esha didn't bother hiding her steps now.

She ran as fast as her feet could take her, bobbing through the outskirts of the bazaar and under stall covers and unfurled blankets. Disgruntled shouts followed her, and she knew from the echoing of curses after her that Kunal was still on her trail, not far behind.

Esha swerved into a small alley, using a woman with a huge basket of jackfruit on her hip as cover. The sun burned into her back even in the shadows of the alleyway, and she hastily mopped her brow with the edge of her uttariya.

She scrambled up the loose stone wall of a building, collapsing on the rooftop above.

Esha stopped for a minute, catching her breath, but continued moving. Moon Lord's mercy, she refused to be caught, not only because she had to get to Amali. The shadows of her days in the dungeons of Gwali loomed, threatened her.

A noise came from below and Esha started off again on the rooftop, nearing its end. Ahead was another rooftop, but there was a gap, and Esha looked around frantically.

Her feet pounded onto a flimsy slab of wood and she used its bounce to jump and roll over into the next rooftop, which slanted downward.

Footsteps resounded behind her and Esha glanced back to see Kunal charging ahead on the rooftop, about to use the same wooden slab to traverse the space.

Her nostrils flared out as she made eye contact with him. She'd do this all day if she had to.

Her feet bounced off the ledge of the slanted roof and she curled her body into itself as she crouched and leaped over, landing unsteadily in a squatted position. Loose rabble dotted the rooftop and she grabbed a few stones, hurtling them behind her to slow him down or throw him off course.

He dodged them neatly, ducking and bending under her throws.

"Esha!" he cried.

She ignored him, pushing her feet forward again. Up ahead, there were a series of windows across the stone archway.

They looked empty—she could finally end this chase. Knock him out and be halfway to Amali before he woke up.

Esha pushed forward, taking care not to look down as she scampered over the narrow stone archway connecting the roofs. These buildings were tall enough that a fall would ensure several broken bones, though perhaps not instant death.

Esha darted into the open window as the archway came to a stop, narrowly missing falling over the edge.

She tumbled into the room, straight into a pile of old, dusty tapestries and rugs.

A violent sneeze itched at the back of her throat but she held it back through brute force of will, clamping her nose closed with her fingers.

She scrambled to the side of the window, waiting for him.

CHAPTER 32

K unal fell into the room, steps behind her, and tumbled onto the ground.

Towering stacks of jute carpets surrounded him and piles of tapestries were thrown across the room. Rows of tall looms and small weaves lined the walls, showcasing vibrant and colorful threads of silk and cotton.

Kunal pulled his foot free from a snag of cotton, to be greeted by a blow to the head from behind and a knife to his throat.

"You're becoming predictable, soldier. Or you just really like me. I thought I had made it clear you would never be able to capture me again when I escaped your ropes," Esha said, standing behind him.

He could hear the smirk in her voice. The scent of night rose wafted over his shoulder, distracting him from the sharp point of steel against the tender skin of his larynx.

"How was I able to follow you, then?" Kunal answered.

Instead of tightening up, she moved closer, so that her arms around him were more of a caress.

"Oh, I've no doubt you've got some ability as a Senap," she said. "But I'm the Viper, remember?" Her voice was edged with steel and silk, softly menacing. "A monster and a murderer."

A muscle in his neck jumped as he clenched his jaw.

He grabbed her wrist, twisting it away from her body and spinning her in. Her body was flush against his now, and he held her other hand with the knife in the air, daring her to try to wiggle out.

Her eyes flashed in annoyance as she found she was stuck.

"Shouldn't you be more scared I'm going to kill you, soldier?" she hissed.

"I should be. But I'm not."

"Mistake," she replied instantly. "You're a fool."

"I'm a lot of things . . . but I'm pretty certain I'm not a fool. Haven't I proven I'm not some savage Jansan soldier?"

The question caught her off guard, her eyebrows flashing up in shock, her lips pursing.

Ah, he had hit a nerve.

His hunch had been right, that there was something behind that anger and hatred. Something real.

"You could've killed me in my sleep. Slid your knife against my throat. Taken away my breath with the end of your whip." His tone softened. "Yet I'm here. Alive, in spite of how much you hate me and my comrades."

"It would've been too much of a mess. What would that poor merchant family have thought, coming home to a dead and decaying body of a somewhat attractive soldier?"

There it was. That confusing, blithe ruthlessness coupled with a compliment.

He gave her a look.

Esha shifted, and Kunal looped his foot around her leg, making sure she couldn't use it to knee him. Tendrils of black hair had escaped from her braid and formed a halo around her face. They tickled the bottom of his chin.

"I don't understand what you want from me," Esha said.

"I'm asking you why you let me live."

"Because—" Esha looked trapped, and not just because she was encircled by his arms. Her eyes darted around and when she realized nothing would save her, she lifted her chin and stared him dead in the eye. "I have my own code of honor, soldier. While I think the concept of a life debt is unconscionably stupid, I do have honor."

"Kunal."

"What?"

"My name is Kunal. Not soldier."

She scoffed. "I know that."

"Do you? I don't like being drawn as only a soldier, just as I'm sure you want to be seen as more than the Viper."

It was a gamble. He had seen only glimpses of that. Flashes of weariness when she thought he wasn't looking last night. A sigh hidden beneath harsh words.

"Do I? And how would *you* know that, sold—" She rolled her eyes. "Kunal."

"I think we're more similar than you think," he said, smiling.

"Except that I'm not trying to kill you."

His brow furrowed as he took in her meaning.

"I'm not trying to kill you."

She snorted, rolling her eyes.

"Great, we've both established we're *not* trying to kill each other anymore. But first of all, you would return me in chains to the Blood Fort. Certain death. And second, I don't see either of us lowering our weapons."

Kunal realized his left hand was still clamped around her knife hand, and though his right arm held her tight, he saw her fingers grazing the top of her whip.

"You're right on that. I have my duty. But you won't die."

Esha blew a curl of hair out of her eyes.

"All right, let's play your idea out. You take me back. I'm set for a trial. They slit my throat in my sleep and celebrate killing General Hotha's murderer before parading my body around to warn all future insurgents. Sound about right?"

He shook his head, about to protest.

"There's no point lying. I've heard of how the Fort treats its own soldiers accused of treason. No trial and straight to death. Pray tell me, why would I be different?"

Kunal was about to protest when he thought back to Udit, how the commander had ensured his death. And before that, the soldiers accused of treason. He didn't even remember their true crimes.

But if he went down that road, he wouldn't be able to do his duty and complete his mission. And murder had a price. To let her go without any consequences, no matter how intriguing and frustrating she was, would be a complete betrayal of the only family he had.

Esha's voice floated in his head, reminding him of his own sins, of the many who had died at his own hand. He tried not to wonder when his payment would be due.

"As commander, I will guarantee you stand trial," Kunal said, becoming more and more convinced. He would see justice be delivered, the right way. "It's clear you hate the soldiers, but we're not one vicious unit. Many of us are fair and just. Do you think I wouldn't stand by my word?" he asked, his eyes locking with hers.

She raised one eyebrow and stared back.

"I think you would, despite barely knowing you. I'm not questioning your honor, I'm questioning your sanity."

She looked away and looked back quickly. "I really should kill you," she whispered. "It would make all my troubles go away."

His heart stopped beating for a second, not out of fear for his life but at the look in her eyes. Anger, frustration, sadness—but no hatred.

He should disarm her, knock her out with a well-placed blow, but he couldn't. Not now that he had seen that she was finally looking at him with something other than disgust.

Without warning, she stomped down hard on his instep, taking advantage of his moment of pain to wrench her arm away and clock him with the hilt of her whip.

The jewels cracked against his skull and Kunal staggered over, seeing colorful spots instead of Esha.

He fell onto a thick pile of carpets, grasping at the side of his head. Out of the corner of his eye he saw her moving across the pile and he tugged, sending her to the ground in a heap.

She recovered quickly, scrambling up and away. He unsheathed his knife and threw it at her moving figure, but she was too quick. Instead, she spun around, charging toward him and landing another blow to his left cheekbone.

He went down again.

A woozy image of Esha peered down at him. She clambered up into the window behind him, then turned back to address him.

"Go home. Forget you saw me. Kill some other poor fellow and pretend they're the Viper. Just . . . don't follow me, Kunal. It's for your own good. I won't stay my hand next time."

He didn't try to get up. But he also knew he wouldn't be able to stop, not when so much was on the line.

CHAPTER 33

Esha let a gust of wind buffet her as she leaped to the next rooftop, looking both ways before she crawled down the side to get back onto solid ground.

Rooftops were useful, but putting solid ground under her feet would make her feel more secure. The dry midday heat was mellowing, a soft yellow instead of burning orange. The altercation with Kunal had set off her entire plan for the day, particularly her plan to be in Amali in two days.

He was a thorn so deep in her side she should consider it a permanent wound.

Esha landed heavily on the siding and she readied herself to land on the next roof. Instead, the siding wobbled and held her weight for only a few seconds before she crashed through into a dank pit. Short metal spikes shot out at the edges and narrowly missed Esha's head.

Dark, packed dirt surrounded her like the walls of a cell

and her breath came quick. At her feet was the braided fence of rope she had come crashing through, and the pit was wider at the bottom, as if to collect more thieves.

Esha cursed. A damn trapper's pit. What sort of half-witted thug lived here that was *that* paranoid?

The tiles of the roof above her shook as heavy steps bounded across, and Esha's eyes widened.

"Wait!" she yelled, but it was too late.

Kunal came crashing through the hole she had left, but wasn't as lucky as she had been. As he fell, his arms grazed the spikes that edged the pit. He landed in a sprawl, half on top of her.

She swore again, this time throwing in a few choice Dharkan curses as well.

Kunal clutched his arm, cut up and bleeding. He got on his knees and turned toward her, his mouth a tense line.

She glared at him. "I tried to warn you," she said.

"You could've done a better job," he snapped back, his amber eyes flashing, turning almost yellow. His voice came out more gravelly than normal.

Esha raised an eyebrow. She hadn't known he had that kind of bite in him. Perhaps the soldier could lose his temper.

"Is there a reason you're still sitting down?" he asked as he rose to his feet, some of the edge having bled out of his voice.

She shook her leg at him and he looked confused. To demonstrate, she moved and was yanked back by a thick, viscous string attached to the ropes.

"Trapping glue. Made of tree resin. It's what thieves or sell-swords use to take their competitors out when following a mark."

Kunal arched an eyebrow at her intimate knowledge of mercenary tactics but said nothing. Instead, he moved toward her and reached for the ropes binding her legs.

"No! Don't come—" she cried.

Too late.

Kunal's legs collided with the rope and it snapped around him, coiling over his foot like a snake. He tripped and fell heavily on her and she let out a small yelp at the impact.

He looked down at her, accusation stamped across his face.

"Don't look at me. Not my fault you weren't taught to be careful in that stupid fort of yours. Or listen to people who know better than you."

He brushed the hair out of his eyes, making sure to pick the sticky residue off his fingers first. "I thought you were exaggerating," he said, looking slightly sheepish.

She snorted. "Serves you right, then."

He was still sprawled across her, and when silence settled between them she could feel the heat from his skin. It made her uncomfortable, and not just because he was cutting off circulation to her arm. She coughed.

"This is very cozy and all, but I really can't breathe," she said, wheezing against his bare chest.

He moved as much as he could, slowly easing his weight off her and falling to his side. It was a task made much harder by his bound and sticky feet.

Esha pulled in a full breath, shaking her arm around to get the blood flowing, resin stretching with her as she leaned forward.

"That's better," she said, wincing a bit.

Kunal was still close to her and it unnerved her. This close, his eyes weren't just amber, but gold and flecks of sun. His gaze lingered on her and there was an intensity in the tightness of his jaw.

Their hands accidentally touched as they moved, their fingers brushing, and Kunal pulled away suddenly, as if realizing where he was and who he was with.

"We need to get out of here. If you're right about this being a trapper's pit, then someone will find us soon and I'm sure neither of us want to be here when they do."

"Of course I'm right. But yes, let's get out of here," she said coolly. He nodded but avoided her eyes as he set upon the ropes with his unsheathed knife.

Esha knew she should help but felt a niggling doubt. Kunal was frowning at one of the knots that had wound its way around his foot. The fence of rope had been woven with loose knots, designed to capture and hold trespassers along with the glue.

"I don't understand," she said.

"You don't understand what? How to untie a knot?"

He didn't look up, continuing to inspect the knot, making faces at the sticky resin.

"No, you lout."

That made him look up. He grinned at her.

She frowned at him. Had he been dropped on the head as a child? She was insulting him.

"Why are you smiling?"

"You reminded me of my friend. He always has a number of creative insults to address me with."

"I can't imagine why," she said drily.

"What can't you understand?" She looked at him in question. "You said you didn't understand," he repeated.

"Oh." She paused, uncertain how to say it. "Why did you come out to help me that first night?"

His hands stopped for a moment, a stillness overtaking him as he quirked his mouth to the side. It looked as if he was deciding whether to be honest with her. A snort escaped from him.

"You mean when I didn't realize I had a snake in my backyard? When you used me to kill General Hotha?"

If it hadn't been directed at her, Esha would've been proud of the snark in his voice.

"I hadn't meant to use you. You just happened to show up."

He said nothing, giving her a pointed look. Putting the knot down, he turned his torso toward her, the glue restricting his movements.

"The cease-fire had been announced, and yet this girl shows up near the Fort only a half hour before we were about to start war exercises. I assumed you were new to the area. I didn't know who you were, but I was worried you'd get trampled underfoot, especially as all the soldiers would be drunk. I decided I didn't want to wait and see what might happen."

Esha bit her lip, thinking that all of her current problems were a result of this soldier's damn bleeding heart.

An utter paradox in her world.

"But I'm not so naive now. I know you could take out half a regiment with that whip of yours. I will admit, I respect that. You fight hard." He pointed his knife at her. "But it doesn't change anything."

The words were spoken with force, but his eyes flickered to her own unsteadily.

He was wrong.

Everything had already changed.

She stared at Kunal, trying to determine when her feelings toward him had shifted. He was attractive, that was undeniable, but there was more to it. There was something small and hopeful and wondering in her chest now.

Esha wanted to know him, understand him—but she didn't see how that was possible in the lives the gods had given them.

She was silent long enough that he turned back to the knots. His brow was knitted as he concentrated on untying the knots, his lip tugged between his teeth in concentration.

"Would you ever leave?"

He looked up at her in question.

"Leave where?" he asked.

"The Fort," she said in a whisper.

He looked thoughtful for a moment, as if he had decided

candor was the best way to go when stuck, literally, in a trapper's pit with one's enemy.

"I never wanted to spend my life there. I told you I hadn't wanted to be a soldier. A year ago, I thought at best, I would become a Senap guard. Worst, I'd stay until I was released out of active duty in five or ten years." He looked at her now, straight in the eyes. "Eventually start a family. Go back to where I grew up and teach combat."

"And now?" she probed.

Kunal turned toward her sharply, searching for something in her face.

He seemed to find it.

"And now? I can't say. I wouldn't have foreseen anything that's happened to me recently or expected the opportunity to become commander. But now that it's here, I want the chance to leave my mark. Change things."

"Like what?"

He dropped his hand to his side, the knife loose in his fingers. "Real justice. A jury of peers like before. Punishment for soldiers if they engage in thievery. Discourse without fear of retribution."

She stayed quiet, letting his words sink in. Painting an image of a future she'd probably never get to see. But sitting near him and hearing his soft voice, Esha let herself imagine it.

Of course, the impossible attracted her. Harun always said she had something self-destructive in her. Maybe this was it. This longing in her to know a boy whose history she should be able to read with two words—Jansan soldier.

She hadn't felt this alive, this curious in a while. All she had felt in the years following the murder of her parents had been anger and unending grief.

Hatred. A thirst for revenge.

They still were there, nestled in her breast. But she also heard her father's words in the back of her mind.

The goal of an ambassador is to bridge the gap, find the similarities between people and cultivate it like a precious bloom in the summer heat.

Esha felt that old grief creep up. He had been a great ambassador for Dharka.

She had taken their life for granted—their ease between cultures and their lifestyle—and it wasn't until they were gone that she understood all that she had. It was why she wouldn't stop until the man responsible for upending their lives was dead.

How many other families had been torn apart? How many other girls had seen their parents cut down, their unborn sibling dead in an instant?

The pain had faded over the years, but it never left, a dull ache she could never cast off. She glanced at Kunal, who had been watching her the whole time. The look on his face was inscrutable.

If he knew the depths of darkness in her soul, he would turn away in horror.

He had never seen her with whips in her hands and fresh blood on her knife. And she wouldn't give up that part of her for anyone. Especially not a soldier of the Pretender King.

He continued to saw away at the knot but locked eyes with her.

Esha felt a spark between them. She took a deep breath, steadying the thrum of her heart.

CHAPTER 34

Esha seemed to look past him, her thoughts far away.

Kunal watched her as he continued his ministrations on the thick, sticky ropes. He would need to give his knives a good cleaning after this. The stickiness made his stomach queasy.

She was biting the corner of her lip, staring a little past his head. Until she caught his gaze in hers. That jolted him. Her eyes were something he would never forget. Not tomorrow and not for years. He yearned to paint them, the bloom of dark chestnut and honey around her irises and the deep arch of her brow.

If only they had met in another world, another life.

Instead she had found him in this one. Bound by duty and honor, sworn to protect and serve.

The old tales always said the gods never gave anything

without taking. It would've been easier if she had never crossed his path.

"And you?" he asked. "Would you stop being the Viper? Would you leave the Blades?"

"The fact that you even know that about me, about the Viper—"

"Who am I going to tell?" Kunal scoffed. "Who would even believe me without you there as proof? Claiming the Viper is a woman would be enough to get laughed out of the mess hall. My knowledge is meaningless."

"Your comrades can try me on, I'd—"

"Answer the question, Esha. It's only fair."

She blinked a few times and looked away.

"No, I wouldn't leave. Not until I fulfill my goal. Even if I die trying."

He didn't hesitate. "What did the king take from you?"

Esha didn't move a muscle, but her eyes grew stormy. "Who said he took anything from me?" she replied, her voice even.

He shifted back, watching her. Kunal wanted to open up, admit to her that the king had taken from him too, albeit indirectly. That he had lost his mother, his friends, everyone he had known.

But he kept his voice even, swallowing the memories.

"You hate soldiers. Maybe you believe in the tale of the lost princess, but that doesn't seem like you. You're some-one who walks easily between Jansa and Dharka. I could believe you were a trader or merchant, as you're clearly educated. Perhaps a rogue unit of soldiers stole your family's shipment—or worse, destroyed your livelihood. Or maybe it's more personal."

Esha looked at him for a moment, as if considering something.

"I'm impressed by your imagination, soldier. And for that, I'll give you a straight answer. I'm here to fulfill the aim of the Blades—overthrow the Pretender King and restore balance to our lands. How can you not see it? The *janma* bond is broken because of him. A Samyad was always meant to be on the throne and he threatens both of our worlds by having taken what isn't his. The gods don't like thieves. But I don't plan on stopping there."

Kunal started. She couldn't hope to kill the king—there was already a line of men outside the palace who had tried and died. King Vardaan relished such attempts, even laughed and displayed them on the outer moats of the palace.

But he was impressed by the passion and conviction with which she spoke. The willingness with which she challenged and fought. His life had been orders and rules, discipline and unquestioning obedience.

Looking at her, he wondered if he hadn't done it all wrong.

He sighed. "I'm not surprised."

Esha looked shocked. "What? No lecture? No admonishments about honor in killing?"

"No. You only know one small part of me. You know

nothing of my past or of my beliefs," he said, the words coming out with sharp edges. "Anyway, it would be like telling a panther to eat roots instead of flesh. Pointless," he continued.

She grinned at him. A look of real delight.

"That might be the nicest thing you've ever said to me, soldier. I like that you've accepted who I am." A sticky string stretched behind her as she moved her body away from the wall and closer to him. "I should tell the boys back home that's the way to speak to a lady."

Kunal gave her a lopsided smile. "A lady? Are we talking about you?"

Her eyes widened. "Was that a joke? Am I rubbing off on you?"

Oh gods, the image that came into his head.

No, she definitely didn't need to know about that. He felt a tension in his body that hadn't been there a moment before and he fidgeted, trying to make it go away.

"I really hope not," he muttered. She chuckled at him.

"Are you sure? You hope I'm *not* rubbing off on you? Most people like me, you know," Esha said, watching him with that look that made his entire body flush.

"I bet most people like you—but at arm's length. Scorpion and frog. Friends until there's a stinger in your back."

Esha laughed but he thought it sounded tighter than before.

"I like that you think that about me and aren't running away in terror." She looked at the sticky glue constricting them to the dirty ground. "If you could run, that is."

She was close to him now, close enough that he could hear her breaths as she blew an errant curl out of her eyes.

Kunal reached out as he looked down at her, brushing the curl away from her temple and tucking it behind her ear.

Everything stood still and Kunal forget everything he *had* to do and focused on what he *wanted* to do. He wanted to cup her face, feel her smooth skin under his calloused fingertips. He wanted to run his hands through her wild curls, letting his fingers get tangled in them.

He wanted to kiss her so hard it took her breath away.

But Kunal did none of those things.

He might've moved, might've acted, except for the sudden squelch of wet mud above them.

Someone else was here.

CHAPTER 35

Esha's instincts kicked into action.

Kunal tried to run to the sides of the wall but was pulled backward, the tree resin holding his feet tight to the bottom.

Esha looked around frantically, pointed at her knife, and whispered, "Our shoes. We need to cut off our shoes."

But he would have to do it—her hands were still stuck. It should've occurred to her before, if she hadn't been busy making moon eyes at the soldier.

Kunal looked at her as if she was crazy but then nodded vigorously. He grabbed the knife at her waist with his free hand and hacked at their shoes and the remaining strands of resin that held her to the ropes.

A voice shouted out, not far away, and Esha shot a look at Kunal. He motioned to move, even though they were still half connected to the sticky ground.

"Lean," he mouthed. Esha jumped to the corner of the pit as a head peeked over the top. She flattened herself against the sloping wall, hoping that the sliver of shadow would cover her, praying that they didn't lean in to see the wall nearest them.

"Aw, you said a big loot. All we got are two mismatched cheap shoes that look like they fell apart. You've really got to set up your traps better."

Esha bristled at that. Those shoes had not been cheap.

Another voice chimed in "I could've sworn I set it for a heavier weight."

"Clearly not, Lai. Clearly not."

"No, I swear. Let me go down there and check. Or at least walk around to the other side. Sometimes little animals hide in the corners. Could be a good dinner."

Esha shot a look to Kunal, who eyed her, shaking his head.

"Not worth our time. Dharmdev will be back soon and it won't do us any good if your fat arse gets stuck down there and can't get up."

The other person grumbled but didn't disagree. The voices faded out and Esha allowed herself to return to breathing normally.

"We need to get out of here," she whispered. *She* needed to get out of here—and before Kunal. But she'd need his help first.

Kunal nodded in agreement. Esha closed her eyes for a moment, listening for any sign of the two men again. Satisfied, she inched over to Kunal.

"The walls are packed in, but now that we're free from the trapping, I can try to get up if you give me a push."

Kunal's eyes narrowed as his lips pursed.

"And then?"

"And then I'll drop a rope down or something."

"Sure you will."

She took a deep breath.

"You'll have to trust me. Think you can do that?"

Esha wouldn't have trusted him if the situation were reversed. But at the same time, he didn't have much choice. She decided to tell him as much.

"We can't switch roles—there's no way I could support your weight or give you a boost. This is the only logical way."

Kunal looked like he wanted to argue, but gave her a tight nod.

She hopped over to him, discarding the remaining pieces of rope that twirled around her feet. The wall of dirt was packed tight, no sign of pockets for her hands to fit in. She'd have to use her knife to climb. There was only a thin outer border of the floor without resin and they had danced around it so far.

Behind her, Kunal stood unmoving. She turned her head back toward him, blowing air out of her mouth. She had her knife in one hand and patted her pack with the other, slipping her hand inside.

"Are you going to just stand there? Give me a lift."

Harun would have called that her bossy tone, but she

preferred to call it authoritative. If she knew the best way to do something, she should be in charge. It was as simple as that.

Kunal grumbled something she couldn't hear and moved closer so that she could feel his presence behind her. Calming her pulse, she gave him directions.

She could feel his muscles tensing around her, enveloping her, and it made her heart quicken. The rest of her warred, unsure whether to keep her word or to flee and leave him in the pit. The latter ensured she would get to Amali quicker, and before he could catch her trail again.

Kunal was an interruption. Something that shouldn't have come into her life, but now that he was here, she was feeling herself change in tiny, imperceptible ways.

And she wasn't ready to change. She didn't want to owe or give anyone part of her.

Not yet. Not when her desire for revenge still burned bright and hot. Until that day, she still belonged to the ghosts of her family and the young girl she had been.

With a grunt, he pushed her up, one hand on the small of her back, and Esha drove her knife into the wall as high as she could reach—and made her decision.

"Hold on, I see a rope. Let me tug it down. Can you balance me on your shoulders?" Esha saw a brief nod out of the corner of her eye. "Look up, Kunal. Can you grab the rope?"

She balanced her feet on both sides of his shoulders and leaned against the wall. It freed her hands and with a swift movement she uncorked the rest of the sleeping draft and splashed it onto his face, the rest falling to the dirt in a cloud of gray vapor.

Esha heard him sputter and knew he would fall in a few seconds—she needed to use his body as leverage before that. She hung from the knife and kicked off Kunal in time to jump up and swing around, landing on the edge of the pit.

Below her, Kunal fell to the floor, sprawling in an uncomfortable-looking position, dirt smudging the edges of his face and clothing.

His face looked peaceful, but when he woke, he would have a raging headache. She had never used that much sleeping draft on anyone. Esha crouched and put her head between her legs before taking a shaky breath and rising to her feet.

So tired. She was so tired.

Beneath it was a faint sadness, but she pushed it down.

The victory was hers. She'd be out of here soon. Somehow, it felt hollow.

Esha looked around and spotted the length of rope and tied it to the cistern nearby. She whipped out the piece of charcoal and paper she always had hidden away, scratching out a note, which she tucked into the smooth interior of the pail. She tugged it down and looped it a few times, throwing the edge into the pit.

It's not like she wanted him to die down there.

She watched the pail land on the soft ground before she turned on her heel and left.

CHAPTER 36

Kunal woke with a jolt, sputtering out dirt. His eyes darted around, seeing only spots. No Esha.

Gone. Of course she was gone.

He lurched into a sitting position, the creak of his bones and joints like a squeaky wheel of a fruit seller's cart, before being thrown back by the pull of the resin. Groaning, Kunal grabbed the knife near him and hacked at the strands to pull himself free.

Once he was free, he rose to his feet and dusted himself off. The only consolation this time was that he had finally managed to grab something. He could only hope it would be useful.

Kunal patted his back, feeling for the scroll he had stolen. It was still in its place, tucked into the back of his pants. He allowed himself a little smile for thinking quickly and grabbing a scroll from her bag when he boosted her up, realizing there was a chance she would abandon him to his fate.

Which was exactly what she did.

Once he was out of this hole, he'd take a proper look at it. With any luck, it would give him some clue as to where she would be next, where the rebels were.

In the corner of the pit was a small pail hanging from a rope, and with a few steps he had the pail in hand and tugged. Inside was a thin scrap of paper, which Kunal almost didn't notice. He caught it before it fluttered to the ground.

A note and a rope. *She* was the one getting more predictable.

Kunal didn't know if she was aware that with each action, she gave away a part of her story. Letting him live, leaving him a rope. This wasn't the Viper who was rumored to have torn through a Senap Guard, leaving only one survivor.

Kunal grimaced. Every time she showed her humanity, his stonelike belief in his duty cracked. Was there a way he could fulfill both of his debts—to his uncle and this enigma of a girl?

Becoming commander was the only way to guarantee a fair trial for Esha—he ignored the small part of him that whispered that even then, it might not be so easy.

Maybe it was time to send another note to Alok.

Kunal closed his eyes as the inside of his head split open in pain without warning. He leaned forward, pressing his thumbs into the soft inner corners of his eyes. After some minutes, the pain subsided to a throb.

He groaned as he moved up the rope, note safely tucked into his pocket. Whatever tincture she had used to knock him out had left every muscle an aching, fraying mess, and his head—it was as if someone was steadily driving hot nails into his skull.

Kunal pulled up to the top of the pit, swinging each leg up and over.

Purple streaks of night bled across the sky like sweeps of a brush. It had been hours since Esha left. Night would blanket the sky soon and he would have no chance of following her. Even now, he had only a vague idea of where she'd go next. It was likely she'd completely abandon her previous route now that she knew he was following her.

He brushed off his hands on his pants and finally drew out the note, frowning and unsure of what to expect. Funny how in such a short time he could read her words and hear exactly the way she would have spoken them.

> *It's a good thing you have an interest in the arts because after this, you might need to look for a new job, soldier. I'm sure the other Senap squadrons would love to hear how you've been bested by a mere girl not once but twice. Maybe they'd regret banishing us from the army. You really should go home. I'm sure you have a cushy room in the Fort with some sweetheart pining away, waiting for you. Who knows?*
>
> *The only thing I know is that you'll never catch me. I'm the Viper.*

He chuckled despite himself, hearing her voice in his head.

You know, that might be what I'm called, but I used to be more frog than scorpion. Life has made me the scorpion. It's easier to betray someone than to trust that they'll do right by you. Especially in this land.

Now, I want a story next time I see you. I expect it will be sooner than I anticipate.

Tell me something I don't know, soldier.

Kunal folded the note up in precise rectangles and tucked it away, coming to a slow realization as the dim light of camphor lamps began to shine through the windows of houses.

He still wanted to take Esha back to the Fort, but now, he also wanted something else too. He wanted more time with her. He wanted to convince her that when he gave his word, he meant it—she would be given a trial and he would fulfill his debt to her. He wanted to change her image of the soldiers by leading them the way they deserved to be led—with honor and by an honorable commander.

To try to show her how wrong she had been and how right he could make things.

Little by little, her eyes would light up in understanding and radiate her complete trust in him. It was only a dream, after all.

A fortnight in pursuit, and he had no Viper in his custody.

But he knew that she loved mangoes and counted the stars when alone to remind her of how far she was from home.

He could envision the look on his uncle's face if he'd been alive—disappointment.

CHAPTER 37

Esha couldn't be sure, but she thought she spotted Kunal a few streets over in the small town of Chinta, her one stop before Amali. She ducked into a colorful stall, letting herself get lost in the rows of indigo silk and white muslin. Esha grabbed a silk uttariya to wrap around her head as a shadow moved toward the opening of the tent, her heart racing.

In seconds, the shadow passed, but her heart didn't let up on its tempo. Instead, at the thought of him, it rose in a thudding crescendo that drowned all of her other senses.

Esha felt her heart turn traitor and she knew it then—the winds had shifted between them.

She was close to the mountains now and knew if she made the trek, she would get to the other side and be on Dharkan soil soon. Esha had sent as much by owl to the rebels a week ago, trying to code some of the urgency she had felt in the note.

How things had changed since then. She just needed to make it through the next few days without running into the soldier and she'd be home and free.

Why didn't the thought make her feel happy anymore?

CHAPTER 38

It had been two days since Kunal had been left behind in Faor, and the next closest military garrison was in Onda, a small town near the river and to the east of the Hara Desert.

The troops were stationed in a sun-speckled stone tower to the west of the town's center. He turned his mare in that direction as he entered the crumbling town walls, a casualty of yearlong battles fought over the town's proximity to the river and iron mines. Kunal could tell his horse was tired from her low whinny and slowed her to a trot, feeling a warmth beneath his fingers as he absentmindedly rubbed her neck.

Kunal got a better look around as they ambled their way through the narrow roads that led into town. He immediately noticed that people looked healthy, whole, unlike in Ujral. His newfound cynicism assumed it was due to the army presence in the town.

It had been a full day's ride since Faor, but the scroll stolen from Esha hadn't left his mind. He knew that it was a military report by the script it was written in, Old Jansan. Only the Fort leadership wrote reports in the dead language.

His Old Jansan was rusty, underused in the past two years as he'd been out on more Senap missions, but he could understand bits and pieces. Enough that he had been able to read the title of the report.

Sundara.

The site of the battle that had led King Mahir to push for a cease-fire. It had been celebrated at the Fort, the victory that had shown the enemy's weakness. But more important to him, this military report on Sundara was in his uncle's strong scrawl.

What could his uncle have written about Sundara? He had said the campaign was Vardaan's order and he had little to do with it. Kunal didn't know, but this would be his best chance to find out. After checking in for the mission, he would go to the garrison's vast library. It would be vital in deciphering the report and whether it had any clues to where Esha might go next.

He arrived at the stable and a small boy ran forward. Kunal dismounted and tried to hand the reins to the boy, but his horse nipped at his head. The boy scrambled back and Kunal sighed. The mare was getting attached. Kunal petted her, blowing softly into her nostrils until she calmed down.

An hour later, after his horse had been taken to the stable and a bath, he was ushered into a small dining room by the housekeeper. After weeks of hard traveling, Kunal rather enjoyed being treated like royalty. He dove into his food, carefully ladling the stew of spiced lentils and vegetables over the cashew-and-clove-studded rice.

Laksh's voice filtered in before Kunal saw him, and he rose to his feet in surprise as his friend entered the dining room. Laksh hid his surprise better, giving him a huge grin. He was tanner, his skin a deep brown from days in the sun, and he seemed skinnier, more drawn in the face. But that twinkle remained in his eyes.

"Been following me, have you?" Kunal said.

"I've had enough of that. It took me two loops around the western hills of the Varulok region to shake off Rakesh," Laksh said, grasping Kunal's shoulders. "You are a sight for sore eyes, Kunal. I know I grew up around here, but it's easy to forget how sand seems to get in about everything."

"If only I could say you were wrong." Kunal grinned, his heart buoying at their easy banter. After all the confusion and uncertainty, Laksh was a beacon of light.

Familiar. Constant.

He ached to tell his friend everything. Spill out the story he had inadvertently started with Esha, the confusion he felt at having to take her back, but something prevented him as they sat at the table and caught up.

Maybe it was the wary undertone that slipped into their conversation. Light, but as if they knew there was still a competition going on. Esha wasn't just a normal girl he could talk to his friend about—she was both of their marks.

"Where to next, Laksh?" Kunal asked casually, holding the tiniest of hopes that his assumption had been wrong and their friendship was still more important than the competition. Kunal was in the lead, yet he had never felt more lost. Or alone.

The skin around Laksh's eyes crinkled and he gave a wry smile. "You know I can't tell you that."

"No?"

"It's a competition. Thought you'd care more as the general's nephew."

Now Kunal frowned, ever so slightly. "Who says I don't?"

Laksh put his hands up. "Not me, that's for sure. I was teasing."

Kunal rubbed his brow and sighed. "This chase is getting to me, Laksh. I'm tired."

"Then turn home. Let me win," Laksh said, grinning. When he realized Kunal hadn't teased back, his face changed. "I know. It actually makes me miss the Fort in some ways. I miss the structure."

Kunal nodded. He felt the same way at times. But he also felt a thrill at making his own path for the first time. Deciding where to go and what to do. He wondered if this was what it would be like to be a full Senap guard. If nothing else, it made him long for his release from active duty, more so than normal. The alternative—deserting—was not an alternative at all.

They moved on to lighter topics, talking of the towns

they had been in, carefully avoiding any details of whether they were any closer to finding the Viper. Kunal was still able to pick out a few details, knowing the location of most of the towns from the map he had drawn. It seemed Laksh was sticking to his path of questioning and following the Crescent Blade's blacksmiths.

"I'm heading to the library," Kunal said, answering Laksh's last question as they washed their hands in the bowls to the right of their plates.

Laksh gave him a look, making a face, as Kunal knew he would. "You're basically giving me a head start out of here."

"You'll need it," Kunal responded, grinning. They rose from their seats and he embraced Laksh like a brother, his heart a bit lighter.

———◄◦►———

This library was nothing like the one in the Fort, which was housed in a vast room but was underused, almost criminally so.

This library was smaller but looked more worn and loved. Small, multicolored stools with embroidered peacocks were settled into the corners, nestled between long rows of scrolls in their small wooden cubbies. The cubbies were part of massive wooden structures, almost like a honeycomb, that stretched to the ceiling of the room.

Kunal traced his finger over the library's categorization system, looking for older translation scrolls. He knew for a fact that each garrison housed specific works of translation, and he hoped the one he wanted was here.

Studying had been the lone bright spot in his first year at the Fort. He had been ahead of the others and it made the other soldiers seek him out for help and tutoring. That was how the "perfect Kunal" nickname had started, had become another form of armor for him to don.

Kunal found what he was looking for and grabbed the scroll, settling into one of the small nooks. He shook out the report he had stolen from Esha's pack, sounding the words out loud as he went.

The dialect was difficult, but he understood enough.

Soon enough, he wished he didn't.

He had been wondering what Uncle Setu might have done, and now he knew. He swallowed roughly, the coldness of the realization hitting his body like ice. It swept into his lungs and his heart as he read.

The writing was his uncle's, and as he translated, he could almost imagine the words in his uncle's voice, low and rumbling. It was a frustratingly slow process, but he was committed now to finishing the translation, if only to no longer be in the dark.

It was a personal account of the soldiers' actions in Sundara, the small Dharkan town in the far reaches of the Aiforas. His uncle had lied about not being there. Soldiers had captured the town, driving the townspeople into the frozen desert in the north without food, water, or shelter. All for "disobedience," which, after his time traveling, he now understood could have meant anything from refusing to give up their crops to active rebellion.

Kunal found himself giving the townspeople the benefit of the doubt, and it was a jagged dagger to his heart, tearing a wound that wouldn't close so easily.

It was one thing to hear of Sundara and the innocents who had perished, but another to hear it in his uncle's clinical, almost pleased voice.

A great victory, he called it.

Sour acid rose in Kunal's throat and he almost couldn't go on reading as the account became more and more detailed. A contingent of soldiers had stayed behind to guarantee the deaths of townspeople.

Kunal couldn't fathom a reason for a massacre.

No matter how hard he tried to understand it, there was no explanation for ordering the deaths of hundreds of innocents. No Rule of Order that forgave it, no god that would either.

He now knew that Sundara was no victory, but a tragedy of epic proportions. Kunal resisted the urge to throw the scroll across the room, to remove the evidence of his uncle's utter betrayal of honor from his sight. Then it wouldn't exist and maybe he could forget it.

But as soon as Kunal closed his eyes, rubbing the bridge of his nose in a vain attempt at *control*, he saw it all, every detail in the report. It played in his mind with no end.

If his uncle had ordered this massacre, it was possible he had done it before.

Kunal had always assumed Vardaan had been the mastermind behind the royal coup and murders that fueled it, but what if it had been his uncle? Had he known, or cared, about the people caught in the crosshairs? Like Kunal's mother, his sister-in-law?

Torn by anger and betrayal and a deep, unending sorrow for all those lives lost, for the memory of a man he had loved, Kunal sat there, unable to do anything but stare at the slowly fading light of the camphor lamp. And in those silent moments, a thousand questions ravaged him, forced him to reconsider his uncle, his upbringing, himself.

Who was he if he held this man in esteem? If this man had created him?

Was he also this monster?

When he looked up, the sun had all but left the sky.

He left the library like a shadow, exiting the garrison quickly before he'd have to converse with anyone. He couldn't bear the thought of talking when his mind and heart were this burdened.

The walk to his mare felt long, and Kunal dragged his feet despite knowing he had to move quickly to get back on Esha's trail to Amali. The heaviness in his limbs had spread, and all Kunal wanted to do was lie down for a nap and wake up with the world back in order.

Esha was a murderer, his uncle a victim. That's what he had believed.

Maybe it wasn't that simple.

CHAPTER 39

Esha breathed a sigh of relief as she wound through the streets of Amali. Finally, she was here, and not a moment too soon—in a week, it would be almost a moon since she had left the Blood Fort, leaving only one more moon before the peace summit.

Amali was nestled right in between the mountains and the desert like a diamond in a jeweled tiara. It was a part of the Parvalokh region, a swath of land that bordered the mountains and was crisscrossed by roads for traders and caravans.

It was a sophisticated system of roads for a region of Jansa whose nobility hadn't allied with Vardaan, due to their distance from Gwali and proximity to Dharka. And it was the perfect region for Dharkan smugglers looking to bring their wares to eager Jansans who missed the days of open trade and borders.

And now with the drought, it was a key town in ensuring supplies got through to people who were in need. Harun had sent the team here more than a few times. It had made finding the scholar easier, knowing her way around this region.

Esha bit down a smile as she passed a frowning couple arguing over whether they needed to buy their young son a new knife as he stood to the side, playing with his own shadow and oblivious to both of them.

The boy reminded her of a friend she had shared a tutor with at the palace—a happy, silly boy who had too much action and joy in his heart for their poor tutor and his mother. She still remembered how they would climb up lemon trees and lob lemons at anyone who dared to pass by and pored over scrolls in the library till their eyes went crossed.

A type of friendship that only children could have— sweet, simple, and hopeful. Esha took a deep breath at the thought. Her rebels were her friends too, but as the Viper, there would always be a part of her she couldn't show them. She had a reputation to keep up.

Esha reached the house she was looking for and knocked on the cracked wooden door to no answer. She had raised her hand to knock again when the door banged open and a stout woman with a round face peered out at her.

"I'm looking for a tailor. I caught my hem while on horseback," Esha said, repeating the phrase Tana had written down for her.

"Yes, in here."

The woman leaned out, looking left and right, before ushering her into the house. It was a rather small home, made all the smaller by the towers of opened and unopened scrolls that seemed to have been sneaked into every nook and cranny of the house.

"Our mutual friend tells me you used to be a scholar at the university in Gwali," Esha said.

"I was a scholar of languages when the coup happened. Haven't been allowed back in the Great Library since then." She said the words straight, without a plea for sympathy, but Esha winced anyway. The scholar waved her over to a table, where she pulled out two chairs.

Esha rummaged through her pack for the scroll, wondering if it was her imagination or she was missing one. She found the one she needed with a relieved sigh and handed it to her.

"These scrolls should have military information, but there's something in this one that has caused a lot of trouble." Esha thought of the Blade who had gone to his death trying to protect it. "There's also a part burned off, but if you can make sense of it . . ."

"Let me take a closer look."

Esha had no reason to believe the scholar couldn't be trusted, but she kept a tight hold on her guard, observing the woman as she examined the reports, as she smoothed out parts of the paper and peered over them. Not exchanging names was only part of that.

After determining there were no weapons—or objects

that could be used as weapons—in their direct vicinity, Esha took a moment to relax. The small house smelled like paper and incense, mixing into a heady combination that lulled Esha's senses. The past few days had been a relentless drive and she was happy to have finally reached Amali. Scrolls overflowed even into the kitchen, and Esha saw a cowherd girl figurine in the corner of one of her shelves.

Minutes later, the scholar raised her head and locked eyes with Esha.

"Tana was right to send you to me." Her voice was soft but had a strength to it. "I'm one of the only scholars left outside of Gwali who can read this dialect of Old Jansan—it's from the region that borders the Yavar's lands. This burned-off part, it's not clear, but it refers to someone who calls himself Dharmdev." The scholar snorted. "Of course a man would call himself the Lord of Justice. Anyway, it looks like this report is about a classified Senap search mission."

The woman continued reading, tracing her finger over the curved letters, mouthing the words. Esha stilled.

A search mission?

Esha could think of only one thing the Fort might be searching for that would be worth killing for—worth framing someone for.

Could it be?

"This phrase, *heen rayan*, I'm pretty sure it's what they were looking for," the scholar said.

"*Heen rayan?*" Esha repeated.

The scholar lifted her head to look at Esha, a deep

sadness spreading across her face as she frowned.

"I never would have believed it had I not seen it written myself," the scholar said. Esha leaned forward. *"Heen rayan.* It's a loose transliteration of 'Lost Princess.' There are a few ways to interpret it, but given what we know, it makes the most sense." Her eyes darted to the cowherd figurine in the corner. "The princess Reha."

The scholar's words instantly made Esha tense. She had assumed the report would inform them that Vardaan had secured an alliance or another reason that would explain the silence from the palace about the general's murder.

But this? This was much worse. This went beyond the truce—this was about Reha, the lost key to saving the land. If the Fort knew about her whereabouts, found her first . . .

"Is it true? Is she alive?" The hope in the older woman's voice nearly broke Esha's heart. The yearning for her, for the lost princess Reha, was strong.

"I don't know," she answered. And that was the truth.

They had their own Blades out all over the Southern Lands, trying to discover if there was any truth to the rumors of the Lost Princess surviving. Even if no one knew her real identity, life in Jansa wouldn't have been easy for the past decade of war. She and Harun would have to double up their efforts to find her.

She had started out hoping to figure out who had framed her and the Blades, who might be against the peace treaty. But she hadn't expected this.

If Reha was found, it would change everything. There

was no chance for peace, no chance for an end to Vardaan's regime if he controlled the only person with a direct claim on the throne. Three droplets of her blood could fulfill the ritual, heal the land.

She'd be a weapon in the wrong hands. Vardaan would simply keep her prisoner until her death, using her blood to maintain the land through the ritual, all while continuing to wage war, growing his borders until he had built an empire under his name.

Esha resisted the urge to send a hawk immediately, knowing that something this sensitive would have to be delivered in person. And Harun might become hasty. She would get to Mathur in a few days, and she'd have a plan of action by then.

"It also mentions that there was actionable information sent to the Fort. In a note? It's a bit confusing. Half the information seems to be secondhand, from some group whose name is burned off." She tapped her fingers against the table. "The only way to interpret this is that the Fort has received and is pursuing information about her whereabouts," the scholar finished.

Moon Lord's fists, she didn't want to imagine what the Senaps might do to the princess if they got to her first. How had they missed this information?

"And the source that is mentioned?" Esha asked, hoping more than she should have that there was something, some clue as to who had been behind all of this.

It had seemed so clear that the person who framed her

was trying to prevent the truce, but what if it had all simply been a distraction for her and the Fort?

And she had certainly been distracted.

The scholar shook her head. "Nothing to go off. I'm sorry. I wish I could've been more useful."

She placed a light hand on the woman's arm. "You've been more helpful than you know."

———◄◦►———

Esha rushed back through the streets of Amali, pondering her conversation with the scholar. She'd developed the outline of a plan, the first step of which was to get back to Mathur.

A man passed by, looking at her a bit too close, as if he didn't quite believe what he was seeing. Esha frowned, pulling her turban down lower. Esha walked faster, throwing a sidelong glance behind her. The man had turned to inspect a stall of small, sugar-coated jellies and was no longer focused on her.

Her stomach growled. She'd been so intent on determining what to do next that she had ignored her need for food and rest. She slowed down, letting herself take a deep breath of the mountain air, crisp and clear.

The fruit seller's stall she had passed in her earlier scouting round was only a few streets away, which also meant she might be able to stop by the market. A new habit of hers— going to the market in every town she stopped in, both hoping and not hoping to catch a glimpse of Kunal.

She was playing a dangerous game, but she was too far

gone to care about the repercussions. Something about him made her want to gamble—and win.

He was the only boy in years who she felt was her match. Offered her a challenge. She wondered what it would be like to sit with him, sprawled on low, plush cushions like the ones in the inn's hearth room below, trading thoughts and stories across the glow of a fire.

It was a dream for another life.

She would be back in Dharka soon enough.

A tiny part of her hoped, against all odds, that if she met him again, she might be able to turn him. That if she turned him, maybe she'd somehow be able to keep him by her side.

Did he know about all that his general had done? Did he deserve to know that she hadn't actually killed him? Would it matter?

The sweet fragrance of ripe custard apples, dried plums, and fleshy peaches peppered the air as she approached the fruit stall. A scrawny fellow leaned languidly against the back stone wall. Esha tossed him a glance. He grinned at her, all white teeth, his eyes shifting around.

"Hungry, young master?"

She nodded. "How much for two peaches?" Esha dropped her voice low, hoping to pass for a teenage boy going through his changes.

The man gave her a sticky smile.

"Two coins."

Esha hid her surprise. A bargain. She handed over the two coins and sorted through the peaches, looking for two that were firm and unbruised. The man leaned over her, pointing out the best ones, and she thanked him, snatching up two.

She bit into the first one, smiling as the juices hit her tongue with pops of flavor.

A cloud of dust kicked up as Esha walked away from the stall and she shielded her eyes with the loose edge of her turban. The warmth and lushness of the Tej seemed like a distant memory and Esha longed to get back to Dharka.

The first thing she would do once home was go climbing for a large, juicy mango, pick it from the tree, and eat it in the sunshine with its juice dripping down her forearms. The proper way.

The mangoes here were anemic, green and pink instead of a rich orange. Firm instead of soft like a woman's curves.

Esha brought up the peach to her lips, imagining it to be that mango, when someone grabbed her arm and tugged her off balance. She caught herself before falling, catching the arm of a passerby who shook her off with a shake of his head. Her attacker was a hefty man in a linen dhoti decked in a green uttariya—which was topped off by the red fury of his face.

"Thief!"

Esha sputtered. Who was this man and how dare he? She was a lot of things, but she always paid for her food and goods. You weren't raised as an ambassador's daughter without understanding how important merchants and their livelihoods were to trade and economics in a country.

She put her hands up and turned toward the man to explain there was a mistake, but he grabbed her by the shoulders, continuing to yell in her face. Esha's blood began to boil and she felt her fingers close into a tight fist. She poked the man viciously in the chest with her other hand, hard and fast.

"You are not listening to me," she said in an emphatic staccato. "I am not a thief. And I do not appreciate your tone." Her eyes had narrowed into slits and she could feel a low rage building in her stomach.

"No? Why do you have two peaches, two of my beautiful peaches, without any coin in my hand?" he asked, his red, sweaty face displaying that he had already decided the answer.

"I gave your attendant the coins. You should keep better track of them," she hissed back, her fisted hand dangerously close to her whip.

"I have no attendant," the man replied, his eyes bulging.

"He's right there—" Esha looked over to see the scrawny man had disappeared, nowhere to be seen. She closed her eyes for a brief second, schooling her features.

"Lies, lies from a thief!"

She cursed inwardly. Unfortunate that she had let herself be duped so easily, but this was an easy solution. She would pay the man and be on her way, before the small crowd became bigger. Drawing attention had not been on her list of things to accomplish today.

Esha held up her hands. "An honest mistake. Let me pay you."

She reached down into her belt, realizing with each empty swipe of her hand that she hadn't just been duped, she had been made a mark. This was what resulted from her daydreaming about Kunal.

She bit her lip and looked apologetically at the man as she drew her empty hands out.

"Let me go back to my room and I'll get you the—"

But the man had stopped listening, fury contorting his features. His hand strayed to his knife and before he could move any farther, Esha took off in a sprint.

Stupid. So, so stupid. Had she always been this careless or had it only started after meeting the cursed soldier? And taking off in a dead heat wasn't exactly a great defense. The past weeks had made her jumpy.

She was constantly looking over her shoulder, wondering if, aside from the soldier, there was anyone else after her.

She was growing sick of having to run for her life. And she was feeling a little restless—and reckless.

Esha came to a full stop and turned, pulling out one of her whips and knife and easing into a crouch. She unfurled her whip, letting it hit the air with a warning flick.

This shopkeeper had picked the wrong girl to accuse.

In the distance, she saw a glimmer of green and behind the shopkeeper, two men armed to the hilt with short swords and maces. The men caught her eye. There was no reason to run after a thief of two peaches with armed men. This was something else.

Before she could continue her train of thought, an arm shot out and pulled her into darkness.

———◁o▷———

A cry escaped her lips but was muffled by a hand over her mouth.

Esha snarled and bit at the hand, struggling against the tight hold on her limbs. She threw her elbow back and it lodged into a soft part of her attacker, who gave a small yelp but didn't let go of her.

"*Stop*, Esha."

She went still. Kunal's voice was a blast of cold air against the heat of her temper, drawing her back into the calm, collected part of her brain.

"And stop squirming like that."

Esha stopped fidgeting, but tried to turn. Kunal caught her arm and spun her around, pressing her against the wall.

"Don't say a word," he growled, his words clipped. She couldn't help the look of offense on her face. She had barely been around him for a minute and he was already annoyed.

"What—"

"I'm trying to help you." He reached toward her turban before pausing and looking at her. "They're looking for a boy in a turban, not a woman." She nodded quickly in understanding.

Kunal yanked at her turban, unwinding the long cloth and tossing it into the darkness of the alley. Esha shivered at the contact, and the smart remark she was about to deliver died on her lips as she looked into his eyes. She noticed his stubble had grown into a full beard. It made him look older.

He cut off her words, unsheathing his knife. "Whatever you got yourself into, it's much worse than you think."

"I know, that man thought I stole from him but I had been—"

"No. There are three men on your tail, and two behind them. And you were planning to take on all of them in the street."

She glared at him and was about to swat away his hand when he pulled at her arm, pinning it above her. Esha was so shocked she almost went quiet, but somehow found her voice.

"I'd be scared for my virtue if you didn't have enough for both of us," she said.

Kunal shot her a tight look. "Just play along."

He drew so close that she could feel the flutter of his eyelashes, pressing his body against hers, mussing up her hair with his hands, fisting his hand tightly in her curls. She leaned into him, unable to control her reaction to his touch, the way her body moved to his. His other hand was pushing up at her loose dhoti, exposing her calf to the sweltering air as he tugged her leg higher around him.

And then he kissed her neck, and her skin was on fire and the heat was no longer coming from the air outside but from the endless pit in her core. She let out a sigh and she felt

Kunal stiffen and then pull her tighter.

"Turn your head down," he whispered into her ear, his lips brushing her earlobe, sending sparks down her spine. Three figures pulled up just then, blocking the only light streaming into their alleyway.

Kunal whipped his head around, angling it so it blocked Esha's face. Understanding flooded her and she quickly tilted her head away, the picture of shyness.

"Get out of here!" he snarled, hurling curses at the fruit seller and his men. They left with a few snickers and an apology, though Kunal continued to throw curses worthy of a fisherman at them until they disappeared from sight. Esha coughed and tugged her torn pants down, turning her face up toward Kunal.

"My, my, where did an upstanding soldier like yourself get such a filthy mouth?" Esha looked at him with amusement, her heart still beating like a hammer, trying to let some of the fire between them dissipate into steam. He stared back.

"A thank-you would be nice."

"For what?"

She knew for what but wanted to see it—see his eyes flash like lightning.

"For saving your life," he said, his teeth gritted. "My debt is paid."

Esha felt her breath catch and she couldn't help poking the bear. And for that matter, she would've been fine without him; she had her whip and knife and that's all she really needed in life.

She didn't need him to honor his cursed debt. She didn't need anyone. That was exactly what she was going to say, but other words escaped her lips.

"It must be nice, to be able to lie to yourself so easily. Pretend at honor and fulfill debts when it costs you nothing." The words were angrier than she had intended, but she couldn't stop them.

"This didn't cost me nothing. You're my mission—"

"Ah, yes. The mission to become commander by capturing or killing me."

His gaze faltered and his eyes flickered away as if he couldn't bear that truth anymore himself.

"I don't want you to die," he said, his words insistent. His gaze bored into hers, and she didn't flinch, holding it just as steadily. "And I don't even want you to be captured, but I believe in justice, and . . ."

Without warning, he leaned forward to rest his forehead against her own, as if letting go of all of his worries, if for only a second.

It took her aback, the change in his voice, the uncertainty in his words. Something, *something* had changed, and Esha wanted to tell him then, admit she was innocent. If she could turn him . . . but she didn't have time.

Not after discovering Vardaan was searching for the princess.

Her own duty, her own responsibility, her own life. They all waited for her across the mountains. But her feet remained rooted here, in the arms of the soldier she would have to leave behind.

"And those men? They were there by a new royal edict. You managed to upset a shopkeeper on the newly instated royal inspection day. There would have been no leniency." Esha opened her mouth. "I know you're not a thief," he said.

She looked up as he drew his head away from hers and untangled his hand from her hair.

"A murderer but not a thief. And I told you before, disguising yourself as a man only draws more attention to you. You couldn't blend in if your life depended on it. And it almost did."

She scoffed.

"And pray tell me how I managed to get by for two years as the Viper?"

"You do the opposite. You stick out so much that it's impossible to think you'd be anything but harmless."

"No, soldier. I think that's just you. I can disappear just fine when I like," she said, arching her eyebrow.

He smiled at that. "Maybe it is just me, but for some reason, I really don't believe that."

"So, was that all acting right there?" She didn't know why she did this, teased and flirted with him until she didn't know when she was getting a rise out of him and when she was digging the knife deeper into herself. "Or were you happy to have my eyes on you?"

A faint blush colored his dusky skin, but Kunal's expression didn't change.

"Why save me?"

"I told you. You managed to get in trouble on the worst day. And my debt."

Esha shook her head.

"That's not enough. Why? That cursed debt you claim can't possibly be worth more to you than the chance of such power as commander. I would think if you returned with my head it would be an automatic promotion." The grim line of Kunal's mouth was all the answer she needed. She hadn't known for sure before, but his silence confirmed it.

"What about those other soldiers?"

Kunal shifted uneasily. He had forgotten he had told her that, hadn't he? He ran a hand through his hair, rubbing the area between his ear and jaw.

"Esha—I can protect—"

"Stop." Her voice became hard. "Don't forget who I am. I don't need your protection."

He exhaled from his nose. "Yes, maybe you don't need my protection as the Viper, but as Esha—you nearly got caught there."

"My mistake." She shrugged. "I would've cleaned it up if you hadn't gotten in the way."

He barked a laugh. "Gods above, you are determined to be hard and unkind. I didn't want to see you in prison or dead because, for some unknown reason, I do like you."

Esha's heart fluttered, threatening to stop, wanting to

hear him go on as much as she didn't.

"And it's the worst decision I've possibly ever made in my life. To believe words that come out of those lips. When it's clear you would toss me to the dogs the moment you could. Every word you speak could be a ploy."

Esha blinked at him, doing a double take. The venom he had begun with had faded into an open, wounded look on his face that she was sure he didn't realize he was wearing. Only a moon had passed and she was entangled with this person so deeply her words could hurt him.

She should have killed him that first night they spent together.

His potential was something she could see with every word, every kind action. She almost believed Kunal when he said he would change the soldiers and bring back honor to the Blood Fort as commander. She knew he would fight for it.

The innocence in her wanted him to do it. The woman in her knew it wouldn't matter, that she could never stop until Vardaan and his regime of destruction was dismantled.

She spoke harshly because he was pure gold and she was tainted black. Her presence in his life would smudge the perfect edges of his goodness, strip his shine.

Wasn't it painfully obvious with every quip and tease and flirting word that he was slowly burrowing into her soul?

CHAPTER 40

Kunal couldn't tear his eyes away from her, in anticipation of her response—and in preparation to flee if necessary.

He couldn't believe he had said those things, brought life to those thoughts. But there was something about her that had plagued him since that first night, a distant memory. Sure, they had reached an uneasy truce of sorts, but the past few minutes had reminded him he wasn't dealing with just anyone.

She didn't need him. But that was part of why he wanted her.

If he could borrow even a little of that strength, that fire in her eyes, he could be the person his mother had always told him he could be, who he wanted to be. Even now, he questioned his orders because of her words. He had discovered the truth about his uncle because of chasing her. He hadn't questioned an order since his first moon at the Fort, when his opinions had been beaten out of him.

Esha reached out, cupping his jaw in her warm hand, and he held back a shudder at her touch.

She hesitated, as if unsure of her own words.

"I wouldn't," she said softly. "I wouldn't leave notes to someone I wanted dead. I would just kill them. I don't even know why I did it."

She paused, shaking her head.

Silky words and silver promises—that's what he'd get for believing Esha, but something about the contrast of her flippant tone and sorrowful eyes told him she meant it. She wouldn't hurt him. But Kunal didn't see how their truce would last.

"And you shouldn't believe anything I say," she said, her voice hardening. "Leave me here and go back."

She was echoing everything he had already thought, but he shook his head.

"No. I can't."

"Kunal, go home. What do you expect to get here? I won't come willingly back to the Fort. Are you going to keep chasing me for moons—years? Look how well that's worked out for you so far." She shook her head. "Best scenario, you get by the border guards after I cross and continue following me in Dharka. There is little love for bronze armor in Dharka. Many have been through much worse than I during the war. You'll die before you find me."

Kunal understood that—as he did pain and loss. The

274

stories of the soldiers' rampage after the usurpation of the throne hadn't escaped a young Kunal, but he had ignored them, wanting to believe the path he had been put upon was a good one, an honorable one.

"What happened?" he asked, his words light and gentle, so as not to scare away this new Esha. The pain that flared across her large eyes almost stopped Kunal's breath.

She moved her hand down to his lips, tracing her finger over them. She was so intent on it that he thought she would ignore his question.

"If you ever decide to stop chasing me, I'll tell you. Until then, you're still a soldier of the Pretender King and I'm still a rebel. Unless you'd think of joining the Blades," she said wryly. "But I know better than to try to turn you, soldier. Even though you'd be a valuable ally with your knowledge and experience."

Esha looked away. "But until that day, if it comes, we're still on opposite sides. We're already endangering more than ourselves here."

Kunal closed his eyes, letting himself bask in the feel of her soft fingertips on his face, tracing his nose and jaw and cheekbones.

Trying not to let the spark of hope in his heart fade.

If he lost being a soldier, he lost his entire identity. But maybe it was an identity no longer worth keeping.

He was beginning to think if Esha left, he'd lose the one thing he had held on to with tight fists since his mother's death—his heart.

Kunal hated how right she was. He was being reckless, endangering lives other than his own, betraying his comrades. To what end? And as for his duty—what end was that for?

He loved Jansa, his homeland, but he was seeing that the soldiers were only the puppets of the king, fed half-truths and convenient stories. Might over loyalty, brutality over compassion, greed over temperance. He wasn't even sure anymore that becoming commander would make any sort of difference, despite how desperately he now wanted it to be true.

But this life was all he knew. He was accepted as a soldier. He didn't know who he would be without the armor. Who he would've been without his uncle, despite the horrors he had perpetrated, despite Sundara.

Esha's fingers had wrapped around the back of his neck, playing with the edges of his hair. He dipped his head forward, stopping inches from her face.

"If I stop chasing you, you'll disappear anyway. Not much incentive for me to stop," he said in a low voice.

"I guess." She smiled at him, and it lit up her face, as if she had swallowed the sun itself. Her fingers stilled but she didn't deny it.

"I won't go back. I will never go back to that gods-forsaken place. You can try if you're willing to drag me back by force. Or just go home to the Fort and say the Viper disappeared. No one else will find me or go against your story. You'll go back to being a soldier and you'll have the prestige of having risked your life for the Fort. No one will have expected you to succeed anyway. The Viper is a myth, after all," she said, her eyes twinkling.

Kunal opened his mouth and then closed it.

"You hadn't thought of that, had you?" she asked.

Her words hit home, ringing with a truth he didn't want to meet. But the Fort had never been his home. It had just been where he lived.

He wanted to tell her, to explain, but he saw in her eyes that Esha was already drifting away and the Viper was returning.

"It's the perfect plan, really. None of you become commander through an unfair game that pits young soldiers against one another to find a spy that no one believes truly exists. It's as if you were set up to fail."

Kunal cocked his head at that. He was desperate to hold her attention, if only for a moment longer, and tugged her closer so that there wasn't even a hairsbreadth of space between them.

Something dangerous flashed in Esha's eyes in response and she gripped his chin.

"What? Have you become mute, soldier?"

Kunal continued to ignore her, his breath hitching as she drew closer. If they kissed, crossed this line, nothing would be the same. There would be no wall of ignorance to hide behind, no stories to tell himself that it had all been a game.

This would determine everything to come.

Kunal had played it safe for so long that he was craving danger with a thirst that surprised him.

Everything around him faded, the sounds of a town alive, the musty scent of the dusty alley and the laundered clothes above. It all vanished as she became the only color he saw.

She tilted her head and Kunal leaned in, hesitating, letting her bridge the gap between them.

Esha raised her other hand to his face and tugged down the clothesline above them with one swift movement. A ball of damp silk tumbled onto his head and he cursed with a thoroughness that would've made Laksh proud, stumbling back.

Through the vibrant colors, he caught a glimpse of Esha leaving.

He let her walk away, listening to his heart for once.

She paused to look back at him, her eyes holding a farewell in their depths, before disappearing down the street.

———◁◦▷———

A faint drizzle of rain splattered the dusty ground like bursts of paint. Kunal crouched on the rooftop, shaking his damp hair out of his eyes as he focused on a pinprick zooming over the horizon.

He had considered it. For a moment, he had truly considered stopping all of this.

Kunal couldn't decide if it was weakness or a new form of strength to directly defy the orders he had been sent out with.

At least, self-preservation or ambition should have driven his hand to simply knock her out and drag her back, as she had suggested. But Kunal had always had a heart, the one thing a good soldier was never supposed to have.

He unclenched his fist, small half-moon indentations left behind in his palms as he shook out his hands. With a grimace toward the fading image of Esha, he pulled his pack into his lap, rustling around to find his whistle and the note he had tucked away.

A sharp two blows of the whistle in his hand and wing beats followed in the distance. The hawk swooped down low, circling around Kunal. It tilted its beak up, as if sniffing the air around Kunal to determine whether it would deign to rest on his outstretched forearm.

He was deemed worthy and the Fort hawk landed with a graceful swoop, its talons clenching into Kunal's bare skin.

Since he was a boy, he had gone bare-armed with his hawks and falcons. Something about the connection of skin to claw resonated deep within him. It was a feeling he couldn't ever quite explain—as if for a second, he got to feel the fierce freedom of being an animal. He felt it in his bones, in his blood, and it never failed to make him feel whole.

He produced a small piece of leathered meat, which the animal snatched into its beak happily. Now it turned its eyes fully to Kunal, willing to engage. He tied the small note to the hawk's claws and watched it fly away, majestic and free in the wind.

He had always wished he could fly as a child, climbing

trees so high that his mother's cries were distant and enveloped by the clear air above. That need hadn't changed as he grew older, and he had often taken the worst shift times so he could be alone at the top of the Fort, a moment of respite and wholeness that he found nowhere else in that massive structure.

It was why he had seen Esha. And how this whole mess had started.

Alok's latest note had arrived earlier that day, before he had found and lost Esha.

> *Hullo Kunal,*
> *The Fort isn't the same without you or Laksh.*
> *I'm hoping one of you comes to his senses and returns home. Is it really worth it to become commander? They always have to work so much. Yes, yes, I can imagine you frowning at me, Kunal. But you'll be happy to hear, I opened your mail and saw that you received your official Senap posting. You'll be in Gwali.*

Kunal felt a little flutter of pleasure at learning of his posting in Gwali. He hadn't expected it, but it was nice to have the option now, with all the uncertainty in his life.

> *So just come back, all right? You're already going to be an important Senap, no need to capture the Viper and add another feather to your turban.*
> *Anyway, we've been told to remain quiet about the*

general's murder, though the commander hasn't said
much about it anyway. The cease-fire is still on, at least.
It's all very odd and there's a tense undercurrent in the
Fort. Normally, I'd say it was in anticipation of the Sun
Mela a moon from now, but my gut says otherwise.

Perhaps everyone is just scared about how badly I'll
trounce them in archery during the Mela games. Mark
my words . . .

The rest continued on like that, and Kunal folded the note away, pondering Alok's almost desperate plea for them to forget their quest and return home. Knowing that Uncle Setu had orchestrated the Sundara massacre, he wasn't sure he even wanted to be commander and follow in his footsteps, his idea of greatness.

Kunal had seen what he was made of—and it wasn't steel and blood. He was neither here nor there, unwilling to let go of his training and unable to let go of his feelings.

He was stuck.

On the bright side, he now had information on the whereabouts of the other three soldiers, after stopping by another garrison and bribing the guards with jellied candies.

Rakesh was the one he had to worry about—the soldier in the last town said he had made his way inland and was boasting his way through each town, sending back tales of his progress in gaining information. Apparently, he had been tracking the tales of the whip after Laksh had shaken him off his trail. Laksh hadn't checked into another garrison since Onda, it seemed. Which could be good or bad.

None of them were here in this town, so none of them were close to the truth regarding the Viper. When Esha had suggested he pretend he had never met her, he had seen a future with that in it. It would be a blow to his ego, but that was a small thing now.

Go back and admit defeat, but admit defeat to a supposed assassin shrouded in myth. There would be ways to atone on his journey back—maybe take in a criminal or rebel to even out the scales of justice.

He could do it. His old life would be waiting for him, like the way the shore welcomed the sea no matter the time of day. Life would go on, he'd take on his Senap post in Gwali, and he might rise to commander in his own time. Or be released from duty and carve out a life for himself, somewhere quiet, with tall trees and a view of the ocean. Somewhere he could paint to his heart's content.

Kunal sighed and sat down on the rooftop, rubbing the tension out of his neck as he let the vision envelop him. He breathed into it and it gathered around him like a haze in the slowly fading swelter of summer.

The scenery was softer here near the Ghanta Mountains; the heat kind enough to allow blooming tendrils of flowers across houses. In front of him, the land stretched out greener than he had seen in many moons. It was a visceral relief to see the land and river thriving and it reminded him of all that he had missed. It would be easy to absolve himself of blame—he wasn't a general or a royal or a son from a noble house.

But he found himself unable to forget.

The images of the shantytowns, the drought-stricken land in Ujral, replaced the greenery, memory tugging at his mind.

Would becoming the commander even allow him to fix these people's lives, or would it simply be another collar around his neck? Would he be forced to order the deaths of innocents? Or had that been his uncle's choice?

He realized he no longer felt that raging ache under his ribs at the thought of his uncle's dishonorable death.

Could death ever truly be honorable? It was always a loss, a period instead of a comma.

And Esha.

She wanted nothing from him but for him to leave. Their story had ended; this was when the hero went home in the tale. But he didn't feel like a hero returning triumphantly. He didn't feel like a hero, period.

Thwarted and outsmarted at every turn, his own heart and conscience turning against him when he needed to stay strong.

He had left the Fort with such a clear idea of what was right and wrong, who was right and wrong, and what the world was. If he returned now, he would return with no such comfort and with an ache in his heart that he supposed only time would mend.

But it would be less torture to turn around empty-handed than watch hatred grow in her eyes when he dragged her back.

Kunal bit the inside of his cheek, pushing away the parts of him that whispered that life after Esha would never be the same.

———◁o▷———

Kunal tugged at his mare's reins, tying them to the wooden post in the stable of the inn as he moved to brush her coat.

He had decided to take his time today, leisurely strolling through the town, stopping to fill up his rations for the trip back, buying an unnecessary trinket or two—which would have made Alok happy. He had found a companion to his marble miniature, a small, delicately carved copy of the Aifora Range, the home of the gods and spirits.

Kunal tossed his horse a few small sugar cubes as he finished up, patting his pockets absentmindedly to check that the miniature was still there. When he got the chance, he wanted to paint it all, every town, all the vibrant colors and people. Maybe even work with marble on his own.

Kunal had an idea where Esha would have to go next, but instead of rushing after her, he had spent the past day in thought, working through every option, every strategy to see how he could still win. Still win and keep his own sense of honor. The idea of getting her a fair trial was uncertain and the idea that he might take her back to her death made him shudder to his core.

He couldn't—wouldn't—let Esha die.

Was this one girl worth his whole future? A future he wasn't sure he believed in anymore, but nonetheless, the only future he had.

For a bleak second, he had considered finding another person and pretending they were the Viper. But he hadn't had the forethought to steal one of Esha's whips for proof and he couldn't stomach the thought of an innocent's death on his hand.

Then he had considered a criminal, but couldn't stomach that either.

How could he be a soldier and start thinking about whether the enemy or a criminal had their own reasons for being there, for making the wrong choice? In battle, he would be killed in the few seconds of hesitation such thoughts would cause.

Kunal longed for those childhood days at the summer palace. Life had been so simple as a boy, with his mother to guide him and his nurse to watch over him. In the stable, he put away the brush and tied his mare up again.

He sighed as he opened the inn door, letting out a cacophony of noise into the street.

The main room of the inn rose into a high domed ceiling with flowing reams of silk separating the large room into quadrants. Red-and-white patterned cushions acted as seats for the variety of patrons, from merchants with elaborate gold necklaces to scholars in pristine white robes to giggling young women with tinkling anklets. He elbowed his way to the back of the room, close enough to the exit and the stairs.

The maid had already found him, glancing up at him through her eyelashes as he sat down on the low cushions. He wore the clothes of a traveler, an uttariya thrown across his shoulders and over his head.

Food arrived in minutes, perfumed with steam and the heavy spiced aromas of Dharkan cuisine. Kunal let a small sigh of pleasure escape. They weren't allowed Dharkan food at the Fort and he had loved it since a child.

Something about the spicy, robust flavors, the heaviness of lentils and rice, warmed his soul. The food seemed to fill a small hole in him that he hadn't realized had been forming, gnawed into place by worry and confusion and frustration.

He closed his eyes for a second, leaning his head against the wooden wall. Light filled the right side of his face but Kunal didn't worry too much. Anyone who would have known him wouldn't recognize him now.

His hair had grown out into soft waves, streaked dark brown by the endless sun, and his beard was becoming thick. He rather liked the feel of it. His father had had a thick, flowing beard and a striking head of hair. That much he remembered of his father—when he had known him.

The maid came to fetch the emptied plate, ever attentive, and as he opened his eyes, thanking her in soft tones, something caught his eye.

A glimmer of bronze cuirass walking straight across the

room. Curls and a red face that despite its disdain seemed hungry, needy.

Rakesh sat down among a group of sell-swords, the rice wine in his hand sloshing out of its metal cup onto the ground. Kunal snapped to attention, straining to hear the conversation. The girl was still standing in front of him and looked startled at the sudden change in Kunal.

Kunal smiled at her and leaned in. "Who is that man?" he asked.

Her eyes opened wide and she played with the valaya at her wrist. A Dharkan-run inn that hadn't been burned to the ground, protected by the town's inhabitants—it was a wonder in this new Jansa. But it was a flimsy protection in the face of a soldier. Kunal understood the expression on her face now. Fearful but uncowed.

"He came in earlier and has been holding court. A soldier come from Faor," she whispered. She flicked her eyes between them and brought herself closer. "He claims to have found the Viper and is planning to bring the traitor to justice." She blushed. "*Traitor* was his word. And to justice for what, I do not know. It seems a bit late to go after the Viper for his crimes after all these years."

She seemed to realize she may have said too much and snapped her mouth shut.

Kunal gave her a warm smile that let her know he wouldn't repeat her words. She relaxed and the shy look returned to her eyes. Inside, he was in turmoil. The question was if Rakesh was on the correct trail or a lie.

Kunal whispered a thank-you to the girl. She turned to leave and his arm shot out, grabbing her wrist. "Could you tell me what else he says?" He thought quickly. "I have no love for soldiers, and this one seems to be one of the worst."

The girl's eyes widened and she nodded, making Kunal wince. Lying was starting to become too easy for him.

The girl hurried over to the corner where Rakesh held court, sending him a small smile.

He didn't deserve her admiration. He had grown lax, underestimating his opponents. How had Rakesh found out Esha was headed in this direction? Did he know who the Viper was?

If he knew it was Esha . . . Kunal had so much to lose now. Considering letting Esha go was different from letting Rakesh win. It made his blood boil to think he could become commander.

And the thought of Rakesh finding Esha, being anywhere near Esha. Kunal remembered what Alok had told him, about House Baloda. Desperation led to bad decisions and in Rakesh, it would turn to cruelty.

She was his. His to capture or not.

And commander, that was also his.

To see Rakesh, of all people, find and capture her . . . He couldn't just step aside and allow her death at Rakesh's hands.

Kunal pinched the bridge of his nose, trying to quell the overwhelming tightness in his chest.

Calm. *Control.* He needed to remain calm and *think.*

Faor. Maybe someone had seen her, put two and two together. Rakesh might know everything or he might only know the Viper had headed in this direction.

From here there were only a few ways into Dharka. The official border pass, monitored by Jansan soldiers, was out of the question. She must be going through the Ghanta Mountains, and that would require her to trek through the Mauna Valley, which would leave her very little room to escape. If Rakesh cornered her in the right spot, alone, she would be in trouble.

It was obvious. Even Rakesh would have figured it out.

Kunal sat and waited, watching Rakesh with an ever-growing fire of hatred filling his belly. Esha could take care of herself if Rakesh managed to find her, but what if Rakesh sent off a hawk to alert the others?

Esha had told him to go home. He had been ready to.

But when faced with it, he wanted to win.

If Rakesh won—if he hurt Esha at all—it would haunt him till the end of his days.

CHAPTER 41

The messenger hawk swooped through the mountains, following the golden mist that tumbled down their sides into the Mauna Valley, obscuring the tops of the tall trees.

The hawk landed unsteadily on Esha's outstretched arm. The ribbon tied around the note slid off into her hands and Esha tugged on the ends, unfurling it. She scanned it quickly.

Moon Lord's curses. She had left one problem behind and had found another.

She could imagine Kunal's reaction at being called a problem—indignation coupled with that little crease in between his eyebrows. Esha still remembered the way he had looked at her, like he was drowning and she could save him. But she couldn't. Not when she still had to fight for her own path.

Her life wasn't her own.

Esha shook her head. If anything was traitorous, it was her own mind. Wanting to run away with a soldier, even if just for a moment, was the ultimate betrayal of everything she was.

The hawk nipped at her fingers and Esha pulled them back sharply, glaring at it. She infinitely preferred the owls. Not only were they sweet-tempered, but Harun never used hawks unless there was an emergency. These hawks were trained to find the scent of the person within a day.

She glanced back down at the note.

I should chastise you for not telling me about the deserter, but I know you won't listen to anything I say once you've made up your mind, so I won't bother. A soldier was looking for you in Faor and overheard the doctor who examined your Tana, making the connection between the whip welt around her neck and your escape. Tana sent us an urgent note as soon as she realized the soldier was on to you—good work developing her as an asset.

She winced, knowing the truth of it. Not that she'd tell him.

The soldier's been trailing you north since, asking questions in every town. We're going to move up our meet and send the Blue Squad.

At the bottom, a postscript.

Stay safe, Esha. I'll only feel at ease when I know you're back home.

Esha crumpled up the note in her fist, indignation her first reaction. She didn't need to be saved. But there was also slight relief in her chest—she wouldn't be alone.

She knew the soldier in the note couldn't be Kunal. He wouldn't have needed to ask around about her and wouldn't be so stupid; she knew that much. It had to be one of the other soldiers from the forest.

Esha moved toward her horse and tugged off the reins and saddle. It was better to go by foot in this jungle and a horse would slow her down now. The horse stared at her for a moment, not believing that it was in fact free. She hit its rump and it took off with speed into the trees, tearing down branches and making her grin.

She climbed into the undergrowth of the jungle, taking care to step over the gnarled roots as she hacked through the thick vegetation with her knife. The branches and dewy leaves caught on the loose fabric of her dhoti and her sticky skin. Overhead, sunlight streamed softly down, like blankets being aired in the wind.

Esha stilled for a languid moment and took in a deep breath; she could smell Dharka again. Jasmine and mango. Banyan trees mixed with taller trees throughout, making the jungle appear as if it were on stilts. Home.

The *janma* bond here was still alive; you could sense its vitality in the way the small streams of water sparkled and the hornbills swarmed together, cackling to themselves. Animals roamed around, living in harmony, one with the land. The thought that it might fade, be reduced to the dried-out forests and hill towns of Jansa, cut her deep.

She shook her head, unwilling to consider the possibility. At least Vardaan hadn't found Reha yet, hadn't found the *heen rayan* mentioned in those reports.

Esha frowned. Not that they had found her either—or a solution to fixing the *janma* bond.

The rebels would meet her tomorrow farther into the jungle, close to the secret trail near the Mauna Valley that cut through the Ghanta Mountains. It was the only way around the closed borders—everywhere else was certain death.

She had to stay alive and out of harm till then.

The words in the note loomed over her as she continued her journey.

CHAPTER 42

The depth of night was upon him but Kunal rode on, using the stars dotted above him as guidance in his path north. Time was of the essence and Kunal refused to let Rakesh win—or let Esha get hurt. For the first time in his life, he had no plan—but he felt propelled forward by something bigger than himself.

He patted his mare's neck as they galloped, soaring over the ground. The air lashed his face and the ends of his turbaned uttariya flew in the air behind him. Kunal leaned in, murmuring words of encouragement into the mare's ear. The night air was a breezy gauze, cool yet comforting against his skin. It belied the roil inside him.

The girl at the inn had proven useful, relaying the rest of Rakesh's boasting. Rakesh knew enough of the truth to get himself killed if he did find Esha. Something told him she wouldn't leave that particular soldier alive.

But he couldn't wipe the image of something horrific happening to Esha at Rakesh's hands—he was a soldier, and trained as such.

A shiver trailed through Kunal. He had watched the soldiers leave the camps at night when campaigning and return with bloody knives and grins on their faces. He had never spoken up, deciding to ease his own path rather than fight for another's.

As a grown man, he couldn't claim powerlessness anymore.

He spurred his mare on.

CHAPTER 43

E sha heard the whinny of the horse before she saw it from her spot high in the asvattha tree. The sky was gray, a harbinger of the storm to come. A few hours later and the early morning sky would be clouded and forbidding. Even now, a mist blew in, covering the mountain's forested slopes with a silvery, opaque haze.

Kunal was a disheveled sight, his turbaned uttariya unraveling and his dhoti dusted with sand and grime. Why in the name of the Moon Lord's spear was he here?

She swallowed a frustrated groan. Did she have to physically hurt him for him to get the message?

As he walked into the jungle, she scrambled to a closer tree, leaping and snatching a branch, rolling herself around it to land nimbly. She leaned forward; his expression was wild and he looked desperate.

The branch snapped in displeasure at her weight, the sound like a shriek in the stillness of the morning. His head whipped up. Not even the trilling blue robins were singing their song this early.

Biting back a curse, she swung herself down through the aerial roots of the asvattha tree, landing on the floor of the jungle, leaves crunching underfoot. Kunal started but showed no surprise.

"I didn't think it would be *this* easy to find you," he said wryly, rubbing his head as if in pain. He looked relieved and it made her blood boil.

"What are you doing here, soldier?" she hissed. "I warned you."

She had let him live, had even given him a way out, and now he was back? How could he be that desperate to make a prize of the Viper?

Well, she wouldn't allow it.

"I came to—"

Esha pushed him roughly against the trunk of the tree, watching with satisfaction as he winced. But he didn't struggle. Slowly, he put his hands up, holding them out.

"I will kill you, Kunal. I don't care about whatever might be going on between us. If you make one undue move, I will wrap my whip around your neck and drive my knife into your ribs before you even draw in a single breath. And I won't feel the least bit of remorse."

She could hear the fear in her voice but she couldn't help

it. The words came out rough, spears of truth. Without his spell around her, Esha had seen with clear eyes what she still had to do.

"Am I allowed to speak now without you threatening me?"

Esha snorted. "The day I don't threaten you is the day you're already dead."

He gave her a crooked smile. "Good to know. But I came to tell you something."

Esha cocked her head at him, wondering if she should trust him. He had come after her, even though she had told him to go.

Which could mean he still wanted to be commander badly enough to capture her—and her freedom could be at stake. That was too much to gamble. She would have to knock him out and run to the low pass to escape.

Esha backed off a step, lowering her knife.

Kunal dropped his hands and she took advantage of his momentary pause. She rammed into him and stepped on his insole, driving her elbow into his side. He groaned but blocked her next blow by grabbing at her elbow. But she was too fast and all he caught was the back of her cotton shirt, which tore away at her shoulder.

Her eyes narrowed. This was the only shirt she had. She raised her hands to land a final blow. Suddenly, Kunal had her arm in a tight grip and the look in his eyes stopped her cold.

"When did you get that scar?" he asked, his words sharp.

His eyes darted between the raised scar that danced down her shoulder and her face. It was an old scar, a reminder of her youth and why one should never lose one's focus when facing a knife.

"Naria?" he said, whispering the word like a prayer.

Esha felt the word like a slap to the face—bold, unexpected.

The last person who had called her that had climbed lemon trees with her in the lazy heat of summer, had been hidden away at the summer palace, away from the prying eyes at Gwali.

Her last real friend.

"Naran?" she asked.

———◄o►———

Shock froze her in place. It felt as if the entire world was moving slower, so slow she could hear the change in her heartbeat as it pounded faster and faster. The names were a distant memory, of playing pretend and legends come to life.

"No, it's impossible. It can't be," Esha said.

Naran and Naria. The founders of Jansa and Dharka. Her favorite game as a kid.

Their favorite game as children.

Kunal was staring at her. "I never thought I would hear that again," he said, his voice shaky, disbelieving.

Esha swallowed hard, the lump in her throat refusing to descend. She felt as if her heart would burst out of her chest and lay itself in Kunal's hands.

No wonder he had felt familiar. The heart always knew more than the head.

"How? Why? How?" Esha stuttered. This was her lemon boy?

"I don't know," he said, laughing. "I want to know too."

They both grinned at each other, drawing so close that she could hear his breath hitch as she touched his skin.

"I thought that girl died, just like my old life," he said.

Esha shuddered slightly. "She did, Kunal. That girl stopped existing on the Night of Tears. When her parents were murdered."

A shadow passed across his face and Esha knew he understood. His mother had also been killed in the coup. His fingers had softened from their previous grip and were now tracing the edges of her scar. It was an ugly thing, raised and puckered. A mark she used to cover out of shame but now hid to make herself more anonymous.

Her posture eased slightly and she closed her eyes, letting him pull her closer.

"I thought you died," he repeated, his eyes rapturous on her scar.

"You already said that."

She shook her head, smiling.

"I really mean it." He looked up at her, his eyes unsteady. "I can't tell you the number of days I thought of you when I was first at the Fort. The other boys looked down on me and all I wanted to do was climb high, escape their viciousness and pity. I thought everyone who had been in my life was gone and I didn't want to be there without them."

Esha felt a small lurch in her heart.

"Your friendship brought light to that summer, the last one before everything changed. I didn't realize till I thought you were dead that I didn't even know your real name."

Esha laughed. "That would be my fault. I dubbed you Naran and no one could convince me you were anyone else. And me? I wanted to be Naria, 'warrior of justice,' so badly I made everyone call me that for those few, blissful weeks."

Now her laugh held a bitter edge.

"Why did you let them dim *your* light, lemon boy?" she asked. How could he have become a soldier? They had killed his mother, and there were rumors the king had seen to his father as well.

Did he not know?

"You used to shine so bright back then it made my eyes ache. I still remember when I first met you, when you jumped down from a lemon tree to scare the tutor," she said.

His fingers tapped an unsteady, unhappy beat into her skin. He frowned. "I didn't think I had any light left in me to dim once I got to the Fort. Not after my mother's death."

CHAPTER 44

Kunal could feel the honesty spill out of him before he could lock it away.

He didn't want her pity. He wanted lost time, years of friendship and warm laughs and stupid fights. She had been big hair and sharp eyes when she had first come to the summer palace, alive in the best way possible and one to never let him get a word in edgewise.

Kunal had loved being bossed around by her, having someone shake the branches to terrorize him as he climbed to the tops of lemon trees and help him hide from their tutors. The summer palace had filled with their laughter and hijinks, putting a smile on his mom's face as well, the first one since his father was gone.

How they both had changed in ten years. A lifetime.

She lifted her chin, gazing at him—not with pity, but with a challenge.

"Cowshit. You have more light in your thumb than any of those soldiers. Don't go back, Kunal. Come with me," Esha said.

Her words made him stop cold; even she looked a bit surprised. He had been about to laugh, tell her that he belonged with the rebels even less than she belonged at the Fort.

But before he could say so, he saw something else on her face: a desire so deep it caught him off guard.

A sharp whistle pierced the air and Kunal's head whipped up.

It was the sound of the iron tip of a copper arrow, an arrow created only at the Fort.

Terror gripped him, and before he could think, he shoved Esha away. She went sprawling on the ground, directly in the clearing.

A look of hurt flashed over her face, hitting him in the core, but then an arrow hurtled past them, burrowing into the tree trunk.

Right behind where Esha's head had been.

He wanted to ask if she was all right, help her, but he was out of time.

Rakesh had arrived.

CHAPTER 45

E sha was back on her feet in seconds.

Another arrow hurtled past her, nicking her ear and lodging itself into the thick tree behind her. She unleashed one of her whips and knocked away another arrow, the crack deafening.

Esha whirled to face the direction of the arrows, flicking the length of her whip up and out toward the noise. A moment and then a shout, deep and male. Anger rose through her throat at the intrusion.

Where had Kunal gone? She glanced back to see him hiding in the cover of the trees, his hand on his knife. It was as if he was frozen. There was recognition in his face, and beneath it, something akin to terror. But why?

She didn't have time for this.

The intruder was far enough away that she was able to

pull her whip up and bring it down sharply, the end of her weapon coiling around his ankle. He landed with a thud and Esha waited, brandishing her knife as she pulled her whip back.

The man in front of her was no more than a few years older than her, with corkscrew curls that reminded her of pigs' tails. But he was the soldier—that much was clear from his armor. She paused, sizing him up, and he took advantage of it, scrambling into an upright position with his own thick sword waving next to him.

Now she got the full size of him and almost gulped. Lying down he had looked like a pig, but upright he was a boar. A very big one.

Was he working with Kunal? The thought left her cold.

Esha scrambled back to where Kunal hid. "Was this you, Kunal? Did you lead your friends to me?" she demanded, panic turning her fury black. Kunal started, his eyes widening in indignation.

"I came to warn you," he whispered back in a rush.

She met his earnest gaze with ice. "You came to capture me first."

"The legendary Viper is just a woman?" the soldier questioned loudly, his lips turning into a sneer. "And she's running away."

She reappeared and laughed, the coldness in her voice surprising even her. "If only you were so lucky."

Esha had a lifetime's worth of experience in dealing with

men who underestimated her—or those who were scared by her refusal to fit their norms.

There was bravado and nothing of substance under that armor. This was the type of Jansan soldier she hated. But judging by his size and the way he held his sword, she would have to be careful.

"A woman who managed to drag you to the ground." She smirked at him, her full Viper mask on. Kunal lingered in the corner of her vision, hidden in the brush.

For the life of her, she couldn't figure out why he was hiding. If they were working together, he wouldn't be standing there, frozen. Maybe he was telling the truth and had come to warn her.

Esha wasn't too worried about this overgrown pig who had boasted of finding her. He may not think much of her, but he'd soon learn.

She was about to grin when a realization hit her like a punch to the gut, knocking the wind from her lungs.

Kunal.

She glanced at him, finally understanding the tension in his shoulders, the way he was keeping so very, very still. If he *had* come to warn her, and if he was caught having done so, saving the enemy, his entire career—and life—was forfeit.

One wrong move and she could damn him to a dishonored life of exile for giving her a chance to live. Her lemon boy from a summer past, when smiles still came easy to her lips and life's opportunities seemed endless. She could kill the man, but Harun would be angry if they had an opportunity to capture and get information from a soldier and she squandered it.

And Kunal. Two soldiers for information would be better than one, and the rebels would act first and question later.

The soldier picked himself up off the ground and was moving closer to her, taking her silence as invitation to find a way to best her. She snapped her whip back and up, knocking him off his feet again and leaving a deep gash in his arm. A howl of pain erupted from him and he clutched his arm on the ground, looking at her with murder in his eyes.

Good. At least he had decided what he thought of her. Most of her opponents realized the power of her whips within seconds of engaging her; he was no different.

She had maneuvered the soldier to face away from where Kunal stood and she finally threw a look in his direction, hoping he understood the pleading in her eyes.

Go. Run. Fly away from her.

Forget what she had said; she wouldn't have his life on her hands.

His expression remained impassive—it was clear he didn't plan on running. It seemed like he didn't know *what* to do.

She had never had a problem with people listening to her orders, until this cursed boy. He defied her at every turn, putting others first and himself last. It was an admirable trait—and a stupid one.

The soldier lunged at her and she dodged, rolling onto the ground away from him. She emerged in a crouched position, her knife held high above her head and her whip low in the other hand. He was faster than he looked, and landed a blow to her side before darting away from her whip's reach. He eyed the metal tip with fear.

Esha grinned, a maniacal one she liked to wear to confuse her opponents. She began lashing her whip out, so quick the soldier danced to escape meeting its touch, focusing in on the weaknesses his body whispered as he moved. He pivoted to the right and she slipped toward the left, digging her knife deep into his side, enough to harm but not kill.

There were dungeons that lived beneath the rebel base where he would be quite comfortable.

He yelped and stared at her in shock, his hands grasping at his side as he fell to his knees.

"You'll be fine," she said, rolling her eyes.

She struck her whip against the ground next to him, startling him enough for her to yank out the knife. She began to clean it daintily as she watched him grow pale at the sight of blood on her blade.

What an embarrassment, a soldier who couldn't stomach the sight of blood. Or maybe it was because it was his own. What a pampered existence, to have never seen your own blood.

She sniffed, watching him. He had probably used intimidation most of his life. With a sigh, she tugged off her waist sash and threw it at him.

"Take this and hold it against your wound." He looked at her and spat. Esha simply stared back at him until he began fidgeting under the weight of her gaze. "Or you can die. Really no matter to me," she said with a shrug.

He grabbed at the fabric with hasty, shaking fingers, squeezing it against his body. She continued cleaning her knife as she crouched down in front of him. He glanced at it and then up at her again, in quick succession.

"Are you going to cut off my nose?" he blurted out. Esha swore she heard a cough, or a laugh, coming from the trees behind them. The soldier was too focused on her to notice.

"I'm not sure why that tale came about. I only did it once," she replied.

He blanched. Esha got up and turned away, but not before clocking pig boy in the face. He passed out cold.

After a moment, Kunal ventured out of the thicket of trees. He craned his head toward the fallen soldier.

"Is this what I've been missing? And poor Rakesh—his ego will be bruised far longer than any physical harm will last."

"Sorry about your friend," she said in reply.

"Not a friend." Kunal looked a bit sheepish. "Can't stand the guy."

"Is it because he looks like an overgrown piglet with those curls?"

Kunal squinted his eyes before they widened fully. "I never realized it, but you're right. Huh."

He did seem to notice the blood staining the ground

around the man. Kunal's eyes darted from the blood to her face.

"Glad I never ended up like that," Kunal said, a faint reverence in his tone.

Esha grinned. "You're too pretty for that," she said. She saw the change in his body language as he came closer, and her breath caught, her skin flushing with warmth. She needed to be getting him away from here, not drawing him closer. And if the rebels found them together in a way that looked too familiar . . .

It wouldn't be good for either of them.

"Kunal . . ."

"This is what I was trying to tell you. I found out Rakesh was coming your way."

"And you came to what, warn me? Save me?"

"I came to make sure he didn't find you." She lifted an eyebrow at him, her knife still in hand. "Not because you needed my help. Clearly, you could have taken him. But still . . . I . . . ." He stopped, seemingly lost for words. She let the silence grow between them.

"I wanted to—" he said, his eyes closing for a brief pause. She cut him off before he could continue.

"You came to capture me before he did. Good for you, soldier. You know what you want." And she meant it, despite the slight twinge in her heart.

"Esha, the minute I saw the scar—and then when you were facing down Rakesh, I—" He sighed, struggling to speak.

"I can't drag you back to win my prize," he said finally, the corners of his mouth turning down. "I realized that the moment I found you today. And I can't leave you here knowing who you were to me." Esha looked up. "Who you are." He took a deep breath and she looked at him sharply.

"This doesn't change anything," she said quickly, echoing his words from the pit. This was exactly what she didn't want. Men like Rakesh would always be after her. Her job and desire for revenge hadn't changed with the realization that a small part of her youth had remained whole.

It only made her want to work harder to avenge it. Her invitation had been selfish, before she had remembered that she was the Viper, not a real girl.

"You asked me to—"

"It was a mistake. You can't follow me. I shouldn't have asked." She blew past the pained look on his face. "It was unfair of me. Go home, Kunal. For the last time, I'm telling you to go home." Her lip curled. "Get your honorable discharge, find a sweet girl, and make a new life. I still have to fight for my old one."

She tried to keep her voice nonchalant as she folded her arms. "You'd just slow me down anyway."

He looked hurt for a moment, but he suddenly pulled her closer, shaking her arms out of their crossed position.

The constant whisper of the jungle, of the various birds and insects and mammals, faded back, as if there had been a disturbance. For a moment pure silence flooded the jungle, and all Esha could hear was the slow thud of their hearts.

A fragment of memory from that sun-stained summer flitted into her mind as his eyes flashed in annoyance, his pale eyes turning a savage yellow. A wildness she had seen only once before, in the eyes of a Samyad queen.

She gasped, memories flooding her as the sounds of the jungle rushed back in. Esha remembered the first time she had met Kunal's mother—the late princess Payal Samyad, the last queen's youngest sister. She had bent down to be eye level with Esha, taking her small hand in her own and solemnly asking her to be a good friend to her son, to take care of him throughout the summer.

It was only later, after the coup, that she had discovered that Princess Payal had been unmarried, that Kunal had been born out of wedlock and had spent most of his life hidden away. Esha supposed it had been her position as the ambassador's young daughter that had allowed her to be his playmate for a summer.

She had never dwelled on it, thinking her friend had been dead for all these years, but now?

Kunal drew back, alarmed, his eyes fading to amber, and raised a hand to his temple.

"You have shape-shifter blood," she whispered. "How could I have forgotten?"

He said nothing, staring at her. Esha grabbed his arm and dragged him into the shadows of the jungle, where Rakesh couldn't see them if he woke.

"What are you talking about?"

Esha doubled back in shock. He didn't know?

"Kunal, you're a Samyad. You have royal blood, shape-shifter blood, from the gods."

"No," Kunal laughed. His face fell when he caught her eye. "No," he said more firmly.

"You've never felt like something was constantly caged inside? Something you had to control for fear of letting it out?" Esha said, recalling how Harun had described being a shape-shifter, the fire before he turned into his animal form.

Kunal's face drained of color.

"You're a Samyad, Kunal. Do you realize the danger you're in? The rebels are on the way. Even my prince—if he finds out you have Samyad blood, he will never let you leave."

Many nobles had claimed some Samyad blood through-out the years in an attempt to build rebellions against Vardaan, but now Kunal was the only true living descen-dant of the deceased Queen Shilpa. He had the best claim to the throne, even if he didn't want it. She grabbed his arm, shaking it, trying to get him to understand. "Your hopes and dreams for your life? Gone."

Kunal shook his head.

"I'm just a soldier."

"Wake up, Kunal. Your mother was murdered along with the other Samyad royal family—your family. You are the only living direct descendant of Queen Shilpa. You are a threat to Vardaan—his enemies will want to have you on their side to bolster their claim to the throne. And you will become a pawn. A very valuable one."

"This is ridiculous. Even if it was true, I wouldn't want

any part of it—Jansa is meant to be a queendom," he said.

"It's not just about the throne, Kunal. The *janma* bond, you know it's broken. You've seen the drought and the dying land. The Blades have been desperately looking for a solution, but we're not the only ones. I've been in contact with the best scholars in Mathur to see if there's a workaround having a Samyad woman and Himyad man for the renewal ritual," she said, pausing. "Your family were the keepers of Jansa's bond with the gods. There's a chance you could use your blood to stem the spread of the drought. It won't solve the problem, but it might help."

"My family?" he said quietly. "My powers?"

Kunal stood still in the breeze and though he stared at her, he didn't seem to see her.

Didn't seem to notice the way his body was vibrating, as if barely contained. His eyes flashed, yellow and gold, gold and fire.

"Kunal," she said, her voice insistent. "Listen to me."

"No," he whispered. "You're wrong. It's impossible. My mother—"

Fury shot up Esha's veins as she looked at him, worry a close companion. She had to show him, prove to him what he was.

Esha pushed him away, causing him to stumble backward and finally look at her, really look at her. She could see the battle raging in his eyes, as he decided whether to believe her.

She just needed to show him, but how?

CHAPTER 46

Kunal struggled to take in what Esha was saying. It was as if his body and mind had gone numb.

"My uncle said I needed to learn control because I was weak, too emotional."

"Your uncle?" she asked. He blanched, having realized what he'd revealed. "The general," Esha breathed. "I had forgotten that your father was his brother."

Kunal saw the way her face clouded over, as if she was torn between shock, dismay, and—regret?

"This whole time—I never knew. Taking me back was about more than just becoming commander, wasn't it?" she asked quietly. "The general was your family."

He stared at her for a beat. "I wanted to honor his memory, but there was so much I didn't know about him."

"But he took you in. How he must have hated that his own brother had fallen in love with a Samyad princess," she said, almost to herself. Her expression shifted and she reached for him, grasping his arms. "Kunal, your emotions make you who you are. You *are* the son of Princess Payal. Own your birthright."

"My mother was a lady-in-waiting; it's why we spent time in the summer palace, away from Gwali. We kept the house maintained for her visits."

Even as he said it, he knew, in that darkest of places within the heart, that Esha's words could be true. The queen had visited only twice in his six years at the palace, and then she had come without her personal court.

He felt that fire, the exact feeling Esha had described, growing within him. His uncle had always said that his anger was the only becoming emotion for a soldier—that the others required fierce control, temperance.

This time he didn't control the emotions. He didn't control the confusion, pain, grief, or *fury* at the idea that everything he had known about his family might be a lie. Instead, he let them settle under his skin. And in that space, he felt something else rear its head.

Grief, so deeply entrenched that it felt like an ocean in itself, engulfed him as he thought of his mother's voice. And without the tight leash on that grief and those memories—

He remembered.

A whisper of laughter, the tinkles of bells.

Being bowed to as a child before the servant was made to stop.

The stories and songs of the Samyad dynasty he knew as a child.

The clarity with which he remembered his mother's face, as radiant as the sun. Her firm voice when commanding their guards to blockade the door the night of the coup and take Kunal away. She had sat on the throne as he had been dragged away screaming.

Every single memory of his had been easily answered by his uncle, so he had thought himself crazy.

The son of one of the royals? Ridiculous.

What a tale from such a scrawny boy.

Soon any sort of past life had been beaten out of him and he had let the memories go, believing them the fanciful tales of youth. The price of survival in a new world.

And now Esha was standing there, confirming what he had so long denied. Staring at him with shock and accusation in her eyes.

He didn't want those stories to be true. They would hang on his neck, forcing a new identity on him that he didn't want and couldn't handle right now.

It was all too much.

But if he buried those memories, he'd have to bury those of Esha too. For his time with her as children couldn't be real if the rest wasn't.

Kunal's heart began to tear in two, his mind following soon after, and the rest of his *control* began to dissipate.

It happened all at once, the pain, the scream, the fear, the *pain*.

He was human and then—he was the beast inside.

CHAPTER 47

E sha almost fell back as Kunal turned into an eagle in front of her eyes, not letting go of her.

It was a sight, the way his features slowly turned and his body rose and fell, shifting into its true form. It reminded her of the tales she had grown up with, the gods who took many forms and ruled the skies and earth.

Here those tales were, in vivid detail, a living story of their land and the gifts the gods had given them. It made her want to drop to her knees, to marvel.

But Kunal hadn't let her go.

His fingers became sharp, turned into claws, and she gasped at the pain as they cut into her skin. His clothes tore at the back, his wings unfurling first, the rest of his body following.

The last time she had seen a royal turn into their animal form was that summer, when Princess Payal had left to complete the ritual. But she hadn't been this close, so close she could see the irises of Kunal's eyes widen and feel his body racked in silent pain as if someone was tearing him apart from the inside.

In the blink of an eye, she was wrapped in the wings of a giant eagle and soaring up, hitting every tree branch in sight. The jungle around them was a blur of green, sunlight weaving in and out.

Another tree branch appeared in their vision, ramming into Kunal, and Esha. The breath went out of her and she gasped as she saw spots.

Her fingers slipped and she was falling, hurtling to the ground as she bit down on a scream.

The rush of wings sounded against the air and Kunal caught her.

They landed on the ground with a jerk, tumbling to a stop.

Esha gingerly got up to her knees, checking her scratched-up elbows for any worse damage. To her left, Kunal was on the ground in human form, a shivering, cursing mess. His clothes were torn where his wings and shoulders had grown, revealing the gleaming bronze armor underneath.

Esha crawled over and grabbed his hand. His shifting eyes settled at the sight of her, turning back to their normal amber.

"You're a royal, Kunal," she whispered, holding his hand as his body continued to shudder.

Esha thought back to the general's final words, of his nephew. The love in them.

He must have known about his blood; otherwise, why had he spent years trying to instill in him the need for control? The general could've easily turned him in—as a direct descendant of Queen Shilpa, bastard or no, he would've been important to Vardaan. Instead, he had spent a decade raising his nephew, protecting his secret.

Now it was on her.

"Your uncle lied to protect you," she said. Kunal's eyes searched her own, and she could sense the war going on in his heart. "Whatever else he has done, he also protected you all these years."

Esha brought him to his feet and let him lean on her as they walked back to the clearing with Rakesh. By now, anyone nearby would know something had happened here by the noise alone. She could only hope no one had seen him turn.

People would kill for what he was, the power of the Samyad blood in his veins, if they knew.

She had thought of him a few times since the drought had started, the Samyad boy who had been one of her first true friends, but she had thought him dead. And his blood dead with him.

He said nothing. Not then and not during the journey. It was as if the turning had caused all the fire, and speech apparently, to go out of him. Esha waited, trying to be patient and give him time to process.

They arrived in the clearing and Rakesh was where they had left him, still unconscious, the waist sash tight against his wound. Kunal caught her by the shoulders, stopping her before she could reach him.

Kunal turned her around to face him, taking her hands in his own. They were battered and cut up where his claws had been, much like her own. He winced as he saw the deep punctures he had left as he had turned.

"I'm sorry," he said quietly. She tilted her head.

"Kunal—"

"How was I to know? I believed my uncle. Every word, every lie. I know so much more now, but I still feel as if I know nothing. I cannot possibly be a royal, even a bastard, yet when I turned I felt free, Esha," he said, his voice breaking.

"You need to leave," she said. The hurt in his eyes was almost too much for her. "The rebels are on their way and after that commotion, they'll know exactly where we are."

"I'm not leaving you. And I still have so many questions."

"Go live your life, soldier. Be free. If you stay here you will become a prisoner. In more than one way."

"Esha, I—"

Everything she touched turned to dust as the Viper. She wouldn't let it happen again.

Esha shoved him away from her, pushed his dragging feet into the brush, his already torn clothes catching on branches.

"Go!" she hissed.

She picked up the sheathed knife of his that had fallen to the ground and hurtled it at him. He ducked and caught it easily, his eyes turning dark.

A rustle breezed through the leaves and branches behind her, and Esha froze.

And a voice she hadn't heard in weeks.

"Need some help there, Viper?"

The rebels had arrived.

CHAPTER 48

Kunal looked at her in confusion, hearing the voice seconds after her head snapped around. He recoiled as it hit him.

The rebels.

He didn't have much time to think. His feet took off toward the forest, but he didn't get far before an arrow punctured his bicep and a bundle of limbs and clothes shot out from behind Esha and flew into him, tackling him to the ground.

The burly boy flying at him landed a hard blow to the side of Kunal's head and the world around him danced in black spots.

Esha's voice sounded like a cloud, distant and far away. "Stop! Bhandu, stop it. I don't need your help."

Kunal tried to lift his head only to be smacked back down into the forest ground. His teeth chattered in his skull and the black spots returned, accompanied by purple and blue bursts of color. Lines of pain ran down his back where his wings had been and the rocks dug into them, making him grit his teeth in agony.

He didn't try to lift his head again, rolling it to the side so he had a better line of sight. Two archers but they looked the same.

Was he seeing double? No, twins. They were lined up behind Esha and she was fighting with someone he couldn't see.

Kunal flicked his eyes up, trying to stay still and keep the pain at bay.

The boy on top of him had pinned him with massive hands that were tattooed up to his wrists. A Jansan brand for war prisoners—only administered by soldiers.

Kunal sensed the danger he was in, and it tasted like metal and rust, blood coating the inside of his mouth. He coughed, sputtering out a trail of blood.

"You'll be fine, pretty eyes," the boy on top of him said, squinting at him curiously. "What were you doing having a knife thrown at your head by our Viper?"

Kunal said nothing.

The boy's eyes raked over his face. "No surprise at hearing that she's the Viper. That's dangerous." He leaned in close, whispering in his ear. "No one knows the identity of our lovely lady without forfeiting their life." The boy's face broke into a broad grin. "That doesn't necessarily mean we'll kill you, though."

Kunal merely stared at the boy, unable to respond even if he had wanted to. The wound in his arm had started burning and he bit on his tongue to dull the pain. The boy chuckled, fingering the edges of the sheathed knife in Kunal's belt.

"Nice knife. Even though it's Jansan made." He began inspecting the rest of Kunal's body and outfit, making comments. Kunal ignored him, straining to hear Esha's conversation in the background. It was faint, but Kunal could make it out.

"I had it under control." Esha's voice was tight.

"Really?" The sardonic reply was in a man's voice, deep and lilting. "We were checking the eastern part of the jungle when we heard a huge noise here and turned around. Good thing we did."

"Do you not see the soldier on the ground, bleeding out? I can take care of myself."

"I see that. I also saw another man that you were standing pretty close to. You know we'll have to kill him. He's seen too much at this point, which is regrettable." He paused. "You normally would have done that yourself. We'll keep this soldier to question, but get rid of the man Bhandu is holding down." Footsteps moved toward him, getting louder by the second.

Bhandu shifted, and Kunal struggled to move, fear overtaking the pain holding him down. Bhandu began to tug out his knife and Kunal wiggled an arm up, wrenching his shoulder around when he was pushed back down. Bhandu's eyes widened as his fingers brushed the smooth line of Kunal's armor, now peeking through the torn cloth on his chest.

"Uh, I don't think he's just a man," Bhandu said. "He's a—" Kunal heard a quick intake of breath from Esha as she interrupted Bhandu.

"He's a soldier," she said quickly. Her voice became terse, as if annoyed. "I don't kill every person I meet, especially if they might have valuable information. I left him alive because I managed to turn him."

The footsteps stopped and Kunal felt himself relax, enough to let his cheek rest on the ground again. He'd let Esha talk and when he could, he'd try to escape. When it didn't feel like he was being pinned down by fire.

"And how did you do that?"

Kunal didn't like that tone.

Esha didn't seem to either. "I have my methods for turning assets, Harun. You don't get to question them when you're never out in the field."

Her words made the archers behind her tense up and move away. Even the boy on top of him cocked an ear.

Esha took a deep breath, the sharpness in her voice becoming calmer. "I always complete my missions. I always get it done. My way."

A sigh.

"Yes, you do. It's been a rough couple of days, wondering if we would get to you first."

"You needn't have worried. I always make it home."

Kunal felt his heart squeeze behind the haze of pain that

was descending on him. Fear gripped him. This was no natural pain.

Kunal blinked up at the sky, wondering why it felt like the ground was disappearing and pain had become every inch of his body. It burned, the wound in his arm burned. Slowly, the color in the world around him began twisting in swirls.

The boy on top of him looked at him, his smirk turning to a frown. He heard shuffling footsteps, and chestnut eyes appeared above him, looking down with worry.

In the distance, he heard shouted words.

"What in the Moon Lord's name did you do, Bhandu?"

"Nothing, I didn't do—"

"It's the poison, Esha," the deep, mysterious voice said.

He heard a low growl and the world faded to black.

CHAPTER 49

She saw red—vivid, raging, furious red.

Her fist slammed into Harun's side and he yelped, jumping back in pain. Bhandu was wagging a finger in front of Kunal's face, slapping him without any gentleness.

"How could you? Poison?"

Harun looked at her in confusion, but his eyes were keen. He straightened to his full height, towering over Esha. She didn't back down an inch. "Why do you care? He's just a soldier."

"A soldier we can get information from, Harun. And when did we start using poison? It's a dirty trick. A soldier's trick. We make that decision together, or not at all."

Esha gave Harun a pointed look and he had the decency to look a little sheepish. He might be the prince, but she was the Viper. They each had their role and this wasn't a dictatorship.

One of the twins flicked a long lock of silky straight hair from his eyes. "Seems fitting, then, doesn't it?" he said.

Esha tried to calm herself. She had to tread carefully. Maybe a dash of honesty would work.

"Normally, I would be all for it. But this might undo all the work I put in to turn him. He came here to warn me about the other soldier in pursuit." She gestured at Kunal, trying to school her face at the sight of him unconscious.

Half-lies but also half-truths.

Harun shifted in his position, folding his arms across his torso. The breeze lifted and played with the edge of the thin uttariya tied around his forehead to keep back his long black hair.

"How did you manage to turn him?" His expression was blank but the words weren't idle. Esha felt the danger and evaded carefully, slapping away his words with a flick of her wrist.

"Later. What matters is I got it done and I even managed to find a potential turncoat for us. A Fort *soldier*. That is, if you don't kill him and waste my weeks of work."

He stared her down, his dark eyes thoughtful and probing. It was a gaze that would have a normal girl blushing in her sandals.

Thank god she wasn't one. She had practiced for years to be able to get past that stare of his.

Finally, he laughed, and the tension in the forest clearing lifted.

"Only you would convince the enemy to turn. Well, if

he's good enough for you, we'll give it a chance. Lift him up, Bhandu. We'll take him back and patch him up." She glared at him. "It's a mild poison. Hallucinogenic. Painful. But won't cause death in the dose we gave."

Esha bit her tongue in frustration. She had revealed too much.

Harun's gaze told her he thought the same, so she changed the subject.

"Why are you even out in the field?" she asked. Bhandu struggled with Kunal behind them, gesturing at the twins to come help him. She tried to avoid looking at Kunal, knowing Harun was watching her closely. "Why didn't you send Arpiya?"

The question was twofold—she needed to know what had been so important to draw Harun out of the palace and she missed her friend. She had hoped to see Arpiya today.

"I did used to go out in the field more, you know. Just recently with my father's worries and night terrors increasing . . ."

"I know." She laid a hand on his forearm, a small reassurance. He looked at it, then her, something softening across his sharp features. "How is the search for Reha going, by the way? Any progress?" She ventured the question with a tentative smile, her eyes focusing in on him, looking for any wayward expression.

Harun shook his head. "Nothing promising yet. There are more teenage girls out there than you'd think." A flash of despair crossed his face despite the humorous tone of his words. "And Arpiya wanted to come, but I asked her to stay back and keep training the new recruits. Without you around to scare them witless, it's been slow going," he said, with that languid smile of his that always made her grin back.

Harun seemed to be truthful, his expression open and almost vulnerable.

He hesitated. "And I wanted to get you. I can't tell you what it's been like. You killed the general, Esha. A victory for the scrolls. And then everything went wrong—you had to change course, there was no communication, and we found out you were being pursued from Tana." Harun closed his eyes for a moment. "I was worried. I wanted to make sure you were safe."

She looked up at him, her tight posture relaxing a bit as she understood. "I never asked you to worry about me."

A look of hurt crossed his face. "And yet here we are. I can't help it." He cleared his throat. "I worry about all my recruits. And you're my greatest asset. We have another performance coming up for a new group of nobles, as you requested."

Esha let it slide. A nice save.

She nodded.

"I'm a little rusty, but I can practice a bit before the performance. I have some ideas. We can talk more at the base," she said, throwing him a smile.

Usually, Bhandu was the spot of light in their small band of rebels.

Esha could always rely on him to have a joke or witty comment on hand. But now, his jokes grated against her skin like sandpaper and his witticisms made her want to cover her ears. All she could think about was the unconscious boy thrown over Bhandu's shoulder.

She couldn't even look back because Harun was watching her like he was waiting for her to slip and reveal something—she didn't even know what at this point.

So many secrets were now nestled in her chest.

They hadn't seen Kunal's shifting—yet Esha still felt a sense of unease.

The sky above them flashed with lightning, teasing the coming of the storm. By her calculations, it was about fifteen minutes out from where they were. That's how much time they'd have to get across the pass before it flooded or border soldiers caught sight of them.

It was monsoon season.

No Dharkan took the monsoons lightly. Water could be as treacherous as the other elements—slow, calculated, unforgiving. It could renew and give life and snatch it away in the next moment.

And now she had another life on her hands. It was an odd feeling. Death had been her companion for so long that life seemed fragile—easily broken.

Bhandu's voice pierced her haze of thoughts. He was

fighting with Harun. Again.

"We should take the low pass. I can't carry this load of muscle and bones through the high pass," Bhandu said, his voice strained.

"Don't be so lazy. And I don't mind if you knock him around a few rocks here and there," Harun replied, his words dry as the Jansan soil. "More to the point, the high pass will be quicker and we don't have much time to get through to the other side before the rains start."

"You wouldn't let me cut off that other soldier's finger and send it back to their Blood Fort," Bhandu whined, trying another tactic. The lone horse, a gelding, the team had brought had Rakesh thrown over it, still passed out, though this time it was from Bhandu's draft. The twins pulled on the gelding's reins.

Esha whipped around, glaring at both Bhandu and Harun.

She pointed at Bhandu. "You need to stop whining, it's giving me a headache." Bhandu threw her a wounded look. "Why do we have you around if not for your big, brawny muscles? I picked you out from rest of the lot during that wrestling match for a reason. You've beaten every black-smith in Mathur."

There, a smile. Esha knew how to play Bhandu like an instrument, strumming him with compliments. Harun was harder.

She faced him. "And you, you couldn't have brought another cursed horse? You knew we'd have at least one body." Bhandu snickered. Harun didn't flinch from her stare.

"But Harun's right." Esha sighed, ignoring Bhandu's pout. "We take the high pass over the hills or we get washed away in the rains or one of the waterfalls. You know what happened to the Green Squad, Bhandu."

"Yes, I do." He hefted Kunal again, readjusting him on his shoulder. "I'll listen to her. Don't think I'm listening to you, oh Prince Harun."

Harun rolled his eyes, easing his crossed arms apart. "No, never that." He glanced at Esha, his eyes insistent. "We'd probably all be better if we listened to Esha."

An apology, then. It was the only kind she would expect from Harun. She barely acknowledged it, meeting his eyes for a moment before breezing past him.

The twins, Aahal and Farhan, watched it all with mild interest, their sharp-boned, thin faces darting between the three of them. They weren't as identical as they looked at first glance.

Aahal's face was narrower and his nose longer, vaguely aquiline. Farhan was slightly shorter and always had an eyebrow slightly raised, as if the world never failed to amuse him. Both had matching expressions of curiosity as they folded themselves around her, falling in step with her after tossing the gelding's reins to Harun.

Farhan spoke first.

"Why did you move up the meet? Harun didn't tell us

much, just that we had to come retrieve you sooner than we had thought—"

"—which seemed pretty bad," Aahal added.

Esha released a weary sigh. The twins were never ones for small talk. She rubbed the point between her eyebrows, gritting her teeth.

"Thanks, boys. Appreciate the vote of confidence. I just got to the border sooner. And didn't Harun warn you guys to stop doing that finishing each other's sentences thing?"

They exchanged looks.

"Sure, he told us," Aahal said, a twinkle in his eyes. "But he tells us lots of things."

"Anyway, you're our squad leader. He might be prince and all, but we listen to you first and foremost," Farhan said, with a firm nod of his head.

The words warmed her and she could feel herself relaxing. She stopped rubbing her brow, instead looping her arms around both of them awkwardly, as they were much taller than her. She pulled them into a quick hug and let go just as quick. Their expressions were of matching bewilderment but they said nothing.

Esha cleared her throat, trying to find the words to explain.

"It's good to see you again. To see my team again. It's been a confusing, difficult couple of weeks."

"But you killed General Hotha. You struck a huge blow to that traitor on Jansa's throne."

Aahal's response was fierce, and Esha understood the ferocity on a visceral level. The general had burned down the twins' village with all of the families still in their beds. The twins had been out, sneaking around with their friends. Their guilt had never left them.

They spoke of her rarely, but a drunken night had revealed that they used to have a little sister.

Esha felt a flash of pain in her heart. She might have had one too—her mother was pregnant at the time of the coup.

"The General saw his own death."

Esha's mouth was a grim line. At least that wasn't a lie.

Once this was cleared up, she would tell them the truth. But until then, she would hold it close to her, until she had more answers. She knew what she had to do.

The slope was steeper here and she could hear the faint wheezes of their lungs as they climbed higher. At least being chased had kept her in shape.

Pride shone in Aahal's eyes but Farhan's eyes were quieter, not shouting in happiness like his brother's.

"Harun wasn't happy you left the whip," he said quietly, glancing back to Harun to make sure he wasn't listening. Farhan tugged at his hair, tucking back escaped strands. He was breathing through his mouth now, clearly feeling the incline. The long, lean lines of the twins bent and unbent with a lanky grace that Esha envied.

"Oh?" Esha asked, her words breathy as she pumped her legs. She had told the team in her message days ago that she had left the whip.

Farhan shrugged. "He thought you'd blow your cover."

Esha held back a cough.

It annoyed her that Harun had been right, even if he didn't know it. But she felt her heart ease a bit. Harun betraying her would make no sense, but she was glad to have the reassurance that he hadn't either way.

The rest she'd reveal to them in person, just in case. The reactions of her team, and the rest of the rebels, would be key to her ferreting out any traitors over the next week.

Anger was good.

Aahal shook his head quickly, his hair swishing across the sharp planes of his face.

"He has to look out for everyone." He shot an annoyed look at his brother, who had never been as enamored with Harun as he was.

Aahal turned back to her, a sheepish look on his face. "And hate to say it, but you did allow two soldiers to get on your trail."

If only he knew all of it. She had jeopardized herself, her identity, and the rebels. She hadn't even told them the truth about the general's death. How could she have known that meeting one boy on one night could change everything?

The randomness of fate once again struck her as being the ultimate cruelty and blessing of the gods. It seemed Kunal truly was her tiger at midnight, there to collect on her missteps.

The old folktales never lied.

"You also accomplished something each of us have

dreamed of doing a hundred times over," Aahal added, his smile so contagiously warm she couldn't help but grin back.

"Thanks, you two."

Aahal eyed her. "Are you going to hug us again?"

Esha grinned wildly. "Do you want me to?"

Aahal opened his mouth to respond but Esha had already jumped on his back, flipping him onto his side and holding him down in a headlock.

"Going to complain about my hugs now? Huh?"

Farhan fought against her hold but she held him tighter until he found an opening and elbowed her. Esha doubled over and he took the moment to escape her arms. He smiled triumphantly at her, even though dust streaked the back of his cotton pants, and his waist sash was undone and dragging in the dirt.

Harun appeared by her side, offering his free hand. She swatted him away.

"All in good fun," she said happily. "I've been alone for a while."

She turned toward Harun as Farhan reached to fix his brother's waist sash.

"Indeed." Harun gave her a pointed look. It made Esha's body tighten with familiarity and she turned away abruptly.

Bhandu was pulling up behind them, Kunal over one shoulder. The horse carrying Rakesh trailed behind, moving faster as Harun tugged at the slack rope.

"Did someone get attacked?" Bhandu asked.

"What happened to pig boy?" Esha asked at the same time.

Rakesh seemed to have gathered layers of dirt since they had started their journey. Bhandu snorted.

"Pig boy. I like that. He keeps falling over." Bhandu glared at Harun's back. "I wanted to leave him behind. Dead weight. Literally. We are going to kill him, right? After we get information?"

Harun shrugged, his dark eyes unreadable. His jaw showed the beginnings of a beard, one that he hadn't been wearing when Esha had left. It complemented the strong angles of his jaw and made him look more like his father, King Mahir.

Esha had always found him attractive, but the last vestiges of boyhood had melted from his face, leaving behind a young man who had become harder to decipher than her old friend.

"Probably. Let's see what we can do with him first."

"And then kill him?" Bhandu was like a cat with a mouse.

"Eventually," Harun said.

Esha watched it all with a faint smile. She had missed them. This was her family. Her eyes drifted back to Kunal, his face slack in poison-induced sleep. Faint purple tendrils curled around his temples, reaching down to his eye like grasping tentacles.

She looked up only to see Harun, who, of course, had been watching her.

"What's happening to him?" she asked, trying to keep her voice casual.

Harun paused, and she knew he was deciding how much to tell her.

Moon Lord's fists, after everything they had been through, this was how he repaid her? Mistrust? She knew she was hiding things from him, but *he* didn't know that. She should be owed good faith.

He seemed to have reached the same conclusion. His face opened up and she could read him again. "It's just the beginning stages. If we woke him, he'd be in faint pain and feel nauseated but nothing more. But we'll need to get him back quickly. We can administer the antidote in small doses when we arrive."

Esha couldn't control her reaction. "*You didn't bring the antidote?*" she seethed. The twins looked over, aware of the danger in her voice. "What if one of us had gotten hit instead?"

Harun scoffed. "The twins never miss—"

Esha cut him off. "This isn't about them. I know they're spectacular." She threw them a sweet smile and Farhan blushed. "This is about you putting us in danger, however unlikely."

He looked back at her, a small frown forming.

"I didn't do it on purpose, Esha. We'll get him back in time, and if you hadn't noticed—we're all fine." Harun moved closer to her, his voice dropping low so that the others strained to hear. He placed his hand on her elbow. "Are you sure there isn't something else going on here?"

She shook her head a bit too hard. What did he want her to say? That somewhere in her cold Viper heart, this enemy of theirs mattered to her? It was laughable. But Harun knew her, and she wouldn't be able to avoid his probing for long. Just for now.

The lie came easily.

"No, I just don't want anything to happen to my team."

His hand was still warm on her arm and she wanted to lean into it, tell him everything, as she always did, just to have someone to tell. But instead, she moved away. They continued the trek up from the Mauna Valley to the rebels' hidden pass.

This valley was known to be one of the most beautiful and magical places in Jansa outside of the Tej. A place where deep ravines met thick, grassy fields, where elephants and tigers lapped at the water streams together at dawn, oblivious to humanity. She had only ever seen a peacock, and those cursed howler monkeys, in her visits so far.

Puffs of breath led the way as they left the valley, the air turning thinner as they approached the highest point of the lowest peak in the Ghanta Mountains. A low cloud, supernatural by the light gold color, enveloped them as they climbed, its soft chill wrapping them in its embrace, turning everything into a light fog.

These clouds always drifted over the Ghanta Mountains, though no one could agree on whether they were elemental spirits or those of the mountain gods.

She turned her head, straining her neck to see if she

could catch a glimpse of the Aifora Range to the north. It was rumored that at the right time, on the right day, the highest peak of the Aifora Range would turn a shimmering, burnished gold and those who saw it would be blessed for the remainder of their lives.

The myths also said the tallest mountain of the Aifora Range, Mount Bangaar, was shrouded in chilled gold clouds that led up to the home of the gods. The bottom of the mountain was a site for holy pilgrimage, or at least it had been before the war had started. Now the path taken by thousands through history was blocked off by border patrols.

Another thing the Pretender King had ruined.

They emerged from the cloud soon enough, frost coating the ends of Farhan's hair and the tips of Aahal's long eyelashes. Harun seemed unaffected except for a small shiver, having given the gelding's reins back to the twins.

Bhandu bounded out, Kunal still dangling from his huge arms.

"That was refreshing," he said, smiling toothily at everyone.

His ears were poking out slightly and the faint sheen on his broad forehead had almost frozen in place. He raised his arm to his head and dropped the reins to the gelding with Rakesh, allowing the horse to whinny and rear up, causing Rakesh to fall.

"Oops." Bhandu stared down at Rakesh, who had landed in a heap, not a whit of remorse on his face.

The moment was so painfully typical of Bhandu—so

lighthearted amid all the dark she had been in—that Esha burst out laughing. Bhandu beamed at her, though he also looked confused.

His eyes darted to her face as he carefully placed Kunal on the ground, before kneeling next to Rakesh and poking him. She couldn't remember the last time she had laughed—not in mockery, not with a smirk, but out of pure joy. Esha let herself be warmed by the sound and crouched down to help Bhandu drag the soldier to his feet.

They had climbed up the mountain, gotten through the clouds, and now all that was left was to descend. Then she would be home.

CHAPTER 50

They were caught by the rain as soon as they got to the base of the other side of the Ghanta Mountains.

Silence fell between them, crackling with unspoken words and orders. They had done this so many times—spoken, fought, schemed together—that words weren't necessary.

The monsoon was ingrained in all of their blood, its melody, harmony, and percussion. They rushed through the damp and squelching mud at the base of the path, slipping and sliding through it like snakes.

Esha took the lead through the mud and low-hung branches of the tight jungle that lined the path, able to easily scout out any obstacles with her slight frame and quick movements. Harun and Bhandu were safe in the middle, and the twins took up the back, each armed with their matching curved longbows and arrows, nocked and ready.

They were like a well-oiled door, working seamlessly at its purpose without ever drawing notice. They finally broke out of the forest and Esha stopped, overcome by the sight in front of her.

The city of Mathur was majestic in the evening twilight, an exquisite painting against the rough wilderness of the Ghanta Mountains and the bright green jungle nestled along its base.

Curved sandstone buildings wrapped around the towering white marble palace at the center of the city. To the east the river wove through the city, carving it in two. Mathur was surrounded and protected by nature since its birth, with fortifications carved into the taller slopes of the Ghanta Mountains to the west and towers peeking out of the thicket of jungle that bordered the city to the east.

Stars dotted the sky like jewels on a scabbard, the moon casting its loving light over it all, illuminating the city against the peaks of the Aifora Range in the far distance.

It was home, and this was what she was fighting for.

They hadn't passed any rebel guards on the path on their way back. And there had been no border soldiers lurking about. She would have to talk to Harun about that later—it seemed Tana's information had been right.

But for now, she feasted her eyes on the city below.

Harun drew up behind her. She knew it was him without looking—the scent of the almond oil he always wore preceded him, his warmth welcome in this moment.

"Beautiful, isn't it?"

Esha nodded.

"Welcome home," he said softly, putting a calloused hand on her shoulder.

She smiled, breathing in the air.

CHAPTER 51

K unal felt coolness against his temples, and he hungered for it.

Inside, he burned. Every edge and curve and point within his body hurt and scorched with a depth that was endless in its misery.

Words croaked out of a dry throat. Had he asked for more?

But the coolness was gone.

A halo of light appeared.

No, someone. Gentle hands. They helped fight the tide of fire in his body. At the edge of his vision he saw purple. His hands were purple, tainted with something he could feel moving in his blood. Faint, in the back of his mind, he remembered the word—*poison.*

The Viper.

Esha.

The same. They had poisoned him. Was that it? His thoughts came in and out, broken fragments and specks of anger and pain.

He was in a dark, dank dungeon. The walls and floor were cool and he had lain against them. He didn't know for how long.

The cool hands had lifted him up.

Now they tilted his mouth open and blissfully frigid liquid poured down the furnace that was his throat. He gulped it down, thirsting for more. But no more came.

"You can only have a little at a time, Kunal."

The voice was kind, gentle.

He tried to speak, to say no, bring more, don't go away, I want more, stay with me. But no sound came out of him.

The halo hovered over him and he reached out. Warm, soft skin. The halo gasped, a soft one, almost imperceptible if his every sense hadn't been magnified by the heat.

She reached out, stroking her fingers against his cheekbones and across his jaw.

His eyes cleared, just a bit, the fog lifting.

Esha was crouched down in front of him, dipping a thin cloth in a small metal bowl of liquid. She wrung it out and turned to him but he recoiled, scooting back and away from her.

He was angry at her and he didn't know why.

Hurt flashed across her eyes.

It hurt him too, a sharp pang in his left side. What had she done?

The fog came back up, swirling and threatening, over-coming his senses so that he was fire and smoke. He didn't want to go. Reached for her.

The last thing he saw was her face.

CHAPTER 52

The shift happened so quickly Esha almost wasn't prepared, her thoughts preoccupied with replaying how he had recoiled from her. How much hatred had been in his eyes.

Was that how he truly felt about her when all artifice was gone? Did he blame her for this? His capture, the poison. It wouldn't have been her choice.

The turning was ferocious, claws snapping at her, his skin tearing open at his back. Like lightning, he turned back and forth as if his body didn't know which form could take the pain coursing through its blood.

Esha pulled as close as she could without coming under attack. She whispered to him, soft and slow, stories of their childhood, holding a hand out.

He stopped flipping bodies like the flickering flame of

a candle, calming as Esha herself calmed. The pain in her chest eased as he turned human, and stayed that way.

She shook her head. The soldier. Her lemon boy. A Samyad prince.

It wouldn't matter that he couldn't sit on the throne or might not be able to perform the renewal ritual any better than Vardaan. Though he was a Samyad, he wasn't a woman, and the renewal ritual required a Samyad woman and a Himyad man. A queen and a king.

He would be royalty in name—and cease to become anything else. Her mind whirred at what it might mean for the rebels—was there a possibility he could delay the full death of the land long enough for them to find Reha? She was no scholar, and the gifts of the gods were wild in nature, unpredictable as the seas. But time was running out. Only four moons now remained before the winter solstice and the last renewal ritual.

The scholars hadn't reached any firm conclusion, but there was a chance that his blood could hold back the tide of destruction. It wasn't much, but it was better than nothing. Could she ask that of him? To give up his dreams for his quiet future? If he helped them, he might never see it.

She wrung out the cloth again and put it to his head. Esha was choosing him over all her other loyalties.

So he better survive.

CHAPTER 53

He still burned, but it felt like a dull roar, a deafening of the pain that had racked his body earlier.

Kunal felt more lucid, aware that he was no longer in the dungeon. He was adrift in a sea of silky red-and-gold sheets, ensconced in a large bed with gold lions carved into the bedposts, staring down at him from above.

The purple fog still hung over him, clouding his thoughts and memories. Every inch of his body felt as if someone had stabbed him with careful and detailed precision, and he could tell by the burning in his throat and chest that he hadn't kept down any food.

All he could do was move his head, a nudge, to the side. Enough to see what was making the noise. He was pretty sure it wasn't in his head.

Kunal's eyes strained to look down the room, where

two faint figures stood. Their words were sharp, hot, furious. The passionate tones moved closer.

"You told me it was a mild poison, Harun. You lied to me!"

"You were being unpredictable. I had to get you out of there, otherwise we would've all continued arguing while the rains descended on our heads."

"And you kept him in the dungeons. He was burning with fever and racked with pain when I found him. You gave him a strain of night rose."

It sounded like Esha. The voice was low, dangerous. The other figure moved back suddenly, as if pushed.

"And now you have him up here, in one of my private suites. I don't care if he's a turned asset, until he proves his worth he's an unknown. He's only alive thanks to your grace, and thanks to whatever secrets he might have in his head. A soldier of Jansa being treated like royalty," the male voice spat, traces of venom in his words. "Have they not done enough to us? Think of Sundara."

"If I hadn't gotten him out of there and administered the antidote to him properly, he could've been paralyzed."

"So what?" Something told Kunal that the voice wasn't being truthful. The man sounded less confident. "And it's not your call to have him moved. Esha, I would give you anything, but do you know how that made me look?"

A hiss. A warning.

"I don't care how it looked. You were wrong, Harun.

You promised me. And you broke that promise. Either you trust me or you don't. Don't live in between."

"Then don't undermine my power," he snapped back.

"Don't try and control me. I risk my life on missions, I kill your failures, I ensure we have patrons; what more do you want from me?"

Kunal heard pain in her words and tried to speak, to reach out to her. He hurt too.

The figures were leaning in, the larger one holding the smaller in its arms.

Kunal tried to clear his vision, to focus again.

The smaller figure—Esha? Her head whipped around.

She looked like someone who had hurt him, but he wanted her happy. He didn't know why. Who was she?

"Did you hear that?"

"No, Esha—"

She was at his side in moments, a cool hand on his forehead. He tried to move his lips but the fog thundered back in and she disappeared in smoke.

◄◦►

The third time he awoke, he was more lucid, and it lasted longer.

He was weak, but he no longer burned. A faint screeching sound filtered through his mind and he could raise his hand and pinch the bridge of his nose to block it out.

The entire room was lavishly decorated in vivid tapestries of gold and silk. The vaulted marble ceilings made it look cavernous and he saw that the room was of gray granite.

Last he remembered, he had been in the forest, an arrow in his arm. And Esha had given him up to the rebels. If that was the case, why wasn't he dead?

He lifted himself up onto his elbows. In the corner, a small figure was curled up into a ball on a long brocaded chaise. Esha was wrapped in a thick red blanket.

"She's been here for days."

His head whipped around and he grimaced from the immediate pain. He reached up instantly to massage his neck. The burly boy who had pinned him down sat to the side of his bed, sharpening his curved blade with long slides of a stone.

Now he knew what that sound was. Kunal rubbed the side of his face, his hands scratching through a newly trimmed beard.

"I don't know what's so special about you or why she wanted to keep you alive. I voted to kill you." The boy grinned at him. "Though you seem like you could be brutal in a spar. Do you have training courts at the Fort? Large ones with maces and spears? Archery targets?"

Kunal was too confused to do anything but nod.

Esha had been here for days?

"I hate the Pretender King and all of you Fort soldiers. And pretty much anyone who thinks the Pretender is anything other than a piece of filthy, heaping rubbish," the boy continued.

Kunal focused in on the boy's face—it was interesting, sharp eyes in a broad face. He would've been a great soldier.

He was strongly built, with a thick neck and strong hands.

"Oi—are you eyeing me? I'm sorry to say, but I'd never be interested in a Fort soldier. But yes, if you were wondering, I *could* snap your neck with these hands. I'm the strongest of the team—I even carried you here."

Kunal thought he muttered, *Though I don't know why.* The boy snapped his fingers in front of Kunal's face.

"Do you speak?"

Kunal groggily tried to snap out of the haze of thoughts he had been getting lost in.

"Yes."

It was a horrible sound, as if chalk met sandpaper and dragged against metal. Kunal decided to try a question. The boy seemed talkative enough—maybe he could make a friend despite his protests of hatred.

"How long have I been out?" Kunal thought carefully. "Why am I here?"

The boy raised an eyebrow at him. "I honestly wish I knew the answer to the last one. The other soldier we found is down in the dungeons. But not my place to say. I don't need to get in the middle of whatever spat Esha and Harun are having."

Kunal had meant why this room and not the dungeon, but tucked the nuggets of info away for later. Harun? Kunal had heard the name before and it rankled at the edges of his memory, a sour note in a song.

The boy continued talking. "I can tell you that you've been out for almost a week."

Kunal started at that. A week. A week of his life gone, disappeared into vapor.

"Oi, soldier with the weird eyes."

"They're not weird," Kunal snapped.

The boy grinned, like he was beginning to like Kunal. "You look like a cat with those pale eyes of yours. Cat-eyed. That's what we call people with your color eyes in Dharka."

Kunal shook his head, thinking his nickname could have been much worse.

"Anyway, cat eyes, stop looking at her like that. She doesn't deserve your anger. Without her fighting for you, we would have left you in a dead heap of bones back in the forest. You might be annoyed she revealed you're a soldier, but it's the only thing that saved you—your potential usefulness."

It registered in Kunal as truth, despite the anger and betrayal he had woken up with. It wasn't logical, and he had no ground to stand on, but Kunal still couldn't shake the feeling.

He flicked his head up, rubbing his forehead again.

The boy stared at him, the candor and grins gone, as if he were trying to figure out the secret of Kunal.

Kunal wished he knew too.

CHAPTER 54

Kunal woke from a fitful sleep, plagued by images of a snake with dangerously beautiful chestnut eyes.

Last time he had woken up, there had been vague sounds in the background, low words, soft shuffles of feet. But now there was only silence.

Kunal eased himself into a seated position, muscles screaming as he rubbed his eyes with the heel of his palm. Today was the first day the burning was gone. His muscles still felt like an achy mass of coiled nerves and tissue, but there was no burning. And for that, Kunal could've gotten on his knees and kissed the floor.

Carefully, he scooted out of the bed and tried standing up. The ground held, but his legs wobbled and he fell back heavily on the bed. He winced, feeling pain down his back as if he had been sliced open.

The pain was so different from the burning he had felt

for the past week that he reached around, tracing his shoulder blades with his fingers. Jagged cuts ran down his skin. He paused, his fingers stilling.

His heart seized in terror, the memory coming at him quick.

He had turned into an eagle. In the forest.

The cuts had been sealed with salve, Kunal could tell that much.

It had to have been Esha. Anyone else, and he would be back in the dungeons. She had kept this secret of his, healed his wounds. A warmth spread through him. He couldn't remember the last time he had been tended to that way, not since he had arrived at the Fort.

A surge of affection rose in his heart for Esha, for the kindness behind the mask, the girl behind the Viper. He would have to find a way to thank her for saving him— many times over at this point.

Kunal still struggled to wrap his head around it. Being in Mathur, discovering he was descended from one of the two royal shape-shifting bloodlines.

His mother had been a princess. He was a Samyad. He had never known—he had truly believed that his mother had been a lady-in-waiting. His bedroom hadn't been draped in gold and jewels befitting a prince; he had lived a simple life following his mother and nurse around.

How could he have known as a child?

And his uncle? Kunal remembered what Esha had said, that he must have lied to protect him. Despite everything else he had done, he *had* hid Kunal, given him a new life. But he had also lied to Kunal about the wildness in his blood, broken him down over needing *control*. It would take him time to unravel his tangled feelings toward his uncle.

But for the first time in years, he felt free.

Until he realized he was on foreign soil and in the royal palace of Mathur. Control would be needed more than ever. Kunal wasn't ready to give up his identity when he was just beginning to understand it.

And what had happened to Rakesh? The boy had said he was in the dungeons, but he didn't know more than that. He needed to be careful here. A deep breath helped him refocus his mind, and he looked around to get the layout of the room he was in.

He tried to get up again, leaning heavily against the golden bedpost. Slowly, he felt enough strength to walk, and a package on the chaise at the foot of the bed caught his eye.

It was covered in drab brown packaging with dark red ribbons. A note fluttered onto the bed when he touched the package.

*Soldier, the clothes are for you. The guards will
show you where to go when you've bathed and changed.*

It was signed by the crown prince of Dharka.

The prince of Dharka. In the barracks, they talked of him as clever, sly, and wholly dedicated to his country. His father had kept him away from the army, as he was his only heir, but it was whispered he had the entire court at Mathur in his palm.

Kunal wasn't keen on figuring out what he wanted with him.

Guards, tall and proud, lined the door down the corridor. Each had a longbow at his side and a more immediate short sword hanging from his waist sash. Not one but three valayas were stacked on their wrists and forearms, the sign of the warrior class in Dharka.

He sighed. He was barely strong enough to shuffle across the floor, let alone think of any sort of escape route. And now he knew he was being watched.

Shame swallowed him, defeat not far behind. He had allowed himself to be captured and it prickled at him like a splinter. A novice mistake and one Kunal wouldn't forgive himself for, for some time.

What soldier allowed himself to be so distracted by a girl that he couldn't hear the arrival of a group of rebels?

Now he was in the most beautiful of prisons with people whose soldiers he had killed on the battlefield.

Kunal was expected by the prince of Dharka.

Bath and clothes it was, then.

———◄○►———

The guards were stony-faced to him but jovial, warm, and joking with each other.

Kunal felt queasy. He was in a place where he would

always be "other," where he had no chance of blending in. It felt like it had when he had been six years old and was thrown into the world of the Fort.

Except this was leagues apart, the soldiers joking with their superior officer, with each other. The only person they had a rude look for was Kunal. It was clear these people respected one another, even cared for each other.

Kunal remembered what the boy had said, that Esha's words had saved him, but he couldn't help the rise of resentment against the back of his throat.

This was her home.

She *had* a home, one that held warm people and fond memories.

He didn't remember much from the past week, but there were flashes—a team had come to get her. There had been jokes and laughter and real affection. It made him miss Alok and Laksh fiercely.

Except for those two, Kunal didn't think anyone at the Fort would care to come after him, unless it was on orders. The Fort leadership didn't believe in one for many—if you were lost or captured as a soldier, you were on your own.

There would be no rescue mission for him and Rakesh.

He felt angry at Esha and himself in turns, resentful and yet grateful to even be here, to be alive. He was once again indebted to Esha for saving him, taking care of him when he had been wild. Protecting his secret. He both longed to thank her and wanted to shout in anger that he even had a secret to protect.

It was a confusing mix of feelings, to say the least.

He and the guards shuffled in and out of taller, marble-capped rooms of various colors—coral and indigo and fuchsia—resplendent with vividly textured tapestries and brightly jeweled walls. Everything in this palace was majestic and opulent. Yet it held a warmth, as if inviting a person to fall asleep in its jeweled bosom with sweet stories of the past.

Each tapestry illustrated a different tale from Dharkan history and myth—the churning of the ocean to create the Southern Lands, the crowning of Dharka's first king, Naran. His teachings of compassion, his founding of natak, the art form that blended story and dance and the birth of the five noble houses of Dharka. It was all illustrated across the walls, the palace a living, breathing story in itself.

He could've gotten lost walking through the rooms, drinking in the splendor of each. One of the guards had let it slip that they were going to meet the prince—and now they were moving faster, Kunal struggling behind them, and he didn't want to know what would happen if he fell behind.

Right now, he was being treated like a guest. It worried him more than if he had been in chains. Then he would know where he stood.

Kunal hated being on unknown ground, with no clear plan of action, nothing to assess.

They veered sharply away from the towering height of the halls and into a wing that was even more lavish, jewels encrusted into the very floors. Kunal wouldn't have ever thought it possible.

A memory hit him, of a pink and gold granite room in the old palace. His mother would sing to him there, tell him stories of the bravest warriors of Jansa.

Every inch of this wing was covered in detailed stonework and mosaics. One of the guards whirled around, crooking an annoyed finger at him. Kunal hadn't even realized his feet had slowed, his gaze distracted. He quickened his pace, tugging at his uttariya around his shoulders.

The outfit that had been left for him was grand—a gold-and-white-threaded uttariya, of the finest-cut silk with a jeweled waist sash and a silk dhoti of the most brilliant cerulean blue. He fidgeted, picking at the golden hem of the uttariya as they entered a new room.

Kunal no longer felt out of place with his outfit.

The hall they had entered was resplendent with color. Bright swaths of silk and gold gauze hung from the ceiling, jewels dripping from where the fabrics met. Throughout the room were men and women in the most spectacular outfits, rivaling his own.

Silks of the deepest purple and red, pearls from the Far Isles, emeralds from Dharka's caves, dripping gold jewelry, all were on display. Some of the women wore peacock feathers in their hair; others had exquisite braided or curled hair. Even the men shimmered, from their shining, gold-threaded uttariyas to the thick jewels that sat on top of their sandals and knife hilts.

The courtiers were chattering among themselves, parrots in a brightly colored enclosure. Their eyes darted to the door at the right corner of the hall, plain compared to the rest of the space.

Rows of seats lined the hall and Kunal gnawed at his lip, wondering what was going to happen next. He didn't think it was normal to be welcomed this way.

No, he was being sent a clear message.

Kunal understood this—he doubted that the prince of Dharka did anything without a reason. What Kunal really wanted to know was how the prince even knew who he was.

He had been dragged out of the dungeons and placed in a splendid room in the palace—which meant Esha and the rebels were not unknown to the prince. He hadn't seen any of them, except for the burly boy, since the jungle.

Kunal moved into the room, blending into the left row of chairs as much as he could. He stayed close to the door, the only obvious exit in the hall, a habit from years of training. The guards who were flanking the door eyed his movements but didn't stop him.

A hush fell over the crowd so that the barest movement of a silken slipper could be heard.

As if breathing together, the room sighed as a figure entered from the left. It took him a second, but even when Kunal refocused his eyes, he saw the same thing.

That boy—no, a young man, the one who had been in the clearing with him and Esha—he was entering the room, and immediately, the room fell into bows. His outfit was similar to Kunal's but more ornate, each inch of his clothing woven with gold threads, and he was dripping with gold jewelry.

Kunal caught on, mimicking the bow and making his palms meet as he bent, like the others did. Inside, his mind was a whirl.

This young man was the prince? The rebel who had poisoned him? This news could change their relations with the Crescent Blades. He understood why it had been kept a secret. If word got out that the crown prince of Dharka, King Mahir's only heir and surviving child, was behind the infamous rebels—it would put the prince's life at risk. It would also make a truce impossible.

It would be invaluable, strategic information for the Jansan army.

And he wasn't sure he'd give it up.

The Dharkans weren't a faceless enemy anymore. Before, he had lived in a perfect hypocrisy—he had loved Dharkan food, culture, music secretly, but had plotted against and killed them publicly. He could no longer reconcile that person with who he was becoming now.

A shudder of whispers drew him out of his thoughts. From a door to his right, a woman emerged, wearing a short emerald blouse that was encrusted in gold beads, a long, layered gold belt draped over her hips to emphasize their curves. Her armbands glittered with emeralds and diamonds, matching her choker.

Her pants caught his attention. The banded cuffs of her dhoti came halfway up her calf and had some sort of embroidery on them—he couldn't tell what. Her dhoti billowed out as she moved, and she was a song of sensual movement.

She wore a mask of golden filigree edged with green, her hair braided tightly back into a crown and covered with a long, gauzy uttariya trimmed in gold.

When she moved forward, the room held its breath, and she held its gaze with a smile. And as she slid down the room, she threw whispers to the nobles like kisses to a lover.

Whoever she was, she knew how to capture a room.

If this was how Dharkans welcomed their guests, no wonder there was such a crowd. But Kunal knew to look deeper. Why was he here, why now? The pretty courtiers around him were here for a reason. Why was he being allowed to witness this?

The music started like the beginnings of thunder, low and soft, but transformed into a powerful beat. Drums echoed against the corners of the room and the woman swayed, undulating with the rhythm and the harmony.

Now Kunal wanted to avert his eyes because he *did* recognize her.

A crack resounded through the hall and Kunal's eyes grew wide as Esha weaved her whip through the air like a floating ribbon, carefully missing its thin end as she twirled and tumbled across the room, the agile notes of a sitar punctuating her every move.

The drumbeat rose in a frenzy and her movements became faster, and she unfurled her second whip, joining in her dangerous dance. It was a performance of strength, grace, and death.

Kunal couldn't tear his gaze away, and it wasn't simply because it was Esha.

He didn't need to see her eyes to speak the language of her body. It spoke like she did—coy and teasing, yet artful.

Kunal didn't realize he had moved forward until one of the guards glared at him in warning. He pulled back to rest his hands on the back of one of the seats.

The woman in the seat turned to him in annoyance. The momentary diversion had distracted him from Esha, and gasps surrounded him. When he lifted his head, he gripped the back of the seat harder, knuckles turning white.

At the end of the room, Esha was deflecting knives thrown at her with her two whips, a spiral of cloth and air and technique.

It was a breathtakingly beautiful sight, but his gaze darted to the prince, a low fury building in his stomach.

The prince's eyes were already on him. He'd been watching him, watching Esha.

So, that was his game.

Kunal's nostrils flared out and he didn't back down from the stare.

The prince wanted Kunal to see this. To see her be the deadly Viper with adoring fans. Kunal could think of only one reason the prince would do this—to scare him or threaten him.

Why? Why did he matter? What harm was he in a

foreign city where he had no friends, no weapons, and no agency?

Kunal looked away as the applause started, searching through the standing crowd for Esha's gold-and-green mask. Her posture was triumphant, her whip raised with knives scattered around her. But Kunal couldn't see her eyes, and he was suddenly desperate to do so.

The claps slowed and Esha swept into a low curtsy, her knees bending to almost touch the polished stone ground with her hands pressed together. She tossed kisses to the crowd, who were desperately clinging to every step of her leather-clad feet as she moved up to where the prince sat.

The prince watched her, unmoving from his high-backed gold seat. Slithering up the steps of the dais, she took her place beside him, resting her forearm on the arm of his throne.

They looked like a fierce pair. The prince and his Viper.

But something bothered him—Kunal still couldn't figure out why the courtiers were here.

"Welcome, everyone. To start off, thank you to our gracious guest of honor, the Viper herself. Some of you have literally been begging me for several moons to have her attend our parties. I finally convinced her—seems she might believe in our cause as well. Who would've known?" He gave a small laugh and the room tittered with him. The coy smirk on Esha's face didn't budge.

"And I thank you all for joining us. A reminder, though: this is *our* secret," the prince said. "If my father knew I was raising money for the Blades, we'd all be in trouble. You know how he feels about my various 'projects.' Though I do think that peacock fountain was a great idea." A number of the younger nobles laughed and the prince winked at them.

"So, let's keep this between us." He smiled and it made his already striking face shine, like rays of sunlight after a storm. "And if it gets out, well, let's just say I'll know exactly who to look for. Or send our friend here after."

That same smile was still on the prince's face, but now it was razor sharp.

Had the guards moved in closer, or was it just Kunal's imagination? He took a step forward, noticing that many of the nobles were sitting a little straighter in their chairs.

"But on to why we're all here. Now is the time for us to act to overthrow the Pretender King and bring balance back when the cease-fire is still new."

Kunal could've sworn the prince sent him a look as he said those words.

"The Pretender King of Jansa, Vardaan. Our dear king's brother—and my uncle. He took the crown by force, disrupting the natural order of the world. Our brothers and sisters across the mountain are suffering as their land dries up, the river no longer held to their land by the sacred bond." The prince's voice became stronger, commanding. "Do not think he'll be happy with just Jansa. He wants our land too, he will *need* our land soon, and we will not let him take it."

He rose to his feet, his palms outstretched toward the crowd, a yearning look on his face.

"Help the Blades, donate to their cause, and together, we will protect our lands, restore the rightful heir, and find my sister, the lost princess," the prince said, beseeching the crowd. Kunal saw a tear run down the face of the woman who sat in the chair in front of him and had scowled at him.

Sun Maiden's shield, he was good.

And now Kunal understood. It was a brilliant move to find patrons among the nobles and merchants who had lost much from the closure of the borders—no longer able to travel or trade as they liked. Some might even be as loyal to their country as they appeared to be, and this would only strengthen their hearts.

Kunal didn't think he could be a good judge of loyalty anymore.

And sister . . . Princess Reha would be his cousin, wouldn't she? Her mother, the late Queen Gauri, his aunt. The thought was a jolt. He tried not to think about the fact that the prince was his cousin too. It just made him queasy.

He turned to watch Esha, finding himself slowly making his way through the crowd so that he could see her more clearly. Her chin, not covered by the mask, was raised as the prince spoke, and she didn't move an inch.

"—and we will accomplish this. Especially as we have the Viper in our lair."

The prince coiled an arm around Esha and pulled her

into him, a position so intimate that there was no doubt as to what he was implying.

Esha's eyes darted quickly to Kunal's. A look of fury flashed in them, barely perceptible underneath her mask, but the prince's hands held her in place and the flash disappeared as quickly as it had come.

The low fire that had been ignited in Kunal was back with a fervor. And there was—had there been something going on between Esha and the prince?

Kunal rubbed his eyes. He was a teeming pot of anger and confusion. Nothing was making sense to him and he wanted, more than anything, to return to those moments in the jungle where it had been only the two of them.

He wanted it to always be the two of them.

Esha had a tight smile plastered on her face as the prince held her, his fingers playing with the snake bracelets twining up her bare arms. Kunal saw the tensing of Esha's grip on the chair and the murder behind her gaze.

The fire in her eyes worked quite well with the image of the Viper. The prince looked at her quickly and Kunal saw that he knew it too.

Kunal would have to reevaluate this young man. He was more than clever, he was a schemer, and that was infinitely more dangerous.

"—first the general, then Vardaan."

The prince finished speaking and the room erupted in noise, the nobles' excited voices rising. In the din, no one was watching the prince anymore. Kunal realized this was because of the long table laden with food that had appeared in the center of the hall, courtesy of the servants now scurrying out.

But Kunal's eyes hadn't left the pair.

Esha flicked at the prince's fingers and he flinched, removing his hand. The smile dropped from her face and she left the hall in a haze of cloth and fury, leaving an emptiness in her wake.

Kunal strode forward to where she had been, ready to follow her. The guards moved with him and he looked back at them, annoyed, his hand going to a weapon that wasn't at his side.

The prince held up a hand to them and locked eyes with Kunal.

"I would leave her alone," was all he said.

Kunal's vision was blurred with outrage—it made him reckless.

"I'm not the one she's mad at," Kunal bit back. The prince's eyebrows rose, considering him—Kunal didn't miss his slight wince.

The prince shrugged and moved away, telling the guards to stand down with a flick of his hand.

Kunal brushed past the guards and the prince into the hallway outside.

CHAPTER 55

He pushed into Esha's room after catching up with her, ignoring the clear message conveyed by its shut door. Esha sat in a corner, her uttariya tossed to the ground, her head in her hands.

Something in Kunal's heart had flipped. He wanted to blame her for the pain he had endured for the past week, for taking away his freedom, but he had made every decision that had led him to being stuck behind enemy lines.

And he had seen that the life she had wasn't wholly her own either. She needed someone as much as he had—as he did. And she had saved him. He understood the prince's warning now.

Esha had saved him and the prince was anything but pleased.

He entered the room, shutting the door behind him.

The creaking gave him away and Esha's head shot up, her mouth a grim line.

"You don't have to do this," he said, moving in closer to her. Slowly, as to not frighten her away. Kunal was about to say more, explain, when she jumped up and started moving frantically, pulling at her pinned hair and clothes. Apparently, she had understood him well enough.

"What do you know? The Himyad royals took me in when I had lost everything. When I was nothing," she said, her voice emotionless.

"You don't owe them your life because they saved yours once."

"Don't I?"

The hopelessness in the question sent a dagger into his throat and deeper into his soul. It was a question he had whispered to himself over and over when he had been younger. It was the question that had led him here, drove him to pursue Esha at all costs.

Esha was avoiding his gaze, instead plucking pins from her hair and throwing them into the silver bowls on top of the dresser. She tugged at her delicate uttariya with rough hands, tossing it onto the bed.

"You can continue bossing me around about a life you don't know and would never understand, but for now, can you turn around so I can get these cursed clothes off me?" There was an edge to her voice. Her jaw was wound tight, her chin uptilted.

Kunal quickly turned, though the motion made him sway, facing the long tapestries adorning the room's walls. He counted the silence between them through his breaths.

The sounds of her undressing—the tinkling of bells, the clatter of jewelry—faded and finally, there was rest.

"All I had was darkness in my heart and rage in my bones. Their family took me in after your general Hotha and his soldiers murdered my parents—when Harun was only a child as well and they were all hurting from the loss of his sister, the betrayal of his uncle. He, and his family, they saw something worth saving in me. That broken and wounded little girl. Yes, I was their ambassador's daughter, but what they did for me, that was beyond polite kindness. Wouldn't you want to give those people everything?" she asked, her voice soft and pained.

She moved to stand behind him, and Kunal felt her small hands on his back in a soft caress. Kunal closed his eyes, fighting back memories of his own, leaning into her touch.

"Yes," he said simply. "But also no. Though that answer is only one I came to recently. Because of you." He took a deep breath. "My uncle was that person for me. He hid my identity, took in his brother's bastard son, and gave me purpose as a soldier. I thought I owed him everything. You're not the only one who lost their family in the insurrection." He paused. "And he's dead. The only man who was like a father to me."

The echoes of fury filled him, but it felt hollow now after everything he had been through.

"He was a horrible man—" she said immediately, her

hands dropping from his back. Kunal cut her off, turning around to catch her hands, tugging her closer. She was wearing a multicolored silk sari now, her waist sash tied hastily. Her black curls tumbled down her face, her eyes bright.

"I never said he was a good man. I said he was the only father I knew."

Kunal dipped his head, overcome. The old guilt was there, the blind devotion that had guided so many of his actions. He tried to wear that old armor, but it didn't fit anymore.

It only deepened his sorrow.

"I didn't kill him."

His head snapped up.

"That isn't something to joke about."

"I'm not joking. Kunal, you have to believe me."

"I have to believe you? You, the Viper—" He almost laughed, as if it was the only reaction possible.

"I lied before." She pushed on as the humor left his face, as he listened. "I won't deny I intended to, but when I slipped into his chambers, someone had gotten there first and left one of my whips behind. I lied to keep the charade going. I needed to know who had framed me, and if the true murderer knew I was searching for them, they might have gone into hiding. I would never find out who did it then."

Was it possible? He had looked for something to damn or excuse her and had found nothing. Now, when he had accepted it all, he got the answers he had been looking for. The irony of the gods didn't escape him.

A weight he hadn't known was there lifted. He might

be tangled up in Esha, but at least now he could look at her without the bloodstained edges of his former life. No more shadows.

Though he still felt confused, he tried to pull himself back to equilibrium.

"It wasn't me—" she started again.

"Then who?"

He wanted to ask her why she lied, why she hadn't told him from the beginning, but would he have listened? Who would be so reckless as to murder the Fort general and then blame it on the Viper?

"I'm still trying to figure that out. I still don't know."

Esha moved forward, putting her hand on his arm. "Kunal." He looked at her, her gaze piercing him. "I'm sorry. The pain of losing a loved one is always deep, no matter what."

He could tell by the crack in her voice that her apology was genuine, and he knew what it cost her to say those words. It eased over Kunal, a salve to the guilt that had been festering at the idea of letting Esha go, of dishonoring his uncle's memory.

"He made me into this soldier. He gave me a future. But he also crushed my past, made it disappear until I couldn't remember what my own mother's voice sounded like. I always felt that the only way he could stand the sight of me was as soldier in his own image. Making me into a proper soldier—not like his brother. Maybe he had been trying to save me from being a pawn, as you said. Or maybe it was selfish. I won't ever know."

"I remember that her voice was beautiful," she said gently.

She took his hand in hers, linking her calloused fingers through his equally calloused ones. It felt right.

"I remember bits and pieces of her songs, but he beat the poetry out of me and left cold steel instead. I still don't know when I forgot the sound of my mother's voice," Kunal said, memories painting his words blue. "But this past moon, these weeks have pulled up years of memories I buried deep inside. Feelings, thoughts I've ignored."

"Because of me?" she asked, avoiding his eyes.

Kunal hesitated. "Because of you coming into my life, yes."

He sighed as she came closer, smelling the fragrance of her curls as they tickled his nose.

She pulled back, looking him square in the eyes.

"What if I agree with you—that I don't owe them. But what if despite that, I still want to do this—be the Viper? What if I consider this *my* duty?" Kunal didn't say anything, keeping his face blank. She continued. "I believe in what I do, in bringing back balance to the land. When I steal a missive, thwart a raid, cut down one of Dharka's enemies, it makes my blood sing," she said.

Esha's eyes weren't avoiding him now. They stared him down. "It brings me that much closer to killing Vardaan and avenging my family."

She glanced away for a second before pulling the full weight of her gaze back to him.

"And you, Kunal. You could help us, if you stayed . . ."

Kunal paused and glanced back at Esha, unsure what to say.

Before he could answer, she grabbed his head and tugged his lips down on hers.

Kunal was so surprised it took him a few seconds to realize that she—Esha—was kissing him, but once it wore off he wrapped her in his arms. He could feel the promise of their kiss in his blood, as if it was answering some unspoken question for them both.

And he wanted more. He drew her in closer until there was no air between them, the crisp silk of her sari crumpling like fine paper.

Weeks. He had been wanting this for weeks. He captured her lips again with ferocity, his hands sliding against her bare skin at the edge of her blouse, his fingers grazing the metal hooks as they moved closer to the bed. Her fingers threaded through his hair, sending shivers down his body, causing him to pause, to glance up at her. Her eyes were dark, hungry, and in that moment, he knew she was feeling the same as him.

He bent his head, brushing his lips against the hollow of her throat, bringing back memories of the alleyway when without warning, she shoved him away.

Esha scampered quickly across the room, putting distance between them just as the door opened and a maid bustled in. The maid started when she caught sight of Kunal but said nothing, turning her head to the side as she scurried past him toward Esha.

Kunal was almost glad for the interruption. He didn't

have an answer for her.

He slipped out the door, casting one last look at Esha before he left. She was sitting at her dresser, combing through her hair, resolutely looking at the mirror in front of her.

Their eyes caught through the silvery glass and Kunal swallowed hard, knowing that a dam had been broken.

He didn't know if either of them would be able to deal with the onslaught.

———◄○►———

She had kissed him to shut him up—before he said something that couldn't be taken back. Of course he wouldn't have an answer for her. It was stupid to have asked and she had realized it instantly when she saw the indecision on Kunal's face.

Her brilliant plan had been to kiss him.

It had been entirely the wrong thing to do. His lips hadn't left her mind since then.

Esha padded along the smooth floor, taking care not to fall in her silk slippers. Silk was a better choice for sneaking around in this cursed palace than leather, which squeaked more than pig boy did. But silk was slippery and more than once Harun had smirked at her at their morning meal, knowing the new bruises on her elbows were a result of her night excursions.

But she had gotten good at sneaking around this palace, and she also knew the easiest way into Harun's bedroom. Esha tightened her grasp on her whip, clenching her jaw.

She hadn't forgotten what had happened at the performance.

Esha hurried down the last corridor, pushing a small doorway to open up the passageway Harun had once shown her. She vanished into its darkness, feeling with her hands until she got to that sharp, rectangular stone. Pushing it, another door swung open and Esha slid out, brushing off her hair and clothes.

She snapped her whip taut between her hands, cracking her neck as she moved closer to the giant bed in the corner of the room. It was a monstrosity, or that was what she always told Harun. Who needed a bed big enough for three people?

His only response was to wink at her whenever she mentioned it.

She moved like a whisper, ignoring the softly spoken "Esha?" that emanated from the bed. Within seconds, she had the prince in her grasp, her whip wrapped around his throat and her lips at his ear.

"You don't own me, Harun, and you do *not* get to pet me in *front* of the courtiers."

She pulled the whip tighter around his neck, applying the right amount of pressure to make him wheeze but not to incapacitate. She wanted his response.

"And you brought Kunal. You brought him to throw me off my performance and undermine me. You made a power play against me, Harun. That's a dangerous game to start. We're supposed to be in this together." Her voice became cold as steel as she shook her head.

Harun's eyes darkened in displeasure.

"If you ever pull something like that again, I will hurt

you, even if you are my prince," she finished, her mouth a grim but set line.

He continued looking at her, his gaze growing deeper and making her blood warm. A smirk curved his lips.

"No, you won't," he managed to cough out.

Esha scoffed. "The Blades will still follow me without you. They like me better anyway."

"Glad to hear you've thought about that. But that's not it." He licked his lips. "*You* like me."

She raised an eyebrow at his words but let the whip slip a bit, revealing a red welt across his throat. He lifted a hand to it, rubbing the spot where the whip had been.

"You like how I make you feel," he continued. She blinked, trying to ignore the rising heat in her belly.

Curses. He didn't seem to care that she still had a noose around his neck. Maybe she should remind him of it.

Esha moved to tighten the noose when Harun's hand shot out, dragging her closer to him. The whip still hung around his neck but he had gotten Esha tangled up in the rest of its length so that they were looped together. His dark, thickly lashed eyes became heavy lidded, and the look he was giving her chilled and fired her up inside. Her body leaned in for a second, used to his touch, before she snapped back to reality.

She was here because she was angry, furious at Harun. This may have been how they used to handle conflict, the fighting, kissing, and making up, but this time she knew better.

He couldn't make a power play against her and get away with it.

He needed to know that.

"You seem to have forgotten I came here for an apology. You almost tarnished the Viper's reputation. Swear you will never do it again," she said, her voice clear in its vehemence.

He stilled, staring her down. Finally, he sighed.

"I'm sorry," he said. Esha did a double take, shocked. "And I swear."

She couldn't remember the last time Harun had apologized, to anyone. She knew he saw it as a weakening of his position as the prince. He took on the responsibility and the ire for any and all decisions within the rebel ranks while she remained unscathed, the beloved of the two.

It weighed on him, but it was a burden he had chosen, no matter how much she had argued. "I promise, Esha. I swear, I hadn't planned it. But Adviser Jehek said . . . and then I saw their reaction to us on the dais . . ."

Harun was stuttering, but it didn't give her as much satisfaction as she thought. Her annoyance still ran hot.

"Capitalize on your own reputation, Harun. Also, I hate that man. I thought we agreed he was a slimy toad."

"He is a slimy toad, but he's also a toad with money and influence." Harun sighed, and she felt it ripple through his body. There was clearly more troubling Harun. "You know why we called the cease-fire. You agreed. A few more moons and our troops would've been decimated, especially after Sundara. Esha, there's so much I need to catch you up on—"

"Same here," she said, thinking of the squad she had just sent out with orders to join the search for Reha.

"—But I never meant to undermine you."

"Doesn't matter. You did. And Kunal—"

He cut her off with a finger to her lips. She started pulling away, her whip uncoiled and fallen on the floor.

"I don't want to talk about the soldier. He's alive," Harun said, his tone biting, his eyes flashing with fury. He trailed a finger up and down her skin in a way that made her shiver. She knew that look on his face, the one that was asking her to stay.

"I have to go," she said with a shake of her head. He may have apologized, but she'd nurse a grudge for another day or so, for sure.

"Do you?"

"I have training with the team in the morning."

"I'm canceling it."

"You can't do that, Harun."

"No, I can't, but it was worth a shot." He looked at her, grinning. "I just wanted to talk."

And in his eyes was a softness she missed. The softness of familiarity and acceptance. And they did have so much to talk about.

But another pair of eyes flashed in her mind, amber and gold.

"Actually, I do have something to tell you," she said, with a frown. "And you won't like it."

CHAPTER 56

Arpiya found Esha as she sneaked back into her rooms in the morning, desperate for a bath and some chai before having to go down for training.

Esha had stayed till the morning and taken advantage of the safe space of Harun's bedroom to finally reveal the truth of the night of the general's death—and to admit to not telling him about what she'd discovered from the report, that Vardaan was onto Reha's trail.

She had apologized for that to Harun, but she had needed the past week to gather information and begin evaluating everyone on the base. Esha had started to check each squad's postings and that someone else, a contact or another rebel, could vouch for them being there.

Once she had cleared the Red Squad, she sent them out to help in the search for the lost princess. They needed to get there before the others did.

Harun might not have acted so rationally when it came to his sister. His response to the truth of the night and her confession had been expected: shock, fury, worry.

And in that moment they had forgiven each other—they realized their own internal power struggles were nothing to the larger game someone had set up around them. Esha still had no idea who the killer was and it bothered her. Her stomach turned at the thought of being a fly in a vicious spider's web. She had asked Arpiya to set up a meeting for that reason.

Arpiya stood outside Esha's room, leaning against the ajar door, which Esha distinctly remembered locking the previous night.

"Sleep much last night? I've been looking for you," she said to Esha, smirking. Esha rolled her eyes and pushed past her into the room.

"It wasn't like that this time." She didn't know why she felt the need to explain herself. It wasn't like Arpiya was Kunal. Or that Arpiya even knew who Kunal was, though she was sure Bhandu had spread the news around. "Where have you been?" Esha asked in response.

"Harun's had me training the new recruits. A bunch of rotten, lazy mangoes, the lot of them."

"We used to be those rotten, lazy mangoes once."

Arpiya gasped. "No, never!" She plopped herself down on Esha's bed, fingering the soft sheets. "Are his any better?"

Esha wished she didn't understand her question. "Of course. They feel like clouds. "

"I don't know why you don't just sleep there all the time."

Esha sighed, tugging off her clothing and pouring herself a cold bath. She wasn't in the mood to deal with a maid and she wanted to talk to her friend in confidence.

"You know it's not like that, Arpiya. It's never been. It's an arrangement, nothing more." She pushed away memories of when it might have been more than an arrangement, when they had stood on the precipice of something more.

Her relationship with Harun had always been . . . complicated.

Arpiya raised her shoulders as if to say, sure, whatever, not my business anyway. But her eyes flashed with mischief and Esha knew this wasn't the last she'd hear of it.

"What have I missed?" Esha asked instead. Arpiya launched into the rundown.

The peace summit was still on and a messenger had arrived just this morning. Surprisingly, not a word about the general's death. Not even a sole squawk of protest that their general had been murdered. That raised Esha's hackles— was silence indication of an upcoming attack? It was the last thing they needed right now. She made a note to inform Harun and send out the Yellow Squad leaders to hunt for information.

Kunal might have information; now that he knew the truth about his uncle's death, maybe he could be a real asset. Despite the kiss and the unspoken words, Esha felt as if they had reached an understanding yesterday. She hoped she was right.

Aside from that, training was going abysmally, in Arpiya's words. But she had never been one for patience and coddling, which was what new recruits needed in the beginning. Arpiya was like a dust storm—unpredictable and ever changing. The fact that she had remained with the rebels was a constant source of fascination to everyone, even Arpiya herself.

Esha thought it was because no day was the same with the rebels. And they had a purpose. Purpose could overcome boredom and fear, two of the biggest problems they faced with recruits at first. It was why Harun was an integral part of the first moons of training. He was the best at boosting morale, and Esha swept in after to whip the recruits into shape after their morning indoctrination.

A brilliant setup. Sometimes Harun's mind frightened her.

Esha sighed, rubbing her eyes. "Moon Lord, Arpiya. I have so much to tell you."

She hesitated then.

Trusting Arpiya was second nature, but Esha had to be careful. Betrayal often came in the least expected packages. There was the truth with the general, but also Kunal. Esha had been pulled between thinking of all the advantages Kunal could bring to the rebels and wanting to pack him far away from here, away from politics and war.

Since coming back a week ago, she had taken on the mantle of rebel leader again, and she found herself hating the way she now viewed Kunal. He deserved better and she needed someone to talk to.

Arpiya rolled her eyes. "I can literally see you thinking, Esha. Is this how you became the Viper? If so, it's a wonder you haven't been killed yet."

Esha scrunched her nose up at Arpiya. "Only you can read me that well. Anyway, I don't want to burden you . . ." She didn't see the flat pillow before it hit her, smacking her square in the face. Esha sputtered.

"Don't ever say that again," Arpiya scolded.

Esha began to protest but Arpiya waved her words away. "Our bond is deeper than mindless gossip and meaningless gestures. You've killed for me, Esha. I'll keep your secrets. It's just a drop in the bucket of what you've given me."

Esha swallowed hard. They didn't speak of that night often, but Esha had never forgotten it, and apparently, neither had Arpiya.

Arpiya's expression lightened. "And you're my friend. Stop looking like you swallowed a prickly jackfruit and tell me everything."

Esha took a deep breath and started with the truth of the general's death. When they came out of the whirlwind of words a half hour later, Arpiya's eyes were wide.

"The general's nephew? Have you told Harun?" Arpiya asked. "This could be a great opportunity."

"No, not yet. It's not like he'd be that useful, especially now that the general is dead."

"It won't matter and you know it; Harun isn't going to let the soldier leave easily if you tell him. It's too good of an opportunity," she said.

And this was only with the knowledge that he was the general's nephew. Esha rubbed her eyes, pressing the heels of her palms against them. She breathed in, heavy and tired.

She *knew* this.

If she was being a true leader to her rebel family, she wouldn't let Kunal leave either.

But something had shifted in her, her allegiance being split in two. Esha sighed, realizing she hadn't even revealed the worst part to Arpiya yet—that Kunal was a Samyad.

"And he'll be even more displeased when he realizes the soldier's halfway in love with you." Esha's head, bowed in thought, shot back up. She sent daggers at Arpiya, who was unfazed. "Why else would he have let you live, over and over?"

"In love?" Esha scoffed, her heart beating faster in spite of herself.

"And now I know it might be mutual."

Esha said nothing but knew she was caught. She had known from the beginning that the feelings blooming in her heart were madness, utter stupidity. Arpiya's words simply confirmed it.

"I barely know him."

"Okay, then maybe not love, but something. Be thankful that the rest of the boys haven't figured it out yet," Arpiya said, her calmness a growing contrast to the fireball burning in Esha's chest.

Was that why Harun had been acting so odd? She had thought he had been trying to assert his power over *her*, but maybe it had been about Kunal. Harun could be dangerous if pushed too far.

Yet again, her presence would cause someone else harm. Kunal deserved that life he had envisioned—a life of simplicity, art, and most important, anonymity. The inklings of a plan sprouted in her mind and she hid it carefully on her face, knowing Arpiya was watching her.

And love? No. No one could love an animal like her.

Immediately, the image of Kunal, talons and torn skin and otherworldly eyes, flooded her mind. If he was a beast, so was she. The first pinpricks of pain started above her heart, and slowly expanded. It didn't matter what could have been.

Everything she touched became ruined. As a rebel, that was a benefit. She refused to ruin Kunal's life, no matter how it hurt to think of losing the one person who could understand her—all of her.

No matter if he could help save the land. It was too uncertain and the cost was too high for him. The decision she had been weighing became clear.

Esha schooled her features into her best Viper face—blank with a smug upturn of her mouth. "I'm good at my job. As a turned asset, he *should* be halfway in love with me. Harun will be pleased."

Arpiya stared at her, her gaze unblinking. "I know you're good at your job, but . . ." She gave a small sigh. "Just be careful. Don't let anyone know how you had the opportunity to kill him and let him live—more than once."

"If the rebels have issues with how I do my job, they can find a new Viper. I always fulfill my missions and if they're angry that I saved one person, one soldier, then . . . ," Esha said with more heat than she had wanted to reveal.

Arpiya's face had softened. "And there we go. That's what you need to avoid. It's clear to me that you care about this boy. Don't let him become a weakness," she said softly.

Esha heard the unspoken words—caring for a Fort soldier in any way was already a weakness.

"Anyway, you asked to go to the blacksmith. I set up the meeting. He's waiting," Arpiya said. Esha nodded, glad to be changing the subject.

She dug out the fake whip, the next piece of the puzzle.

CHAPTER 57

Arpiya dragged her through the early-morning haze of light, winding their way through the narrow stone passageways of Mathur.

The city was just beginning to wake, a slow yawn before dreams finally faded away into the distance. The merchants were already out, the denizens of the city just now making their way to pick up their food and goods for the day.

Esha loved this time of morning. People were more open, their worries clothing they hadn't yet adorned.

They stopped to smell the ripeness of a jackfruit or ask after a shopkeeper's newborn. Esha was out of the city too often, but Arpiya's face was known and respected—stall keepers went out of their way to talk to her. These rounds kept the morale alive within the city. Arpiya dropped little hints of the successes and exploits of the Crescent Blades, propping them up in the minds and hearts of the people.

The city of Mathur wasn't as colorful as some of the towns in Jansa, but its soul was old and bound with nature. You could see it in the reverence given to every animal and plant, from the large tree roots of the banyan that the bazaar was centered around to the sparrows that came to feed at the small stone bowls that had been laid out near the well.

Dharka was home, and for a moment Esha felt truly at peace. Centered. Her people were like the moon whose lord they claimed as their own, calm and steady.

When they finally stopped walking and Esha could catch her breath, she saw that they were standing in front of a set of double doors, carved with gold and silver depictions of the gods, that reached two stories high, uncommon in the short buildings of the city.

She raised an eyebrow at Arpiya, who responded with twinkling eyes and a tug at her arm, her delicate features giddy. They stepped through the massive arched doors into a huge courtyard, opened up to the peeking rays of the sun and warm breeze.

They hurried through the courtyard and through a secondary set of passageways until the sun was hidden from their view and all they could see in front of them was darkness. Arpiya looked back at her before pushing through the door in front of them.

The wave of heat that escaped hit them like a barrel, rolling over Esha and out into the passageway. Esha popped her head inside, her eyes wide at the rows of kilns set up along the room. Arpiya was already talking to a man in the back, a short, sturdy blacksmith with dark brown skin, his sweaty brow shining in the firelight.

She ventured forward, taking care not to disturb any of the other blacksmiths at their kilns, garnering a few uninterested glances up.

"Esha, I'd like you to meet our new blacksmith," Arpiya said. "He can be trusted."

Esha pressed her palms together in the Dharkan greeting, bending slightly. He returned the gesture—and she took stock of him. Kind eyes, strong hands, a passing resemblance to Arpiya with his low cheekbones and square jaw.

"It's a pleasure to meet you, Esha. I've heard a lot about you from this one here." Esha didn't miss the look the man threw Arpiya; it spoke of familiarity and affection. "First, I've something to show you."

Esha put aside her curiosity about this man who was obviously Arpiya's kin for a moment and followed him around the table, tossing a questioning look at Arpiya. Arpiya just smiled. The blazing warmth of the kiln had started to make her sweat, and she pulled at her sari to get some air. He noticed and chuckled.

"You get used to it after a while."

The blacksmith indicated that they should come closer. Esha moved to his side and almost gasped at what was in his hands.

He held the most beautiful curved gold bracelet, one that was a perfect replica of the valaya she had been gifted by her parents when she was a child. Esha reached out, unable to hold back, to caress the smooth metal of it. He had even gotten the clasp right, a small snake engraved on the underside.

"It's yours," Arpiya said simply. Esha picked it up, cradling it gently. "A gift from Harun. He wanted to bring you here, but I made him let me. He stuck me with the recruits after all, so I figured he owed me."

"It's beautiful," Esha breathed. She marveled at the valaya. She had never replaced it after she lost it on a mission. It hadn't felt right, plus it had given her the ability to pass as whoever she needed to be for the rebels.

On the inside was an inscription written in Old Dharkan.

Never afraid.

Her father used to whisper those words to her at night, her own personal chant to keep away the monsters and terrors from her sleep. She was surprised Harun remembered.

"You deserve it." Arpiya cleared her throat. "Even if things didn't go the way we planned, you were willing to risk your life and freedom for our cause. It was Harun's idea, but it's from all of us."

Esha looked up at Arpiya in gratitude, clasping the bracelet onto her wrist. Her heart surged with affection for her rebel family.

Something wasn't clear, though.

Why were they here, underground? Who was this man who had created her gift?

"Do you remember how I mentioned my brother,

Chakor, was coming to Mathur? Well, he's taken on the role of our lead blacksmith as we build out the second base," Arpiya said, her voice almost shy at first.

Esha smiled, understanding. She reached out and grasped his shoulder. "Welcome to our family, Chakor." His tentative smile broke into a broad one that overtook his face.

"And this will be the entirety of the second rebel base?" Esha asked.

Arpiya nodded. "The front part will become a storefront or a home of some sort. We're still working out the details, but I wanted to show you."

"Good work," Esha said as she dragged her fingers along the wooden worktable beside her.

She had missed so much over the past moons since she had left for this mission. Esha had fought hard for the better part of the past half year to have this base. Their current base in the palace was secure, but its presence constantly put Harun and the royal family in danger of discovery.

It would be much easier to keep an ear to the ground outside of spiraling marble walls. To be on top of news and maybe prevent what had happened to her, being taken unawares and framed. After weeks of uncertainty, Esha finally was on solid ground. Back on the offensive, no longer on the run.

Esha pulled at the pleats of her sari, lifting them up as she stepped over various finished maces and short swords cooling on the floor. She tugged the whip out of her waist sash and placed it on the table.

"Chakor, this is between us three—on pain of death. Someone made this replica of my whip and used it to frame me in the eyes of the Fort. I've spent moons away from home, being chased for a good part of the time. I want to know where this might have been made."

His face remained enviably still even as he nodded, but the tension along his jaw gave his unease away. It made Esha like him more.

She watched him while he worked, examining the heft and shape of the replica, eyeing it under a large piece of refracted glass and feeling it in the grip of his hands.

Though her feet were on solid ground, Esha felt as if she were walking a tightrope, hoping to all the gods that he would say it wasn't made in Dharka.

They already knew they had enemies outside, but wasn't that better than those within? She couldn't keep looking at and talking to everyone within the base as if they had something to hide. It was slowly breaking something inside her.

Chakor was melting down the hilt now, examining the liquid metal with scarred hands that looked at ease in the glow of the kiln. He turned to face them both.

"This wasn't made in Dharka, if you were worrying. Definitely not in Mathur, and not by any rebel-associated blacksmiths. I know all of their signatures as well as the metals and alloys they use."

The relief hit her like a shock wave. Arpiya put a hand

on her shoulder, her friend sensing what this meant to Esha.

Chakor's face didn't look pleased, though, his mouth still a straight line.

"The alloys used in this replica, which are lighter than what we have here, are only traded to certain areas of Jansa. Those that are close to maritime trade routes with the far west," he said.

His face loomed bright even in the darkness of the underground smithery as he moved closer.

"Whoever made this, made it in the Blood Fort."

CHAPTER 58

Kunal strode quickly toward the training grounds, watching the sun pulling itself from the grasp of the horizon.

They trained early here, something he understood in his bones. The early morning sun streaking across a sanded ground had been a constant image in his life, and he was looking forward to rediscovering some of that in this foreign city.

Kunal hadn't been able to forget about the kiss, and he had tried. It had been days since it had happened and other than a brief conversation, he had barely seen Esha. She had cornered him for a few minutes two days before, telling him quickly about the cover story she had given and why. Kunal was to pretend to be a soldier who had decided to turn away from the Fort, help the rebels.

It was easier than he would've thought.

He had made up a story about seeing the ravages of war on the towns and the destruction of the land for the team. Esha had nodded along in the back when he told them, clearly happy with his acting.

He hadn't had the heart to admit—to her or himself—how much truth there was in the story. Everyone seemed to buy it, though, except for Harun, who just stared at him. As long as his secret wasn't revealed, he'd deal with a number of stares from the prince.

He tried not to think about the other secret that had been revealed, of his uncle's death. He had turned it over and over in his mind, wondering and questioning and hurting. But thoughts of his uncle still felt heavy, especially after what he had learned about Sundara. After Esha's assertion that his uncle had been protecting him for years. He struggled to reconcile the two, his heart burdened with the new knowledge of his parentage.

In spite of all of that, he was excited for the training ahead of them this morning. Moving his body in familiar motions would bring clarity to the confusion in his mind.

And he'd see Esha again . . .

What was worse about the way they left the kiss was that he understood Esha—her desire to see her plan through, that she enjoyed her role as the Viper.

He had seen it with his own eyes, and how could he speak against something that seemed so much a part of her? At the same time, he had seen how it affected her, how it weighed on her. He wasn't sure if she even realized that.

He pushed aside his thoughts, knowing that her kiss had saved him from saying what he knew was true—that he still identified with being a soldier of Jansa, in spite of his uncle. It was the part of him that he had to be careful about here, in the palace.

Part of him still wanted the simple life in the countryside. But he also wanted her fire and warmth.

Another part of him yearned to do what he'd sworn an oath to do. To protect Jansa and his people.

There were so many paths in front of him, and he had not a clue which one was the right one. If he was being honest, he hoped someone would beat the answer out of him today.

Kunal wasn't sure what to expect, having just received a note telling him to come down for training with the squad. He had worn the loose cotton dhoti that had been left for him, slapping on his own leather forearm guards—which had mysteriously reappeared in his belongings.

Kunal had climbed up to the parapets at the top of the palace earlier that morning. Of course he had found the tallest point of the area, reveling in the feeling of weightlessness so high above the ground, the way the buildings below looked like ants.

He'd also spotted the training grounds. They had been hidden in the east gardens of the palace, in an area that looked to be overgrown to the point of neglect. From above he could see how it was just a deterrent—beyond the thicket and crumbling walls was an open area dedicated to training.

The guards who appeared, yelling at him to come down from the parapet, indicated that the area was watched.

His body was still weak and it had taken him a half hour longer than normal to climb, but it had been worth it to feel so free. Even though he might not be in a prison cell, like Rakesh was, he was a prisoner in this palace, despite the beautiful room and lack of chains.

After the *rightness* he had felt while turning, almost everything felt confining now. There was still a bud of disbelief in his chest. How could he be a Samyad? A shape-shifter?

He thought back to the clues that now made sense, how being in the air had always given him a sense of peace that felt raw, natural. And those headaches he got while tracking, was it his body's desire to turn? Or was it from his uncle's conditioning to control his emotions, therefore delaying the turning? And how did one control one's turning?

He had so many questions and had no idea who to ask, or where to go to get answers. It was a gnawing tension in his chest, all of this curiosity. His thirst to understand.

If he had a moment to himself, he could sneak to the library. But he longed for someone to talk to about his new-found family.

Kunal felt alone again, adrift in this huge palace. Playing the role of someone he wasn't, in more ways than one.

At least he knew where to go without having to ask any of the guards. He hurried out toward the east garden, following them through hidden doors into a large, open space with sanded floors punctuated by short stone columns.

Targets lined up in rows along the edge of one side and figures with curved longbows took turns aiming and letting their arrows fly. At the far corner, a square was outlined in chalk on the floor, and two men danced across it with wooden practice maces swinging at their sides. Dharkan shield fighting was being practiced in the other corner, two girls dodging and ducking each other, armed with a round silver shield and thick curved swords. Around the perimeter, boys and girls were running drills.

Kunal looked through the chaos for Esha but instead caught sight of the burly boy—Bhandu—near the targets.

He weaved his way through the other rebels, who ignored him in turn. It was a mark of dedication, or solid training, that no one even batted an eyelash at his intrusion. Though he had been invited, he felt as if he had sneaked in— privy to the workings of the rebels' inner circle.

It was both terrifying and exciting because he knew the deeper he got, the harder it would be to leave, or escape. He tried not to take note of the number of recruits, or the strength of their fighters—things he would've tucked away to report back to the Fort.

As he drew closer, he caught sight of Esha, who was adjusting the foot positioning of one of the twins from the jungle who had long hair that brushed his collarbone. His twin was to the left of him, imitating the change in footwork.

They both regarded Esha with a curious intensity, hanging on to her every word despite looking to be about her age.

Esha was dressed for training, in a cotton blouse, loose cotton dhoti, and thick-soled leather sandals. Leather forearm guards were laced up both arms and her hands were wrapped in linen. She hadn't caught sight of him yet and he took the moment to observe the group.

A tall girl was on the other side of Esha, with dark brown skin and short hair. She was going through the motions of a block and jab combo with Bhandu. Kunal admired the move for its simplicity and brutality.

Bhandu blew out a breath with the ferocity of a boar, his eyes suddenly on Kunal.

"Oi, cat eyes. Come over here," Bhandu said, calling loudly for him over the sounds of clashing swords, swinging maces, and grunts of pain.

Kunal sighed, shaking his head as he walked over.

"My name is Kunal, not cat eyes," he said in response, taking up the spot next to Bhandu.

The girl's eyes snapped to him, pausing her demonstration to give him a once-over. He felt himself flush as her gaze raked up and down his body. She seemed to approve, giving him a small nod.

Bhandu laughed, a sound like a roar. "Kunal, then. Despite being a 'former' soldier, you've got the makings of a person I might like. Let's see if you pass the test. Arpiya, toss me your sword."

The girl—Arpiya—shook her head. "No, challenge him and measure the length of your swords later, on your own time." She smirked. "I have to go back to the new recruits anyway, so this is the only time I can show you this move, and if you're not somewhat decent at it by the end of training, Esha will give us that look."

Bhandu grimaced. "I hate that look."

"It makes my insides churn and feel like jam," Arpiya said, her hair bouncing as she shivered visibly.

Kunal looked between the both of them. "Esha's on your team? I thought she worked alone," he said carefully, thinking back to his earliest assessment of the Viper.

Bhandu looked at him sidelong. "You shouldn't even know that, cat—Kunal. She's not on our team."

"She leads our team," Arpiya cut in. Bhandu frowned at her interruption.

Kunal looked over at Esha, watching her line up her toes to the chalked line on the ground, notch her arrows, adjust her fingers, and let the arrow fly. It landed just outside the center of the target. An impressive shot from where she stood, and with a bow that looked to be too big for her.

When he had known her, she had spent more time in the libraries and with the visiting performing troupe than at the sparring courts. But she looked like a natural. Once again, it hit him how much ten years had changed the two of them.

"She never mentioned that," Kunal said, his voice quiet.

Bhandu rolled his eyes. "And why would she? Give away her secrets to a soldier? Even if you are on our side now."

Bhandu didn't notice his hesitation, having already turned his attention toward the twins. He was shouting some obscenity at them.

Arpiya gave him a sly look, having caught him looking at Esha again. He kept his chin high, trying not to let on how his thoughts had begun to turn in another direction entirely. He had noticed the way Esha's clothes contoured to her body, her hair blowing softly around her face as her brow creased in concentration.

It was an arresting image, and havoc on his mind and body after their kiss.

She wore her conviction like armor. Right now, Kunal wished he had his own set of armor. At that moment, Esha looked over and a smile lit her face as their eyes met. It disappeared just as quickly but Kunal took note of it, tucking it away in his mind.

Arpiya poked him, pointing toward where Esha, the twins, and now Bhandu stood. They walked over.

"Glad to see you up and doing well," Esha said, her voice light.

Kunal cleared his throat. "Yes, I'm feeling much better." He couldn't help his voice softening. "I was told that was thanks to you."

"And me," Bhandu interjected. Esha rolled her eyes but laughed, a low chortle.

"We helped too," one of the twins chimed in. He reached out a hand to Kunal. "Aahal. And this is Farhan." He pointed to his twin brother. "Don't worry if you get us mixed up, it'll only devastate us slightly."

Already, Kunal could see a difference. Aahal had a twinkle in his eye while Farhan looked more serious, considering Kunal with all the friendliness of a prowling panther.

Kunal bent his head toward them both, repeating their names. "I'll try my best," Kunal said.

"I certainly hope so," Farhan replied, his voice no friendlier than his demeanor.

Esha clucked her tongue at him and his hard expression softened. Arpiya motioned at the other boys, drawing them away with a challenge for closest shot, winner buying wine for all.

It left him alone with Esha.

She moved to the side of the row of targets, indicating that he follow her with a hand gesture. Kunal felt awkward, unsteady, in this training ground that felt so familiar but also not his own. She clearly had a solid presence here, and it drove a small pin into his chest.

He had thought after seeing her performance that he understood her life, but seeing her here, in her element? It only reminded him of how little he really knew her.

Esha balanced a short blade in her hands before handing it, hilt forward, to him.

"What, I'm allowed a weapon?" Kunal said, before he could help himself. "I'm really getting the royal treatment compared to Rakesh."

Esha snorted. "Yes, don't make me regret it. If you'd like to join your fellow soldier . . ." She shrugged, as if saying that could be arranged. "If you're going to be here, might as well train. Would be a shame to let a perfectly good warrior go to waste."

He accepted the sword, hefting its weight in his hands. A good make, but a different feel than Jansan metal. Made for precision rather than simple brutality.

"Is he all right?"

"Pig boy? He's fine. Despite what Jansa leads you to believe, we do have honor when keeping prisoners of war. He's in a cell with daily meals. Since the cease-fire is on, Harun hasn't decided what to do with him yet, but who knows, he could prove useful later."

"Thank you," he said. "For saving me. I know I wouldn't be alive without your help. I remember that much, at least."

"You remember?"

"Bits and pieces. Enough."

Esha looked like she was about to ask more when someone jostled Kunal, tumbling out of the chalked lines of an ongoing spar. She shook her head quickly and settled a smile back onto her face.

"How do you feel about a spar, Kunal? Let's see what you can do."

He wasn't sure if she was serious, but he couldn't deny he was itching to get on the sparring floor. Anything to stop thinking.

"Weapon?"

CHAPTER 59

They settled on using long knives, curved and fiercely sharp. Esha had almost looked gleeful when she had picked them up. He understood why—they were fine knives.

Before, he would've thought twice before fighting a girl, but if he'd learned anything over the past weeks, it was to not underestimate any girl. Esha was dangerous and skilled.

He let a small smirk escape and Esha latched on to it as she set up their perimeter.

"Feeling cocky?"

Kunal laughed. "Oh, I don't think I would ever feel cocky around you."

He heard a sound of approval from behind him. "At least he knows that much," Bhandu said, raising his eyebrows.

They hadn't yet attracted the attention of the other trainees, but Esha's team had settled themselves down to watch.

Kunal forced their chatter out of his mind, zeroing in

on Esha. The perimeter was set and she was crouching, her knife low near her belly. He met her in the middle, taking up his own stance. He kept his knife low as well, hoping to deflect and dodge more than use the knife.

Neither of them moved, sizing up the other. Esha lunged first, so fast that her knife caught the edge of his dhoti, tearing into it. He ducked, hitting her knee as he moved to slow her down.

"I need to ask you something. And I wanted to talk," she said softly. They danced around each other. Esha landed a hilt-down blow of her knife to his jaw and he stepped back, rubbing it.

"So, you challenged me to a spar? Couldn't you have just pulled me to the side?" he asked, his mouth twitching. He pushed his knife a bit farther forward.

"There are eyes and ears everywhere. And we haven't told everyone about this," she whispered back, her eyes insistent. She was being serious. He swept her leg and she tumbled to the ground, rolling away before he could land another blow. "Harun wants us to keep this quiet."

"Harun?"

Esha popped up to her feet in front of him.

"The prince."

Within seconds, she hit him in the side, knocking the wind out of him and sending him straight to the ground before he even saw it coming.

She straightened from her crouch, holding a hand out to him. He grabbed it, dusting himself off. "You should adjust your stance when wielding this type of knife. Have a wider stance, especially for an opponent who might not be clad in armor. Your center of gravity was too high, letting me knock you down."

"I don't see myself fighting anyone who wouldn't be in armor," Kunal said, bristling. The look Esha gave him was pointed, and he understood what it said. Life hadn't really turned out the way he had thought.

She shrugged. "I'm used to teaching here, and if I see something during spars that can be adjusted, I fix it immediately. Now, do you want my help?"

Kunal hesitated for a moment but then nodded, and she moved toward his feet. He *was* unfamiliar with this make of knife. Behind him, Bhandu was expressing his displeasure that Esha was letting their fight be a teaching spar, instead of one to the death.

"I was going to ask before. Did you see anyone else the night of the general's death? Or anything else unusual?" she whispered.

Esha wrapped her hands around his arms, adjusting them into a lower grasp. Kunal blinked, unsure why she was asking. He thought hard.

"No," he said. "But we found a soldier who was accused of letting in the Viper."

"I remember him," she breathed. "And the Fort, are weapons made on site? Who might have access to a smithery at the Fort?"

"Yes, they are made in the Fort. As for access, only the

blacksmiths and soldiers." Kunal paused. "It's uncommon, but some soldiers do take a liking to making their own weapons and the Fort allows it, as long as it doesn't distract them from their duties.

"What's—" he stopped, in sudden pain. She had kicked at one of his legs to move it out and Kunal felt a few muscles scream in the process.

Esha was behind him now, and he could feel her warm breath against his skin. Images of her mouth, of kissing her, flooded his mind. He turned his head, and their faces were so close Kunal could see the widening of her pupils.

"Kunal, I wanted to say . . ."

Was Esha blushing? The softness of her voice and the smolder in her eye told him the topic had changed. She didn't finish and he took advantage of it, jumping in with a question that had been niggling at him.

"You and the prince—if you're promised to him . . ."

"No," she said quickly, fixing him with a stare. She pulled away, moving to face him, and took his hand, adjusting his grip on the knife. He thought about explaining himself to her, the confusion rolling around in his stomach about his identity, his future, and whether he could be who she thought he was. "I'm not promised to anyone but myself."

The tightness in his chest relaxed. "Esha, about before." She lifted her head. "I'm—"

She shook her head ever so slightly, darting her eyes to the side.

"No, I need to—" he tried to say, but he cut himself off

at the warning on her face. And turned around to see where she was staring.

The prince now stood behind the twins, leaning against the wooden rail behind the targets. He was clad in a dark green dhoti, his cream silk uttariya worn around his neck and tucked into a thick gold belt. His muscular upper arms were wrapped in gold armbands with engravings of a lion, the sigil of the Himyads, and more gold hung from his neck. And he was watching them with intense eyes.

All in all he looked like a prince, a regal warrior. Kunal tried to not let it intimidate him. Though technically a bastard, wasn't he a prince as well? Kunal dismissed the idea, feeling uncomfortable.

Harun strode forward, startling Bhandu out of his seat.

"Looks like a cozy training session. You've got an incredible teacher there, Kunal."

Kunal bristled at the use of his name but hid it. It felt unfamiliar and strange in the prince's mouth, as if he was deciding what to do with it and it might not be pleasant. Kunal clenched his hand around the knife.

"I am quite lucky. She's showing me how to use a knife to better attack an unarmed man—or woman," Kunal said.

The prince flashed him a smile, teeth bared, before dismissing him with his eyes and turning to Esha and Arpiya. "If you both have a moment."

He didn't wait for a response, striding to the side of the court. Esha followed him and so did Arpiya, after throwing a menacing look at Bhandu and mouthing "Practice" at him.

Whatever they were talking about led them to argue.

Or that was simply how they interacted. Kunal couldn't tell.

Minutes later, all three of them walked back and Harun stopped in front of the rest of them. "We have another mission."

"Do we get to go?" Aahal asked.

Kunal almost laughed at the excitement in Aahal's voice. Bhandu seemed as interested in the answer.

Harun shook his head. "No, just Esha. This is just an information grab. She'll be meeting with a source we've found. There is a *situation*, but I'll explain it to you three later, when it's just the team." He looked at Kunal when he said it, as if waiting to see his reaction. Kunal kept his face impassive. "All of you is overkill for this mission."

Aahal's face fell and Bhandu's scrunched up. Harun seemed to notice. "Next time, I promise," he said, his voice soft and disarming.

Kunal saw it then—what it was about the prince that made people stay loyal and devoted to him and his cause. It wasn't just the commanding, masterful actor he had seen before.

He genuinely cared about his people. Which made him all the more dangerous.

"Kunal will come with me."

Kunal's head whipped around to look at Esha. Her face was blank and she said it calmly.

Harun immediately opened his mouth to respond, and

she interrupted, looking over at Kunal. "You're part of the rebels now, so you'll earn your keep. He'll be useful in bolstering my cover. If not, I'll bring him back in chains," she said.

Kunal furrowed his brow. He had no idea how he would be useful.

But one angry look from Harun was all it took to convince him to keep his mouth shut. He'd be grateful to not be under his watchful eye—which was currently turned on Esha with barely contained annoyance.

In a flash, the look was replaced with a placid smile.

"Whatever you say, my Viper. I expect a full report and I give you permission to use any force necessary to make sure the soldier stays in line. You asked for him, you get to deal with him," Harun said, his foot tapping. "Don't let him murder you in your sleep," he murmured, his words biting.

Kunal blanched, ever so slightly, even though he knew the prince wanted him to react. Harun moved closer to Esha, settling his hands on either side of her shoulders.

"Be careful?"

"You know I always am," Esha said, looking up at him. Something passed between them and Kunal fought back the urge to grimace.

Bhandu clasped him on the shoulder as the prince left, his hand clenched on the hilt of the knife on his belt. It jarred him out of his thoughts, which were swirling in confusion, trying to decipher what had just occurred.

"Good luck, Kunal. I know the prince mentioned

attempted murder on your part but if you touch a hair on her head, I will find you. Anyways, I'm more worried about you, cat eyes. Try not to get killed—by her," Bhandu said with a grin, the twins looking at him with matching expressions of envy. Arpiya was silent, her head going between Esha and the retreating Harun with an eyebrow quirked.

"If she hasn't killed me so far, it'll be harder than you seem to think," Kunal said in response.

Bhandu let out a deep-throated laugh, the sound rumbling. "That's because she's never truly wanted you dead. Make sure it stays that way."

———◁◦▷———

The rest of the morning training session passed quickly.

Kunal jumped into the training with ease, appreciating the distance and clarity it gave him. With every lunge and blow, he felt clearer, more sure. If nothing else, his body and skills were the same, a constant in the changing storm that had become his life.

His clothing had become torn and dirtied by training, but Kunal felt a lightness he hadn't known in a while. The rest of the group was laughing and joking about Bhandu's newly acquired set of bruises, a gift from Arpiya for failing to learn the correct move, as they walked down the corridor. Esha caught his eye as he turned to leave to his room.

"Clean up and meet us back here for dinner after," she said, looking up at him.

His core warmed at her mussed, disheveled state. Her skin was flushed and sweat shone on her temples and neck, dripping lower. Kunal pulled his thoughts away from its descent, trying not to imagine what was under the neckline of her shirt.

He nodded and she sent him a small smile as the others trailed ahead, out of earshot.

"I see why you were a big shot at the Fort, Kunal. It wasn't all your uncle. We could use someone like you on our side if you ever decide that bronze armor isn't worth it." The surprise, and slight horror, must have shone on his face because she continued on hastily. "We can always use good men and good fighters."

The open warmth on her face had disappeared, her expression shuttered and almost—pained? He let her go, watching her jog down the hall, before turning back toward his room. The kindness behind those words was clear, but all Kunal could think about was that armor.

Would he ever have a chance to wear it again, or would his entire life consist of him being here, as a prisoner, living a lie someone else had created? Fear rose in his throat. This mission might be his chance to escape, but to leave would be to leave Esha as well.

Back at his room, the prince was lounging against the door.

He was dressed in the clothes from before, and twirled a small knife in his hand with indolent grace. Kunal slowed, not bothering to hide the suspicion on his face.

Harun looked up at him, nostrils flared.

"If you do anything to harm my mission, or my asset, I

will set my most brutal men on you, soldier. Esha will look like a pretty scrap of silk compared to them. And you will suffer. She may trust you, but I don't, despite your story. You're here, alive, by her grace. Don't make me regret giving you that antidote. This is your chance to prove that you *are* a rebel now."

Kunal tilted his head, the barest acknowledgment.

"I know," he said simply.

He understood. He wouldn't do a thing to hurt Esha, but he still hadn't decided whether he *wanted* that chance to prove himself. Kunal knew himself enough to know his limits.

Harun let out a breath. "Good. Makes it easier on everyone. Gods know why she wants you on the journey, but my Viper has never led us wrong."

He watched Kunal for a long moment, the only sound in the hall the whoosh of air as he twirled his knife.

"You might be fine being here at our base, training with us, maybe even helping us on a mission. Maybe you see the truth and nobility in our cause. Maybe it's for a girl."

Harun sent a vicious grin toward Kunal. Kunal felt stunned, rooted to his spot.

He had hit some truth—bit by bit, Kunal did see the nobility in their cause. The good. Maybe he always had. And now he had the chance to do something about it.

"She's a heartbreaker. You'll think you know what she needs, that you can fill that hole in her heart. But the only thing that will fill that heart—that she needs—is cold-blooded revenge."

Time stood still for a few seconds, in which every doubt and fear and worry Kunal had experienced since meeting Esha rose to the surface, clawing at his throat. Kunal had let himself see, for the briefest of moments, a future with the girl who was *something* to him.

How had Harun known?

"But do you think your little soldier heart can stand by and watch her kill the pretender, your king, and raze through your comrades? Could you defy every oath you took and every vow you made?" Harun continued as Kunal tried to ignore the bile rising in his throat.

Something like triumph passed across Harun's face, and Kunal's gaze shot up, angry.

"How is that any business of yours?" Kunal said, his voice taut.

He kept a tight leash on his temper and his control, not wanting even a hint of turning in front of the prince.

In a second, Harun was close enough that Kunal could hear the prince's deep breath. "Anything that goes on here is my business." The fury leached from Harun's eyes and he adopted a wry smile. "Consider it a helpful warning. From a friend."

Before he could respond, Harun swept away down the hall, vanishing into the darkness.

Kunal's hands immediately went to his eyes, rubbing

the growing tension between his eyebrows away. He had started to consider the alternative to escaping—that he might be able to train, adjust to a new life, and let go of his duties as a soldier for Jansa.

But that wasn't the worry blooming in his heart like a weed. Harun's words had started to slither into his already tattered brain, clawing hooks into his thoughts.

Could he let go of all he'd known for a new future—for Esha?

CHAPTER 60

Esha looked everywhere for Harun, only to find him in the peacock gardens, trying to get one to eat from his hand. It kept nipping his fingers instead.

"Having fun?" Esha asked.

He jumped up at her voice and cleared his throat, a faint blush covering his cheeks. Harun, blushing? The world was really on its side these past few weeks.

"I was waiting for you and got bored."

"You could've joined us for dinner, instead of sending me a cryptic message."

"I would've, but there's a reason I'm dressed up like this," he said. "We just received a messenger from Jansa, who delivered this."

He thrust a small scroll into her hands. Esha unraveled the scroll and read quickly.

"An invitation. To the Sun Mela. 'To honor our shared

ancestors' before the peace summit." She frowned. "Dharka hasn't been invited to the games since the war started."

Esha snapped it closed and looked up at Harun.

"It's a trap. Especially after what we discovered from the whip," she said.

Harun nodded, closing the distance between them to take the scroll back. "Those were my first thoughts."

Esha paused, looking between the scroll with the royal seal and Harun.

"Why are you receiving messengers, opening mail? That's for your father."

"Father is . . . not well." Harun shifted uncomfortably.

"The night terrors?"

"The night terrors are not real; I couldn't say much else in front of everyone else. The drought is still concentrated in Jansa but Esha, it's moving. Father's been experimenting with the university scholars, using his blood to see if there's any way to slow the drought from spreading. He's growing weak. If there's a chance Vardaan or his scholars will work with us to find a solution, then we have to go to the Sun Mela. The last ritual is only four moons away."

"No," Esha said immediately. "You can't trust him. Invite them here to Mathur for the summit. We can keep a better eye on them. Don't let the king go."

She grabbed his elbow, shaking it, as if that would show how against this she was. Her worry for his father, especially after knowing the toll of trying to maintain the *janma* bond, was as strong as his. But this?

"My father won't be going. I will be."

"What? No. That is reckless and stupid."

"I know—"

"—And dangerous and *stupid*."

Harun placed his hands on her shoulders. "Esha, I know. But that's why I'm sending you on this mission. I'd rather go into that traitor's den with some knowledge of what's happening."

"I can't convince you not to go?" He began to shake his head. "Then I'm coming too, to Gwali."

Harun looked like he was about to protest but then bowed his head.

"I expected as much. Go to your meet, pack light. We'll be traveling with the court, which means you'll have plenty of time to gather information and meet up with us on the road. I'll have the rest of your belongings packed and brought along."

He tugged out another scroll from his waist sash and handed it to her. "Here are more details on the meet. Our contact will be dressed as a beggar but with a large green hat."

"Hat?"

"Don't ask me," Harun said, sighing. "I don't set the terms for these meets. I'm just happy the Yellow Squad found someone willing to talk. Any information will be valuable. I'm worried about Vardaan's silence on the general's murder, Esha. We need to know more."

Esha nodded, tucking the scroll into her pack and turning back to him.

"No excursions this time." He raised an eyebrow at her and she laughed. The last time she had gone to a meeting with a source, she had ended up running into, and breaking through, a Jansan blockade. That port city still spoke of the Viper with awe. "I'm serious. Stay safe. I'll lose my mind if something happens to you."

"Oh, no Viper to clean up your messes then?" she joked.

"No, the Viper can hang itself. I mean you. Don't do anything stupid, okay?" Harun leaned in and quickly kissed her forehead, taking Esha aback. "Good luck."

Esha nodded, her quick retort dying on her lips.

Luck hadn't been by her side recently and she was hoping to woo it back.

CHAPTER 61

Esha and Kunal left at dawn as sunlight filtered across the sky.

The plan was to move fast and be back within a day or two. Harun had stressed that part. Their contact would be in town for only one day before he disappeared.

Esha threw a glance over her shoulder at Kunal, who was taking in the countryside as they bounced along the dirt road on two mares. They were dressed as a married couple, Esha wearing the necklace of gold and black beads that signified her status, as did the wide gold ring on Kunal's right hand. He had been quiet, as if lost in his own world.

She supposed it was odd to be traveling together—both of them awake, uninjured, and neither chasing the other. They were at a peculiar impasse. Neither had mentioned the kiss, as if waiting for the other to be the brave one.

The soldier and the Viper.

Both could cut a man down without blinking but couldn't talk about a kiss.

He caught her eyes this time, holding her gaze steady with clouded amber eyes. For a moment, neither looked away.

Heat rushed into Esha's limbs and she broke their gaze.

———◀o▶———

"We're almost there, but let's stop for water. I'm parched."

The words jolted Kunal out of his thoughts and he threw Esha a quick nod. She dismounted gracefully and he followed suit, taking his mare's reins in hand as they moved off the path and into the rocky terrain as they neared the bottom of the Ghanta Mountains.

Kunal heard a sharp intake of breath and looked over at Esha. Her round eyes were wide and he caught where her gaze went.

The ocean was laid out to the west, a brilliant blue that sparkled and took his breath away. The press of thoughts and decisions and burdens faded away for a few moments. He stopped worrying about the life he left behind or Esha and stared out in the vastness of the ocean.

"Every time," he whispered. Esha tilted her head toward him.

He repeated his words. "Every time. Every time I see the ocean, I have the same feeling. My heart squeezes at the beauty and its absolute enormity. And I think again how I will never be able to paint its majesty or capture its every facet because I'll never be worthy of it."

Kunal fought the tightness in his chest.

Esha looked at him with those inscrutable eyes. "Why do you need to be worthy to capture the ocean's beauty?" she asked, her brow furrowed.

Kunal struggled, unable to find the words. "Something so raw and untamed? Pure? Hundreds will dedicate their lives to art, to capturing the beauty and passion in the land around us." His mouth hardened and he felt the words spill from his lips before he could stop them, a soft whisper. "I will never be worthy."

She shook her head at him, her lips pursed. "That's stupid." Kunal felt the hairs on his neck bristle. He scrunched his forehead together, hot words on his tongue. "It's not about being worthy. It's about respect. Do you respect this land? Your people? Then you are entitled to it the same as everyone else. We're not born perfect and we don't die that way."

The words on his tongue melted away as Kunal considered her.

In a few words, they had both exposed themselves to each other in a way more intimate than any brush of lips.

Once again, he had no answer, which he covered with a question.

"This person, do we know why they framed you? What they want?" Esha had filled him in before they left with the basics of what she had discovered, about being framed and the scroll that detailed a search of some sort. But she kept it short, as if not wanting him to know too much. As if she didn't trust him.

"As my father used to say, the simplest answer is often the correct one. They didn't want any of us to know about what the Fort was searching for and framing me was an easy way to distract us."

Esha sighed and rubbed the bridge of her nose, which he had noticed she did when tired.

"And the cease-fire, you think Vardaan has been using it as a cover for this thing?"

He remembered thinking it was odd that the Fort hadn't announced the general's death. Kunal couldn't help but feel like he'd be more useful if Esha told him what this thing was that everyone was searching for.

Esha nodded. "A source told us he's consolidating troops from the borders."

"He wouldn't do that lightly. You're right, something is definitely up," Kunal agreed.

Esha slowed her horse, tossing him a half smile, but offered nothing else.

Kunal wanted to ask her more, about why she had inquired about the smitheries and that night. It was clear to him that she was holding back, but who was he to say she was wrong?

He didn't even know his own heart.

———◇———

Esha had hoped their last moments together could be light-hearted, hearkening back to their time as kids. Instead, Kunal was getting deeper into the labyrinth of being a rebel, where alliances were constantly shifting and you didn't always know who to trust.

It tempted her, the idea of what he could do in the rebels, how he could help them. But she wouldn't be his captor, no matter his title or abilities. If he had a chance of a life away from all of this, he should take it. She would give it to him.

Esha steered their conversation away as soon as she could, and Kunal didn't resist, having developed a far-off look in his eyes.

They reached the edge of a small pond and watered their horses. Esha reached down to fill her small flask, splashing water across her face and neck.

The air was cooler as they approached the coast, a sea breeze mixing in. Kunal had turned away, filling his own water, and Esha took advantage of his distraction to sneak a look at him.

Burn his face into her memory.

———◄○►———

They stopped in the road, a grassy patch of trees leading off into the jungle on the right. The ruins of an old, abandoned temple to the Earth Mother, evidenced by the fire trenches and broken statues, spread out over the jungle here, intertwining with the undergrowth.

With a wave of her hand, she motioned him to follow her, and they moved farther into the jungle until they were surrounded by a green canopy, the ruins just behind them.

He regarded her warily and moved toward her, his hand on his sword that hung off his belt.

"What is it? Did you spot raiders?" he asked, his voice low.

"No, no raiders." Esha tugged on his horse's reins, his mare neighing softly at the tug, and held them out to Kunal, who gave her a questioning look.

She grabbed the collar of his cloak and pulled him close, shoving the reins into his hands.

"Go. Go home. I won't keep you here."

His heart froze in his chest and he couldn't speak, confusion and joy warring in his body as her words resounded in his head.

Was she really giving him the chance to go home?

As if answering his unspoken question, she said, "You were never supposed to be captured and, well, you already know too much. Harun would never let you leave without a fuss, so I'm giving you the choice now."

Kunal began to shake his head but she pushed the reins back into his hand, almost toppling him. He looked up sharply and saw the seriousness in her face.

This was no joke. It seemed a stroke of luck, not having to plan the escape that was but pieces in his mind.

He would return in disgrace, but it would be his life. One where he had control, one he knew. And he could work his way back to respect.

He barely thought before he took the reins in his own hands, feeling the hard leather cut into his palms.

"What about the meeting?"

"Does it matter?"

"Won't they know?" he asked.

She shrugged, her shoulders dropping. "I'll tell the team you knocked me out and escaped. Or I'll tell them you tried to run and I buried a knife in your ribs. I'll figure it out and I'll make it good. You can rely on that."

She wouldn't look at him anymore, averting his eyes.

His former life beckoned. He tried to fight back the guilt and sadness he felt at the thought of turning away from her.

If only they had met at another time, in another life.

The Fort was his home, had been his life for ten years. It would be wrong to give that up so quickly for a girl he barely knew. Right?

"And what about . . . you?"

He wanted to say *us* but found himself unable to. Her face remained impassive.

"I'll be fine, as I've always been. I've got my team—and Harun will think it was another one of my Viper escapades gone wrong."

Harun. He felt the walls around his heart shooting up.

She had the team and *Harun*. The prince.

Kunal didn't have the strength to fight back at the jealousy inching into his heart. He remembered their kiss, their conversations, the day at the market, and so many more moments. Deep inside, he knew they had a connection.

But why would she hand him the reins if she wanted him to stay?

Why give him the choice when he was already here? He was a prisoner to her in more ways than one, and she was telling him to go.

The wave of stubbornness hit him hard, in the soft part of his heart where pride and fear mingled together.

This wasn't his life, these weren't his beliefs, his desires. These were hers, and no matter how much he wanted a chance to be with her, becoming a rebel?

Kunal choked on the thought. Impossible.

He would never see her again. Kunal pushed that thought down, along with all the soft, happy moments she had given him over the past moons. Getting to know her and seeing her and tasting her.

He pushed it all down with expert soldier training, ignoring it all to focus in on one image.

Home.

His old life. What did he want?

The next few moments would determine his future.

<o>

She saw him open his mouth but she barreled on.

"Don't tell them you know the Viper when you get back. Forget my face." Esha bit her lip, swallowing hard as she steeled her mind. "They'll use it against you," she explained. "I didn't release you just to see you killed. Say you were tricked and thought you had found me but had been misled. Lose your pride but don't lose your life—or the future you want."

His lips had flattened into a thin line.

"Why?" he asked, the single-word question hiding its depths.

She stared back at him, wondering if her gaze revealed what she had been trying to hold herself back from saying.

Don't go, don't leave. Stay. With me.

She wouldn't say those words or the many others at the back of her throat. That she cared, that he had brought back light to her past, that for some reason his presence made her heart beat faster and brought a genuine smile to her face.

Esha didn't want to hold him prisoner in a life he didn't want, with people who might never trust him. She had told him to go two weeks ago, and now she was forcing his hand.

Either the future he had dreamed of, free to do as he pleased, safe from the machinations of others. Or the life of a rebel where he would have her, but all else he had known would be lost. Where if anyone discovered who he was, he would be lost as well.

She wasn't sure she was worth the trade.

"You're the only spot of good in this world that gives me hope. I believe in you. I believe you deserve that simple life you wanted, lemon boy," she said instead.

Esha thought she might have seen a flicker, a sign of regret—or something in Kunal's impassive face. But if it had been there, it left as quickly.

"Take the path along the edge of the banyans east to the base of the mountains. You'll avoid rebel patrols and be in Jansa soon enough," she said.

He nodded, walking into the lush foliage to the east. At

the last moment, he turned and gave her a long look.

The forest enveloped him as he left.

———◄○►———

The elation at being free, at deciding his own path for the first time in weeks, washed over him as he turned away from her, leaving the Viper, the ghost of his uncle, and the schemes of the rebels behind.

He crunched through the leaves and branches, leading his horse gently over the rocky undergrowth. Kunal took a deep breath, and a few more as he and the mare continued their journey.

The happiness didn't last long, slowly twisting and turning into ash as he considered what he had chosen. With every breath the truth washed over him, bit by bit.

Soldiers who had ripped away his family, had taken away his passions and turned him into a weapon.

Who had left him to die at the hands of the Viper.

Left Rakesh rotting in the dungeons of the rebels.

A Fort that was soaked with the blood of its queen, whose heart had been ripped out to be replaced by men with blades and gruesome smiles who believed in *duty*.

What had duty brought him?

All he had ever wanted was for someone to accept him and welcome him, all of him. He had found that person and walked away from it all for an easy future that might never come.

Even if she . . . didn't want him, he was realizing he couldn't go back to the Fort.

Not when he had seen what it was like in Dharka, the real kinship the rebels had, the vibrancy of its people. They fought not just for themselves but for their brothers and sisters in Dharka.

A true nobility.

And for the first time, he felt every facet of his emotions—the confusion at what to do, the elation at being free, and the despair as he realized what he might be leaving behind—and he didn't hear his uncle's voice. He didn't try to control the emotions, shut them down, hide them away.

It left him feeling raw, exposed—but also powerful. In *true* control.

He knew what he had to do now.

Kunal tied his mare to the tree and turned back, his movements desperate as he flung himself through the jungle, retracing his steps to find her. He held a hand to his side as he ran, as if to hold in the hope that was crushing his heart, hope that she hadn't left, that she'd stayed.

As he got closer to where he had left her, the hope became a slowly searing pain as he realized that all he had ever wanted had stood in front of him—and he let it go.

All because he was scared.

Kunal had known what every day at the Fort would be and what his duty as a soldier was supposed to be, yet it hadn't stopped his life from taking another path. There was no guarantee in life, even in safety.

But he had been given the chance for happiness, if only he had been able to see past his fear to grasp it.

If he had any luck, any luck at all, he would catch her in time. He had only traveled a quarter of a mile. He would comb through the forest till he found her. And when he found her, he would grab her and pull her into him and say what he should have said then, because now he understood.

Kunal ducked under another branch, knocking aside stray leaves as he raced back.

She hadn't asked him to leave. She hadn't let him escape.

By letting him go, she had been offering the chance to be a part of her world, but only if it was his choice. Esha had been giving him the gift he had thought to give her before— the chance to hold a memory of her that didn't wither over time with hate.

He saw the clearing ahead of him and pulled up, coming to a full stop, an invisible hand holding him in place as he stared out at where he had been standing previously.

What if he had been wrong? What if she really had wanted him to leave?

But the question had been so naked and raw on her face, if only he had been able to see beyond his own fear when it had been asked.

Will you stay?

Now he just wanted the chance.

And in the back of the clearing, a flurry of movement rustled through the leaves. Esha was in the shadows, crouched low to the ground. She brushed the back of her hand across her cheek as she finished packing.

When she turned in the light, he saw the glisten of tears

in her eyes and his body finally unfroze, his heart clenching painfully.

He pushed forward, so desperate to talk to her and explain that he didn't notice the soft footfalls behind him until a hand closed over his mouth.

Kunal heard himself yell for her, a single cry before his words were muffled by a sharp blow to the head.

His vision turned to black.

CHAPTER 62

Esha stood there after he left, the wind gently whipping around her.

She couldn't move. She felt rooted to the spot, as if moving would cause the heavy weariness that had descended on her soul to fully crush her.

And that inner voice she hated, telling her she had been stupid to give a piece of herself to a soldier, to anyone that was alive. She wasn't supposed to have any heart to give.

Then why did her chest ache and beat with such ferocity it threatened to rip out her chest? No, she had a heart. If nothing else, she couldn't deny it anymore.

The Viper had a weakness. And he had walked out of her life. But she felt no joy at the thought, despite having achieved part of her goal. Or that's what she was telling herself.

She had given him a choice, and he hadn't chosen her.

With the realization, she felt her body unstick. It had been inevitable, him leaving her, and yet the knowledge didn't prevent the tears from bubbling up. She brushed them away hastily, crouching down to inspect her pack. To do anything that would distract her from the pit in her heart.

A small, hated part of her whispered to her that maybe he would come back. It kept her in the clearing longer than she should have been, throwing sidelong glances at the trees with undue hope. It was a preposterous thought, yet one that kept hitting her.

But minutes passed and she remained the only one in the clearing. With a heavy sigh, she gathered her pack and stood up, shaking off her clothing.

Esha almost thought she had imagined it, her name shouted through the quiet hum of the jungle. She whipped around in the direction of the sound in time to see Kunal's bright eyes close as he was pulled into the darkness of the forest, his head hanging limply.

This time her legs weren't frozen. Esha sprinted to where Kunal's body had fallen, but when she arrived, he was nowhere to be seen.

It couldn't be the rebels—she knew exactly where every Blades squad was stationed now. Who, then?

She fell to the ground, inspecting the tread of sandals against the soft earth. The misplacement of branches and broken twigs. Whoever they were, they weren't trying to be careful or hide their tracks.

Esha frowned, her mind racing to sort through every-thing. Maybe it had been a mistake? But he had come back and been steps away. And he had called her name.

She was sure of it, would stake her whips on it. And the look on his face as he fell—it was surprise. She wasn't even able to feel the joy that he had returned, knowing he was unconscious somewhere. Questions swirled in her head but she chose action.

Esha traced the outline of the sandal imprint with the tip of her finger, an image emerging in her mind. Of flat-edged sandals with sharp metal bottoms—military issued as part of the Jansan army uniform.

But relief at knowing he was with his own soldiers didn't come. The depth of the imprints in the soft ground told the truth.

Whoever had taken Kunal here had been lying in wait, had possibly seen Esha with him. Esha's heart pounded, thudding in her ears with a vicious clarity.

Her cover could be blown, her true connection to Kunal revealed.

And if they had heard their conversation, Kunal would be a known deserter and traitor to the Pretender King.

———◁◦▷———

When Kunal came to on the soft dirt of the ground, he sprang upright, hand on his knife. The last thing he remem-bered was being knocked out, the pain in the back of his head a reminder that he hadn't been taken of his own will.

Esha.

He pushed aside the thought, blinking as he acclimated himself to his surroundings.

"Hold up there, Kunal. You can put the weapon away."

Kunal whipped around, ignoring the accompanying sharp stab of pain. He must be imagining things. He shook his head again. The image held.

Laksh leaned against a tree, and he saw Amir and two more soldiers—Saran and someone new—sitting around the fire to his left. Amir looked over and his face lit up. He stood and moved toward Kunal, gathering some of the rations that were near the fire.

"Good to see you awake," Amir said cheerily, handing him a chunk of crusty bread and dried meat.

Kunal took the food from him, staring at him in bewilderment. Laksh hadn't moved from his spot against the tree, continuing to watch Kunal.

"What in the Sun Maiden's name am I doing here?" Kunal asked shakily.

"Sorry. I'm happy to see you all again—and some other brothers—" He nodded at the other soldiers, who dipped their heads in response. "But could someone tell me how I ended up here with a sore head?" He drew the words out into pointed jabs.

"Ah, that might be a better story for Laksh to tell," Amir said with a rueful expression. "He found you deeper in the jungle when he was hunting."

Kunal rubbed the back of his head, and Amir winced. Laksh remained unmoving, his mouth quirking into a quick grin. If Kunal didn't know better, he would have described it as almost gleeful. Laksh had never been that excited to see him before.

"Sorry about the blow to the head. You weren't wearing your armor, so I didn't recognize you at first. You know our motto. 'Attack first, questions later,'" Laksh quipped. "We've been in need of food and rations."

It didn't look like it bothered him to admit to thievery. Kunal put down his bread, his appetite gone at the mention that it might be stolen goods. "When I noticed it was you, I brought you back to camp immediately," Laksh said, finally looking a bit guilty.

Kunal didn't know how else to respond but to nod and force the smile he knew he was supposed to have on his face. His heart began to sink. There was no chance he'd get back in time to find Esha still in the clearing. She was not easy to track.

The irony. He no longer wanted to be back at the Fort.

"How are you here? We're technically within the Dharkan border," Kunal asked.

"We could ask you the same thing," Laksh said wryly.

Amir jumped in. "We met up a few towns back at one of the garrisons, me and Laksh, by pure accident and found those two in town as well. The border soldier regiment has thinned out, so they were almost glad to see us. We said we'd keep an eye on things during our journey back to the center of Jansa." Amir threw a reproachful look at Laksh.

Amir's face softened as he turned toward Kunal. He had

always been a kind boy and Kunal was glad that hadn't been ripped from him over the past two moons of the competition. Kunal's mind whirred with thought, hearkening back to his conversation with Esha. He had the chance to press for information here, but he would have to be delicate. Offer information of his own.

"The center of Jansa?" Kunal asked casually.

"Lagor," Amir said, referencing a city close to Gwali, the capital.

"We've been recalled from our coastal posts and thought we would enjoy a night in town before heading in," Saran said. "Ran into these two fools and decided to take the short-cut to make up for the night."

"Recalled? I thought maintaining our hold over the borders and ports was a priority," Kunal asked.

Saran nodded. "It was. And there are still some soldiers there, but some of us have been redirected for the king's newest directive now that we're at cease-fire." A faint pounding filled Kunal's chest. "We don't ask questions. All I know is that there is precious cargo we've been assigned to protect."

"Jewels?"

Saran gave him a look that indicated he might be acting a bit too curious.

"No. I heard from one of the other guards in his cups that it's a girl. He's kept the cargo under lock and key, won't let anyone near it at pain of death. If it is a girl, maybe it's a potential bride. I'd lock her up too."

He snorted and laughed at his own joke as the others rolled their eyes. Kunal tossed him a chuckle to soften him up, trying to mask his disgust.

A girl? Lock and key? He wouldn't put it past Vardaan to "protect" his future bride, but something didn't fit. He'd see if he could press him more later, when Saran was in his own cups.

Saran continued. "I got to whet my sword in town, though. We were tipped off about a deserter—a small, weak man. Infantry, of course. I wouldn't have pegged him as a smuggler. He was hanged wearing the ridiculous hat we found him in." He rolled his eyes. "He kept babbling something about the *heen rayan*, as if the Lost Princess was real."

"Good memory on your Old Jansan. But as Master Nambudh would've told you, *rayan* can mean princess or prince, depending on the context," Kunal said, a small smile escaping. Saran had been in his class, despite being a few years older.

He made a face at Kunal. "There was a reason I always looked off your work. I don't give one whit about these dead languages. That's not why I joined the Fort." He shot a grin over to the young soldier, Jageet.

Jageet joined in, a new recruit by his armor. "At least you got to see some action this time. I would have loved to fight a Dharkan or two. My sword is aching to slice through a few of them. Their blood would be a nice decoration, don't you think?"

The younger boy grinned as Kunal felt a dull roar in his head. This was what he had been fighting for?

"I hear the Dharkan women aren't so bad on the eyes, or rough to the touch either," Jageet continued, winking.

Kunal's vision turned hazy—the dull roar had become deafening in his mind.

"Are those remarks really fitting for a soldier of the Fort? Of Jansa?" he snapped. Kunal stopped himself in time from saying what he was really thinking.

The rebels I met were worth more than all the bronze armor you proudly wear.

The sharpness of his tone brought a flush to the young soldier's face, his fingers curling, looking as if he was about to fight back with his fists.

Amir jumped in, ever the peacemaker, changing the topic to who would be on guard duty that night. Kunal continued to fume, but schooled his face into a blank mask that would have made Esha proud. The thought sent a pang through his heart.

He needed to figure out how to get out of here and find her—if he could find her. If he moved quickly, he might be able to catch up with her before she reached the rebels' contact for her meeting.

Kunal raised his head and caught Laksh staring at him with a thoughtful expression, his face shadowed in the twilight. When his eyes connected with Kunal's, he looked away, engaging in the others' conversation. Kunal furrowed his brow.

He had to figure out how to escape without drawing attention, and it had only been due to Amir's grace that his carelessly antagonistic remarks had been brushed aside.

What worried him more was that Laksh hadn't mentioned to the others how he had found Kunal—or asked why Kunal had been there in the forest. It was a weapon waiting to be used.

Kunal looked at Laksh, really looked at him. His face was shut off to him as it had never been before. Part of him wondered if it was him; had he done something wrong? But Laksh's bite was sharper with everyone, it seemed. Had it only been a few weeks since they had met and had dinner together at the garrison? Anyway, Laksh's moods he could deal with later.

He had the clothing on his back, the weapons at his side, and his pack. Now he needed a plan.

◄◦►

Esha hurried through the wood, following the tracks as best she could. The sun was beginning to set and soon twilight would be upon them, leaving it nearly impossible for her to track Kunal.

She inhaled the jungle, breathing deeply of the leaves and earthy scent as she examined the dirt and branches. The footprints faded in and out but thankfully, there were other tracks for her to follow. The broken branches and debris on the ground indicated someone being dragged at first, and the subsequent deeper footprints spoke of the traveler carrying a heavy load.

Esha kept thinking back to her realization outside of the clearing.

Why would the soldiers take Kunal? The tracks showed signs of struggle.

She supposed he hadn't looked like a soldier without his armor. But given the depth of those footprints, she could tell that whoever took Kunal had been watching him from a distance.

She moved faster, her breath ragged as she pushed herself through the forest as quickly as she could. In the distance, she heard faint sounds and slowed down, holding a hand to her side cramp.

All this for a soldier. If she had any sense, she'd let him go. He was probably in good hands anyway, as he was with his own kind, and he had left the second he had the opportunity. Esha shook her head, bracing her hands on her knees as she stopped to draw in breath.

But his face when she had looked up . . . why had he come back? That was the only thing making her move forward and not leave him, and all of this mess, behind.

She needed to know. That and whether his captor had seen them together. That information would be imperative. If they had been seen, the witness needed to be taken care of.

She hadn't worked this hard for ten years to let every damn Jansan soldier find out her identity. And since discovering that the replica whip had been made in the Fort, Esha had determined that the murder of the general had to have been an inside job. Whoever had taken Kunal might've seen her, might reveal it to the wrong person.

The sounds grew louder, and Esha made out distinct

voices—one of them Kunal's. She tiptoed toward them, keeping herself hidden behind the stout mahogany tree trunks. A large one's branches loomed over the fire that danced ahead and Esha climbed it, knowing it would give her a better vantage point.

Her heart beat like a sky drum as she pushed closer and heard the next words, that Vardaan's soldiers were protecting a girl.

The young soldier spoke of Dharkan women and instantly Esha's blood boiled and she ached to jump down and drive her knife into his throat. He looked like a young fool on his first mission, but Esha knew they could be the most dangerous and eager to prove their worth.

Kunal's voice rang out in rebuke of the soldier, surprising her enough to stay her hand.

It warmed her heart. Maybe soldiers could change.

She watched Kunal sit in the hollow beneath a large banyan tree, his face losing its heat and becoming a mask.

He was becoming more like her, but it only made a part of her sadder. Already, Kunal would be forced to hide his blood from the world. Harun had grown up reveling in his shape-shifting birthright and he could never see it as anything but a blessing. If Reha had been around, at least Kunal would've had someone to talk to about it all.

Reha.

The world became a haze as Esha thought back over the words of the soldier.

Vardaan's precious cargo was a girl. What if? And as Esha

put it together, she felt an anchor drop around her chest.

The Blood Fort had found Reha.

It was the only answer that made sense of everything. The search, the continuation of the cease-fire, the soldiers moving away from the borders. Vardaan was confident because he had found the only thing that would guarantee his hold over Jansa—the lost princess Reha.

She was alive. And the Pretender King had her in Gwali.

Esha shook her head to clear it. Kunal had said something, but she had missed it, and now the young soldier was speaking.

"I didn't come out on duty to stand watch and meander through towns," he said, glaring at the others.

"Even the most exciting tours of duty can become slogs. Laksh, Kunal, and I set forth to find the Viper," the boy with a soft voice chuckled. "And look where we are now."

"Didn't four of you set out, Amir?" the young soldier asked, fidgeting in his armor.

The other boy—Amir—nodded. "There was another. Rakesh. He was also ahead of you. Our cadre."

The soldier from Faor, Laksh, spoke up. "Speaking of Rakesh, any idea what happened to him, Kunal? Last I heard from base, he had sent word that he had found the Viper. You had been traveling in the same direction. Did you happen to cross paths after we met at the garrison?"

Esha's ears perked up, her heart beginning to race. Kunal knew this soldier. From the look on his face, he knew him well.

It was an innocuous question, but Kunal could damn himself with a few wrong words.

Kunal seemed to realize the delicate situation he was in, a tension marking his brow that Esha recognized and hoped the others didn't.

"I ran into Rakesh a few towns back. He had claimed to have found the Viper and was making a nuisance of himself throughout the town," Kunal said. Esha released a bit of her breath. Every successful lie needed to have more truth than not. "I chased him down and it was there that the Viper found us."

A sharp intake of breath—she didn't know from who—but Kunal had succeeded in capturing their attention.

"Why didn't you tell us that immediately? What was he like? The Viper?" Amir asked, his eyes wide in awe. "Was he a human?"

Laksh let out a bark of a laugh. "Of course the Viper is human. Kunal is here alive, isn't he?" His intelligent eyes narrowed. "Say, Kunal, how *did* you get out alive?"

———◀◦▶———

Kunal pushed down his rising unease.

He had to believe this story or no one else would. He couldn't reveal the Viper's connection to the Blades; he at least owed that to Esha.

"It wasn't easy. The Viper led us into an ambush by the Blades and Rakesh and I were taken and captured because we were too focused on winning over the other." He tried to look contrite. "The Blades took us captive and I only just escaped. As far as I know, Rakesh is still imprisoned."

Saran spoke. "He's alive?"

Kunal nodded. "I think so. But I don't know if he'll get out alive."

"You did," Laksh said plainly. Terror gripped Kunal's heart for a second but he kept his face expressionless, guileless.

"I did," Kunal said in the same tone. "I wasn't stupid enough to wear visible Jansan armor and go around boasting of my prowess. I was dressed as a townsperson and that's who the Blades thought I was after the Viper ran away. Someone in the wrong place at the wrong time."

Kunal heard a snap of noise in the trees around the camp but forced himself not to look away from Laksh's eyes. The noise wasn't the heavy tread of a man but spoke of something lighter. Hope rose in his chest.

"I had to fight my way out." Kunal let a small smile play across his lips. "Took out a few rebels, but had to run for my life. You know the rules. We don't go back for anyone."

The soldiers around the camp nodded solemnly. It was a stupid rule and one Kunal had always hated. He could see a similar feeling in Amir's eyes—he had never been cut out for this life.

Laksh murmured in light agreement. Amir turned shining eyes toward Kunal. "So, what was the Viper like? Are the stories true? He's clearly wily, leading you to the rebels and escaping."

Kunal paused, analyzing how much to reveal before he spoke.

"I can't speak to all the stories. But the Viper I met was a woman." A murmur went through the soldiers, and Laksh watched Kunal carefully.

The young boy gasped in disbelief. "No, she must have been a decoy." Kunal almost let out a sigh of relief. He latched on to the idea, nodding firmly.

"That's what I thought. The real one had discovered us on his trail and had set us up."

Amir sat back heavily, a frown on his face. "Maybe the real Viper hadn't even been in the area. I heard that the Viper can take on multiple forms and one is of a wily woman." He sighed. "Either way, I'm happy to see you alive, Kunal. It was lucky we found you. I know this is a competition and all, but I frankly don't care anymore. I'm ready to go back to my warm cot and thrice-daily meals at the Fort."

Laksh tilted his head. "It was lucky, indeed. Escaped, no vicious Crescent Blades after you, at least from what we can see." He smiled, though it seemed a little cold. "You're here now, though. We should celebrate."

Kunal took it all in, the lightning-fast shift in Laksh from cold to warm. Had he guessed Kunal had lied at the garrison? Was that the reason he was acting so odd?

Laksh handed him a small metal cup with wine and Kunal took it, tilting his head in acknowledgment. The soldiers grew loud, trying to outshout each other as they drank.

Kunal resolved to keep an eye on him.

For now, he was on his own.

CHAPTER 63

Kunal rose in the early morning, when night was still bidding farewell to the world, only tendrils of light hinting at the morning to come.

The others had gotten drunk but Kunal had turned his cups into the grass when no one was looking, thinking of a plan all the while. He had always thought of his fellow soldiers as good men at the core, but he was beginning to realize that stemmed more from his own hope for the world than reality—Laksh and Amir being exceptions.

His weeks away had turned something in his belly. The blood and death and war—he couldn't take it back.

But he no longer felt that single-minded duty or only saw things in black and white. It was as clear in his heart as his mother's voice. He had spent a night trying to fit back in with the soldiers, but it only led him to realize he would never fit in again.

Kunal moved like the breeze, his movements quick but silent as he stole some of the soldiers' weapons. He paused and left Laksh's weapons by his side, taking a long look at him.

And right where Kunal had sat, he nestled the whip he had lifted from Esha's pack into the dirt. Let them think he was taken again to be killed.

After all, he had seen the Viper.

They wouldn't follow and memory of him would fade—soldier's rule was not to return for those captured. He hoped Laksh, and Alok back at the Fort, would forgive him one day. He would've given anything for a chance to explain to them, but he had only a small window of opportunity to act.

One day he would. Kunal lodged that hope in his chest as he prepared to leave.

What would come next for him? He didn't know, but he was ready.

Kunal set his jaw and strapped the remaining knives onto his belt, gathering up one of the packs—the young soldier's. Inside it had enough provisions for a few days until he found Esha.

The soft morning dew decorated the tangled undergrowth of the jungle, bugs swarming around, and Kunal took care not to slip as he padded away from the camp, heaving a sigh as he escaped the first ring of trees.

A rustle. He froze.

Kunal glanced up to where the sound came from and

caught a glimpse of movement in the trees above. It had looked like a young woman's face shrouded in a hood. He changed direction and padded back a few steps to confirm what he had seen. Her face was one that would never leave his mind. If she was here, he would need to get her out before the soldiers woke.

Another rustle behind him startled him, his hand flying to his knife as he whipped around.

Curses, Esha.

But it wasn't Esha's laughing brown eyes that stared back at him.

"Going somewhere?" Laksh asked, coming out of the shadows.

He had an odd expression on his face.

"Just heard a noise and went to scout it out." Kunal shrugged, thinking quickly. He tried to loosen his limbs so he didn't look as guilty as he felt.

How much had Laksh seen as he had been preparing to leave? Would his friend believe him if he lied, hate him if he told the truth?

He wanted to feel relieved that it was only Laksh, but it was a weight instead. So, he did what Esha would do, reverting to that quipping humor she always used.

"Looks like Jageet fell asleep on guard duty," Kunal said with a small chuckle, keeping his stance loose.

"Animal or human?" Laksh asked quickly.

Kunal shook his head, not wanting Laksh to wake up the other soldiers. His friend stepped closer to him, his gold cuffs glinting in the dim light of morning. He stared at Kunal, crossing his arms around his torso.

"Or perhaps it was a snake? I hear they're common to this area of Dharka. Especially Vipers."

Kunal's head snapped up to meet Laksh's eyes. He swallowed hard. Laksh smirked, revealing that his choice of words was no coincidence.

Esha. In his haste to leave, Kunal had forgotten what this whole trip had been about, how four of them had set out with one goal—to capture her and become the next commander of the Blood Fort.

Clearly, Laksh hadn't forgotten.

"No, no snakes. Just a deer. I was heading back to camp, actually, but stopped for some water. Sorry to have woken you up."

Kunal began to edge closer to the tree, where the rustle had come from above. Laksh nodded, staying rooted to his spot.

He hoped he had imagined Esha's face and that she wasn't nearby. If she was, and Laksh realized, she would be in grave danger. They both would be.

"Do you always scout out noises with all your belongings?" Laksh asked, startling Kunal, who had been focusing on the sounds within the jungle.

"It never pays to be too caref—"

Laksh cut him off. "You can stop, Kunal. It's painful. You are a horrible liar." Kunal said nothing. "I saw the whip and more important, I saw you with her."

Kunal felt that knife edge of fear.

He knew. Laksh knew Kunal had defied his orders, but worse, he knew Esha's identity. Still, Kunal tried to keep his voice even, steady. Lie through his teeth. There was a chance he could convince Laksh he was wrong.

"That girl?" Kunal scoffed.

"Don't you mean that girl with the beautiful eyes, the one who's also secretly the Viper?"

"What?"

"No point denying it. Stop pretending you didn't know. I know you, Kunal, like a *brother*."

Kunal coughed, trying to give himself a second to think, wondering if he was imagining the note of hurt in his friend's voice. He had wanted the time to explain his choice before, but would Laksh listen? Or would his hurt at Kunal's deception cause him to finish the task he had set out with?

"Laksh, it's not what you think."

"No?" Laksh smiled, a wry one. "What I think is that you've been lying to me, maybe since Faor, maybe since before. I saw you two in the clearing yesterday looking cozy and then made the connection when you mentioned the Viper was a woman. Leaving a whip this morning was the final clue."

Kunal couldn't spot the right path forward. If he admitted it, he revealed Esha, endangered her. If he continued to lie, he'd lose Laksh's trust, maybe even his friendship.

Either way, he'd lose something precious.

"You've been holding out on me, Kunal. How long have you known?"

"You have to believe me, I never meant to lie to you but you said yourself, it was a competition."

"It *was* a competition, but I thought we were friends, Kunal," Laksh said, the first sign of a break in his facade showing through. It only drove the knife deeper into Kunal's gut.

"We are, Laksh."

"I eavesdropped yesterday when I found you both in the clearing. Your conversation was touching, heartbreaking almost when you turned away . . . but you *did* turn away. You turned back to the Fort. I brought you back to keep an eye on you. Hoping I was wrong."

Kunal started. Laksh was hoping he wasn't returning to the Fort?

Laksh shook his head. "I almost can't believe it. You, Perfect Kunal, deserting."

Kunal's mind raced as he tried to figure out how to explain in a way that Laksh would understand. But would he? Or would he see a failed soldier, one who had abandoned his duty? Despite the certainty with which he had turned away from the camp, Kunal knew those questions would haunt his own dreams for many moons to come.

"I'm not deserting, I'm just—"

"Then what? Just taking an early morning stroll with your pack and weapons?"

"I always carry my weapons."

"You should be glad it was me who heard you and not one of the other soldiers," Laksh said with a little shake of his head.

And Kunal was. If it were any other soldiers, they would have attacked first, not bothered to ask questions. Laksh's questions were sharp weapons in themselves, but they were buying him time to figure out what to do next. If only Kunal knew what to say.

"Laksh, I—"

"I just don't understand why you wouldn't tell me. That the Viper is one of those—that you're joining those Dharkan rebels, the *Blades*."

"Those Dharkan rebels?" Kunal said, before he could help himself.

Weeks verbally sparring with Esha had trained him to hear the nuances in words he would've missed before. Kunal snapped to attention, focusing on Laksh's face. Where he thought he would find disgust, shame, horror, he saw—nothing.

At the Fort, they never referred to the rebels as the Dharkan rebels. They were just "the rebels" or "the Blades."

"Don't you mean *the* rebels?" Kunal said again, trying to maneuver around any verbal trap.

Kunal thought back to his conversation with Esha on their journey here, about how someone had wanted to distract the Fort and the Blades. And the venom with which he had said the *Dharkan* rebels. Could there be a new resistance group, a Jansan one?

"Because there are no other rebel groups, that *I* know of, anyway," Kunal continued, his voice steady. A muscle jumped in Laksh's cheek but otherwise, his face remained impassive. Kunal finally felt like he had gained an inch in this conversation, even if Laksh was closer to the truth than was comfortable. He ignored the little feeling of betrayal that seemed lodged in his throat. "Right? Only the Dharkan rebels. And how do you know the Viper is one of them? Unless there's something else *you* want to tell me, Laksh."

"Time with the Viper has changed you," Laksh said, with a tsk of his tongue and a smile.

Laksh reached forward to Kunal, who shook his head and backed away a pace.

"Did you know that our land is dying? Not just growing a little weaker in spots as they told us at the Fort, but wasting away? This wild monkey chase has only made it all the more obvious to me," Laksh said.

Kunal watched Laksh pace in a half circle. It was as if a new person had replaced the hurt Laksh from before. He had always been a chameleon, but this whiplash change left Kunal mentally scrambling to catch up.

"I did." Kunal figured this was a time for honesty. Lies were hanging over both of them. A spot of truth might salvage their friendship. "I saw it firsthand in some towns. The hunger and death."

Laksh gave him an approving look, raising his hands.

"You noticed. And from your tone of voice, you don't approve."

Kunal shook his head. "No, but I don't see how this answers my question."

"Vardaan is killing our land, our people. He is not one of us, so what did we expect?"

Laksh had never been a soldier of choice, but this was more than a disgruntled soldier. His words held the ringing surety of someone converted.

An eager look spread over Laksh's face. "I'll admit it, I felt a bit betrayed at first when I saw you leaving, but more that you chose those Dharkan rebels. I've been looking to turn you for a year now. Alok would be an easy one to turn, but you? You held your duty above yourself. How would I convince you that there was more to the world? So much more that had been hidden from us? But I still hoped that one day, you'd awaken to the truth."

Laksh grasped Kunal by the shoulder. "I'm glad in an odd way. You are a true Jansan and you've fought hard for your country." His voice grew softer, more cajoling. "But you've been led astray. We all were. Ever since I saw the light of justice under Dharmdev's guidance, I feel like I've found purpose."

"Careful, Laksh. You're talking treason," Kunal said, his voice quiet.

His mind whirred, making connections with a speed only fear could usher in. Laksh had mentioned this man, Dharmdev, "the Lord of Justice." He must have been converted into this apparent new group of Jansan rebels.

Or was that a ruse to catch him out? Have him admit to treason only to take him back? Kunal didn't want to believe that of his old friend, but having been so close to freedom, he grasped at it that much more. He said nothing.

"Kunal, do you know what the Fort soldiers did just moons ago to my village? When I went back, nothing was left but ribbons of clothing from my sister's dolls. Everything else had been set aflame."

Laksh's voice broke, a storm of pain shuddering across his face, and it was so deep Kunal almost had to look away. Laksh had returned from his last visit home different, changed. Kunal had assumed it was maturity making him more serious. He had never known, never asked.

"I'm so sorry, Laksh. I wish you had told me—"

"How could I tell you what I saw when I went home? The last thing I would've wanted to hear was you forgiving your cursed uncle, excusing the soldiers who had destroyed my village, my family," Laksh said sharply.

Kunal reached out to Laksh but his friend held a hand up.

In seconds, his composure was back and he let a little smile shine.

"That is why we need you. Join us, join the rebels of your own motherland. We want what you want. Dharmdev wants what you want."

"Which is what exactly?"

"A free Jansa. Our country and land returned to us. King Vardaan doesn't care about the Jansan people. He's burning villages, raiding already poor towns. All for his own needs."

Kunal stared at him, unsure whether to ask the questions popping up in his mind. A free Jansa? What of a healthy one, a whole one? One thriving under an unbroken *janma* bond? And who would take charge if they brought down Vardaan? How did these rebels plan on addressing those concerns?

Kunal understood then. The first mask of Laksh *had* been a ruse, trying to use his guilt against him. And when that didn't work . . . But why? It hit him.

He was the general's nephew, a beacon of what the Fort was. Was this even about him? Or what he might stand for? The thought left a sour taste in his mouth.

But that wasn't the only danger lurking. Kunal could hear Esha's voice in his head. If these Jansan rebels found out his true identity, he would have no peace. This fleeting freedom he had found, the ability to choose for himself, would vanish.

Despite that, Kunal couldn't deny the appeal of Laksh's words. Laksh seemed to notice it.

"We need you, Kunal. Our cause needs you," Laksh continued on, his voice lowering, becoming more urgent. "Take me to the Viper and we can take her back. You can become commander of the Fort and we will effect that change you dreamed of, that you told Alok about. We'll take back the country from the inside out, take back the Jansan army. Our group is true to Jansa and we're getting closer and closer to the key to healing our country. Think of what we could do together."

Laksh's words caused an ache in Kunal's chest, answering an unspoken need he had felt for years. Hadn't that been one of his goals? To remake the army in a way that would befit mother Jansa?

The ache only grew deeper as he realized it was an old need, an outdated dream. He couldn't give his new life up, give Esha and even the team up, just to fulfill an old, wild dream of his. If he knew anything, he knew that.

And the key to healing their country? What did Laksh mean by that? Could he mean the broken *janma* bond?

"Are you boys talking about me?"

Esha dropped down from the trees, her hair a crown of fury around her as she landed lightly on the ground, whips in each hand.

Laksh laughed, his face crinkling in real delight.

"Pleasure to meet you again, Viper. I've got to say I'm impressed—it looks like you've turned our Kunal. For as long as I've known him, I'd only ever dreamed of doing it." He gave her a blinding smile. "Now, if only I had known it would be so easy to get an audience with you back in Faor. No dancing monkeys required."

"The pleasure's all yours. Though I'm sure we could've made time to chat if I had shown up at the Blood Fort just a little bit earlier, right?"

Kunal's head snapped up. What did she mean by that?

Laksh locked eyes with Esha but said nothing.

Esha nodded to Kunal. "He's been lying to you, feeding you sweet words." She turned to Laksh. "Why don't you tell him?"

"I'm more curious how you figured it out," Laksh said, tension in the line of his jaw. Kunal noticed his hand was drifting to his waist sash. Kunal stepped closer to Esha, slowly moving his hand to the knife in his own sash.

"The whip, it was a fake," Esha said encouragingly. "A very good one, but a fake, immediately detected by my blacksmith."

"I heard you left yours behind instead. A bold move," Laksh said, his voice light, his fingers still dancing along the inside edge of his waist sash.

Esha wasn't playing his game. She pursed her lips, tapping a finger against them. "You know, once I found out the whip was made in the Fort, I knew I was looking for a soldier. I overheard everything, about this Dharmdev, your new vision for Jansa—and your attempt to recruit Kunal. Does he know? The blood on your hands?"

Laksh laughed. "As if you don't have plenty on your own."

"I'll take that as a no. You said leaving my whip was a bold move?" Esha's face tightened, and Kunal froze at her expression. "Yours was bolder. Killing the general in his own bedchamber. If you hadn't revealed that you knew the Viper was a Blade, I might not have been sure."

Her words swept over Kunal, the links clicking together in his mind. Whoever had framed Esha had known the Viper was one of the Blades, had been the one to leave the pin and whip, had murdered his uncle in cold blood.

Had he truly killed Kunal's uncle, his own general?

Could people change so much, so deeply, that you could wonder how you ever thought you knew them? Or had it been a lie from the start?

Laksh faced him, but Kunal didn't know if he could trust this new mask any more than the previous ones. "You must know by now all the atrocities he committed. My family . . ."

"You killed him?"

Something in him wanted the confirmation, needed it.

Laksh hesitated but nodded. "Kunal, it had to be done. We had to protect the intel we had gotten."

When Kunal said nothing, Laksh continued, "Kunal, you were one of my first friends at the Fort and that was never false. But this? This is bigger than us. Bigger than your uncle. Even then, I'm sorry to have hurt you."

Kunal felt in his bones that Laksh's words were heartfelt. Laksh must have seen the flicker of doubt in his eyes.

He held a hand out to Kunal.

"Join me and let's end this. No one else has to lose their family."

And for a second, Kunal got lost in his words, the promise in them.

But were these new Jansan rebels any better than the Blades? Any better than the Fort?

Kunal looked up at Laksh and caught sight of Esha as she moved closer toward them. She was the reminder he needed.

"No." Kunal shook his head. "You know I can't."

Laksh let out a sigh, taking a deep breath as if he was readying himself to go another round to convince Kunal.

"I thought you might say that," Laksh said, before throwing his knife straight at Esha's chest.

CHAPTER 64

Esha ducked, rolling across the jungle clearing. The knife nicked her ear and skittered away from her.

"Stop!" Kunal yelled, rushing forward to block Laksh from taking another shot.

His friend backed away, holding out a second knife. It seemed leaving him with his weapons had been a bad move.

"She's the key, Kunal. We take her back and this cursed mission has been worth it. We'll have a commander in the Fort. It could even be you. And I may have killed the general, but the Blades were planning the same thing. They're no better."

Kunal knew this, understood it, but he wasn't choosing Laksh's rebels or the Blades. Right now, Kunal was choosing Esha.

He dove at Laksh, tackling him to the ground long enough to yell at Esha to run. She looked furious at the mere suggestion, shaking out her whips instead.

It was a good move, for in a few heartbeats, there was the sound of pounding footsteps heading to the clearing.

Saran, Jageet, and Amir emerged from the brush, looking quickly between the three of them. Laksh tossed Kunal off and staggered to his feet.

"It's him! Laksh is the double agent you suspected, Saran," Jageet said quickly. Laksh sneered at him.

"Seems the commander was right and we did have a traitor in our midst, though I think we caught ourselves two extras today," Saran said, a note of pleasure in his voice, his hand sliding up and down his sword.

"You're the Viper? Kunal wasn't lying?" Amir stuttered out, his large eyes turned toward Esha. "But you're so pretty. You don't have a forked tongue."

Esha grinned at him. "I like this one."

She snapped her whip against the ground. The crack made Amir jump back, but the awe remained on his face.

"Capture the traitors," Saran commanded. "And as for the Viper, the commander said dead or alive."

Saran charged at Laksh as Jageet rushed Kunal, leaving Amir to Esha.

⟨◦⟩

Esha twirled her whips in her hands, striking them against the ground with loud cracks that made Amir visibly wince. He was obviously reluctant to attack. Within a few seconds, she had knocked him out cold and dragged him to a corner under the shadow of the tree.

She hadn't forgotten the kindness of the boy the night before at the campfire, or the way he had talked wistfully of life after fulfilling his active duty. Even if he didn't realize it, his soldier days were at an end.

Tana, Kunal, and now this Amir. She was really going soft. But the thought didn't hold the venom it used to.

Quickly, she turned to assess the clearing.

Saran had tossed Laksh to the ground and was about to knock him out when Esha lashed him with her whip, pulling him down so that Laksh could scramble away. She might not be fond of this Laksh, but she wanted him alive and she wanted him as *her* capture. The information he had in that mind would be a treasure for the Blades.

He was the only one here who could tell her how the Jansan rebels had discovered their plans to assassinate the general. A moment of unease had passed through her after she revealed Laksh's involvement in General Hotha's murder, but Esha had seen the look on Kunal's face. The belief he held in this stupid "friend" who lied as easily—no, easier—than she did.

Saran was up again and he staggered back, fury on his face.

Esha raised her knife up as Saran charged forward. She faced off with him, dodging his blows and landing a few of her own. But she was slower than him and her knife wasn't doing much against the soldier's cuirass.

The next blow of his fist landed and Esha doubled back, trying not to fall.

Esha pulled up every ounce of strength she had, knowing she would have to rely on her speed, whips, and dirty tricks to get Kunal and herself out of this alive.

This soldier was bigger and stronger—and now too close for her normal tricks to be of any use. Esha rolled away, ignoring the pain in her side. When she put enough distance between them, she readied her whip again.

Time to play.

———◄○►———

Jageet came barreling at him, pulling him down with a strength that Kunal wouldn't have expected.

Kunal landed heavily on the jungle floor, all the breath knocked out of his lungs. A well-aimed kick sent Jageet flying. Kunal rolled to his feet, trying to keep his breaths steady. He took as much air into his battered lungs as possible. He ended up with gulping, painful breaths, but he was on his feet.

Jageet had gotten back up, but this time Kunal was ready with his attack and swept his leg out as he crouched. The young soldier fell heavily, hitting the hard ground with an oomph.

Kunal took the moment to assess Esha and the field. He noted Amir knocked out cold to the side. Laksh was diving forward, knife pointed at Esha, who was dueling with Saran.

Kunal intercepted him, narrowly missing the knife, which grazed his bare forearm. Laksh took a second to regain his balance and Kunal took advantage, kicking him in the chest.

"You do realize they're trying to capture you?" Kunal said as Laksh struggled back up to his feet. Kunal bounced on his toes, bringing back memories of Laksh and him sparring under the red-tinted sunlight of the Fort.

Laksh shrugged, wiping his nose, which had a trickle of blood.

"Which means I need to capture her first."

Before Kunal could react, Jageet tackled him from behind. They wrestled, the sharp edges of the soldier's cuirass digging into Kunal's torso.

He grunted and tried to toss Jageet off again, but the young soldier yanked Kunal into a firm chokehold.

As Jageet choked him, Kunal looked up in time to see Laksh approach Esha from behind.

His entire body went still. She wouldn't spot him in time.

Kunal stretched his arm out to the rock nearby, fingers stretching and stretching as Jageet squeezed his hand around Kunal's neck. Finally, Kunal grasped the rock and swung it up, cracking Jageet's skull. The young soldier fell in a heap.

Kunal looked up in time to see Laksh's face turned cold as he readied himself for the shield attack, the one Kunal had taught him almost two moons ago with Alok.

Except Esha had no shield.

Kunal rolled to his feet and lunged to intercept him, but was too late. Esha took the blow to her side, crumpling to the ground.

His anguish caught him unaware, hitting him like a typhoon, breaking down his control as the seconds dragged on and she still didn't move.

The wild *thing* inside of him clawed at its chains, battering down the shields he had put up. Kunal felt himself beginning to turn, the transformation striking like a gale of wind.

A ferocity—raw, primal, hungry—coursed through him and he grasped at the edges of his humanity, fighting off the animal inside of him.

A glance at Esha's unmoving form was the last straw.

He lunged at Laksh, talons flashing out, and threw him to the ground, rivulets of blood dripping down the punctures he had left in Laksh's arms. The skin on Kunal's shoulder blades became taut and burned.

Kunal paused for half a breath, horrified that he had been the cause of Laksh's wounds, but the ferocity in his blood raged even as he tried to pull back his control.

But it was too late.

Laksh had gone still, staring at Kunal in fear—and awe.

———◇———

Esha had felt better, that was for sure.

She had taken the brunt of the blow to her right side, falling into blissful black. But now her vision was back, faint words flitting around the edges of her consciousness.

"*Heen rayan,*" Laksh was saying reverently. Esha pulled herself to full consciousness, pain replaced by terror. "We've been looking for you. Of all the secrets we thought the general was hiding, I never thought you would be one of them."

Esha rose up unsteadily. She saw Kunal breathe a visible sigh of relief, which only made Laksh chuckle.

A sharp crack startled Esha, who winced only to realize it was the hard tread of Saran, who was also staring at Kunal wide-eyed.

Esha felt her strength coming back, determination to end this giving her the power she might not have had otherwise. She had the advantage to take Saran unawares.

She made sure her tread was soft as she approached Saran from behind.

————◄○►————

Laksh's words rang in Kunal's head.

Heen rayan.

In seconds his identity, his story, his freedom had been stripped bare. Fear had abated the roil in his blood, pulling him back from a full transformation.

"We need you, Kunal. Our cause needs you. With you, the *heen rayan*, a rightful Samyad, we have the key to power. Birthright. Think of what we could do—what you could do with our group," Laksh said.

Kunal paused, wondering why Laksh hadn't tried to escape yet, when he felt the blow hit his head from behind. He collapsed, his talons digging into the dirt as he skittered across the jungle floor.

Kunal's body shuddered in confusion, fighting to stay human as Jageet's shadow loomed over him.

Esha had finally knocked Saran down with her whips, and she felt exhaustion setting in, making her limbs scream.

She was about to wrap her whip around his neck when she saw Laksh moving toward Kunal—no, toward the jungle now.

Trying to live to fight another day.

Well, she had no compunction about not letting him live anymore, no matter how valuable he might have been. Not after he had seen Kunal turn, knew the secret of his blood. This leader of theirs, this Dharmdev, would know within days, and Kunal would never live in peace again.

She drew out the knife she had hidden in the sole of her sandal, specially wrapped due to the poison it was dipped into.

Laksh turned at the edge of the clearing, locking eyes with her.

"I'd stay longer but I'd rather not be taken back as a traitor. I always rather liked my head," he said. "I'll be back for Kunal. You know he'll always be one of ours, right?"

Laksh sent her a wicked grin before dodging into the underbrush.

Esha bristled at his words, tamping down her instinct to follow. She couldn't leave Kunal to the two soldiers.

She threw the knife.

It missed his heart, but found his arm. Laksh pitched forward but kept running, disappearing into the darkness of the jungle.

Esha cursed, hoping the poison would at least slow him down.

Someone yelped and Esha jerked around, finding Kunal on his back and Jageet standing over him. Saran was struggling to his feet, his eyes on Kunal.

Esha launched herself up and toward them and within seconds she was behind Jageet. With one brutal motion, she drove her knife into his back, right underneath the gap of his cuirass.

"You wench," Saran growled as the young one fell, blood drenching the sides of his cuirass. He changed course, charging toward her now.

———◄◦►———

Once again, Esha had saved Kunal.

At the sight of her, Kunal's body settled and his training and survival instinct snapped back into place.

He got up unsteadily, to move to Esha's defense, but she yanked out the knife she had used to kill Jageet. She sent it flying through the air and it landed in Saran's neck.

The soldier staggered back, surprise etched across his face, and Kunal rushed forward, knocking him out with a final blow to the head.

He dropped to the ground, lifeless as stone.

Kunal whipped around to face Esha, who was staring at the soldier's body, regret on her face. And even after everything, she moved forward to slit each of the soldier's throats—taking care to ensure a merciful death, instead of the slow pain of bleeding out.

When they locked gazes and Kunal saw the weariness and pain and guilt in her eyes, he realized something with every thud of his heartbeat.

She was a risk, the biggest risk he might ever face, but Kunal knew in his bones it was one he wanted to take.

The reward might be everything he had ever wanted.

———◆———

A sharp intake of breath made her turn.

Kunal's eyes bored into her and her replying gaze was weary.

This was her—violent, broken, ugly. Laid bare.

Her hands fell to her side, the knife dropping onto the ground with a soft thud as she walked toward the nearest tree. She braced herself against it, closing her eyes for a moment to master the churning sea within her.

Kunal had looked at her with an expression she couldn't identify, but it had curled around his face, blooming into an intensity that hurt her. She could feel his gaze burning into her skin and she knew if she opened her eyes, he would still be staring at her.

But one thought kept swirling around in her head.

That it was disgust on his face and he would leave. He had seen her viciously killing a boy—a soldier too, but still a boy. Who would love the animal, the Viper?

She wanted love that warmed the coldest corners of her soul, that whispered into her darkness with words of welcome.

But she didn't believe it existed. Or that she deserved it if it did.

She began to turn, not wanting to see the transformation on his face when Kunal recovered from the shock he must be in.

She opened her eyes. Kunal walked toward the tree and grabbed her wrist, pulling her back toward him like a whirlwind. She nearly stumbled over her own feet, she was trying so hard to avoid his eyes.

He tugged her chin up and she braced herself for fear and disgust.

In seconds, his lips were on hers with a ferocity that almost made her step back, catching her off guard. It didn't take her long to respond in kind, meeting his storm with a crashing wave of her own. She pulled him closer so that there was no separation between them, no point where their bodies weren't touching.

Skin on skin. Fire to fire. His fingers curled in the matted tangle that was her hair, leaving trails of blood across her chin, jaw, neck, collarbone. Her eyes fluttered open in a small gasp as he kissed the hollow behind her ear.

Behind him she saw the gleam of bronze armor on the ground.

It was enough to break the spell. She pulled away. He frowned at the new distance between them and she threw a shrug in the direction of the bodies.

"I'm happy we're the ones who are alive," Kunal said,

his voice fierce. "I'm lucky to be alive. You came back for me."

Esha couldn't hide the shock on her face. It sounded like he hadn't expected her to. She couldn't help herself from asking the question that was on her mind.

"But they were your comrades."

"I know, but they weren't the friends I thought I had." Esha heard the pain in his voice. "You have been more of a friend to me, Esha." His arms tightened around her, refusing to let her go.

"If I'm a friend, I've been a horrible one," she said. Esha tried to walk away again, unable to face him to tell him the truth of it.

She was no such friend. All she had done was bring destruction and death to his life. That's all she had done to everyone she cared for.

"Stop. *Stop.*" He tried to tug her back but she fought him. "Esha, stop!" The ferocity of his words stopped her. "Stop running away. You let me live a dozen times over, you came back for me. You know who else has done that in my life? No one. No one has fought for me, ever." The ferocity lessened, a small grin appearing on his face. "We may have had a small rough patch where we tried to capture and kill each other. So what?"

Esha snorted, wiping her nose with the back of her hand. Blood came off her cheek.

"And this? You like me like this? My knife freshly blooded from killing soldiers like yourself?"

She waited, expecting another pithy comment, a sly retort, a smart evasion.

"Yes. I'm more than just a soldier. You're more than just the Viper."

Esha saw the truth of it in Kunal's eyes, shining at her so bright and eager. It made the hard steel edges of her heart melt.

She shook her head. He was insane, but who was she to question it?

It was what she had always wanted, deep in a secret place. Someone who saw both Esha and the Viper and ran from neither. She had a hard time with that herself.

"I had come back. I realized what you had offered me, that it had been my choice." He hesitated. "I was coming back to you when Laksh found me." Esha tilted her chin up at him, trying to show him with her eyes that she understood. She *had* seen his face at the clearing. "And as long as it's other people you're trying to kill and not me, everything will be fine between us," he said, smiling.

The laugh that burst from her was free, unencumbered, a sparrow taking flight in clear skies. Lightness was returning to her world and she noticed the breeze on her skin, the warmth of Kunal's fingertips against her temple, the feeling of knowing someone *saw* her.

And something began to fill the hole that had been in her heart since her parents died. Bit by bit, grains of sand in an hourglass, Esha realized that maybe she would be healed and it wouldn't be solely through revenge.

The thought confused her after years of the dark hurt in her soul and she pushed it aside, leaving it for her future self to unravel. Could they truly overcome their pasts?

Reality loomed over the lightness and Esha returned to it.

"Laksh knows you're a Samyad now, for sure. I saw it all."

Kunal shook his head. "I should've known about Laksh, what happened to me."

"How could you have known? If anyone is at fault here, it's me for letting him escape. Now he might return to this new rebel group, to this Dharmdev, and your life will be forfeit. The poison will slow him down, since it grazed his arm, but it likely won't kill him. That'll be up to us."

Esha let out a sigh. "And Reha," she continued. Kunal gave her a questioning look. "The girl, the precious cargo. It has to be her. Somehow, Vardaan has found her."

"Of course you were eavesdropping," he muttered, but there was no rancor in his voice, only faint amusement. He quirked an eyebrow. "But how can you be sure she survived? That this isn't a false rumor they've started to manipulate us?"

She cleared her throat and he gave her a questioning look. Now was as good a time as any for honesty. "I kept something from you earlier. Not just that the Fort was looking for Reha. But also that I knew there was a possibility she was alive. I was there with her, on the Night of Tears. I helped her and her nurse to escape."

Kunal said nothing, his mouth in a tight line as he waited for her to finish.

"We've had rebels out looking for her since, for her nurse, for any sign. Only bits and pieces here and there, never a full enough picture until now. Vardaan is *scared* of her, Kunal. She is the rightful heir and when she comes into her powers . . . Even if there's only a small chance that the cargo is Reha, we can't leave her there."

He pulled her close and kissed her again, but it was soft, a balm on her soul rather than one to set her aflame.

She pulled away before the kiss became unbreakable, knowing their work wasn't done.

"And we need to track down Laksh, find him before he tells the rebels. They've already been searching for you."

Esha hoped he understood what she wasn't saying, that they'd have to do that without the team.

———◄◦►———

It shouldn't have surprised him but it still did, this newfound closeness between them. He could almost see her mind working in tandem with his own.

"The soldiers said the cargo was still en route to Gwali. If we go now, we can intercept Reha. Rescue her before she reaches Vardaan," Kunal said.

"If we go now, we can capture Laksh and make sure your secret stays secret. That you stay free," Esha countered. They stared at each other. Neither willing to break the gaze.

It would be dangerous either way, going into the heart of Jansa alone.

A cadre of soldiers protected Reha on her journey to the capital and Laksh was still out there, left to his own machinations. And now he knew Kunal's true identity, how valuable he would be to any side. How long before Dharmdev and his rebels came after Kunal?

If they tried to capture Laksh first, Kunal might stand a chance at a real life, one without becoming a pawn of powerful people.

If Reha fell into Vardaan's hands, it might not matter. She would become their pawn instead.

His own freedom or the freedom of the people he had sworn to protect?

Kunal didn't want to be passive anymore, living a stolen life. He would rather take his chance out there, risking himself for something he believed in.

This would be his first decision unencumbered by the shadow of the Blood Fort. The first step toward his new future.

He heard a rustle in the underbrush to his right, and out of the corner of his eye, he saw a flash of orange and black. A tiger.

Kunal turned his head to look, but only the fluttering leaves of a banyan remained.

It was only midmorning, but Kunal recalled the fable of the tiger at midnight, of the two friends at a crossroads, choosing between virtue and vice. He glanced at Esha, whose eyes locked on to his. He didn't back down from her intense gaze.

It was clear what he had to do.

He stepped forward, taking her hand.

Acknowledgments

Bringing a book to life isn't a solitary endeavor, and I couldn't have done it without the help of a number of incredible people. They have my eternal gratitude.

First, to Amma and Nanna. When I said I was going to become an author, you never questioned me. Not when I was five and not when I was twenty-five. Your constant support and love is a gift I have and will always cherish. To Nidhi and Neelima, you both are the best sisters (and cheerleaders!) a girl could ask for. Your encouragement gave me the conviction to keep working hard and to never give up.

To my agent, Kristin Nelson. I'm so lucky to have you on my team. Thank you for being one of the first people to believe in this book and to never waver. I'm continuously grateful that I have you in my corner. And thank you to the wonderful and patient staff at Nelson Literary Agency: Brian Nelson, Angie Hodapp, Lori Bennett, James Persichetti.

To my wise and sharp-eyed editor, Alex Arnold, who saw something in this book and worked tirelessly with me to bring it to life. Thank you for helping me shape and polish this story into a real book. To the phenomenal team at Katherine Tegen Books and HarperCollins, I couldn't have asked for a better publishing home. Thank you to Katherine Tegen, Ebony LaDelle, David Curtis, Jon Howard, Tanu Srivastava, Rebecca Aronson, and all the tireless sales, marketing, and publicity people who have worked on my book.

To Aakash, for spending hours discussing royal lineages, plot holes, fantasy geography and linguistics, and so much more with me. Thank you for being my rock and for always seeing the best in me.

To my Wildcats, for not only being incredible critique partners but for becoming my friends. Thank you to Rosie Brown, who was the first to read this story and see a spark of brightness among all the first-draft rubble. Thank you to Chelsea Beam, Tanvi Berwah, Nikhi Prabhakar, and Crystal Seitz for being there through everything.

To Nikki, Mayura, and Meghana, my best friends. Thank you for not only reading my drafts but for loving me throughout the years.

To Axie Oh, my mentor. Thank you for nurturing me as a baby writer and always being there throughout my publishing journey.

To Meg Kohlmann, inimitable friend and fearless champion of this book. Thank you all for spending your weekends with me, ensconced in coffee shops.

To the wonderful people I met through writing: June Tan, Elizabeth Lim, Kat Cho, Christine Herman, Katy Pool, Akshaya Raman, Claribel Ortega, Ashley Burdin, Alex Castellanos. I've loved our adventures in (and outside of) New York and I'm so grateful to have met all of you.

Lastly, to all the young writers out there, imagining their stories. Don't give up. I believe in you.